SOME WOMEN DREAM

£1=30,

VmJ

Helene Mansfield is the author of many previous books, published in the USA. Her most recent novels include *Some Women Dance* and *Skin Deep*. She lives and works in the South of France.

GW00695925

by the same author

SOME WOMEN DANCE
SKIN DEEP

HELENE MANSFIELD

Some Women Dream

FONTANA/Collins

Collins/Fontana gratefully acknowledge permission
to quote from *Leave it to Jeeves* by P G Wodehouse,
published by the Random Century Group Limited and
from *The Scarlet Tree* by Osbert Sitwell, published
by Macmillan.

First published in Great Britain by
William Collins Sons & Co. Ltd 1990

First issued in Fontana Paperbacks 1990

ISBN 0 00 671509 0

Part One

CAMILLA

Death is the only pure, beautiful conclusion of
a great passion   D. H. LAWRENCE

ONE

London, 1926

Camilla took one last look in the mirror and swept on to the catwalk, a tall, reed-slim blonde goddess with violet eyes. Moving forward with confidence, she smiled inwardly at the gasp of admiration and shock her outfit produced. It was even shorter than the previous season's style, almost backless, with a wisp of chiffon for modesty between the breasts. The waist was at hip level, the stockings of blonde silk, instead of the traditional black. The audacity of it all provoked a round of applause, that was interrupted when the designer, Lucille's, Siamese decided to do a bit of cat walking himself. Looking down, Camilla saw the danger, scooped up the cat and continued on her way to the dressing-room to change into the bridal outfit that would end the parade.

While pressmen took pictures of Camilla in her white, semi-transparent bridal dress, Lucille made a speech.

'Ladies and gentlemen, this is Camilla's last day on the catwalk. She's leaving us to marry Lord Invergordon and we're very sad indeed to lose her. But we wish them both well and if you'd like to join us in the reception area, we'll drink a champagne toast to our girl.'

Camilla heard it all as she hurried to dress, glancing from time to time at the newspaper on the table. Aunt Flora had put an announcement in *The Times*, telling of her forthcoming marriage. By an unfortunate mischance, it had been printed next to another mention of Lord Invergordon, in a paragraph reporting his apology to the Foreign Secretary, after punching him on the nose for allegedly flirting with Camilla. Camilla shook her head, smiling indulgently. Charlie was impulsive and always convinced that men were in love with her. She put on some pearl clip earrings, inspected her new, extra short hair cut, then hurried to the reception area to shake hands, kiss old friends and answer questions from the reporters.

'The date of my wedding is the twenty-fourth of April, in three months' time. We'll live in London and Kent, and go to Scotland for the grouse shooting season . . . I shall miss being a mannequin, but I'll still come and see Lucille and Captain Molyneux to buy my clothes, of course . . . Children? I hope so, three or four. We met at Ascot . . . No, I wouldn't like to tell other young ladies how to marry a millionaire. I'm not sure that wouldn't be in the worst possible taste. Now, if you'll excuse me, I'm going to drink some champagne with my friends.'

In the tiny Belgravia apartment that was home, Camilla looked out at London in the twilight. On the pavement outside the house, a boy was selling the evening paper with her picture on the front page. The wireless was introducing hits past and present. Camilla sang to 'Ramona', 'Margie' and 'Ain't We Got Fun'. Glancing at the book she had bought, she thought how nice it would be to be tucked in with *The Great Gatsby*. Then she made herself a White Lady and drank it as she unpacked the fabulous gifts Lucille and the Captain had given her for her trousseau. They had done her proud, donating a two-piece knitted suit in dogtooth tweed with a matching fox fur to drape around her shoulders. Camilla thought the fox looked so real, she wondered seriously if he could bite her. The matching cloche was delicious and she tried it on and laughed at her reflection in the mirror. Lucille had made her a wonderful negligée with a slightly medieval look in palest blue chiffon, its low waist marked by a *ceinture* of embroidered and beaded lace. For the evening, Captain Molyneux had given her a diaphanous creation, very short, very complicated in its construction, with a kerchief skirt and low draped back, its bodice picked out in tiny motifs of geometric design that he had said were influenced by the Bauhaus. Camilla did not know for certain what that meant, but she wrote on her list to look it up in the morning. The Louis-heeled shoes were comfortable and elegant, the box of silk stockings in black and suntan quite perfect. Camilla was moved almost to tears by the gifts and suddenly conscious that for seven years she had gone to work. Now she would never work again. The finality of the break was worrying.

While she ran a bath her elation turned to a savage loss of confidence. She might have been the most applauded mannequin in the country, but as a woman she knew nothing at all! She had never been kissed, except by Charlie, never travelled and knew nothing about life. As she stepped into the bath, Camilla fell to wondering if she would miss the challenge of the catwalk. Would being a wife and social butterfly be enough? Panicky, reluctant to be alone, she rose, wrapped herself in a bath towel and ran to telephone her Aunt Flora, the woman who had adopted her, loved her, raised her since her mother's untimely death from tuberculosis when Camilla was nine.

'Aunt Flora, it's Camilla. I'm in a tizz.'

'Not surprised. You're on every front page this evening. Have you got an attack of pre-wedding nerves?'

'Could be that, I suppose. I'm afraid that being married might seem empty after the hectic working life I've had. Will I just be an ornament with nothing to do except spend Charlie's money? I'd hate that. I hate idle women.'

'Camilla, it's normal to worry, but marriage isn't empty. You'll have new challenges to face. You'll have to learn to manage Charlie's houses, to be the perfect hostess, have children, raise children, solve the servants' problems . . . That's not an empty life.'

'I suppose you're right, as always. I'm a bit overwhelmed by the idea of changing my routine.'

'Absolutely normal. Eat your dinner and go to bed with a good book. You'll be fine in the morning.'

Camilla put on a silk kimono and wandered barefoot to the tiny kitchen. Normally, after a show, she was ravenous and ate everything in sight. Tonight, she felt tired and empty. She made an omelette, sprinkled it with grated cheese and ate it while reading the new copy of *True Confessions*. Then she made coffee. Captain Molyneux had taught her to make it black and fragrant like the Parisians drink it and she was very proud of her skill. When she had cleaned her teeth and put Vaseline on her eyelashes, she got into bed with *The Great Gatsby*. Her concentration was particularly low, so after a few minutes she turned out the light and slept almost at once.

At ten to three, Camilla woke, soaked to the skin with sweat and frightened to death because she had had a nightmare. Struggling to remember the details, she realized that it was a nightmare she had often had since her engagement, a terrifying image of being trapped in a coffin and buried deep in the earth. The more she tried to get out, the smaller the coffin became, until the moment when she began to suffocate and woke screaming in horror, because the dream had seemed so real. She had had the same nightmare as a child, when her mother was ill. What did it mean? And why was she for ever worrying about things that might happen instead of things that *had* happened? Impatient with herself for her highly strung nature, Camilla went to the kitchen, made a pot of tea and settled back in bed with *True Confessions*. She was being silly. She had pre-wedding nerves, as Aunt Flora had explained. It was probably a form of stage fright, only worse. She wondered what making love was like and asked herself if *that* was what was really bothering her. People seemed quite happy until they got married and started making love. Then, suddenly their lives seemed so complicated. Camilla sighed and returned to her magazine. No doubt Charlie would teach her all she needed to know. She just hoped that she would be a quick learner. The thought made her laugh and as Big Ben struck four she turned out the light and slept peacefully.

The marriage took place at Westminster Abbey, with six bridesmaids, two flower girls and a Scots Guards Pipe Major, whose rousing greeting woke every baby for miles. A train load of jasmine arrived as a gift from Captain Molyneux, who was on holiday in Grasse. This was used in the Abbey and throughout Charlie's town-house, giving its heavy Victorian interior the fragrance of a seraglio. The service was attended by eight peers, two Russian princes in exile and the Duke of Windsor, who had been a friend of Charlie's since childhood, when they had fished together in the summer holidays.

Camilla wore white lace by Lucille, a dream dress of pearl-embroidered silk chiffon, knee-length but with a trailing floor-length veil. The motifs around the hem were in the form of the Invergordon coat of arms. Her head-dress was a tiara of pearls bought from a Romanov survivor. Camilla wore the tiara low over the forehead, the frothing veil framing her beauty like a cloud. She carried a bouquet of white lilies that matched her white silk stockings. Generally it was agreed that she was the most beautiful bride of this season or any other.

One of the peers watching the newly wed couple, turned to his company and spoke wryly.

'She's lovely and so nervous. Pity she's fallen for mad Charlie Invergordon.'

'Is he really mad? Rob Hayes Briton told me that when they were at Eton Charles ate tadpoles for breakfast washed down with champagne if you please! The other night at Boodles he got so stewed he tried to eat the goldfish! There were worse, of course, in that family. His great-grandfather was considered homicidal and went into a state of complete insanity after their gamekeeper died mysteriously. He was guarded by four men round the clock! And Charlie's father's violence was legendary. Hope to God he doesn't take a bad turn. That young lady deserves better.'

'Think she'll tame him?'

'No hope. She's too innocent and too cold. Typical English rose.'

'Still waters run deep and all that.'

'Charlie'll tire her out in six months. He runs on the wild side, always has and always will.'

The reception was held at Claridges, lunch for eighty specially chosen guests, who gossiped furiously about the couple.

'She's changed from her wedding dress into the most divine pink satin with embroidered stars. I swear Charlie's hypnotized.'

'Is he sober?'

'Difficult to tell.'

'If not he might have a bit of difficulty with his conjugal obligations.'

Camilla ate with relish. Now the ceremony was over and her future decided, she felt quite calm. She enjoyed her lobster, her saddle of lamb with new potatoes and the fine English stilton. A few glasses of red wine made her feel distinctly relaxed, so even the idea of undressing in front of Charlie was not as daunting as it had been.

Aunt Flora smiled across the table, her rosy face and large, expressive grey eyes flattered by a marvellous cartwheel of biscuit straw heavily weighed down with cabbage roses. Camilla blew her a kiss. Then folk began proposing toasts and were riotously applauded. An Arab potentate arrived, sat down and was swiftly ushered out to another reception to which he really had an invitation.

When the toasts were over, it was time to cut the cake. Camilla let Charlie guide her hand and together they made an incision straight across the middle of the white and rose icing, provoking cheers and cries of 'Hurry and pass the slices.'

From Claridges, the party was driven to the Invergordon estate in Kent, an ancient priory of fifty acres of walled land with lakes, gondolas, Chinese pavilions and a great fourteenth-century house with cloisters large enough for a thousand phantoms. Guests from the lunch in London were joined by members of the local gentry, older members of Charlie's family and a few peers of the realm. Friends' wives arrived in their most beautiful gowns and family jewels to join in the toasts to the couple and then stay for the gala dinner. The décor theme was springtime, the walls festooned with lilac and cherry, orange blossom and pink roses transported with the jasmine from southern France. Pots of lily of the valley scented the air and a thousand Japanese water lilies had been imported to decorate the fountain of the inner courtyard.

Charlie was overcome by relief at the thought of being married. He had been terrified that Camilla might be tempted to run off with some French Romeo or an American millionaire. Relief ran through him like hot tea in an empty gullet, calming, warming, making him relax. He watched Camilla wandering among the weeping willows in a dress of violet georgette with a fichu of silk violets. She looked like a dream, the most beautiful, intriguing creature Charlie had ever known.

Impulsively he hurried towards her as the orchestra began to play a selection of Strauss waltzes, while the guests filtered into the dining hall.

'Shall we dance, Lady Invergordon?'

'I'd like that but dancing's difficult in the long grass.'

'I'll lead the way.'

'I know you will, Charlie. You'll show me everything.'

Pride made him feel ten feet tall and as he waltzed with her, he kissed her gently on her pale shoulders. She was a beautiful woman and yet childlike in her innocence, which was as it should be. Charlie wanted to protect her, to lock her away where no one could ever harm her. The trouble with Camilla, he thought, was that she never realized when men were bewitched by her. She was never on guard, always dreaming. She drove him and every other man mad with desire, without seeming to realize it. Charlie smelled the violet perfume on her body and whispered in her ear.

'We'll eat dinner, lead off the first waltz and then disappear with a bottle of champagne. Agreed?'

'Of course, Charlie.'

'How's Aunt Flora?'

'Looking forward to dinner and then dancing the Gay Gordons.'

'Wonderful woman, built like an ocean liner!'

'She was Mummy's best friend and since she became my guardian she's been the most perfect friend for me too.'

'How does she live?'

'She was married once and widowed at twenty-eight.

14

He left her money, a house and some very fine paintings. She has enough money to last her for the rest of her life. She owns that lovely house in Sussex and what you call the dungeon in London. She's only fifty-one and she could marry again someday.'

'Be a brave man that proposed to her!'

'There are quite a few who tried, but I think Aunt Flora likes her independence. She's at least two decades ahead of her time.'

They ate a feast of royal venison with sour cranberry sauce and great Spode tureens full of new potatoes, peas and tiny glazed carrots, all grown on the estate. English and Scottish cheeses were followed by syllabubs served in long crystal glasses with tears in the stems. Liveried servants moved like phantoms in the great hall, with its carved and gilded wood panelling and its staircase bordered by family portraits by Romney, Gainsborough and Van Dyck. Jewel colours, rich and deep, gave the scene the patina of a bygone age and as Camilla looked around her, she wondered, as she often had since meeting Charlie, if it were all true, or if she were living in a world of make-believe. Her eyes took in every detail of the scene, her brain registering the emerald and gold of the tooled leather that ran the length of the stairs wall. It had been created for the house by a team of Italian master craftsmen imported from Genoa by an Invergordon ancestor. The vivid colours of the leather formed a backcloth for the dresses of the women present, many in black with diamonds, some very daring in the newly popular 'hard' colours – scarlet, violet and saffron. The most beautiful outfit was worn by a Frenchwoman, the wife of Lord Paget: a Poiret black and white striped evening coat and ebony gown with a head-dress of pristine ospreys that raised a gasp of awe from everyone present.

The orchestra struck up the first waltz. Charlie rose and took Camilla by the hand.

'After this, we're free. I'm not much for big dos myself, but as I'm only intending to marry once in my lifetime I suppose I can't grumble.'

'Me neither!'

'You dance like a dream, Camilla, you always did. I never met a woman with so many accomplishments.'

Other couples drifted on to the floor and suddenly the air was full of scented petals, as thousands of dried roses fell from nets in the ceiling. Those that fell on the dance floor were swept aside between dances into fragrant piles at either side of the bandstand. The rest lay on tables, chairs and shoulders. Charlie grinned mischievously.

'Copied that idea from the Burmese wedding of a great friend, Trumper Hazlehurst. He married a princess and the guests were showered with rose petals and then with thousands of scarlet butterflies that formed clouds. Couldn't find any scarlet butterflies in Kent, I'm afraid, and I'm not sure those rose petals are a very practical idea once they get crushed.'

'When they crush they'll smell even more wonderful. It was a lovely idea, Charlie.'

Smiling contentedly, he led her outside to the terrace, where a hundred-year-old wistaria's scented fronds were filling the air with the sensuous intoxication of another time, another place. Under the fronds that matched her dress, he kissed Camilla tenderly.

'Follow me. I've prepared a surprise for us.'

She ran after him, towards a mysterious amber light at the edge of the woods that formed a boundary to the land. On nearing the light, Camilla realized that it was the glow of a fire inside the hunting lodge. Charlie took her by the hand.

'This lodge was built by my great-grandfather,

Gordon Invergordon. He was as mad as a hatter and believed that if he slept under the same roof as the rest of the family they might infect him with their mediocrity. So he lived in the main house in the daytime and slept here at night.'

'Mediocrity's only catching in the dark, evidently.'

'I think he was scared of sleeping with Great-grandmother Halliday, who was American, rich as Croesus and world champion buffalo shooter. She was a foot taller than he and frightened him to death!'

Inside the lodge, the walls were of panelled oak decorated with deer antlers, hunting trophies, rifles and tiger skins. The fireplace was large enough to take tree trunks, and a zebra skin sofa stretched the length of the main wall. There were wild flowers in copper vases and a tray of champagne glasses nearby. Charlie went to the kitchen, returning with a bottle of Krug in an ice bucket.

'This is for our private toasts.'

'Why don't we sleep in the main house, Charlie?'

'Frightened of some fellow creeping around and seeing you in your nightdress. Count von Arnhem follows you around like a lapdog. I shall speak to him if it continues!'

Camilla looked hard at Charlie to see if he was joking.

'Don't be silly Charlie, he's Katy's fiancé and he follows me around because Katy and I are the only people in London who understand his priceless accent. It's really *very* funny. The poor darling can hardly make himself understood!'

'I can't understand why he came alone.'

'Katy's ill with mumps, if you please. Caught them from her nephew, I think Freddy said. He came because she insisted that my special friends were represented and she knows I haven't got much family.'

Camilla thought of how they would be leaving for Paris in the morning and the tour of France that would be their dream honeymoon. Then Charlie began to hum the new Charleston tune, 'Running Wild'. Adoring it, Camilla got up and danced furiously, pleased when her husband joined her, both of them singing to keep up the beat. The heat of the fire and the dancing made Charlie sweat and he took off his dinner-jacket and his bow tie and helped Camilla out of the frilly fichu of silk violets. When he saw her breasts exposed in outline under the transparent material, he sucked in his breath.

'I didn't know you were half-naked under that thing, Camilla. You could have provoked some fellow to take liberties!'

'I was expecting it.'

'Really? Tell me who and I'll kill him.'

'You, Charlie, who else?'

He kissed her once, twice, three times. Then he carried her to the bedroom, with its giant four-poster covered in a patchwork made by the redoubtable Halliday. When he began to take off her clothes, Camilla lay quite still, afraid and yet trusting, watching wide-eyed as her husband threw his things on the floor, as he had since childhood. When he jumped into bed, she almost lost her nerve. But Charlie was reassuring, kissing her, titillating her body and, when the time came to enter her, speaking gently.

'Might hurt for a couple of seconds, but after that we'll be all set for a fine canter.'

Camilla cried out at the moment of penetration, but Charlie's love was so urgent, his kisses so ardent, she forgot her fear and let herself be whirled along on the tide of his desire. When he reached a climax, she shuddered, closed her eyes and, holding him in her arms, stroked his head and smiled down at him with love in her eyes.

Charlie spoke anxiously.

'Was it good for you, Camilla?'

18

'It was wonderful, Charlie. You're the perfect husband and I hope no one ever steals *you*.'

'Impossible. I'm your slave for life.'

He slept almost at once, as trusting as a child. Camilla lay, staring at the red, coral, black and gold of the patchwork and wondering if Great-grandmother Halliday had found marital obligations as exhausting as she. Then she slept, dreaming of running away from a large black shadow with antlers on its head and a zebra skin over its shoulder. She woke at five, pale, tired and shivering in the bitter chill of an English spring dawn.

In Paris, they stayed at the Ritz, where the Invergordons had always retained the Green Suite. The deluxe quarters had two bedrooms, two bathrooms and a salon with tiny drawing-room, all decorated in almond-green and gold, with amber mirrors and wondrously arranged flowers. Camilla loved it, found the service perfect, the food delicious and her husband quite the handsomest man around.

Within two weeks, the couple fell into a routine: breakfast at eight, then the arrival of the bouquets Charlie had ordered for Camilla the previous day – camellias, yellow roses, gardenias or his favourite bronze and amber orchids. When they had dressed, they went shopping, for jewels at Cartier and dresses from Poiret or Rouff. They lunched at Maxim's, or, if the sun was shining, on a bateau mouche that sailed up the Seine garlanded with daisies. Camilla was so happy she had difficulty believing that she had ever felt apprehensive about marriage. Charlie's gifts had thrilled her: a Cartier watch in gold, platinum and diamonds, a tallow jade frog, a necklace of perfect emeralds in the form of a choker, a bracelet of mixed stones set in zigzag lines in topaz, peridot and diamonds. Charlie had chosen her perfume, Adieu Sagesse, from Patou and had insisted that she buy some of his beach clothes and the new suntan oil, so she could expose herself a little when they reached Antibes. But for the moment, they were in Paris and Paris was the city of lovers.

For six weeks Charlie spent every minute with his wife, flattered by the envious glances all around, because Camilla was never out of his sight and he had no time to become jealous. He loved to watch her dressing for dinner, putting on her jewels and swaying before the mirror, her long, lean body showing to perfection the fabulous wardrobe she had brought with her, to which he was always adding.

One morning, he was flattered to find a photographer from *The Times*, asking permission to take a photograph of him and his wife in their suite. Charlie spoke expansively.

'Of course you can. Come up and join us for breakfast.'

Camilla had always had her photograph in the papers and he was terrified that she might miss that.

After breakfast, at eleven o'clock he hurried out of the hotel, intent on a secret mission. Camilla always went shopping at eleven-thirty and he did not want her to be bored. He had heard of a shop that sold the most exquisite lingerie and was going there to make sure it was respectable before taking Camilla. Delighted to find an erudite woman owner, who offered to make everything his wife might like in any colour she chose, Charlie hurried back to the Ritz, looking at his watch all the time. He must not be late. Camilla hated to be kept waiting.

At eleven-thirty sharp they strolled together along the rue Royale. Camilla was smiling merrily and Charlie was the happiest man in the world. He was telling her about the tour they would make before returning to England.

'We'll go on the Blue Train to Nice, where my cousin Binkie's going to meet us and take us to his house at Cap d'Antibes. Fabulous place. I once got lost there and arrived half an hour late for dinner.'

'Is it near the sea?'

'*Near* it? It's damn near in it! The pool's a hollowed out rock. After Antibes, we'll go and see my friend Cuthbert Rollins in Monaco and then we'll make our way back to Le Touquet and a dinky little plane to Hastings.'

'It's really a dream honeymoon, Charlie. I'm so *very* happy.'

'So am I, always am when I'm with you. If I could, I'd get myself glued to you like a Siamese twin!'

Camilla laughed delightedly at the idea. Then she walked with Charlie to the lingerie shop, where they spent an hour choosing three sets of lingerie, three nightdresses, some lawn blouses hand embroidered in Venice by nuns of a convent on the Giudecca and a marvellous rose kimono embroidered with seed pearls shaded from rose to claret.

On the way back to the Ritz, Charlie turned sharply and scrutinized a passing stranger.

'Thought for a horrible moment that was Count von Arnhem!'

'Oh no, Freddy's in London. You know he and Katy were married a week ago. Pity we couldn't be there.'

'Can't stand the fellow. He's mad about you but you won't believe me.'

'Charlie, if you start talking nonsense again about poor Freddy, who's one of the greatest gentlemen I ever met, I shall *not* eat lunch with you. He's the husband of my best friend and I'll thank you to remember it.'

'Yes, Camilla, I'm sorry I spoke. But when a fellow's madly in love he sees rivals *everywhere*.'

That evening, Charlie and Camilla went to a nightclub

and were astounded by the decadent atmosphere, reminiscent of Berlin. Though he had seen it all before, Charlie's eyes opened like saucers when a black dancer wriggled her torso in a jelly-roll jazz display that made some order more champagne and others hurry home to bed with their wives or lovers. Charlie glanced at Camilla, wondering what effect all this was having on her. He was pleased to see her cheeks very pink, her breath coming rather fast.

'Want to go back to the Ritz? We could have another bottle of champers in the suite?'

'I never saw anything quite like that, Charlie!'

'Come on, Camilla, let's hurry. I'm especially in love with you tonight, even more than last night, though not as much as tomorrow night!'

They made love with more than usual fervour and Camilla felt sure she had conceived. Excited by the idea and eager to please Charlie, she said nothing and the honeymoon continued with the four-week tour of France.

The return to London was almost three months after the wedding. Camilla was already suffering from morning sickness and a trip to the doctor confirmed what she had already suspected. Charlie was jubilant that she was pregnant, treating her like a princess and guiding her to his Rolls. Camilla teased him gently.

'Charlie, I'm just pregnant, not ill!'

'Have to be careful. I don't want you to get ill. I'm very anxious that you're happy and well, so the baby will be perfect.'

From that moment on, Camilla was rarely in the house. When she was not learning to breathe deeply, she was shopping for baby clothes, buying books on child care, seeing friends or walking in the park to keep fit. Ill with morbid fears that another man might steal her, Charlie sent Howes, the chauffeur, everywhere with Camilla 'to carry things'. His instructions to the chauffeur were succinct.

'Go everywhere with my wife. If Lady Invergordon goes in a shop, you wait outside, where you can see her. If she lunches with friends likewise.'

Then the morning sickness stopped suddenly and Camilla began to feel so well she wanted to be pregnant for ever. She lunched with Aunt Flora, Lucille and Katy, now an Eaton Square neighbour with her new husband. She bought bonnets and boots and jackets and nappies for the baby and had the nursery decorated by a Royal Academician, with giraffes and zebras and a merry-go-round of giant animals. Charlie fumed inwardly.

It came as a shock when Camilla's happy times came to an abrupt end. In the autumn, when the leaves turned sepia and scarlet and fell to the pavements, making scratching sounds in the gutter, Camilla stepped out of the car and came face to face with Katy's husband, Count von Arnhem, Freddy, who clicked his heels and kissed her hand.

'My dear Camilla, you're looking wonderful. Being pregnant is obviously good for you. My wife and I were thrilled to know you're going to have a baby.'

As the Count kissed Camilla's cheeks, the calm was shattered by a blood curdling cry.

'How *dare* you kiss my wife! Leave her alone!'

Freddy looked up aghast, to where Charlie was standing at the first-floor window, waving a Purdy rifle. The Count moved away without a word. He had met Charlie once, at the wedding, when it had been more than obvious that he was insanely jealous and probably less than normal. He had no desire to meet Lord Invergordon again. Pitying Camilla, he entered his home and locked the door.

Camilla flew up to her room and bolted the door. She

was trembling uncontrollably and incoherent with anger. When Charlie knocked and asked to come in, she shouted at him in a fury of hurt and shame.

'You're a disgrace! Go away! You've shamed me in front of Katy's husband.'

'Please let me in, Camilla.'

'I don't want to see you. I don't know if I shall *ever* want to see you again. I'll tell you one thing, Charlie. If you ever do that again I shall leave this house, pregnant or not, and I shall never come back. *Never!*'

While Charlie's footsteps receded, Camilla burst into tears and sat on the bed, trying to still the violent shaking of her limbs, the uneven beating of her heart. She could never leave her husband now she was pregnant. But what did a woman do with a spouse so jealous he screamed out of windows like a madman? She tried to make allowances for Charlie, but she could not. The Count was a friend and a gentleman. How could she ever face him and Katy again? And what to do about Charlie's ridiculous and unfounded jealousy, that had seemed amusing at first but was gradually becoming a source of anxiety and tension?

When the housekeeper came and asked if she wanted dinner, Camilla refused everything but a glass of hot milk and honey. Then, when the clocks struck eight, she went to bed alone, afraid and still horrified by what had happened. Unable to sleep, she rose at midnight and looked out at the square, lonely, needing affection and reassurance, but unable to support the idea of talking to her husband. Aunt Flora was in Egypt, seeing the pyramids and hoping to find a mummy or two. Camilla sighed, wishing she could be more independent, but resigned to needing Charlie's presence in her life.

She slept, finally, at three and woke at seven, when the housekeeper brought breakfast. The boiled egg had been placed in a Fabergé egg-cup that Camilla had admired the previous week in a Regent Street jewellers. The toast-rack was decorated with a seven-string pearl choker, the tea-cosy with a butterfly enamelled brooch from Cartier.

When Charlie knocked at ten, Camilla let him in, heard his apologies and his promises never to do the same thing again. She let him kiss her tenderly on the cheek and for the moment peace reigned again in the house. But in Camilla's heart the hounds of apprehension were baying uncontrollably.

TWO

London, 1927

Louise Elizabeth Floralie Invergordon was born in February. The birth had been difficult and Charlie and Aunt Flora were the only visitors allowed during the first week. Two weeks later, Camilla left the clinic accompanied by her husband and the baby. Aware that photographers were waiting outside, she put on a slim silk dress and coat and a straw cloche trimmed with petersham and did her image proud.

Charlie had suffered all the pangs of hell while his wife had been in hospital, watching her being cared for by adoring doctors and knowing that every man was subjugated by her charm. His only consolation was that he knew that Camilla had little natural sexuality. It simply never entered her head that men might want her, because she never wanted them. Still, Charlie heaved a sigh of relief that she was home. Now the baby would occupy her and she could stay in the house where she was safe. He finished the bottle of whisky in the library and slept until the following day.

As soon as she had recovered from the birth of Louise, Camilla began to go out to lunch with friends. Charlie had never been so wrong in his estimation of her routine, which included visits to Lucille, Captain Molyneux, the von Arnhems – all with the baby, of whom she was inordinately proud. In contravention of convention, Camilla simply took the child everywhere instead of staying in the house.

Then she invited the doctor who had officiated at the

birth to take tea with her and Aunt Flora at Fortnum's, sending Charlie into paroxysms of silent rage. More beautiful than ever, Camilla agreed to pose for a set of photographs in Lucille's new season's clothes, with baby Louise attired in some miniature versions. The photographs were wonderful; Camilla and Louise in sailor collared dresses and straw boaters; Camilla in the newly fashionable black, a dress so slim and shimmering she seemed to be enveloped in a second skin; Camilla and the baby in short dresses with a buttoned back fastening. The tiny jet buttons were enticing and letters poured into the house demanding photos, meetings, more photos and professing love, admiration and adulation. Charlie lost control and protested.

'This house is inundated with letters, phone calls and men prowling the area looking for you!'

'Funny the photographs had such a strong effect.'

'I don't want you to pose for more.'

'Then I won't, Charlie. I only did them because Lucille's been so kind with clothes for me and the baby.'

'I can pay for your clothes.'

Camilla looked at her husband in puzzlement.

'But Charlie, last week your uncle told us very firmly to economize.'

'Economy be damned! I'm not an accountant and I don't like restrictions.'

'No one does, but perhaps they're necessary. This winter the stock market went mad and the estates in Scotland haven't brought in the revenue expected, at least that's what Uncle Ferdy said. It was one of the reasons why I did the photos. I thought getting clothes free and lots of them was a very good idea.'

'We'll leave for Scotland on Monday. I must have a chat with Uncle. In any case, I can't stand all these fellows hanging around outside trying to see you.'

'But, Charlie, I'm married and I love you and I adore

our child. I have no interest at all in men. You only need to worry if *I* seem unstable or given to infidelity. If all the men in London follow me it doesn't make any difference.'

'It does to me.'

'I'm so looking forward to getting to know your Scottish home. You must make me a list of all your principal members of staff and I'll learn their names before we leave.'

'You're a miracle, Camilla.'

'No, I'm not, but I'm your wife and I wish you'd remember how seriously I take my responsibilities.'

That night, while Camilla slept, Charlie stood looking down at the silence of Eaton Square. In the private gardens in front of the house, there were rose bushes, hedges of variegated box, and lilac trees. Camilla loved to sit there with the baby in her pram, chattering gaily to Louise and trying to catch butterflies. She loved the idea of having a butterfly sit on her hand, but Charlie knew that if ever she did catch one she would let it go for fear of hurting it. Deep in thought, he paced back and forth. In Scotland, they would be far from pursuit by Camilla's admirers, far from the problems of London life that included her old friends and former employers. Camilla was a faithful wife, but if she continued to attract men like moths around a flame, someday, surely, she would be tempted.

Unable to sleep, anxious for a drink, Charlie went downstairs to the drawing-room and poured himself a whisky. Glancing at the paper, he saw that Al Capone's gang had earned sixty million dollars from bootlegging in prohibition-torn America. *The Times* said Paris was the place to go to economize, its cost of living considerably cheaper than London. Charlie frowned on reading the publicity for Al Jolson in *The Jazz Singer*. Camilla would be mad about talking pictures. She would prob-ably go to the cinema five times a week, running the risk of being molested – or worse – in the dark by some man. He drank another whisky and closed his eyes. Camilla was beautiful but not earthy or sexual. Her kisses were as light and delicate as butterfly wings. Her body responded, but she was never avid for sex. On a certain level, her coolness comforted him. If she had been a sensual woman, Charlie knew he could never stand the strain. As it was, male and female adulation of her drove him to despair. Jealousy had always been a malady with the Invergordons and he knew well that with him it was reaching unacceptable levels, but try as he might Charlie could not control the unquiet demon in his soul. He poured himself another whisky, drank it and slept almost at once, alone, on the sofa, next to an empty bottle.

Over breakfast, Camilla read to her husband from the fashion pages.

'Curves are coming back, Charlie. That's a relief, because my breasts are bigger since I had Louise. And look at that, vamps are just fabulous. It's fun, but very difficult for a blonde.'

'I refuse to discuss the subject!'

Camilla laughed delightedly, clapping her hands like a child.

'I love you when you stand on your dignity, Charlie.'

'I must go now. I'm going to buy the seats for the Flying Scotsman.'

'Howes can see to that.'

'No, Howes must stay with you.'

'Whatever you say, Charlie. I'll go and brush my hair and put my hat on. I'm going to an exhibition at the Royal Academy. It's the Pre-Raphaelites. I love them because they're so romantic. They provoke my imagin-ation like nothing else in the world.'

'Are you being deliberately wanton this morning, Camilla?'

'Of course not. Now off you go, Charlie. Tootle pip. If you're going to behave like a bear be a bear outside the house.'

Charlie bought the tickets and was returning home, when he saw Camilla being driven by Howes up Piccadilly in the direction of the Royal Academy. He followed, noting with annoyance that his chauffeur stayed at the entrance, instead of accompanying Camilla through the galleries. Charlie followed her, thoroughly bored by the exhibits. It took almost an hour to pass through. Then, as Camilla was nearing the final gallery, a handsome man appeared, bowed and kissed her hand, as if she were royalty. Charlie heard Camilla speak.

'Well, what a surprise! It's such a long time since we met. How's the Marquesa? Are you still living in Jerez de la Frontera?'

Charlie was straining to hear the conversation, when he was hailed from across the room by Bertie Stevens, one of his best friends.

'Charlie! What the hell are you doing here? You always said art was for cissies!'

Turning, Camilla saw her husband and waved for him to come over.

'Charlie, I want you to meet the Marques de Huelva. Adolfo, this is my husband, Lord Invergordon.'

It was as much as Charlie could do to be civil. Had the meeting been deliberate? Had the Spaniard come to London specially to see her?

Charlie went straight back to the station and changed the tickets so they could depart the following evening. At the end of his tether, he could not refrain from thinking of the handsome Spaniard with the slumberous eyes, who had known Camilla in her days as a mannequin. Back home, he drank a large whisky and then broke the news to Camilla that they were leaving sooner than anticipated.

She loved the Flying Scotsman, which was all she had imagined a great train to be. Its Victorian atmosphere was perfect, the food delicious and the sleeping accommodation direct from Proust's *A la recherche du temps perdu*. On arrival, Howes was waiting in a canary-yellow Rolls, as large as Belgravia, to drive them to Kilconquhar in the Kingdom of Fife and then to the castle beloved by all the Invergordons.

Once they had crossed the Firth of Forth, the countryside changed and Camilla saw fishing ports with pink granite harbour walls built high and wide to keep out the cruel sea. Tiny villages had kilt makers, glass blowers, blacksmiths shoeing horses and here and there whisky distilleries. There were meadows of rose-edged white daisies and cliffsides rich with sea pinks. Sailmakers and ships' chandlers vied with gentle farmland and men with old sheep dogs teaching young sheep dogs their tricks. There were thatched cottages and some with coral-tiled roofs, all painted white with a line of black around the windows. Camilla gazed in rapture at the sheer beauty of the scene. She had expected austerity and a dour grey landscape. She was looking into a kaleidoscope of pine and larch, sea poppies and wild cotton, thistle, foxglove and cuckoo flowers. Immediately receptive, she listened as her husband spoke.

'Soon we'll be in Kirkcaldy, there on the map. It's pronounced "Kercoddy". You'll have lots of new words to learn.'

'It's just beautiful, Charlie, not at all like I expected.'

'Wait till you see the house. I just hope it doesn't rain. If it does, we'll be knee-deep in mud.'

It did not rain, though a sea mist blew in, shrouding the landscape in layers of what looked like pale tulle. The house seemed to Camilla to be something out of a fairytale of medieval times, a six-storey building of grey-pink granite with turrets supported on a tower resembling a giant tree trunk. Built in the early seventeenth century, it had withstood storm and siege to become a focal point in the area. When the Invergordons were troubled, they came to Black Gordon to recover. Camilla asked the origin of the name, surprised when Charlie shrugged.

'Damned if I know. I think it relates to the black armour one of my ancestors wore. He was called Gordon Invergordon. Some say it was because of the sky, that turns black in these parts when there's going to be a storm.'

'It's an unreal name but a poetic one, like the house.'

'The house is real enough inside, you'll see.'

Mr Craig, the butler, had lined the staff in the castle's great hall. Each one shook hands with Camilla and the women bobbed curtseys. Mrs Craig, who acted as housekeeper and regimental sergeant-major for the staff, eyed her new mistress and decided she was too thin and too fine a lady for the likes of Mad Charlie Invergordon. Thus, she needed protection. She said nothing, but from that moment took it on herself to keep an eye on the situation. In the meantime, she could not resist a smile when Charlie led his wife up the staircase to her room, his face wreathed in pride.

In the staffroom, next to the kitchen, everyone spoke at once.

'She's as pale as a phantom, but lovely. Did you see her hands? All white and long like a ghost.'

'She needs feeding.'

'She needs calm and the quiet life. She's delicate, that's obvious.'

'She'll never have a quiet life with *him*! Do you think she knows how he is? Perhaps that's why she's so pale?'

'I thought the baby was lovely.'

'Charlie never even looked at it! She did. She loves it dearly. We must make her comfortable. Did you gather lucky heather for her room and pansies too? Shall we take her some tea? Mrs Craig, shall we take the mistress afternoon tea?'

'Aye, and some of those spice and lemon cakes you made this morning.'

The furniture in Camilla's room had been made locally, in pale pine cut into chests, chairs and a bed with a Russian-style headboard, its twin doves of peace intertwined with Slavic grace. The hangings were of Indian crewelwork in cream and coral, the beautifully worked linen brought back from Johor in the nineteenth century by a colonial service Invergordon. Camilla felt immediately at home and certain Charlie would return to being his old self now they were out of London. For an hour she explored the galleries and staircases that led to the turrets. Then she went down to the living-room with its stone walls decorated with carved heraldic designs. Outside, seagulls swooped and screamed their lament. In the courtyard, a piper was playing a selection of rousing tunes. Camilla kissed her husband and hugged him to her heart.

'Are you happy, Charlie?'

'I'm tired but relieved to be here. At Black Gordon I always believe peace is possible. In London everything drives me mad.'

'Why?'

'I just can't stand all those men who follow you everywhere with their tongues hanging out like bloodhounds.'

'No one follows me, Charlie. It's all in your imagination. I think you have to try to control your jealousy or it'll make us unhappy. There's no reason for it.'

'What about that Spaniard who you met?'

'I haven't seen Adolfo in years. His wife was one of Lucille's best and most beautiful clients.'

'He's in love with you.'

Charlie's face had turned very red and Camilla knew that she must change the subject quickly. An arpeggio of panic hit her and she wondered momentarily if Charlie were losing control of himself. Then she remembered that they were in Scotland and at Black Gordon everything would be fine. He had always believed that in Scotland nothing could ever go wrong.

That night, they made love for the first time since the birth of Louise. In the months that had passed by without any physical contact, Camilla had imagined that it was her husband's way of showing consideration for her as a woman. Then, after a while, she had been obliged to accept that he preferred to drown his sorrows in a whisky bottle instead of talking them out with her. She had not protested when Charlie started to sleep alone, when all pretence of affection disappeared. She had tried to accept that he was tired and anxious about the family fortune, that someday, somehow, things would return to normal. Now, as he made love to her with urgency and a certain violent longing, Camilla realized that Charlie's jealousy had been responsible for the sudden cessation of intimacy. Looking into his face, she thought him almost possessed and his passion frightened her. The pounding piston of his desire intimidated every fibre of her body, almost repulsing her. Once, he cried out in seeming despair.

'Camilla, I want you to want me as much as I want you. God dammit, woman, don't you ever cry or scream and *need* a man?'

Suddenly, she felt his body explode in hers. Then he was quiet at her side, caressing her cheek and whispering with infinite sadness.

'You're the most beautiful thing I ever saw. I wish to God I knew how to make you love me.'

'I do love you, Charlie.'

'You don't yet know the meaning of the word. I can't even scratch your surface. But someday you'll love a man. I'm just torn to pieces by the fact that it won't be me.'

Suddenly exhausted, he slept, leaving Camilla feeling more alone than she had ever felt in her life. In the small hours, she rose and walked to the window, staring at the white breakers of a rough sea on the distant shoreline. Somewhere in the woods an owl hooted eerily. Camilla went to the bathroom and washed all trace of her husband from her body. As she thought how rough Charlie had been, a solitary tear fell down her cheek. She wiped it away, too afraid to admit that sometimes dreams die and sometimes they become living nightmares.

Camilla was walking on the shoreline the following morning, when she saw a familiar figure. It was Katy, her friend from mannequin days. Ecstatically happy, she ran towards the slim young woman in the waterproof jacket and rubber boots. Katy too was delighted to see Camilla, but not really surprised. So many London friends had places in Scotland.

'Camilla, I'm so pleased to see you. I'm in dire need of advice.'

'Hello, Katy, do show me what you've caught.'

'I've caught nothing but a cold, I can assure you!'

'No sharks or whales?'

'Listen, Camilla, this is my very first fishing expedition. I want to surprise Freddy with a huge fish, but I must be doing something wrong. I'm frozen and I haven't even *seen* a fish!'

'You don't see them. You have to go out in a boat or

fish from the pier. You don't fish from the beach like that.'

'I'll be seasick if I go in a boat!'

'I have a better idea. Come with me.'

They returned to the house, took a salmon from the cold store and Katy went off in triumph to show Freddy her catch. Neither she nor Camilla knew enough about the facts of country life to realize that the odds on catching a salmon on the beach were approximately the same as catching a Scotsman spitting on his sporran.

Camilla rushed upstairs to tell Charlie the good news.

'Guess who I just saw. Katy. She was trying to catch a fish from the beach! She's staying in the gatehouse belonging to your neighbours and we're invited to lunch on Friday. I said we'd be sure to go. You'll come won't you, Charlie? I do *so* want us both to have the von Arnhems as friends. That way you won't be jealous any more.'

Camilla did not tell him how long it had taken her to persuade Katy to invite Charlie to lunch. She had almost pleaded with her friend, knowing there would be a row if she went alone. She was therefore shocked to see Charlie's face turning the now familiar dull, dark, angry red. She flinched when, instead of replying, he gripped the whisky glass so hard it broke, cutting his hand. Panic stricken, she rang the bell for Mrs Craig, who appeared, took in the scene, ran away and returned with an enormous red painted tin medical box.

'What have you done, sir?'

'My wife informs me that one of her admirers and his wife have rented the Bruces' gatehouse and had the temerity to invite us to lunch.'

Camilla rounded on her husband.

'When I was a mannequin for Lucille, Katy was my very best friend. She still is and has been for over ten years. She's married to Freddy von Arnhem and I think what you just said is low, disgusting and a disgrace. You'll apologize at once.'

'He's in love with you and you can't deny it.'

'I only ever met Freddy von Arnhem three times, when he came for lunch with Katy, to our wedding, and the time he stopped me in the street to congratulate me on expecting the baby. And you opened the window, shouted insults at him and brandished your ridiculous rifle. I won't tolerate your jealousy any more. It's insulting and it's unfounded.'

Mrs Craig sighed as Camilla ran to her room. When Charlie tried to follow, the housekeeper pushed him back in his chair.

'You've done enough damage for one day.'

'I don't need your advice, Mrs Craig.'

'It's true, what you need is a new brain. The old one got pickled in whisky years ago, that's why you talk nothing but jealous rubbish. I've cared for you since you were born and you've always acted like a madman. Now you're going to lose that fine girl. Go and apologize to her immediately. She's an innocent wee child and any fool can see it except you.'

Camilla was nowhere to be found. Charlie searched the entire estate, but there was no reply to his cries. She returned a few minutes before dinner was served and retired an hour later without saying a word.

Charlie called Howes to the study and gave him instructions to follow Camilla everywhere, ignoring the chauffeur's protests completely. Then, he locked the door and finished all the whisky in the decanter. At three in the morning, he sang the Invergordon Lament, so loudly Mr Craig appeared and tried to restrain him. But Charlie sang on, until he fell to the ground in a drunken stupor.

On Friday, Charlie learned that Camilla had kept her lunch date with the von Arnhems. From that day, after lunch, she would disappear to pick wild flowers, paint, sketch, ride her horse or just sit in the heather on one of the nearby hills, quite unaware that Howes, with sandwiches, binoculars and a bicycle was following on her husband's orders. For Camilla, the only thing that mattered was to try to still the panic in her unquiet heart.

Sometimes, she walked with Louise in her arms, sometimes alone. Once, she was followed by Mrs Craig's two cats, the fiercely independent Flora and MacDonald. Alone, the tiny Kingdom of Fife seemed like paradise, its tan and yellow brush, its purple hills, its scent of old tweed, heather and log fires all pleasing to the heart.

When she was in the house it was hell, because of Charlie's unpredictable moods. Ignored by him, observing that he seemed increasingly to live in a world of unreality, where everyone was his enemy, Camilla felt herself dying a little. When she tried to work out what to do, she came up against the brick wall of convention. She was Charlie's wife and the mother of his child. She could not leave. She could never go back to work at almost thirty. Divorce was social suicide. She would be unemployable.

Gradually, the kindness of the staff and the locals, the support of Katy and her husband, the picnics prepared by Mrs Craig and the housekeeper's gentle reassurance helped revive Camilla's spirits. Each day she walked further. Often, she learned something new, like the afternoon when Alfred, the gamekeeper of a nearby estate, taught her the basics in the art of fishing. After that, Camilla rarely did anything else but cast her line in the small freshwater lake at the periphery of the Black Gordon estate.

One evening, she told Charlie proudly how she had

caught the trout they were eating for dinner. He did not reply. Camilla spoke gently.

'Charlie. This is your home and your land and I'm *so* enjoying learning to live a Scottish life. You're eating a trout I caught myself. Aren't you just a little pleased?'

'I don't believe a word. The Count caught it for you.'

Stunned by his venom, Camilla fell silent, suddenly conscious that nothing she could ever say or do would cure Charlie of his jealousy and that it was going to sour and even break up the marriage. Without another word, she rose and went to her room, locking the door behind her. Experience had taught her that argument was useless. When Charlie had an idea lodged in his head, there was nothing to be done. Camilla took Louise in her arms and kissed her tenderly. At least she was not alone.

For a while there was calm at Black Gordon. Charlie went out shooting grouse, came home exhausted, appeared affable enough but slept alone. Camilla began to hope that at least his explosions of temper were a thing of the past. But this was the calm before a storm and one day when she ran home, soaked to the skin by a sudden downpour, he was waiting in the hall.

'Well, what happened? Didn't your lover have the grace to bring you home or at least lend you an umbrella?'

Camilla recoiled in horror, uncertain if Charlie were completely losing his mind.

'I went fishing, like always.'

'With whom?'

'Alone, of course. I always go alone, except once in a while when I take Louise with me. Mostly it's too cold or wet to take her in my arms. And I'm sick of your innuendoes, Charlie. You seem convinced of my infidelity, but I've never been unfaithful to you. Only a very unfaithful person could be as concerned about fidelity as you are.'

Charlie hit her so hard, Camilla stumbled and fell to her knees, tears of shock and anguish pouring down her cheeks.

'Who were you with? I demand to know.'

'She was alone, as she told you, sir. I was watching Lady Invergordon, as usual, as per your instructions and I can assure you that she was alone. She has never at any time met anyone, except for her friends, the Count and Countess von Arnhem, and when she's with them they can all be seen quite clearly sitting in the conservatory eating lunch.'

'Silence! I didn't ask for your opinion, Howes.'

'You attacked your wife, sir, and I feel bound to defend her. Lady Invergordon's a virtuous woman, who merits better than a husband who has her followed morning, afternoon and night.'

Incensed, Charlie took a violent swing at Howes, who swayed to the right and dealt him a blow to the chin that felled him like a chopped oak. Mrs Craig appeared at the crucial moment, looked at the chauffeur and sighed.

'What happened, Mr Howes?'

'Lord Invergordon just hit his wife. She needs your attention, Mrs Craig. I shall go and pack. I hit him – and if I stay a minute longer I shall surely kill him.'

'You'll be dismissed without a reference, Mr Howes.'

Camilla struggled to get up.

'I'll give him a reference. Bring pen and paper to my room, Mrs Craig.'

Camilla wrote a glowing reference and gave it to Howes with the only cash she had in the world – sixty pounds. He was gone by the time Charlie woke and started shouting like a madman for Mr Craig.

'Call the constable, Craig. I intend to have Howes arrested.'

Craig's impassive pale face and bald pate seemed even more tallow coloured than usual.

'I imagine Lady Invergordon has already called the constabulary, sir. You hit her a savage blow, sir. We've had to call the doctor and she may wish to make a complaint against *you*.'

Charlie took the stairs two at a time and started hammering at Camilla's door.

'I want to see you.'

She swung the door wide.

'You see me, Charlie.'

Charlie saw with a start that Camilla's right eye was swollen and black. The coldness in her voice made him flinch.

'I shall be leaving shortly for London. If you try to make any complaint against Howes, *I* shall make one against *you*. I have a statement in writing from a witness to your violence and another from the doctor as to the nature of my injuries. Now I need money for the journey and someone to drive Louise and me to the station. From today, if we stay together at all, it won't be as man and wife. I shall stay because of the child, but I shall do so only if *you* promise to do something about your jealousy. I want a meeting of the Invergordon Family Council called in London, including Tomkins, your lawyer and Dr Vernon LeGrice. I have my doubts that you're in a normal state of health, Charlie, and I want the family's advice for my sake and for Louise's. Now let me pass, please. I'll wait for you at the house in London. You have one month to organize the family meeting. After that, I shall leave you.'

When she had gone, Charlie thought hard. First, he

contacted the family and summoned them to a traditional Invergordon Council, held in times of dire straits and major calamity. Then he called a friend in London, who was about to emigrate to Canada, and asked to take over his chauffeur. Wilson would start surveillance on Camilla immediately on her return to Eaton Square.

That evening, as he drank until the small hours, Charlie decided that Howes had been his wife's lover. Why else would he defend Camilla's infidelity and she his security? Tears fell as he thought how much he loved her. But Camilla was a woman and all women were unfaithful. The tragedy of his life was that he still adored her and would never be free of the chains that bound him to her.

THREE

London, 1933

Time flew and as Camilla prepared a party for Louise and her friends, she thought of her daughter's first Christmas party. It had been the occasion of her first Invergordon Family Council, when the subject of Charlie's jealousy had been raised, debated and decided. On that occasion, he had been sent to Black Gordon for a year, to work the estate and reflect on his errors. On his return, he had been calm for a while. Then, as the city got on his nerves, his jealous outbursts had returned and in the autumn of 1930 he had been obliged to return to Scotland for another year of exile.

Now Charlie was in more serious trouble. In January he had met a young American painter, guest of their near neighbours, Lord and Lady Erskine. There had been heated words and punches over the appointment of Adolf Hitler as Chancellor of Germany, Charlie's admiration of the gentleman being equalled only by the American's detestation of the new leader. In church the previous Sunday, Charlie had met the American again. This time they had come to blows when Charlie had accused the visitor of flirting with Camilla. When Charlie had punched English 'rivals', the Invergordons had hushed up the error with money and gifts of land, but the American, who had never met Camilla, had a fiancée of great beauty and enormous wealth. So incensed was he by the accusation, he had called the police, issued a complaint and engaged a King's Counsel of immaculate credentials, well known for his detestation of Charlie Invergordon.

Today, the day of the commencement of Louise's school holidays, was also the third meeting of the Invergordon Family Council. There would be no banishment to Scotland this time because that had not worked. Camilla expected grave consequences for her husband from the High Court and from his family. She sighed wearily.

Louise ran into the kitchen and kissed her mother.

'Aunt Flora's arrived. I'm taking her to my room.'

Camilla embraced the woman who had raised her.

'I hear my daughter's already requisitioned you.'

'Before I go with her, I'll give you the evening paper. Page one is the news you're waiting for, I'm sure. Couldn't you go and stay with the Liveseys for a while, till Charlie comes back to his senses?'

'They've gone on a tiger shoot to Chitwan.'

'Dear God, what an idea! Binkie's as short-sighted as I am. If he sees a tiger he won't realize it till he gets eaten!'

'He won't care. It's all the rage at the moment and they do *so* like to be fashionable.'

Camilla hurried back to the living-room, closed the door and read the headlines. Lord Invergordon guilty . . . A three-month prison sentence suspended . . . first offence . . . one year probation. Costs awarded against the defendant with damages of twenty thousand pounds. Camilla shook her head in despair. Whatever would Uncle Ferdy say? And would Louise suffer at school? Twenty thousand pounds! It would come from the Invergordon estates, but since the Wall Street Crash everyone had had to tighten their belts. The rich talked as if they were poor and some really were.

Having hidden the paper, Camilla went to her room, sprayed herself with perfume and inspected her new Molyneux suit with its wide shoulders and raglan sleeves. In shimmering grey silk, it went perfectly with the platinum necklace Charlie had bought her for her birthday, five strands of chain links of the newly fashionable metal, that gleamed in chill splendour against the pale skin of her throat. Camilla thought wryly that the form of the necklace was prophetic, given that Charlie had always longed to imprison her in the house, far away from her legions of so-called admirers. And now, impoverished by the enormity of the damages, Charlie's expensive presents would become a thing of the past. He would not like that, fearing that he would be superseded by a new, richer man.

At that moment the door bell rang and Fergus, the butler, ushered in Uncle Ferdy and the members of the Invergordon Family Council. They were all very pale and solemn.

'My dear Camilla, we won't stay. We're going straight to the Savoy to wash off the grime of the journey, but we wanted to see you for a moment and to bring Louise her Christmas present.'

'You're very kind. I'll ring for tea.'

While Aunt Flora settled the children to their tea in the blue room, Camilla entertained her husband's family.

'I saw in the newspaper Charlie's been convicted of assault.'

Uncle Ferdy spoke for everyone, as usual.

'We've arranged with Charlie to come in the morning at nine-thirty, Camilla. We have to talk with him and we'd deem it a pleasure if you'll be here too. In the past five years, Charlie's impetuous behaviour has cost the family over a hundred thousand pounds. Now this. It can't go on.'

'What can we do?'

'We feel he needs a spell far away from England, a new start with you and Louise. We'll discuss all that tomorrow, but we didn't want you to be too shocked by the idea. Mull it over a wee bit before morning.'

That night, while Charlie drank whisky in the library, Camilla went to see their child, but Louise was asleep with the bright red teddy bear Aunt Flora had given her. Camilla thought ruefully that the only person who really counted in her daughter's life was Aunt Flora. It had always been like that and always would be. To Louise, Mama was a dream creature, nothing more. Louise loved spraying on her perfume, listening to her tales of mannequin days and putting on her hats. Aunt Flora was reality and security, because she lived far away from Charlie Invergordon. Above all else, the child feared her father and tried to avoid him. She loved Camilla, but held herself back from prolonged contact, because in her mind Mama and Charlie were irrevocably interlinked.

The following morning, Camilla sat in on the family meeting. Charlie was pale and suffering from a hangover. Uncle Ferdy spoke for the elders.

'We cannot go on as we are, so we've made a decision we hope you'll be able to accept, Camilla. We want Charlie to go out to Kenya and farm the Invergordon holdings there. The house is beautiful but remote and we've a hundred thousand acres of prime land. If the only problem Charlie has is the jealousy, which he shows at every instance here in London, the possibility of being jealous in Kenya is very remote, because he'll never see anyone.'

Charlie beamed.

'That could be wizard. I like the idea.'

Camilla said nothing at all. She was thinking how empty life would be without Aunt Flora and all her London friends. She was shuddering at the thought of the heat and the flies and the terrifying animals. Uncle Ferdy continued.

'Tell us your thoughts, Camilla.'

'I'll try it. But for me and Louise to be far away from everyone we love will be very, very difficult.'

'We're grateful to you for saying you're willing to try at least. We'd like you and Charlie to leave in two months' time and we've already arranged everything here in London hoping you'd agree. The house will be let and the rent sent out to you along with a fine allowance.'

Charlie was pleased.

'I'll be a remittance man!'

Uncle Ferdy turned on him with a cutting riposte.

'Silence! If you were capable of behaving like a normal human being there'd be no need for all this. Don't *ever* joke about it, Charlie. Your wife and child'll be unhappy to be uprooted and I don't blame them. Try to remember that they'll be doing it to keep this family together and for no other reason.'

Charlie fell silent and Camilla left the room. Trembling from reaction and shock, she hurried to the library and took down the atlas, searching for Kenya with her finger and frowning, because it really was at the other side of the world. Probably there would be crocodiles and lions and deadly insects that killed with their sting. She sat in the armchair, tears rolling down her cheeks, conscious that her life was suddenly out of control.

Then, walking to the window, Camilla looked down with longing at the peaceful scene of Eaton Square, with its fine grey houses and its residents' park full of dark and empty flower beds and the luminous sunlight of an English winter day. Everything and everyone she loved was in England. Her whole life and that of her child was here. But what choice had she? Charlie was her husband and Louise's father and they could surely not stay in London, where the scandal of the court case had made a mockery of the Invergordon name.

* * *

The packing was done by men of a company used to the expatriation of British colonials. Camilla had bought mosquito nets big enough to cover a football pitch, hats with veils, rifles, knives, a veritable armoury of rat traps and enough tropical gear to outfit a regiment. Before her departure, she talked at length with Aunt Flora.

'If it's dreadful, I shall come home at once.'

'But it'll be wonderful.'

'You've never been there. How can you be so optimistic?'

'How can *you* be so pessimistic? You worry about things that might never happen, you always did. It's time to stop that. If Kenya's hateful, of course you'll come home. If it's beautiful, you'll stay and love it. Charlie may or may not be better when he gets out there.'

'He'll have no reason whatsoever to be jealous. We'll live miles from civilization.'

'Like you did in Scotland? Face facts, Camilla. Your husband has no reason to be jealous now, but he is. I personally think he's mad.'

'How can you say that, Aunt Flora?'

'I'm only saying what you've thought a dozen times and you know me well enough to know that I always say what I think. Charlie's bonkers and he'll get worse when he's older. You must think *very* hard whether you really want to continue your marriage.'

On a dull, grey February day, the family sailed from Southampton bound for Mombasa. The dockside was muddy, with the black wetness of a winter downpour. A band played merrily and passengers sang 'Auld Lang Syne', but nothing relieved the interminable charcoal, ebony and anthracite of an English winter scene.

Frozen by a skin-stripping wind, Camilla went to her cabin with Louise. Charlie went to the bar and relieved his tension with a couple of Glenlivets. Then he hurried to his personal cabin to dress for dinner. He had expected to feel depressed at leaving England, but he felt precisely the opposite, because he was putting behind him all that rankled, all the men who pursued Camilla, all the members of his family who dictated his every move, all the routines that bored him in London, with its bowler-hatted businessmen and strictly conventional social life. He decided to surprise Camilla and, having put on his dinner jacket, called the ship's florist and sent her a bouquet of bronze orchids, following them with an invitation to a very special celebration dinner. He seemed so like the old Charlie that she stared, dumbfounded, when he arrived to pick her up like a beau and not an often drunk and always disillusioned husband.

'Suddenly you look ten years younger, Charlie.'

'So will you, at least by the end of the voyage. Come on, we're going to drink champagne and eat a wonderful dinner and then sleep like logs. We must use the voyage as a holiday that will get us both into the best form for our arrival in Mombasa.'

Camilla put on a slim-fitting dress of oyster satin and the Invergordon pearls. She had aged since the marriage, but remained beautiful, remote, ethereal. Charlie stared in admiration as she walked past him to the door.

'I'm going to make a big effort to start a new life and a good life out there, Camilla. I'm sure now I'm out of London things will go well for us again.'

The voyage was long, the weather changing gradually from grey thundery skies to golden sunshine and then to the alizarine sunsets of Africa. Gradually, they became accustomed to a different scent in the air, a different atmosphere, and by the time they reached Mombasa, they were almost acclimatized to the heat.

Camilla felt like her old self again, full of questions, *joie de vivre* and the desire to hurry to their new home.

Charlie had not been drunk once on the voyage and she was hopeful that he might have found himself again.

Elephants in dark silhouette against a beige-pink dawn, Masai faces painted white around the eyes, a sepia lion hidden in long sandy grass, only the brightness of predatory eyes betraying his presence, a thousand pink flamingoes on an opalescent lake at twilight, Kilimanjaro with its crown of clouds and snow. These were Camilla's impressions of her first unforgettable day in Africa. Against all expectations, she fell in love with a country she had never wanted to visit.

The last few miles to Ruiru led them through dawn lit countryside of beige terrain, thorn bushes and pines, palms and dead trees, where vultures perched like comic characters from a cartoonist's pen. The sky was blue and palest peach. The clouds seemed to move twice as fast as in England. And everywhere were the fragrances of African daphne and a tiny cream blossom bush that smelled of lily of the valley. The dew was silver, the air chill and on the hill where the farm was situated, a pale grey mist hung low, reminding both of Black Gordon at its most beautiful. To their right, a section of undergrowth and small trees had been cleared. As the car bumped up the drive and the sun rose like a golden ball, thousands of butterflies flew from the newly cut section and fluttered around the couple's heads before disappearing like a speckled scarlet cloud. Camilla held Charlie's hand.

'That's a good omen. Even the butterflies came out to welcome us.'

Louise held tightly on to her mother's hand as a lion disappeared from view, his jaws still red from the kill. The silvery grass parted, swayed and he became invisible, a reminder that Africa is a land of extremes, of scarlet butterflies, luminous sunsets and predators with blood on their jaws.

At the door of the farm, a tall Somali dressed in white stood to attention, waving for the family's baggage to be carried to their quarters.

He marched forward, saluted and said in a sing-song voice of infinite charm: 'Sir, madame, miss, I am Jogona. I am head of staff and this is Bilea, my wife, who cooks for the household. General Sir William Orme left only last week. He taught us all the British way of life and I hope we shall please you.'

Before Charlie could reply, Jogona turned, blew a whistle and called: 'Present arms!'

Two young girls, two young men and a stubborn-looking old lady appeared to be presented. Camilla shook hands with everyone while Charlie talked to Jogona. Then they were shown the house, followed by a tour of the estate. Lunch was roast guinea fowl with Yorkshire pudding. Charlie and Camilla looked across the table and laughed at the combination. They laughed even louder at dinner, when muligatawny soup preceded an omelette of wild asparagus and then a local fish served with Yorkshire pudding.

Bilea explained that Yorkshire pudding had been served at every meal, except breakfast, at the request of General Sir William Orme, who loved it more than anything except soaking his bacon and eggs in Worcestershire sauce and reading old copies of *Punch*, which he kept in the attic in boxes labelled with military precision.

That night, the Somali couple whispered their observations in the uniquely oblique way of native staff.

'His ears are purple like a storm sky.'

'His nose also.'

'He rings the bell with anger.'

'His fingers are very fat.'

'Probably he is like Colonel Carruthers, the best friend of General Sir William Orme.'

'The one who swelled like a gourd before bursting and being buried in the English cemetery? She is beautiful and she laughs with her eyes.'

'She laughs only with her mouth when she speaks to *him*.'

'She put cream on the burned finger of Malindi. She will be our doctor.'

'Teach her about the sky.'

'And how to find honey.'

'Help her. She is surely not a woman to be married to a man with purple ears.'

The rains came and the air smelled of magic. Then, after the rains, in the first week of June, the fireflies appeared in the wood and Bilea showed Camilla how to catch one and hold it in her hands, so the skin glowed green. She also gave her lessons on how to hang ropes on the branch of a tree, like the Kikuyu, to make bees build in them and get honey. She explained the sky and how to forecast the weather. She showed Camilla the flora and the fauna of the area, the kapoka tree, the giant lobelia, the thorn bushes and the astonishing baobab or monkey breadtree, that could store up to a hundred thousand litres of water in the soft wood of its trunk. A black mamba was identified and, on the same day, a puff adder hiding in the grass. Sounds of the night, often frightening to newcomers' ears, were identified from the safety of the house and became a private joke between the two women. The howl of a jackal, the hoarse laugh of a hyena, the barking of wild dogs and the soft whoosh of the long grass as a cheetah ran after its prey. Night sounds no longer made Camilla sweat with fear. Like a marvellous canvas of life itself, Africa was showing its colours.

Camilla changed the menus, after learning what was available to the household. She opened a dispensary and each morning tended cuts, stings and small wounds for her staff. There, she made many friends. Often, in the evening, she found fruit, flowers and tiny gifts from the countryside, left on the doorstep for the pale, beautiful creature with whom everyone was in love.

The couple rarely, if ever, had visitors, except a distant cousin of Charlie's, Edna, whose husband farmed an enormous spread ten miles from their own. Then, one morning, an Englishman appeared, introduced himself and asked if he could fill his jerrycan with water. His car had broken down two miles from the farm and he had had to sleep in it.

'I'm John Saunders. I have a farm at Fourteen Falls. I do hope you'll bring your wife to visit, Lord Invergordon, so I can repay your hospitality.'

Charlie smiled but said nothing. He was too busy weighing the newcomer's big, strong, bronzed body, the way he wore his casual clothes with such style. He had walked here through the countryside alone, surrounded by danger, carrying a rifle almost carelessly on his shoulder. Suddenly, Charlie rose and poured himself more coffee, watching Camilla closely as she sent Jogona, who was good with engines, to see if he could fix the car. She was smiling endearingly at their visitor.

'Jogona loves to drive, but it's against his principles to reverse. He goes in a straight line or not at all. Have some more sausages, Mr Saunders. Charlie, you want some more bacon?'

'No, I'm not hungry. I have to go into Nairobi in any case. If you'll excuse me, Saunders, I must be off.'

Camilla looked after him, her face suddenly uneasy. Saunders watched the thoughts racing through her mind and understood. Her hands were slim and pale. She looked more fragile than ever in her loose, light clothes. When she turned back to him, he realized that her eyes were violet-blue and that she was greatly troubled by the departure of her husband.

'Is Lord Invergordon angry that I came?'

'We've never had a visitor since we arrived, except for Charlie's cousin, Edna. I don't think he's angry, but one can never tell. He doesn't see things as other people see them.'

'Is your husband jealous?'

Camilla looked at the broad shoulders, the handsome face with its hazel eyes. She had never met the man before, but was sorely tempted to tell him everything. She answered as diplomatically as she could.

'The Invergordons are a family who suffer from bouts of completely unreasonable jealousy. They call it the family illness and at least four of them have been confined to institutions because of it.'

Camilla thought how she liked his jacket and the very English cream cotton of his shirt. His hands were long and thin and strong and as she gazed at him she felt herself blush, suddenly, at her thoughts. To hide her confusion, she poured him more tea and asked if he would like some more toast.

'Don't run away, Mr Saunders. If you do, Charlie will think you're guilty of something awful.'

'How will he know?'

'He either watches me himself or asks one of the staff to do it. I live under constant surveillance.'

'Then I'll have another round of toast, if I may.'

'What kind of farming do you do?'

'I have cattle at Fourteen Falls. My sister and I live a very quiet life. She's more sociable than I am, but not much, which is lucky, because we're very far from other English expatriates.'

'Have you never married?'

'No. I'm forty now and it's too late to hope. I won't find the woman of my dreams in Kenya. Women here are either Happy Valley types or worked-to-death martyrs trying to grow coffee on farms where the conditions aren't suited to it. Either way, they're not the women of my dreams.'

'You'll find her someday.'

'Perhaps, but I've always had two left legs with women and I'm not sure my charm's high octane enough to inspire a dream woman.'

Camilla smiled.

'I think you'll get by, Mr Saunders. After all, for a lot of women you're a *real* dream man, strong and solid and able to get by alone in this beautiful country. A lot of women would love to have a stable life and a strong man like you. They'd love it more than anything in the world.'

Despite her rigid self control, a solitary tear fell down Camilla's cheek. Saunders pretended not to have noticed it, rose and extended his hand.

'Your man's certainly a very fine mechanic. I tried for ages to get the car going. I hope he knows how to operate the brakes and that he has no scruples against applying them. Otherwise he'll demolish the wall!'

They walked outside and Saunders got into the car. Camilla ran back in, took a picnic basket Bilea had prepared and a gallon of pure spring water.

'Take these, Mr Saunders.'

'John.'

'John, in case you break down again. At least you'll have food and drink to help you through the night.'

'You've been so very kind, Lady Invergordon.'

'Camilla.'

'I'll try to repay the favour someday. Thank you for breakfast, Camilla.'

Their eyes met and held each other. Then he moved out, waving as he went down the hill, until the black car was a speck on the horizon. Camilla went back to the table and poured herself another cup of tea. She sat without touching it for an hour, until Bilea came in with a new pot and a clean cup.

Eyeing her mistress, the Somali smiled, cleared the table and poured the tea.

'Dispensary in half an hour, madame.'

'Is it eleven o'clock already?'

'Yes, madame. Time has flown because you had a visitor.'

'I didn't hear Lord Invergordon drive away. Is he still here?'

'Yes, madame. He didn't leave. He went to his room with the headache, as usual.'

In the months that followed, Camilla became more and more engrossed in her work and ever more loved by her staff. Louise liked life on the farm, her tomboyish ways profiting to the full from the wild environment, the lack of visitors and the animals of every variety, who came to eat at the door and stayed on as her personal pets. When she was not dreaming of riding Edgar, the ostrich, Louise was taking her father's car to pieces or trying to build one of her own, so she could drive it through the fields and then back to London to see her beloved Aunt Flora. She became so uncivilized, Camilla sent a letter to the Invergordon family, asking for a Scottish governess to be sent out at once to supervise her daughter's education.

Miss McTaggart arrived on a bright spring morning, a thirty-eight-year-old Presbyterian with the spirit of adventure, who began to teach the ever unwilling Louise the joys of algebra, Latin and French. Howls of protest came from the schoolroom and one night Miss McTaggart found a lizard in her bed. A lady of sterling character, she picked it up, put it outside her window and then announced to a crestfallen but mightily impressed Louise that the school day would be two hours longer for a week as a punishment for frivolity. Order established, Miss McTaggart quickly became an accepted member of the household.

Things continued well that first year, until the day when Charlie decided to take Camilla to dinner in Nairobi at the Muthaiga Club. It was his way of celebrating their first anniversary in Africa. Camilla had never visited the city before and was overcome by the strangeness of it all. Walking at her husband's side, she stared wide-eyed at masses of men and women with different coloured skins. Dark Kikuyus mixed with Indians, elegant Englishmen in linen suits with barefoot children. The dusty streets were lined with eucalyptus trees and everywhere there were scents of Arab incense, overripe fruit and fried fritters sold in the street markets, where haggling was not only the rule but one of the pleasures of the day. Camilla tried to analyse the sounds, but there were too many languages, the widely spoken Swahili mixing with Bantu and Nilotic.

Outside the Thorn Tree Café on Kimalhi Street, hunters and travellers had pinned messages on the trunk of a huge acacia with yellow bark. Camilla watched as Charlie took a message in his name. Then, smiling, he hurried her back to the car and drove to the club.

'Table's reserved and I've a surprise for you. General Sir William Orme's returning to Kenya and I've rented the farm to him. We're going to move to a regular dream house in the Happy Valley. There's a lake with flamingoes and it's much nearer Nairobi, so you'll be able to shop here and show Louise the civilized side of life.'

Camilla's mind raced, her longing for some civilized company and playmates for Louise battling with her fear that Charlie's jealousy would be rekindled if they began to lead even the most limited social life. Then, as they reached the Muthaiga Club, she stopped worrying and began to enjoy herself. The building was in the colonial style, with pebble-dash finish and Doric columns. As they entered, she glanced around at parquet floors, deep armchairs and chintz loose covers. It was just like an English country house and she liked it very much. When they had registered, they put their things in a room that was decorated in the modern style, with bird's eye maple furnishings, somewhat bare and strangely curved to Charlie's eyes, but which enchanted Camilla, who was tired of everything that reminded her of their home in London, with the heavy Victorian gothic pieces she had done her best to relegate to rooms that were little used. Discussing the decor, they hurried to the bar, where pink gins, fizzes and White Ladies were being mixed for a large crowd of expatriates.

'What'll you have, Camilla?'

'A Trinity, I think. I was thrilled you booked the room, Charlie. I adore surprises.'

'It's not very luxurious, but the bed's good and the bathroom's big as the Taj Mahal.'

'Maybe we should sleep in the bath!'

Charlie looked at his wife in admiration, thinking how perfect she was, with her cool English personality and her pale creamy skin. Dressed in dusky pink, she was every inch the great lady and Charlie thought what style she had, what class. There was no one in the world quite like Camilla. He was admiring his wife, when he became aware of a woman watching him from the other side of the room. Her hair was black and drawn back sharply from her face in a large pearl-studded bun. Her skin was bronzed and she seemed half naked, but for the scarlet and gold silk kekoi wrapped around her body negligently, carelessly, with insolence. She had huge, dark, hungry eyes and a wide red mouth, high cheek-bones and the longest legs Charlie had ever seen. He returned his gaze to Camilla, starting when the woman laughed conspiratorially with her friend, a tall, handsome Englishman with blonde hair. Charlie ordered another round of drinks to be served at table in the dining-room, relieved that Camilla seemed blissfully unaware of the woman in red.

They were eating their mutton chops, when Eira Athoby entered the dining-room with her husband and two friends. Camilla looked up, weighed Lady Athoby's clothes and looked across the table to Charlie.

'There's a most beautiful woman just entered the dining-room. I never saw anyone quite like her. I'm sure her husband's English, their friends too, but she has a Spanish look.'

'Probably Lady Athoby. I've heard a lot about her husband. They say he'll be Governor-General someday.'

'Do have a look, Charlie. She's quite sensational.'

'I can't turn around without being unmannerly. I'll glance at her as I go out.'

They ordered strawberry fool and coffee with Drambuie. Then a second round of coffee and Drambuie. Camilla was already drowsy, as they walked from the dining-room to the hall, took their key from the receptionist and retired. After a bath, she put on her blue silk nightdress and got into bed. Charlie was already sound asleep. Camilla kissed him on the shoulder and was asleep at his side within seconds.

Charlie woke at three with a raging thirst, headache and palpitations. He went to the bathroom, took some Rennies to help his digestion and some aspirin to help his head. What he needed was a walk in the fresh air. He put on his dressing-gown and walked down the corridor to a door leading to the garden. When he had taken a dozen turns around the lawn, he sat on a rocking chair, looking towards the horizon and thinking of Eira Athoby. There were no lights on in the hotel, except the distant reception area, though there were fireflies on the lawn, tricking the eye with their bright light. Camilla adored fireflies. Camilla adored everything that was pretty and mysterious. Pity she had never adored *him*!

Charlie was about to light a cigar, when he smelled Eira's perfume, the heady, heavy iris and orchid scent he had smelled in the dining-room. She was lying in a hammock nearby, still in the red and gold kekoi and it passed through Charlie's mind that she had waited for him. She smiled mockingly at his uncertainty and spoke in a deep, husky voice.

'I couldn't sleep. It's so hot and humid. Anyway, I *hate* sleeping. I'll sleep when I'm dead, but until then I'll do other things with my nights.'

'Gad!'

'Are you going to keep puffing that cigar?'

'Clean forgot about it.'

'Why? Were you looking at these?'

She let the kekoi slip from her body. It fell like a shiver around her, revealing large, firm breasts, their nipples hard and searching. Charlie threw his cigar on the lawn, advancing like a sleep-walker, unable to stop when Eira moved to the ground, naked, before him and raised her pelvis in a blatant invitation. Her voice penetrated his senses, so low, dark, brooding and conspiratorial.

'I want you to love me. I need to be loved, every hour of every day. *Please* take me. If you want me to beg, I will.'

Something snapped in Charlie's head, a violent, vibrant desire that assassinated reason. He had longed for Camilla to desire him like that, but knew that she never would. He felt Eira unbutton him, push him back and impale herself on his hardness. She writhed like a serpent on heat until his body dissolved and he wanted more and more and more. Charlie took her again and again until dawn lit the horizon with the scarlet sabre strokes of betrayal. Then he looked hard into Eira's eyes, before hurrying back to his room.

She said nothing, not even goodbye. Eira never said goodbye. Once hooked by the intensity of her sensuality and the bewitching body she used with such power and finesse, no man had ever escaped her nor wanted to. She went to her room, well satisfied with her nocturnal adventure.

Charlie went to the bathroom, bathed, cleaned his teeth and said his prayers. Dear God, he had brought Camilla here to celebrate their first year in Africa and the fact that they had not had any grave troubles since their arrival. Now this! As he thought of Eira, his penis rose like an accusation. Panic stricken, he stared at it, stepped under the cold shower and then hurried back to bed. Mercifully, Camilla was still asleep. Charlie closed his eyes, trying to wipe out the tantalizing image of Lady Athoby. *Take me*, she had said, as if she could not wait another second . . . *If you want me to beg, I will*. His body began to harden, his penis and muscles tensing. Charlie knew he must see her again. He must find out how to meet her, where, when. Guilt made him wretched and his head began to throb. He had feared Camilla's infidelity, had thought himself her captive for life. But now he was another woman's willing prisoner. Where would it end? Could he find the strength to resist?

FOUR

Kenya, 1936

Sunset cast a blood-red light on the shimmering lake, turning the flamingoes from pale shell to deep coral, the walls of the house from white to vermilion. In the sky, a vulture wheeled, its outline black and menacing against the scarlet and charcoal clouds. Camilla was alone on the terrace. Since their arrival at the house, Charlie had rarely been home and then only to change his clothes and go out again. They no longer slept together. They rarely even ate together. The shock had been sudden and brutal. One minute they had been toasting their first year in Africa, the next renting the new property. In the months since their arrival in the Happy Valley, Charlie had disappeared for varying periods. First he had gone back to the farm to bring their possessions and with them, Bilea, Jogona, Miss McTaggart and Louise. Then, on his return, he had gone for weeks on end and Camilla had been forced to admit that her husband was unfaithful. From being an object of adulation, she found herself completely ignored. The effect on her confidence was devastating. She had only stayed with Charlie because his love had seemed so strong, so unreasonable, his need so touching. Now she had the impression that every minute he spent in the house was a minute he spent unwillingly away from the other woman. She felt helpless to do anything about the fact that her husband no longer loved her.

Camilla read Aunt Flora's letter again and laughed

out loud when she saw that cycling was the latest craze, wondering if her aunt would be pedalling up the lanes. Then she studied the fashion page and thought how terribly out-moded her clothes seemed when compared to the surreal shoe hats of Elsa Schiaparelli and the new wide shouldered look. She decided to grow her hair into a long bob, so at least she could have something in the latest style.

Camilla settled to thinking of Louise, who still dreamed of returning to England to live with Aunt Flora. Probably that was exactly what they would have to do. Louise would be ecstatic. But Camilla would be obliged to stay alone for the rest of her days. Charlie would never give her a divorce and she would remain a rejected wife in a world that had little interest in discarded women with husbands who rarely came home.

Breakfast the following morning was interrupted by a cry from Louise.

'Mummy! Mummy! Do come at once and *look*.'

It was a long, red Mercedes, resplendent with shimmering chrome trim and a cream leather interior that matched the livery of the black chauffeur, who sat like a statue at the wheel. Lady Athoby stepped out, smiled enchantingly and moved to shake hands. Camilla was not at all surprised to see that the lady was wearing the latest Chanel suit, its white tweed trimmed with black, its saucy hat setting off to perfection Eira's beauty and the gleaming gold chains that were the designer's favourite touch.

'I'm Eira Athoby. Sorry to pop in without an invitation but in Kenya we don't stand on ceremony like in England.'

'Come in. Would you like some tea? Louise, you are *not* to touch the car.'

Lady Athoby looked appraisingly at Camilla, smiling at the pastel knitted skirt and sweater.

'I'd love some tea.'

Her black hair was dressed in a severe chignon, in contrast with the curls of every other woman in the area. The eyes were malicious and full of humour as Camilla poured the tea and sat facing her.

'What can I do for you, Lady Athoby?'

'I came to invite you to our party.'

'My husband's not here at the moment.'

'Husbands are never home when you need them! Come alone, it's just a group of friends and neighbours, ours and yours. No need to worry about being solo.'

'I'll think about it, but I'm not used to socializing without Charlie.'

'Ah, you have the English papers.'

'You can borrow them if you'd like. The fashion pages are marvellous, but I see you already buy from Chanel. I wish I dare wear something like that.'

'Of course you dare! Do you go back to England often?'

'I've never been back since I arrived.'

'Oh you must, otherwise it's like living in Siberia! In Kenya you have to learn to make your own fun. Without it, you'd go stark raving mad. Now I must dash. I'm sitting for my portrait at nine-thirty, can't think why I agreed to get up so early. I shall have puffy eyes, that's for certain.'

'They seem wide open to me.'

'Do come to the party. I shall expect you at eight. Ours is the gate with the dolphins in black iron over the arch. About two miles from the entrance to this house, you'll see a little road to the right. We like to be in the wilds, but we're pretty well hidden.'

* * *

Scents of musk, papyrus and spice. Vendors of carpets, carved heads, scarabs, ivory and aphrodisiacs. Camilla searched the crowds for Charlie, but he was nowhere to be seen. She went to the Muthaiga Club and asked if he was there. The receptionist gave her a curt 'no'. Then, when she was gone, he sent a boy with a note to one of the bungalows in the garden.

Charlie was sniffing white powder that was better than any snuff ever invented. His head was clear, his penis hard and he was happy. Turning to Eira, who was lying on the bed, wearing nothing but a necklace of mimosa, jasmine and hibiscus, he sniffed her perfume and began to suck her nipples.

'Camilla came looking for me.'

'She's a sweetie, we should have invited her in.'

'Don't be disgusting!'

Lady Athoby laughed merrily at his reaction.

'Is she really as green as she seems?'

'My wife isn't a subject for conversation. And of course she's innocent.'

'You wouldn't know if she weren't! She probably has a lover.'

'Certainly not. I couldn't stand that.'

'What's sauce for the goose is sauce for the gander, Charlie.'

'You're detestable, Eira, truly detestable.'

'Move a little closer and I'll show you how detestable I can be. Deliciously detestable, unforgettably detestable. Put it there for a change, Charlie. For you, all roads lead to Rome!'

'Gad, Eira, must you be so decadent.'

'Don't be such a hypocrite. You love it. You've made love to me day and night ever since you arrived in Nairobi and to all my girlfriends too. You're a man who can't live without it.'

'I was never like that before.'

'Well, you are now and look at you, sniffing cocaine as if your nose can't live without *that* either.'

'It has a dramatic effect on my genitalia, if you must know.'

'I've noticed, that's why I like you. You're a degenerate too, Charlie. You weren't made for a sweetie like your precious Camilla.'

'Leave her out of the conversation or I shall get up and go!'

'I adore you when you're pompous.'

'You adore every man in Nairobi.'

'Why not? I love them and they love me and everyone's happy.'

'Doesn't your husband ever protest?'

'Why should he? Binkie adores young girls – and young boys even better. He likes anything that makes him come like Niagara Falls.'

'Now you're being disgusting.'

'You'll come to our party, Charlie?'

'Of course I will.'

'Stay over the whole weekend.'

'That's very royal of you, Eira.'

'I'm your friend, Charlie. You're a man after my own heart.'

'I don't think so, but I like to hear you say it.'

For the party Camilla chose a Molyneux dress never worn since her arrival, in silk chiffon shaded from palest blue to midnight. Draped in the Grecian style over one shoulder, the fastener was a pair of twin doves made of feathers and pearls. She was breathtakingly beautiful as she waved goodbye to Louise and drove off towards the Athoby estate.

White-robed servants stood like sentinels on either side of the front door. Camilla saw that the house was built in the form of a quadrangle with interior courtyard.

Eira and her husband, Binkie, were on the veranda, waiting to welcome her.

'Come and have some champagne, Camilla. This is my husband, Binkie. Darling, do run and bring Camilla something delicious to drink.'

Camilla gasped when she saw the surreal living-room of the house, the predominating colour of which was scarlet, the motif, giant lips. A Dali sofa in the form of a slightly open mouth held two landowners, a French visitor and his wife and a solitary, pale-faced woman. On the far wall an eight-feet-long Man Ray painting showed a pair of vivid red lips floating in a bluish grey sky over a twilight lunar landscape. Stools with seemingly real legs held two Italian visitors and Charlie, stupefied and breathless, when Camilla walked in. Embarrassed by his presence, Camilla flinched when he protested.

'Dammit, Eira, Camilla's my *wife*. She doesn't belong here!'

Eira poured him a tumbler of whisky, which, to Camilla's horror, he drank down like water. Anxious to be invisible, Camilla sat on an armchair shaped like an upturned hand, surprised that her glass was refilled as if by magic every time she took a sip. Feeling hungry, she looked around to see if there were any signs of dinner being served. There was no odour of cooking and nothing to indicate that a meal was among the hostess's intentions. As she gazed at Charlie's puce face, Camilla began to panic. When Charlie began to snore loudly, he was promptly picked up, carted out and put to bed by the two Italian guests. Camilla sighed. Evidently her husband was a regular visitor to the house. Maybe that explained the mystery of his absence from her life. She looked at her hands, trying to keep back tears as she remembered the night at the Muthaiga

Club when she had urged Charlie to look at the sensational Lady Athoby.

Dinner was served at ten, by which time the guests were so drunk they had no idea what they were eating. Coffee was served in the lounge.

Then servants appeared with bowls of cocaine, and the guests started to sniff. Camilla had been warned about a white powder said to drive British settlers insane. She wondered momentarily if that was what had sent Charlie off the rails. Then she rose, saying with a forced smile that she must leave. At that moment, Charlie appeared from the bedroom.

'Is dinner ready? I'm famished.'

Eira smiled malevolently at his dishevelled appearance.

'We've eaten, Charlie dear, but cook's left a cold plate and dessert in the kitchen for you. I'll ring for Nandu to bring it.'

Eira handed Camilla a drink with a winning smile.

'One for the road, neighbour.'

'I really must go.'

'A toast to Lady Invergordon, ladies and gentlemen.'

Obliged to drink one last glass, Camilla looked wistfully at the eager faces of the friends of Lady Athoby. The Frenchman was handsome, but bored with life. Athoby was a rake and probably a scoundrel. Camilla was looking into his insolent blue eyes, when she became aware that there were two Lord Athobys, two Charlies, two Eiras and two of everything in the room. She sat down suddenly, afraid that she was going to faint. Then, disbelievingly, she watched as the guests began to play a strange game.

First they tossed a feather in a sheet. When the feather landed, the sharp end pointed to one of them. When it landed again, it pointed to another. The couple were paired off and would sleep together. Panic hit Camilla and she made a valiant effort to rise, but the sedative Eira had put in her champagne had robbed her of all physical strength. She looked appealingly at her husband.

'Take me home, Charlie. I'm dizzy.'

'Drunk a bit too much, my dear? Me too. Best if you lie down for a while. I'll take you back in the morning.'

'I want to go now!'

The feather landed before Lord Athoby. Then, as the guests laughed hysterically, it came to rest before Camilla. Charlie looked dazedly at the feather and then across the table to Eira.

'Look here, Camilla's my wife! She doesn't play games of this sort and she's unwell, needs to lie down.'

Eira laughed delightedly.

'She needs to lie down, Binkie. Shall we help her? You know, Charlie, it really *is* time you cured your infernal jealousy. I've an idea. Drink your whisky like a good boy and then watch and you'll never be jealous again.'

Eira walked over to Camilla and unzipped her dress. It fell soundlessly to the ground, leaving her naked, but for a pale silk underslip. Two of the women lifted the slip over her head. Then, as Charlie roared his protests, his wife was placed on the coffee table, naked, pale, her limbs trembling, her eyes vacant. Drugged, dazed, Camilla was barely conscious, though she saw two men holding Charlie back and then his sudden collapse in an unconscious heap on the ground.

Somewhere in the distance a cymbal clashed and Camilla heard voices chanting and a naked man who looked like Lord Athoby approaching her, parting her legs and amid cries of excitement, penetrating her. Panic stricken, she fought, but her arms had no force, her legs no muscles. She cried out, but the oscillating man above her continued to pump his lust, as fellow guests caressed her breasts and tried to give her more champagne.

When Lord Athoby had gone, the lights were extinguished and scented candles lit. The guests sniffed more of the white powder and Eira stuck a needle into the vein in her arm. Camilla tried desperately to get up, but she could not make her body work. A suntanned Italian began to caress her, suckling her nipples like a hungry child. Then he lifted her in his arms and carried her to the room he shared with the other Italian. There, Camilla screamed in anguish, as the two men began to undress.

Outside, thunder roared and flashes of violet lightning filled the house with the strange and surreal atmosphere of Valhalla. In the living-room, Charlie was still unconscious. He would not return to full awareness until noon of the following day. Eira's guests were drinking, making love, watching each other make love and finding oblivion in the drugs she recommended above all else, as a panacea for boredom.

Camilla woke at dawn alone, her head aching from the aftereffects of the sedative, her body wracked with pain. She rose, looked at her black and blue limbs and then at the chalk-white face and empty blue eyes in a mirror. Her dress had been placed on a chair in the room. Camilla regarded it with horror. Searching the drawers, she found white shorts, a shirt and a pair of white leather sandals. She ran a bath and scrubbed herself clean, thinking sadly that she would never be really clean again. Then, having dressed in one of the Italian's clothes, she took her bag and car keys from the table and, leaving the blue dress behind her, walked slowly from the room.

In the lounge, Camilla stepped over the sleeping forms of those who had been too exhausted or too drunk to go to bed. Everywhere there was the heavy odour of Java lilies, cigars, semen and vomit. Camilla looked down at her husband, sleeping with his mouth wide open, his cheeks flushed to their now habitual pink. For a moment she almost hated him. Then, she pitied him for destroying his life, hers and the happiness they had once known together. They would never be together again. From this moment on, for her, Charlie Invergordon had ceased to exist. Camilla walked like an automaton to the car, shock dawning on the horizon of her mind. She was sure of only one thing. Before the end of the day she would put distance between her and the Happy Valley.

On arrival at the house, Camilla called the servants and Miss McTaggart to her study and explained that she was leaving and why. Bilea ran weeping from the room, returning with a small valise of clothes and a good luck amulet. Stunned but courageous Miss McTaggart was supportive and practical.

'I'll leave also, Lady Invergordon. I'll go back to Fife and tell the family what's happened. It's absolutely essential and urgent.'

'Thank you, Miss McTaggart. I'll give you your wages till the end of the month. You already have your return ticket for the boat from Mombasa. Get Mr Drummond to drive you there on Friday to have it dated.'

'If you ever need me again, the Invergordons will know where I am.'

'Bring Louise down, please. Tell her we're leaving.'

'Where will you go?'

'I don't know. Far away, that's all.'

'You're terribly bruised. Shall I call the doctor?'

'No, just bring Louise.'

Camilla hurried to the car and sat waiting to leave, unable to bear the anguish of more farewells. When Louise appeared, she started the engine. Then she saw Jogona standing alone at the door, tears streaming down his cheeks. She stopped the engine and got out of the car.

'I almost forgot to say goodbye to you, Jogona, and to thank you for all you taught me when I arrived. I've given Miss McTaggart your wages. Return to the farm where we first met. I'm sure General Sir William Orme will be so very pleased to have you back.'

'May God speed you on your way, madame.'

'Goodbye, Jogona. Go now, before Lord Invergordon returns. He'll be in a very difficult mood when he comes home.'

Camilla drove away, knowing only that she wanted to be far from the area. There was a small landing field where a plane could pick up passengers for Mombasa. That would save a drive she was in no condition to make, if only she could find it. But where was the landing strip? Increasingly, shock deadened her memory and Camilla wondered if she were driving in circles. She barely replied when Louise asked where they were going.

From Riuru, she drove to Thika and then to Fourteen Falls, knowing in her heart that she was lost. She had no idea where the airfield was, but had found her way by instinct to the only man she had ever really wanted, the only man she had thought of, dreamed of, since the morning when he had arrived at the farm with a jerrycan because his car had broken down. Camilla pulled to a halt outside a massive ranch house of cedar-clad construction. While Louise ran to ring the bell, she stayed where she was, too tired to move, too shocked to think. She did not notice Saunders' sister, Cecy, letting the child into the house. She simply sat, staring into space, trying not to think of the events of the previous night, trying to still the silent screams in her head, as tears fell like thunder drops down her bruised cheeks.

Saunders took one look at Camilla, bit his lip hard and lifted her gently in his arms and into the house.

'You're safe now, Camilla. Trust me.'

The words made her cry, but she said nothing at all. When Saunders put her in a guest bedroom, his sister and the housekeeper, Madame Nbo, were waiting to undress her, bathe her and put her to bed. Saunders ran to the kitchen and sent a boy for the doctor. Then, anguished by his guest's condition, he sat on the veranda, watching the sun as it sank over the horizon in a striking scarlet sky. Saunders wanted to kill whoever was responsible for hurting her, but was conscious that the priority was to keep Camilla safe, hidden and secure enough to recuperate her health.

When the doctor arrived, from his house on the estate, the two men hurried upstairs to the guest room. Saunders waited outside on the landing, pacing up and down, wincing when he heard Camilla sobbing.

In the kitchen, Louise was telling Cecy the story of her life.

'We've been living in the Happy Valley and, before that, in the mountains. When we lived in London we were in Eaton Square. Aunt Flora used to come and see us often, but now we never see her at all. I hope we can go home to England, so I can repair her car. I've always loved machines and Jogona taught me how to dismantle lots of parts and put them together again.'

Cecy looked with interest at the child, with her big green eyes, curly blonde hair and Liberty smocked dress.

'Do you like repairing cars, Louise?'

'Oh yes, and tractors and any machines.'

'My brother's a fine mechanic. You must get John to teach you all he knows. I'm not bad myself, have to be mechanically minded when you live in the wilds.'

'Can we start learning now?'

'No, not tonight. It's eight o'clock and time for dinner. You can stay up and have it with us as this is a special occasion. Then you must try to sleep. You've had a very tiring day.'

'Mummy's tired and she has big bruises everywhere!'

'The doctor's with her now. She'll be lots better in the morning. We'll all go and pick flowers for her before breakfast and deliver them with her tray.'

That night, Saunders and his sister sat on the veranda discussing their visitors. Saunders remained on the veranda until long after midnight, thinking of Camilla, as he had thought of her every minute of every day since that first meeting. The doctor had explained what had happened and had forbidden Camilla to travel for at least a month, warning Saunders that her state of mind was fragile and that she had suffered greatly, not only at the home of the Athobys, but from years of living with a madman. Saunders knew that Camilla was a rare flower to be cherished in a calm environment. He had one hundred and fifty thousand acres of tranquillity and he would give her shelter and look after her for always. Full of plans, he slept almost at once but awoke with a jolt at 3 a.m., when Camilla screamed in her nightmare.

Saunders rose, put on a dressing-gown and ran to cradle her in his arms. Tears were running down her cheeks and she was only half awake. She spoke as softly as a child.

'Don't leave me, John.'

'I'm here and I'll stay. You're safe now, Camilla, close your eyes.'

She stared at him, registering the words but unable to show any emotion. The shock had so profoundly taken her in its grip, she felt she would never be able to laugh and sing and shout again. But instinct told her she was where she belonged, where she had always wanted and needed to be. Destiny had brought her to Saunders.

FIVE

Louise was tinkering with a car parked under a jacaranda tree. At her side, Charlie could see a tall, thin woman of about thirty-five, with black curly hair and round glasses. Saunders was leading a horse into the stables. There was no sign of Camilla, but Charlie had heard the rumours and had come to see if they were true. Hidden on the hill, he watched the simple, domestic scene with narrowed eyes, sucking in his breath when Camilla rode in on a snow-white horse and led it into the stables after Saunders. Charlie took another swig of whisky from his hip flask, got in his car and drove to Nairobi to see his lawyer.

Saunders listened as Camilla sang 'All the King's Horses', amazed by the change in her condition. After the shock and apathy, she had become impossibly angry, violent and self-destructive, shouting at Louise, crying without reason and generally being unstable. Cecy had resolved the problem, setting Camilla to work breaking a wall. With a sledgehammer in her hands and a crumbling wall to destroy, Camilla had taken her anguish out on plaster and pebble instead of herself. The therapy had worked wonders and she had been back to normal in a week. The experience at the Athoby house would never be forgotten or forgiven, but at least she was singing again. Now, she was blossoming, like the jacaranda and mimosa, which grew in abundance around the farm.

Each day Camilla and Saunders rode or picknicked or

swam in the lake. Each night they dined together and told stories of their youth. Both had been orphaned young and raised by an aunt. Both had rejected the British social life of Kenya but loved the country.

Saunders sighed. He had never been in love before and was for ever debating if Camilla had been permanently affected by her experience in the Athobys' home. His desire for her was now so intense he could barely sleep at night. Often in the small hours, he descended to his office to look over the accounts, but he could not concentrate on them either. Tomorrow was Camilla's birthday. There would be a special dinner and presents, which Cecy and Louise had been discussing for days. For his part, Saunders had bought her a beautiful pearl on a chain. He was planning to take Camilla to see the Fourteen Falls, after which the estate was named, a sight so beautiful he knew it would take her breath away. She loved picnics and this would be the most spectacular picnic she had ever had.

Hearing her singing, Saunders called out: 'Shall we have tea?'

'Yes, I'm hungry. Ask Madame Nbo to make a gallon of tea and some of her nutmeg biscuits.'

'Coming up.'

'John, after my birthday, we must talk. I can't stay here for ever, you know that. I must return to England and put Louise into school. I can't just live here, people will start talking someday.'

'Why?'

'People love to gossip and if they do I'm afraid my presence could bring problems for you.'

'Do you want to go back to England?'

'No, I'd like to stay for ever, but I have to put Louise into school.'

'Then you shall. Afterwards, you demand a divorce

from Invergordon and we'll be married. That's settled. Now pour the tea, there's a dear.'

'Is that a proposal, John?'

'Of course it is, but I never proposed to anyone before and I already warned you I have two left feet with women. You have to be patient and teach me the niceties of all that. It could take fifty years. At least I hope it will.'

Camilla walked towards him and looked up into his eyes. Then she kissed him on the cheeks and gently on the mouth.

'I've got two left feet with men, so we should make a good team. I have so much to learn, it could take more than fifty years.'

The falls were spectacular, their sound deafening. Surrounded by a fathomless arch of green branches, lianes, parasol ferns, noisy with chattering birds and monkeys, it was the perfect hideaway from the sun-scorched landscape of summer. First they swam in the rock pool. Then they walked a little distance from the falls, to where the noise was merely a background murmur and Saunders spread a blanket under the tree. He was about to get out the food, when Camilla took off her swimsuit and stood naked before him.

'I want to make love, John. I want to know how it feels when you love someone with all your heart. I need to be reassured that those men in my nightmares haven't robbed me of my capacity to be a real woman.'

'You're a remarkable person, Camilla. I don't know if I shall be a good lover for you, but if desire and respect and admiration count for anything, you have them.'

She kissed him then, as she had never kissed anyone before, a tiny cry escaping her lips, as her body caught fire and she felt the need to lie back and wind her legs around him, letting him take her. In all the years with

Charlie, she had thought love an obligation. Now, suddenly, she realized that it was a necessity. As Saunders entered her and smothered her cheeks with kisses, Camilla cried out, because her body had come alive as never before. Then, as they achieved the mysterious harmony she had heard about but never experienced, she felt her muscles tensing and the sudden explosion of what felt like a firework deep within her body. She cried out and held Saunders in the vice of her passion. She was trembling and could barely speak, but as he took her in his arms, covered her with the blanket and kissed her tenderly, she told him the truth.

'I know very little about making love. Charlie was the first man in my life and I thought making love was something you did to have children, a kind of necessary evil. I felt nothing and I was upset when Charlie soiled me. With those men at the Athobys' house I felt nothing either. I lost consciousness after a while. I'm not a woman who has ever felt things very forcibly, at least that was what I thought.'

'You were wrong. A philosopher called Taine once said that no one was as capable of passion as a man who keeps his emotions hidden. The same goes for women. No one's more capable of deep passion than a woman like you, at least the woman within you, the one you hide from the world.'

'I love you, John.'

'And I love you, have done ever since our first meeting.'

Charlie watched their return. An hour later, his lawyer arrived at the house with a letter Charlie had written, asking Camilla to come back to him. The lawyer left two minutes later, the letter still in his hand. Saunders stood like a huge rock on the veranda, watching until his visitor's car was out of sight.

Camilla was very pale, but Saunders was adamant.

'If your husband wants trouble he can have it, but I think you should ask for a divorce. If he won't agree, we'll live together for ever and to hell with convention!'

'Charlie's unstable and I'm scared for you, John.'

Cecy entered the room and took her place at table.

'Camilla's right. Invergordon has a reputation for being unstable. I know it's difficult to decide who's mad and who's sane, but the Invergordon family are not famous for their lucidity and Charlie's had a reputation for violence ever since his youth. I talked with Lord Hayes-Farquhar about him this morning. He's known throughout Scotland as a rather dangerous young man.'

Saunders spoke with decision.

'I won't be threatened and I won't run. This is my home, Cecy. What can I do but stay here? If he takes a pot shot at one of us, we'll have him arrested. In any case, I'll give orders to the boys to search my land for sight of him.'

Charlie slept in the open, on the hill, waking at midday, his face burned by the sun. He had little left to eat, but two bottles out of a crate of whisky in the car. From the dishevelled folds of his shirt, he took out an old photograph of Camilla, the one where she and the baby had posed for Lucille's new season's fashions. Louise had not been six months old. Camilla had been truly divine, still was. Tears ran down his cheeks and he cursed the madness that had made him link his life with Eira Athoby's. It was too late now for regrets. All that mattered was to get Camilla back and start again, together. They would leave Africa and go no matter where. Charlie wondered if the family would let him live at Black Gordon. Thirsty, he drank from one of the whisky bottles. Then he looked again through the binoculars, an ever present but hidden presence, torturing himself by watching the wife he revered with another man.

Louise was delighted with the day's work. She and Cecy had fitted shelves in the garage for car and tractor spare parts and reserves of everything the estate could possibly need. Then Saunders had shown her how to drive. Louise was almost beside herself with excitement, remembering the moment when she had taken the wheel and controlled the car for fifty yards. She decided to go and tell her mother the news.

'John taught me to drive, Mummy.'

'Were you tall enough to reach the pedals?'

'He put me on a big cushion and put blocks on the accelerator, clutch and brake. I'm nearly tall enough in any case.'

'You'll be a great driver someday.'

'Like Sir Malcolm Campbell?'

'Probably. I shall be very proud of you, you know. I'm always proud of you.'

'I love you, Mummy. I wish Aunt Flora could see me. Will she be coming over soon?'

'I've written and asked her to come.'

'I hope she arrives. She'll be so surprised when she sees me drive. And we'll be different, won't we, Mummy? You're so pretty now, prettier and prettier and Daddy's never ever coming back, is he?'

'No, Louise, he isn't.'

The following day, Camilla and Saunders went out into the wilds. They saw a huge herd of buffalo on the plateau of the Masai Mara and exchanged gifts and greetings with the warriors of the tribe, who came often to Fourteen Falls, to pass with their cattle to Kithimani. Tall, reed slim, they were an impressive sight, the women's hair dressed with animal fat coloured with ochre. Leaving the Masai behind, Saunders moved around the edge of the forest, showing Camilla the birds of his domain.

'That's the crowned crane, see the tuft on his head. That one's a secretary bird.'

She looked at a long-legged pale grey bird with black flight feathers, who hunted in pairs in the grasslands for snakes and small mammals. Saunders continued.

'That's a weaver bird. He's a spectacular fellow and look over there, a flock of ostriches. Here, take the binoculars. Those are the most stupid birds in the world, once drove twenty miles on a track behind a group of terrified ostriches and not one of them had the sense to divert and avoid running in front of the car.'

On the way home, they passed the cadaver of a young zebra, killed by a lion. Vultures, maribous and ants were removing carrion until the bones gleamed pale in the sunlight. Camilla shivered, imagining the cadaver as her marriage and the animals of prey as the Athobys and their like. Seeing a cloud of doubt pass over her eyes, Saunders paused at the side of a small lake and opened the picnic hamper, handing Camilla a leg of chicken glazed in honey.

'Thought we'd eat here so you could watch your favourites.'

Camilla looked in the direction he was indicating, but saw nothing at all. Then, against the earth at the side of the lake, she discerned movement and realized that there were crocodiles in abundance, big, long crocodiles with mouths like giant rat traps. She laughed delightedly.

'I'm glad they're far away.'

'They feed mainly on fish you know.'

'I'm not eager to put your statement to the test!'

They arrived back at six in the evening, under a violet evening sky. Tired, hungry, they were nonetheless euphoric with happiness in each other's company. Dinner was Camilla's favourite, tomato and purple onion salad, followed by steak and kidney pudding.

Cecy laughed delightedly as both of them ate second helpings.

'I'll never know how you stay so slim, Camilla. You eat more than three Irish navvies.'

'I'm probably descended from three Irish navvies. I've always thought I had a bit of Dublin blood in me. I'm either euphoric with happiness or in the deepest despair.'

Laughter mixed with glasses clinking and then the low murmur of conversation as they took their coffee and Cecy's wild blackberry liqueur on the veranda. Fireflies darted in a magic sky. Stars twinkled like tiny lights and far away there was the faint, luminescence of the crown of snow on the summit of Kilimanjaro. Camilla yawned, rose and spoke sleepily.

'I know it's only nine-thirty, but my eyes are determined to close. See you in the morning, everyone.'

She kissed Cecy and then turned and embraced Saunders. She had had a wonderful day and as she walked slowly upstairs she knew that tomorrow would be another wonderful day and after that endless happiness under the blue sky of Africa.

Silence. Distant howl of a jackal. An eery stillness like the end of the world. Then, the soft crunch of footsteps in the long grass and a startlingly loud thump at the door. A long pause. Finally, the lights were lit and Saunders descended the stairs and opened the door.

'Lord Invergordon, are you aware that it's two in the morning?'

By way of a response, Charlie discharged both barrels of his shotgun in his rival's face. Then, with a crooked smile, he walked back to his car and drove to Nairobi. He took out the letter Camilla had written and sent on to his lawyer. Every word of it was etched in acid in his mind . . . *If you want a divorce, I agree without condition. If you want me to return to you, that can never be. I shall never see or speak to you again. I'm sorry.*

Charlie re-loaded the rifle and sat for what seemed like an age, watching dawn come like a scarlet search-light over the horizon. He had parked the car outside Eira's cottage at the Muthaiga Club, but he did not enter. Instead, he wrote a short note. *I am truly sorry for all that has happened. I only ever loved you, but we Invergordons are mad and the mad only know how to destroy. Charlie.* The sun was so strong, it almost blinded him and his eyes filled with tears of profound sadness. It was the first time he had been sober in over a year. He glanced wistfully at Eira's cottage, sighed and then put the rifle in his mouth, looped his toes around the string fixed to the trigger and pulled.

Camilla ran from her room, only to hear Cecy shout.

'Go back, Camilla. Do *not* come down!'

'What's happened?'

'There's been a terrible accident. Madame Nbo!'

Men were sent for the doctor, the priest and the constabulary of Nairobi. Then Cecy hurried to Camilla's room and found her chalk-white faced and rigid in the armchair.

'I want to see John.'

'He's dead, Camilla. I believe Lord Invergordon shot him.'

Camilla rose like a catapult and ran to the front door, faltering when she saw Saunders lying in a pool of blood, his face unrecognizable. Fiercely, she knelt at his side, kissed his hands, whispering, as if she believed he could hear her, even in death.

'I love you, John. I love you for always and beyond.'

Cecy led her to her room, undressed her like a child and changed her clothes, because there was blood everywhere. Camilla said nothing at all. She could not accept the fact that the good life, the beautiful life was over, that the future was just another black tunnel, as it had been with Charlie Invergordon. She did not cry or scream. Her body felt limp and the light had gone from her eyes as the dreams had vanished from her heart. In a moment of total destruction, the person who had been Camilla vanished from the scene. Unaware of Cecy's anguished gaze, she sat on the edge of the bed, looking with vacant eyes at the ferns she and Saunders had picked together the previous morning. He had told her they would be dead in twenty-four hours, but she so loved ferns they had picked them anyway. Now it was John who was dead. Cecy left the room unnoticed, wondering if Camilla would ever really recover from the second great tragedy of her life.

Later, when she had seen the police, the doctor, the priest and received news of Charlie's suicide at the Muthaiga Club, Cecy went to Camilla's room and found her sitting in exactly the same place on the edge of the bed. She handed Charlie's suicide note to Camilla, who looked at it briefly, barely read the contents and then tore it into tiny pieces and threw it to the floor.

Cecy took Camilla in her arms, hoping she might cry, but she just continued to stare at the ferns and then, after an hour, towards the horizon and the scarlet sunset of an African evening. She was dreaming of the man she loved, talking to him within her brain, holding his hand and trying to forget the bloody pulp that had been all that remained of the handsome face she had adored.

In the still of night, Cecy sat on the veranda looking at the sky and thinking of the brother she had loved. Tears ran down her cheeks as she remembered the day when he had returned home after his first meeting with Camilla, in love as she had never seen a man in love before. For months he had dreamed of Camilla, talked of Camilla and then, as if by magic, she had arrived at the farm. Cecy wept softly at her brother's tragic destiny. To die like a dog at the hands of a madman was a death unworthy of any man. For Saunders it was unthinkable. Cecy had the sudden desire to run away, to leave Africa, to put everything behind her. But she was old enough and wise enough to accept even now that nothing would ease the pain of her loss, except time. When the funeral was over, she would return to England for some months and stay with the family. She would sell the farm and on her return to Kenya would buy her own coffee plantation well away from Fourteen Falls. She would never see the farm and the estate again.

Dawn came blood red over the horizon. Cecy wiped her eyes and went to the kitchen to make a pot of tea. She could not eat. She could not keep the tears from falling like rain down her cheeks, but she had made her decisions. She wondered in silent anguish what decisions Camilla would make, what the future held for a woman and child alone.

Native voices sang a hymn. A hundred white settlers came to pay their respects. The whole area around the farm was covered in flowers, the flowers of Kenya with their strong, sensuous perfumes. As the voices rose in a last hymn, Camilla, Cecy and Louise stood at the graveside, listening to the words of the priest and the eulogy of Saunders' friend, Dr Brady. Louise knew he was dead, but had not been told how Saunders had died. She did not know that her father was responsible nor that Charlie had committed suicide. Standing very still, she held her mother's hand, wondering why Camilla was so pale, almost white, like a madonna made of marble. Cecy also watched Camilla, worried by the lack of tears and the strange emptiness in the violet eyes.

The frail body trembled, but English discipline kept her head high, her emotions under control. Cecy rightly thought that the emotions were too controlled.

By sunset, when the mourners had gone and the tangible silence returned, Cecy poured Camilla another after dinner coffee.

'What are you planning to do, Camilla?'

'I want you to take Louise back to England and deliver her to my Aunt Flora. She needs to be put into my old school in Sussex. Mending cars might be fun, but it's not an occupation for a young lady.'

'But what will *you* do?'

'The estate has to be wound up, sold and probate granted to you and John's family in England. I desperately need to keep occupied. May I do that for you, Cecy? At least I'll feel I did something to repay all your kindness to me. When it's done, I'll return to England.'

'You'll be better when you get back. And I'm grateful for your offer. I'll give you my power of attorney and when you've sold the estate and come back to England, I'll be waiting to help you get settled in again.'

Camilla drank her coffee, smiling wistfully at the words.

'I want to thank you for all you've done for me and Louise. She views you like she views Aunt Flora, as someone stable in her life. She loves me, but I'm unreal to her. I always was. I was always someone who lived with the father she feared. But no regrets. I'm glad she's as different from me as chalk from cheese.'

'I think I'll leave on Friday. Major Carruthers has agreed to fly me to Mombasa and there'll be no problem getting a cabin at this time of year. Can Louise be ready?'

'Of course she can. She'll be ready in an hour if she thinks she's going home to Aunt Flora!'

Cecy sat, as she had sat each night since Saunders'

death, on the veranda. She could not bear to be in her room in the hours of darkness. She found it difficult to remain in the house at all and was profoundly relieved to be leaving. As she ran over all Camilla had said, she wondered at the sudden calm that had taken possession of the seemingly fragile creature her brother had loved. would Camilla do what had to be done to repay her debt to John or to delay the inevitable parting from Kenya? Cecy sighed, exhausted, suddenly, by what had happened. She slept in her chair, waking with the dawn as it came, violet rose, over the horizon. She was one day nearer the day when she would leave the estate for ever. She prayed silently for the strength to leave without showing Camilla the profound depth of her torment, her regrets, her burning fury at the destruction wrought in all their lives by the madness of Charlie Invergordon.

Major Carruthers was in goggles and an aviator suit, that looked as if it were made in medieval times. Camilla drove the car to the edge of the clearing, kissed Cecy and took Louise in her arms.

'This is a special gift for Aunt Flora. It's the pearl John gave me for my birthday.'

'It's lovely, Mummy. I'll put it in my toolbox so I won't lose it.'

'This is a letter for Aunt Flora and a very special present for you. Open it when you get on the boat.'

Louise kissed her mother resoundingly. Then, she stood for a moment, looking up at the beautiful creature in the dusky pink dress, the most wonderful Mummy in the world. As rain began to fall, the child ran to the plane and took her place next to Cecy, both of them waving to Camilla, who remained beside Saunders' old Austin. As the plane wobbled into a turn, they exchanged kisses and raised both their arms in a final goodbye.

Raindrops splashed Camilla's cheeks, mixing with the tears that fell like a cascade as she stood in a sudden shower, watching, waiting, straining until the plane was a mere dot on the far horizon.

As she drove back to the estate, she looked at a field or a road or a hillside, where she and Saunders had picnicked or made love. Memories filtered through her mind like pieces in a kaleidoscope, memories of a happiness so vivid and unforgettable she wanted, above all, to keep them fresh, vibrant, never faded to sepia like old photographs in an album.

In the weeks that followed their departure, Camilla used the power of attorney given to her to put Saunders' affairs in order, and repatriated all monies owing for cattle and equipment sold. When she was not occupying herself with the business, she went and sat at her lover's graveside, decorating it with fresh flowers every morning and then walking where they had walked, watching the clouds as they had watched them rush by, as life had rushed by with sudden and brutal urgency.

One day, her tasks were finished and Camilla knew that she had done all she had promised Cecy she would do. Suddenly, she felt happy, as if a great weight had been lifted from her shoulders. She had repaid the debt to the estate, inasmuch as it was possible. She had done her duty to Saunders and to her child.

That night, Camilla ate alone and retired early. She had decorated her bedroom with dozens of scented lilies, picked, as she and her lover had often picked them, in the wilds. She had put on her favourite sheets, of white linen embroidered in palest cream and green with the Saunders initials. She bathed, washed and set her hair and put on her most beautiful dress, a white and grey lace with long sleeves and a sweetheart neck-line that had been Saunders' favourite. As the clock struck nine, she wrote a letter to Aunt Flora.

I am so sorry for all this. I feel John's presence everywhere and I can't resist the desire to hurry to join him. Tell Louise her Mummy loved her dearly and look after her like you looked after me. I send you all my love.
                    Camilla.

When the maid took breakfast in the morning, she found Camilla dead, a sleeping beauty who would never wake again. By the bedside, there were two empty pill bottles. On the table a note in Camilla's neat hand. For her, the nightmare of solitude and despair was over.

Part Two

LOUISE

She was rather like one of those innocent tasting American drinks which creep imperceptibly into your system, so that, before you know what you're doing, you're starting out to reform the world by force if necessary, and pausing on your way to tell the large man in the corner that, if he looks at you like that, you will knock his head off. P. G. WODEHOUSE

SIX

England, 1946

Louise looked at her watch and smiled with pride, remembering the day when she had won it in the Downhill Skiing Championship at Cortina d'Ampezzio. Glancing at her photograph in the local paper, she grinned mischievously, re-read the article, ate another black market chocolate and wondered if she should go on a diet. She had lost most of her puppy fat in the last two years, but if she kept eating the chocolates Aunt Flora bought from spivs who frequented the American base, she might well weigh enough to break her skis by Christmas.

'I'm going for a spin in the Rolls, Aunt Flora,' she announced.

'Try to remember it's a Morris Minor Rolls and there isn't much petrol in the tank and don't drive so fast you end up in the ditch!'

Louise took off merrily, singing at the top of her voice . . . *Run Rabbit, run Rabbit, run, run, run*. As she had not taken her driving test, her idea of a spin was a few high-speed circuits of the field. Accelerating past the red telephone box on the other side of the hedge, then the cemetery with its grey tombstones, she wondered if someone with a macabre sense of humour had put a telephone box at the entrance to a long-deserted country graveyard, as if to enable the dead to ring the living to give them the latest news of the hereafter! Then, finding a bag of aniseed balls on the passenger seat, Louise put one in her mouth and began again to hum her favourite songs, 'We'll Meet Again' followed, when she had swallowed her aniseed ball, by a lively rendition of 'Give Your Scrap to the Scrapchap'.

A greenfinch flew from the hedge, its yellow chest vivid in the sunshine. Louise glanced in its direction and then slammed on the car brakes. What was *that*? Leaping out of the car, she ran to the hedge, climbed over the stile into the field.

It was a little plane painted red. The door was open. Louise walked around the plane a dozen times, taking in all the details and admiring its seemingly fragile lines. Then she climbed on to the wing, passed through the open door into the tiny cockpit and sat in the pilot's seat. She pretended to be flying it with gusto, making roaring and revving noises in her throat and putting on a special flier's hat and goggles, found on the floor, for good measure. She was imagining herself in the clouds, gliding like an eagle over the estuary, when a voice brought her back to reality.

'Get the hell out of there right NOW!'

Louise took off the flier's hat and the goggles, peered out of the plane and saw a young man as tall as a telegraph pole, with jet-black hair, big blue eyes and a very vexed expression. She jumped out and walked towards him, wishing fervently she were not wearing her old school uniform of navy and white with ankle socks, like a six-year-old. When they were face to face she thrust out her hand, smiled like an angel and introduced herself.

'I'm Louise Invergordon. Who are you? I *love* your plane.'

He opened his mouth to admonish her, took in the huge green eyes, the curly blonde hair, closed his mouth again and shook hands.

'Joe Tanner, Captain USAF, stationed down the road. The Tiger Moth belongs to a friend, borrowed it so I could take a look at the countryside on the other side of the estuary. You shouldn't tinker with planes, they're dangerous.'

'I didn't touch anything. I was only pretending to fly. I'm very fond of mechanical things, always have been. I was friendly with Daddy's gamekeeper and he started me repairing tractors in Scotland when I was four. I can repair Aunt Flora's Morris Minor, Lord Lorne's Rolls Royce and Mr Coleclough's tractor. Taught myself, you know. If you bring me a mechanics' manual for your plane I'll probably learn how to service it too.'

'You're a regular boffin!'

'I'd rather learn to fly it, I suppose. When I was little, I wanted to drive a car as fast as Sir Malcolm Campbell. Now I can drive a car, I'd like to learn to fly. I read the other day that flying's the escape route of the future.'

'How old are you?'

'I'm nineteen. How old are you?'

'Twenty-eight. Do you need an escape route?'

'Oh, no! I'm very happy, but I think I'm one of those people who likes to go where no one can follow. If I couldn't be me, I'd be a seagull. What's the matter? You look a bit stupefied. Tell you what, you can show me how the plane works.'

'No!'

'Why not?'

'Because . . .'

Joe looked at her face, couldn't find a logical reason not to show her, climbed in the plane, increasingly astonished when she followed and listened with rapt attention as he spoke.

'It's very simple, there are two principal controls, the rudder and the joystick. The rudder decides right and left and the joystick sends you up if you pull it back and down if you push it forward, tilt it right and you turn

95

right, tilt it left and you turn left. The rudder also gives the angle of tilt.'

'Show me the rudder and the joystick.'

'That's the rudder and this one's the joystick. Then there's a form of control to start the engine, but you don't need to know where that is!'

They climbed down, Joe helping her to the ground. As he stood near her, he thought that Louise smelled of hayfields and wild flowers. She was no flirt, that was certain. Probably when she was older she'd be a mechanic. Or maybe another Amy Johnson. He thought her capable of absolutely anything. He was amused when, suddenly, Louise said goodbye and walked towards her car.

'You're a very interesting person and I've had the nicest afternoon since I was in Cortina for the championships. Come to lunch on Sunday. That's our house over there, the one with the big chimneys and the yellow washed walls. Aunt Flora's the best cook in England and as you've given me my first flying lesson, she'll be thrilled to meet you and listen to all your stories of the war and your exploits in the plane.'

'I wasn't in this plane. This is for fun flying. I was in a Thunderbolt.'

'Sounds even more interesting!'

'What time shall I come?'

'Come at midday and tell us all about your life. Tootlepip for now.'

Louise got in the car, started the engine and took off over the springy new grass. Joe watched her until she disappeared through the gates of the distant house. Then, shaking his head uncertainly, he got into the plane. He wouldn't go on Sunday, of course, because she was just a kid living with some old woman. He'd probably take Marjorie Knowles to the cinema to see *Brief Encounter*. Women loved a good cry. But what if he

96

cried too? Joe sighed and taxied his plane for take-off. Marjorie Knowles was said to be hot lights on the back seat of the cinema . . .

Maybe he'd go to Sunday lunch with the kid after all. Funny how she liked machines. What was it she'd said about Cortina? Perhaps she could ski. He remembered reading something about an English girl who'd caused a sensation at the Games. He decided to look at the back numbers of the *Daily Mail* when he got back to camp.

Aunt Flora drew herself up to her full five foot ten and boomed in astonishment.

'You've invited a *Yank* for Sunday lunch?'

'Yes. He's very handsome and his name's Joe Tanner, Captain, US Air Force. He flies a Tiger Moth for pleasure and a Thunderbolt for battles, or at least he did.'

Flora eyed Louise and then suggested a look in the linen cupboard, the recipe book and a long session polishing the family silver. They decided to impress Joe with a meal in the traditional country style, the table dressed in Victorian lace, etched glasses decorated with the Invergordon crest and a bowl of old-fashioned pink cabbage roses. The menu would be difficult, because food was even scarcer than during the war. Dried eggs had gone out of the shops and the prize at the church raffle the previous week had been one egg! Flora was worried because she had no tea or coffee, no bread, and no chocolates, as Louise had eaten them all.

After much deliberation and consulting of ration books, they decided on nettle soup with oyster bread, because they could find the ingredients for that in the garden or from Tom the fisherman. Aunt Flora had one sack of flour left in her store and she was prepared to use all of it if necessary. The main course would be wild duck stuffed with sage and onion, served with baked potatoes from the garden. Finally a raspberry fool fortified with home-made wine, in case they couldn't find any cream. Louise went into a tail spin of excitement at the very idea of receiving a young man and her enthusiasm communicated itself to her aunt.

When Saturday came round, Flora sent Higgins, the gardener, to shoot a wild duck 'or anything resembling one'. After breakfast on Sunday, they picked vegetables in the garden and Louise went to try to find some cream, returning with a bowl given as a gift by the vicar's wife, who kept a Jersey cow at the bottom of her garden and was delighted to contribute to Aunt Flora's 'war effort'.

At midday Joe drove up the drive in a Jeep. He was immaculately uniformed and bearing gifts. Having greeted Aunt Flora, he shook hands with Louise and handed over a large box full of tinned milk, chocolate powder, sardines, peas, pilchards and a jar of chicken breasts in aspic. Then he remembered he'd left a slab of butter, four steaks and a side of smoked salmon in the Jeep. Aunt Flora flushed puce with excitement at the very prospect of such gourmandise and kissed him resoundingly on both cheeks.

'You're a very fine young man. Pour yourself a whisky. Food's impossible to find in the shops these days, worse than in 'forty-two. Louise is perpetually hungry. I dream about bread, bread and more bread, but there's never enough available. At least we have plenty of whisky, because my sister sends it down from her distillery in Scotland.'

Louise and Joe sat on the sofa, studying a drawing of the interior of the Tiger Moth he had brought. Aunt Flora drank another double whisky, to aid her recuperation from the shock of seeing Louise with a young man. She had been so worried that her charge would never think of anything but tinkering with machines.

Now she was happy, because Joe had attracted with his good looks and perfect manners, not only with his Tiger Moth.

They ate and laughed and had second helpings, before adjourning to the conservatory for a pot of nettle tea. Aunt Flora reminisced about the days of her youth.

'I was a spoiled brat, always perfectly dressed and whimpering for something. Then Papa was killed in South Africa and I learned that you have to work to survive. I married and when Nathaniel died, he left me enough to live on but I got bored, so I took a job with Lady Mendellsson. She had an interior decorating business in London. One day, I bought a painting at a country auction and offered it to her. She was furious, told me in no uncertain terms to go to hell and take my execrable taste with me.'

'What did you do?'

'I went home with my tail between my legs. I had enough to live on from my husband's pension and the trust fund he'd set up for me, but I was always one to be active. Then, a year later, I decided to do up my own house, which hadn't been decorated for thirty years. I sold a number of paintings that I was tired of, among them the funny little oil that Lady Mendellsson had hated. It turned out to be an early Lautrec and brought a king's ransom at Christie's. So I didn't have to work or *ever* worry about money again.'

Louise smiled shyly.

'Aunt Flora never stops working. She raised my mother when *her* mother died and she's raised me since my parents were killed in a car crash in Africa.'

'Did you live in Africa, Louise?'

'Yes, for a while. I always longed to ride wild animals as if they were horses and once I put a lizard in my governess's bed!'

'Funny you should say that, I once found a snake in mine.'

'What did you do, Joe?'

'It was in North Africa. Desert's very cold at night and very hot in the daytime, so you cover up to sleep or you get in a sleeping bag. I found a huge snake sleeping under my eiderdown. I'd spent the whole night with him.'

'And what did you do?'

'No point in running, because snakes can move faster, so I shot him.'

'Did it make a hole in the mattress?'

'Yes, but it seemed like a good idea at the time!'

They all laughed delightedly. Time flew and after tea Joe sat by the fire telling them about his childhood.

'I'm a New Englander, from Vermont. I used to ski to school and skate on the village pond. In summer we picked blueberries and chokeberries and loganberries on the island near the house and Mother made jam and pies that we stole till there was none left for dinner.'

'Are you from a big family, Joe?'

'No, Aunt Flora, I was the only son but I had two sisters. One was killed when her ship went down off the coast of Hong Kong. She worked as a translator for the US Embassy there. The other sister's alive and living in Boston. She has seven kids and she's married to a doctor.'

'What are you going to do now the war's over?'

'I'll go home in six months' time. Then I want to get married and go into civilian flying. There's money to be made there and it's what I like doing, so I'm a lucky man.'

As Joe had brought steaks, Aunt Flora invited him to stay on for dinner, thrilled when he cooked the meat wild-west style on an outdoor fire. The break in routine was welcome after the dark days of wartime monotony and the steaks were wonderful. Aunt Flora had found an old pot of home-made horseradish sauce to go with them and Louise wolfed even that down. They ate apples from the trees as dessert, with a tiny glass each of raspberry liqueur as a digestive. Joe sang some of the songs he had learned from his grandfather, who had emigrated from Newcastle-upon-Tyne. Then, on leaving, he promised to bring supplies of coffee, tea, sugar and flour on his next visit. Aunt Flora and Louise were thrilled at the prospect of seeing him again.

Sunday lunch became a cherished date for all concerned. Sometimes they ate at the house, sometimes in the pub. Once, they went mushrooming, then, finding themselves near the beach, picked kale on the shoreline and threw stones in the water, howling with laughter when Aunt Flora went paddling. Joe selected some seaweed and explained how it could be made into a fine jelly, to be eaten like jam with cream or custard.

Louise linked her arm in his.

'We have no milk to make cream or custard.'

'I'll bring some next time I come.'

There were oyster plants with tiny purple flowers, spreading among the beach stones of beige, grey and ochre. Joe picked a bunch of sea pinks for Louise. Then they hurried back to the house for their lunch, singing the songs Joe had taught them and laughing at his jokes. Aunt Flora forgot she was seventy-one and felt sixteen. Louise forgot she was nineteen and wondered when Joe was going to propose marriage. She would wear white lace and real nylons, wartime rationing or not! And why had he never kissed her? Did he think of her as a child he must never touch? He had bought Aunt Flora a copy of *Forever Amber* and *she* had read every line. Louise blushed furiously at the memory. It was very odd that Joe had not kissed her, thrown her down on the sofa and had his wicked way, whatever that meant. She decided to think about the problem when he returned to base. For the moment, he was at her side and talking about planes. She smelled his skin, loving the fresh odour that had become familiar to her. She blushed again, unable to work out why she was so strangely emotional and chagrined when Joe teased her.

'You're a regular traffic light today, Louise!'

'Don't say that!'

'It's fascinating. What with the Sloppy Joe in red, yellow and green stripes, like the traffic lights, and your face that keeps illuminating every five minutes . . .'

The following week, Joe read in the newspapers, a young woman with a voice like a ship's horn stormed to stardom in *Annie Get Your Gun*. He noted the name, Ethel Merman, so he could tell Louise about her on Sunday. He cut out a photograph of Raymond Loewy's dream car with Plexiglas top. She would whoop with joy when she saw that. And he bought her a huge shoulder bag, that she had been coveting for weeks, pinned an American USAF badge on it, in the latest fashion and put it in a fancy paper bag. Louise would be able to carry all the paraphernalia of life in that, identity card, ration books, mechanics' manual and her mascot, the supremely battered teddy bear named Kenya.

On Sunday, he gathered together all these presents and the mechanics' manual he had ordered for Louise, changed his clothes, Brylcreemed his hair and hurried to the house.

He was surprised to find Aunt Flora alone in front of the fire with only two glasses and a bottle of her finest Scotch.

'Hello, Joe. Do come in. I'm *so* pleased to see you. Without Louise this house is a mausoleum.'

'Where is she?'

Aunt Flora looked in surprise at Joe's stricken face.

'Didn't the child tell you? She always goes out to Kenya for a month at Easter. She stays with her Aunt Cecy and visits her mother's grave. This time she's going to be away slightly longer, because they're visiting Paris together on the way back to England. Cecy thinks it's high time Louise was exposed to the Ritz Hotel and the French couturiers. Heaven only knows what they'll make of the only female mechanic in Sussex!'

'Is Louise's father buried in Kenya?'

'Yes he is, but we don't talk about Lord Invergordon. I'll tell you the truth, Joe, the marriage of Louise's parents was very unhappy and she feared her father, for reasons that are understandable. She loved her mother and still reveres Camilla, but they were never very close. I think the child saw her mother as a kind of untouchable dream character, under constant threat from the father and she was afraid to love Camilla too much in case she ever lost her, which is exactly what happened in the end. That's why Louise can't bear the moment of parting. If she didn't tell you she was going away it was to avoid saying goodbye for a few weeks. She still remembers the day when she said goodbye to her mother in Kenya, near Fourteen Falls, and then never saw Camilla again.'

'I'm sorry about all that, Aunt Flora. I had no idea.'

'Louise never asked questions about her parents' death. She never complained, but she's been wounded and the result is she's very sensitive to leaving on a trip. Once, when I went away for the weekend and left her with my sister, she cried all day till I got back. Don't be angry with her, Joe. She's suffered a lot in the past.'

'I'm not angry, just disappointed. I brought her the mechanics' manual she's been dying to have.'

'Keep it and give it her when she comes back. She

promised to write often, so if you come next week you can read her letters.'

'I'll be here.'

Joe ticked off the days that passed too slowly for his liking. Each Sunday, he and Aunt Flora laughed at Louise's letters and made their plans for her return. They decided to have a really grown-up dinner-party to celebrate her arrival.

Joe made a list of things to bring from the PX to help Aunt Flora's good humour. Of late she had been tense and difficult, perturbed by the rash of hideous looking 'prefabs' being constructed down the lane from her home. She rarely grumbled, no matter what the problem, but the ruination of the countryside was something she felt most acutely. Joe thought of the homeless and knew that the prefabs were necessary. One old couple, bombed out of a cottage near Aunt Flora's, had commandeered a double-decker bus, parked it in her field, thatched it and resisted all the local council's attempts to evict them, saying the thatch made it a permanent residence. Aunt Flora had supported them in their fight and they had won. Since that day, she had helped the couple paint the bus cream and had donated clematis to grow around its 'walls'. The landscape had not suffered at all in Aunt Flora's estimation, because the bus had been countrified.

Joe marked another day off the calendar, impatient for Louise's return. She was the kid sister he had never had, a spirited, affectionate girl of whom he was inordinately proud. He got out his cuttings of her triumphs at Cortina, her tennis championship at Brighton and the wonderful day when she had attended a local gymkhana and won all the cups on a horse with more size than sense. The horse had achieved his unlikely victory because Louise's expertise had inspired him. Was she ever going to get back? It seemed like years since he last saw her.

Joe was sent on a special course the following week and returned a fortnight later, on the day of Louise's dinner-party. He had not seen her since her return and had suffered agonies in case he could not get back in time for the party. He collected together the presents he had bought her over the last few weeks – the mechanics' manual, *The History of Aviation* with illustrations, *A Manual of New England*, so she could learn about Vermont and the areas around where he lived, an ancient silver bracelet with poison compartment, found in an antique shop in Brighton.

At seven that evening, Joe drove to the house at a speed in excess of Sir Malcolm Campbell's. As he parked the car, he saw a dozen notables of the region also arriving. They were offered real French champagne in the garden. Aunt Flora hurried to meet Joe, her rosy face and generous figure wreathed in smiles and a somewhat ancient Captain Molyneux black suit.

'Come and say hello to Louise. She's been champing at the bit to see you. She had a great time in Kenya and she adored Paris. She and Cecy went shopping and bought half the Faubourg St-Honoré, I can tell you. Do remember to say you like the dress, she . . .'

Joe's mouth opened and he stared in stunned amazement as Louise approached, dressed in a white silk dress with an off the shoulder frill, simple, elegant, perfect. Her hair had been cut in a bubbly halo and she was wearing silk stockings with high-heeled shoes that accentuated her perfect legs. Around her throat was a Saunders family heirloom, an emerald necklet that exactly matched the colour of her eyes. Joe did not notice when Aunt Flora gave him a nudge. He simply kept on staring at the vision before him, blushing furiously when Louise kissed him on the cheek.

'I brought you the mechanics' manual and some other things for your return,' he stammered, handing them to her.

She put the manual in her room, returning wreathed with smiles and wearing the bracelet, which she had understood at once.

'I shall pretend I'm Lucrezia Borgia every time I wear this.'

'God dammit, Louise, you look like Betty Grable! What happened?'

'I grew up in Paris and Aunt Cecy bought me some new clothes and taught me how to walk in high heels. I fell all over the place at first, but now I've got the hang of them.'

'You're beautiful.'

'Thank you. Have some more champagne, Joe.'

'I need it. I never thought I'd see you in a dress like that. Are you good and sure it won't fall down?'

Aunt Flora disappeared, hooting with laughter at Joe's stupefaction.

That night, in bed, Louise re-ran every minute of Joe's reaction. It was perfect! She had really impressed him, just as Aunt Cecy had promised. She put on the light and read a bit of her mechanics' manual, but her attention kept wandering to a more personal machination. Suddenly, she wanted the intangible, mysterious, unknown pleasure that she did not dare put into words. Mechanics' manuals were no longer top on her list of priorities.

A few miles away, Joe tossed and turned. Louise was beautiful, the most beautiful girl in the world and she liked planes and cars and tractors. What more could a fellow want? He rose at two and made a pot of coffee. Then he took a cold shower. Then he went for a walk around the periphery of the airfield. Back to bed by three-thirty, he lay awake, thinking, making decisions, wishing it were time to get up.

Joe arrived at the house at eight in the morning and found Louise repairing Aunt Flora's increasingly decrepit but much loved Morris Minor. She was in dungarees, the emerald necklet still around her neck, a smudge of oil on her cheek. It was the moment when he knew that he loved her more than anything in the world and that he always would. He took her hand in his and spoke with due solemnity.

'Louise, let's get married. I love you. I want to be with you always. I'll be leaving here in a few months' time and returning home to the States. I want you to come with me as my wife. I've got good prospects for a job and I think we can have a fine life together. Do you accept?'

'Yes, on one condition.'

'Granted.'

'You don't know what it is yet!'

'What is it?'

'That you teach me to fly.'

'Granted.'

'I accept, Joe. I love you ten million and I'll try to be the very best wife in the world.'

'Me too.'

They hooted with laughter and went inside to present Aunt Flora with a *fait accompli*. They found the old fox already pouring the champagne.

'I heard every word because the window's open, so we'll have a champagne breakfast and be drunk for the rest of the day. Just imagine, Louise a bride. I always thought she'd end up a spinster working as head mechanic for Brighton Corporation!'

The sun shone. Sheep in the meadow baa-ed. Joe and Louise walked together through the woods, pausing here and there to admire dew that shone silver on spiders' webs in the pale light of morning. There was honey fungus growing in the old tree stumps, and somewhere in the distance a skylark sang only for them.

SEVEN

Sussex, 1946

It was a country wedding, held at summer's end in the village church, where Louise had been confirmed and Aunt Flora had reserved her burial plot. The church was decorated with thousands of white marguerites, ferns and sweet-smelling, old-fashioned roses that gave the place the atmosphere of a bygone age.

Uncle Ferdy came down from Fife to give the bride away, with the only remaining members of the Invergordon family, two aged aunts with desiccated faces. The catastrophe of Charlie's madness and the double suicide in Kenya had caused such anguish in the clan that many had simply gone into declines and never recovered. Uncle Ferdy had sent regular cheques for Louise's upkeep, but he had not come to see her. Only now, for her wedding, had he left Black Gordon to arrive in his Rolls, a tall, stately man with military bearing, who led her proudly up the aisle.

Uncle Ferdy's hostility at the idea of Louise marrying an American had vanished the moment he met Joe. The young man was rock solid and well mannered and Louise was the most beautiful girl he had ever seen, like her mother in some ways, but different in personality. Where Camilla had been fragile, passive and uncertain of everything, Louise emanated energy and determination. The jut of her chin gave Ferdy confidence that she would face the future with courage and never give in. Perhaps there was hope yet for the Invergordons.

As the priest pronounced the vows, Aunt Flora lost

her battle not to cry and finished the ceremony red eyed. It was bad enough to suffer from pinched feet and a severely corseted waistline, but to present red eyes to the world was difficult. She tried to control herself, but the sight of Joe and Louise, so innocent and elated, moved everyone to excesses of emotion.

As the couple moved from the vestry towards the door of the church, Uncle Ferdy took Flora by the arm.

'Now Flora, stop crying. If you keep on like that I swear I'll cry too and I haven't cried since I was in my cradle sixty-five years ago.'

'How are things at Black Gordon?'

'Everyone's dead or dying. Soon there'll be no Invergordons left and the curse of the McGregors will have taken its full toll.'

'You surely don't believe in curses, do you?'

'I didn't, but since the events in Kenya I've been obliged to change my mind. Charlie's death sent everyone into their shells and some of us have never succeeded in emerging into the light of day.'

'Curses can be broken.'

'Only by a child. There's always Louise to give us hope.'

The house was filled to overflowing, so they ate in the garden on trestle tables borrowed from the village hall. The tables had been dressed in white linen, and decorated with marguerites and roses like the church. The guests relished fresh asparagus and stuffed pigeons with vegetables from the garden. There was no bread, because bread had been rationed since July, shocking everyone to the core, as it had never been rationed before, even in the wartime. The sweet was a concoction of Aunt Flora's that resembled fudge but tasted like melted down chocolate flavoured with whisky. Some found it more intoxicating than the punch, the champagne and the atmosphere of jubilation.

The sunny day became a riotous celebration when villagers formed an impromptu orchestra to serenade the young lovers, who danced together under the apple trees to the tune of 'We'll Meet Again'. Then, when tears began to flow at the thought of the imminent parting, Joe's American Base friends got up and did a demonstration of the jitterbug that had everyone shouting for more. The noise was so intense, Aunt Flora's rabbits escaped from their hutch and Mr Coleclough's hens flew up and sat in the hedge. Joe looked contentedly into Louise's eyes.

'I like your Uncle Ferdy. He's a great gentleman.'

'He likes you too. I'm so glad he came down from Scotland. He was very, very perturbed by my parents' death and he never came to see me again. Sometimes I felt as if I were being punished, but Aunt Flora told me it was just that he couldn't stand to be reminded of the past. The memories were too painful.'

'What time do you think we can leave?'

'I like it when you're impatient, Joe.'

'In an hour we'll say our goodbyes and drive away into the sunset like cowboys do in westerns.'

'The hotel in Brighton's lovely. You'll like it there.'

'I'd like it on a sewage farm if I were with you, Louise.'

They forgot the onlookers and kissed tenderly, laughing, when a spontaneous burst of applause echoed in the misty warmth of the afternoon. Then Louise ran to kiss Aunt Flora and Uncle Ferdy.

'It's a lovely wedding. I never had such a lovely day in my life.'

Aunt Flora started to worry that the hour of departure was near. She had protected Louise all her life and could barely imagine that the child was going, for ever, far from her home, land and those who loved her.

'Now don't go doing anything foolish after you leave

Brighton. Deauville's foreign territory and exhibitions of aerobatics are dangerous.'

'Joe and I are both qualified pilots and Joe's a great aerobatics performer. I shall only be watching, Aunt Flora. In any case, I won't ever do anything silly. I know the dangers and Joe has taught me about the responsibility of being in control of a plane.'

Uncle Ferdy shook his head in bewilderment.

'I can't believe it's little Louise. Last time I saw you, you were an expert daisy-chain maker and you took apart Angus's tractor and then put it together again. You forgot the starter, but he was mightily impressed by your four-year-old's enthusiasm.'

Twilight came and Aunt Flora switched on the fairy-lights in the trees. Joe and Louise had gone to change into their going away outfits – his a Prince of Wales check suit, hers a sugar-pink tunic dress with scalloped hem bought in Paris from Lelong. She looked like a dream, with her curly blonde hair, radiant smile and tiny white hat perched over one ear. When the time came for them to leave, they said their private goodbyes to Aunt Flora in her living-room.

'We'll be in Brighton and then on to Deauville and then we'll be leaving on the *Ile de France* for New York. We're going to stay with Joe's parents in New England for a while, until I get my aerobatic qualifications. Then Joe'll find work and we'll do exhibitions together. We want to live in the sun if we can, and once we're settled we're going to send you an invitation and a plane ticket.'

'Wild horses wouldn't stop me from coming, Louise.'

'I don't ever want to lose you, Aunt Flora. You're all the world to me, you always have been and you always will be.'

'You'll lose me when I die, like everyone does, but

not before. Look after her, Joe. She's the best in the world.'

'You're quite something yourself, Aunt Flora.'

After kissing Uncle Ferdy until he turned a fine beetroot red, Louise hurried after her husband to the car and they drove off, waving merrily until the tall chimneys were thin parallel lines in the distant green landscape of the Downs. Aunt Flora wept as if her heart would break. Uncle Ferdy went and sat in the orchard, trying not to do the same. To all of them it seemed like the end of an era and perhaps the end of the Invergordons.

That evening, after dinner, the young couple undressed in the bathroom, each in turn, emerging with a certain trepidation, Joe in his striped green pyjamas, Louise in a nightdress of pristine white satin. Joe poured them each a glass of champagne, then another. The heat of summer hung heavy in the evening air and he felt suddenly extremely nervous. He took off his pyjama jacket.

'It feels hot, I'm sweating. Can't figure out if it's nerves or an Indian summer!'

'I'm sweating too.'

Louise took off her nightdress, smiling when she saw the admiration in Joe's eyes. Then, to her delight, he picked her up in his arms, carried her to the bed and stood, looking down at her with all the love in the world. She was of medium height, long legged and with a tiny waist. Her breasts were full, her arms and shoulders perfect. Joe took off his pyjama trousers and kneeled at the bedside, kissing her feet and her knees, her thighs and her stomach, her nipples and the curves of her underarm. The kisses were exciting and Louise clutched him to her body, feverish in the heat of her desire.

113

'I want you to love me and teach me what to do and we'll do all the things you ever dreamed of together. You have to show me, because I never did all this before.'

'Could hurt a bit at first, but after that it'll be okay. Jesus, I'm nervous, maybe even terrified.'

'Love me, Joe. Love me *now*.'

Her excitement was so intense, her desire so urgent, he took her at once, surprised and pleased that she suffered no pain, that her reaction was one of vibrant sensuality. With each thrust of his body, she reacted, fitting her movements to his by instinct, by a desire to be one and in perfect unison. Outside, darkness fell. Inside, in the lamplight, two glasses of champagne stood neglected as two bodies achieved their moment of glory. Louise cried out her ecstasy as Joe held her close, understanding, at last, what it was to be adored.

After love, they sipped their champagne, laughing because it was warm. Louise poured away the leftovers in the glasses.

'Best have another one out of the ice bucket.'

'Your word is my command, ma'am.'

'I think I like making love. I imagined it to be a kind of obligation, but I feel as if I could become very fond of it.'

'Good, lots of girls hate it.'

'Have you made love with lots of girls, Joe?'

'Sure, maybe a thousand.'

Louise burst into peals of laughter.

'How many? Tell the truth.'

'Four.'

'I don't think I'm jealous.'

'I don't figure you need to be. I only ever wanted to be married to you and I don't ever intend to be married to anyone else.'

'I wonder if I've already forgotten how to do it.'

'What?'

'You start by climbing aboard the aircraft.' Louise climbed astride his body. 'Then you manipulate the joystick to make the plane go up and up and up.'

'Jesus, Louise, you want to give me a heart attack!'

'And the rudder to get your sense of direction.'

They rolled around the bed in mock flight, searching rudders and joysticks and starters and doing loops and spirals of a new dimension, until their bodies hastened towards the climax of sensuality. Then they lay, hand in hand, heart to heart, panting, smiling, teasing, laughing and finally sleeping, until the sunlight of a late summer day provoked them to get up and ring for the biggest breakfast in town.

On arrival in Deauville, they registered at a small comfortable hotel with dark green shutters and ivy that climbed up its grey stone walls. Delicious smells of dinner filtered up from below and Louise wondered if she had ever been so happy. First they wrote a postcard to Aunt Flora telling of their safe arrival. Then they inspected Joe's plane. The aerobatics demonstration, which he and four other experts would give the following day, had been well organized and the town, with its glamorous shops and casino had attracted a large number of visitors. Every hotel was booked solid for the three days, every ticket sold.

Louise was filled with the excitement of it all. She had her pilot's licence and would learn aerobatics when she arrived in the States. Joe had even promised to buy her a plane of her own with his demobilization pay if she did well at the new craft. She dreamed of the day when she would be good enough to do exhibitions with him, but for the moment was content to watch, learn and admire the aviator she had married. Tomorrow would be Joe's day and Louise was happy to be just another fan.

The next morning, the field was decorated with the flags of all nations, fluttering merrily in the stiff breeze. Around the periphery of the aerodrome, cars from Paris and all parts of France mixed with Mercedes and Ferraris of enthusiasts from other parts of Europe. All had come to see the five great practitioners of the aerobatic art: the veteran Frenchman, La Salle, the flying Scotsman, McGill, Joe Tanner, the Canadian Red Rogers and the English Battle of Britain ace, Mallory Ellacott. British and French language posters proclaimed, 'THIS IS THE AGE OF THE MACHINE'. Planes of all the leading makes were on display, closely watched by salesmen eager to sell the tempting idea of freedom after years of the claustrophobic confines of war. Images of flying doves, eagles, seagulls and smiling begoggled faces appeared on every wall in the town and there were few who did not dream of taking a spin on a curly white cloud.

La Salle did a classic demonstration of clean lines and perfect spins, culminating in a loop and reverse loop that seemed to defy gravity and every other scientific theory. The flying Scotsman, McGill, specialized in suicide dives, a manoeuvre that put maximum stress on the plane and the man at its controls. During the dive, the pilot weighed three times his normal weight, because of the speed of descent and the pressure. There were gasps and cries and then a round of relieved applause from a field of stunned spectators. They gave him a big cheer, though, when he got out of the plane in a swinging kilt and red tam-o'-shanter.

When Joe and his friend, Red Rogers, took off together, the spectators craned to see what was happening. Two pilots flying together? Then, as the two interlaced and did wing touches and alternate spirals, rolls and dolphin-like flying on their back, they saw patterns emerge that thrilled every onlooker to the bone. In the middle of the demonstration, one pilot let a red smoke flare loose and the other a blue. Wild applause broke out and some of the French spectators rose to their feet to blow kisses. Then, in a moment of breathtaking simplicity, the two pilots flew low, entering the airport hangar and emerging from the other side in a joking, charming, astounding finale of the pilot's art.

The spectators broke loose and ran to help the two men from their machines. Joe and Red were hoisted up on willing shoulders, dosed with champagne and kissed by everyone from small boys in their Sunday best to the Mayor of Deauville. Flashbulbs popped. Reporters asked questions. And everywhere planes took off and landed to riotous applause.

Louise watched in wonder and admiration, so proud of her husband that tears fell down her cheeks. She dreamed of the day when she would be his partner in the air, when she could stand at his side and be as proud of herself as she was of him. Then, suddenly, her mind went back to that distant moment in the field in Kenya and the little plane that had taken her and Cecy to Mombasa, leaving Camilla behind, never to be seen again. Tears ran freely as Louise thought of her mother and how she would admire Joe. Camilla would be proud that her daughter was happily married, not at war with her husband as had been *her* tragic destiny. Smothering her desire to cry like a child, because Joe's triumph had stirred up memories she had done everything in her power to bury deep within herself, Louise ran to his side and kissed him resoundingly.

They were photographed like that for the local paper, a picture they would keep framed with the hundreds of others that would come in the future, after their triumphant arrival in Joe's home town. Already Louise knew that the people of White River Junction had decided on

117

a public celebration of the return of their own personal war hero and his bride.

The ship had suites, rooms, cabins, dining-halls, a ballroom and even a hospital, chapel and prison cell, in case anyone misbehaved. Louise went into overdrive when she saw it and Joe ordered champagne, enjoying her flushed cheeks and the look of delight in her eyes.

'You're the most exciting and excitable woman I ever met!'

'Everything's so new and it's such a contrast to England in the war and the shortages we've had for so long.'

'France has had a war too and they've had rationing even worse than England and problems they won't ever forget. But this trip'll be special, because it's the company's way of celebrating the end of the war, their return to passenger service and the Chairman's fifty-eighth birthday. My guess is that we'll be spoiled to death.'

Before dinner, they wandered wide-eyed around the *Ile de France* that had been redecorated, restored, cleaned and made as beautiful as only the French could make a ship. Bas-reliefs by Janniot, ceilings by Picart le Doux, paintings by Levy, Bouchaud and furniture by Leleu, Ruhlmann and Montagnac created an art deco effect that in the post-war period was fast becoming a memory instead of a reality. The dining-room was mirrored in amber, so every woman looked beautiful. The food was perfect, if not copious. After dinner, the couple danced and Louise murmured the English words of 'J'attendrai'. Cheek to cheek they whirled around the floor, until they were the only people left. Then, after a last glass of champagne, they went back to their cabin.

In the dark, they lay in their narrow beds, holding hands and whispering.

'I love you, Louise.'

'I love you, Joe. When we live with your parents, how shall we make love?'

Joe laughed out loud at her puritanical streak, loving it all the same.

'Like always, I suppose.'

'*Where?*'

'In our bedroom.'

'Is it a big house? What if they hear?'

'It's pretty big.'

'I wouldn't like your parents to hear the bed-springs creaking. I don't think I shall be able to do it at all.'

'Well then, we won't. We'd best do it all the time on the voyage, so we're ready for a period of abstinence when we arrive.'

Louise bit his ear. He pecked her shoulder. Then, smelling the faint scent of lavender on her skin, he bent and kissed her breasts. Outside, fog drifted in thick, white banks past the ship and the hooter sounded, its muffled, eery tone echoing in the night. Joe and Louise were hastening towards the climax of their love, exhilarated by the champagne, the beauty of the ship and their love for each other.

The town band had been augmented with the bands of four neighbouring villages. There was bunting across the main street and, at every gate, an American and British flag. Children, wild with excitement, ran back and forth, stealing pies or sweets from a long buffet table outside the Mayor's house. Dogs barked, birds sang, the children's choir got the British National Anthem wrong for the fiftieth time. Then someone shouted, 'Train's coming in!'

Everyone forgot what he or she was doing and ran to meet it. The band regrouped. The children's choir likewise. Then, as friends craned to see, Louise appeared on the observation platform, beautiful, striking in spring green and white, with a French hat of spotted veiling tilted over her right ear. Joe stepped up behind her and they waved as a great cheer rose from the crowd. At a signal from the conductor, the band struck up and the children sang 'God Save the King' and got it right, making everyone blush with pride and shock. 'The Star Spangled Banner' followed and then, as the crowd parted, Joe's parents came forward to embrace their son and new daughter-in-law.

Louise saw a tall, slim man with grey hair and a shy smile and an equally tall woman with brown hair and kind eyes. Joe made the introductions.

'Mum, Dad, this is Louise. Louise, say hello to Bob and Martha.'

As she hugged them both, there were tears in the crowd. Then Joe took his mother in his arms and kissed her pale, thin face, before linking arms with his father.

'It's been a long time, Dad.'

'And a hard one, Joe. You've got thin.'

'So have you.'

'I've had bronchitis and I need a rest, but not today. Whole town's gone mad. We'll be eating till Saturday if the women have their way.'

The Mayor was waiting to deliver his speech of welcome.

'Ladies and gentlemen, we're here to welcome home our very own war hero and his new wife. God dammit folks, I'm not much for formality. Joe and Louise are home and we're going to have a party. Come on, let's get to it!'

There were roast sheep and wild boar stuffed with sour apples, twenty varieties of home-made wine, baked potatoes, sausages and johnny-cakes by the score. Louise stared in amazement at the luscious sponge cakes loaded with cream, the piles of bread rolls newly baked. Aunt Flora had written to say that food was even harder to find and rationing more stringent than in 1940. Twenty families had immediately squatted in the American Base, on the day of departure of the personnel and another forty prefabs had been built in the lane. No one knew when rationing would end and some were unable to make ends meet, even with vegetables grown in the garden and eggs swopped from their henhouses in return for other rare commodities. Louise decided that she must send food parcels to Aunt Flora each month. In America, the war had scarcely been felt and she was almost guilty when she saw the spread the women had prepared for the arrival of their local hero and his bride.

Days turned into weeks. Joe worked at a local machine parts factory, returning home each evening at six. Their routine was quickly established. From Monday to Friday they drank a few beers with Joe's parents on his return, discussed ads in local and national papers, for ever trying to find two identical planes at a price they could afford. The search filled their lives, that of the family, their neighbours and even the Mayor of the little town. Folk telephoned from time to time with news of second-hand planes for sale by companies in the vicinity. Each lead was followed up, each disappointment acutely felt. Everyone in White River Junction was involved. Everyone wanted the couple to succeed on their home ground.

Joe's methodical reckonings on endless notepads became the butt of frequent family jokes, particularly from Louise and Martha, whose laconic humour made everyone laugh.

'Joe, you figure if you keep writing totals down your money'll grow?'

'Quit teasing me, Ma!'

'How many planes can you buy right now?'

'About one and a half, depending on the price.'

Louise kissed his ear and handed him another beer.

'Who gets the half?'

'I do. I'm the more experienced pilot, so I guess I have to learn to fly half a plane.'

'How long before we can afford two full planes?'

'Another four to six months at the most.'

Every day, on Joe's arrival home, this scene was replayed until it became a much loved and reassuring part of life.

Saturdays were spent plane hunting, returning at nightfall tired, hungry, full of tales of their endeavours, to be treated to a grand family dinner that was the high point of the week. Then Joe's cousin, Ted, his old schoolfriends, the Greyson twins, and Martha's mother contributed their information on the all-important, all-consuming family passion, the search for the planes in which Joe and Louise would fly.

Sundays and two afternoons each week were spent flying. Louise's lessons in aerobatics started badly, because she was terrified of crashing the borrowed plane. On returning home each time, she burst into tears, took to her bed for an hour and then lay like a zombie on the sofa, unable to talk to anyone about anything. It was Martha who helped restore her confidence.

'Lou, you have to stop being scared. Worse thing that can happen is you both get killed. That way you go to heaven together. If you get injured, you go to the hospital together. If the plane's a write-off the insurance company pays. If you can't get the hang of aerobatics, Joe'll do his demonstrations solo and you'll organize the tours. Okay?'

'I do *so* want him to be proud of me.'

'But he is proud of you. He's so full of dreams for

your future he can't keep his feet on the ground. He thinks you're a natural-born flier.'

'Did he really say that, Martha?'

'Sure did. Listen, Louise, when you're real scared of something, think of the worst that can happen and work out what you'd do if it did. Then you can be plum certain it'll never happen. We just did all that. Now you can settle down and make your errors like everyone else, pass your test and go right ahead with your plans.'

'I might be a natural flier, but I don't know if I'm a natural for aerobatics.'

'Joe wasn't either. He only passed his aerobatics third time around, so he'll be impressed if you pass first time. Bob and I'll be downright overcome!'

Louise's flying hours spent in aerobatics mounted – five, ten, fifteen. She still took to her bed if she had made too many errors, but the faults diminished little by little until it dawned on her that she was at last getting the hang of the new art. At twenty-five flying hours she took her test, passed with distinction and ran all the way back to the Tanner house, shouting like a dervish so everyone in the small town knew.

'I passed! I passed! Is Joe home? Where is he? I passed! I did it first time. Oh Martha, oh dear, oh dear me. I passed. I can't believe it. I must send a telegram to Aunt Flora.'

'Telegram's already gone.'

Louise halted in her tracks, wide eyed.

'How did you know? Is Joe back? How did *he* know?'

'He came home early and telephoned the field every ten minutes. Damn near wore out the carpet pacing up and down and then, when he heard you'd passed, he ran out to beg the Mayor to give him the town council's special reserve for celebrities bottle of champagne. He's near puce with excitement. I had to tell him to calm down or he'd burst a blood vessel. He'll be back in five minutes.'

'Oh Martha, this is a great day!'

'Sure is. Joe was barely home when the twins called to tell him they think they've located two planes. We're all going to Concorde Saturday to see them. If they're in good condition and the right price the Flying Tanners'll be in business and this family'll have a celebration dinner that'll be long remembered!'

Louise and Joe stood gazing at the two yellow planes. The machines were in working order, not in the finest exterior condition, but the price asked was only three hundred dollars each, less than Joe had estimated. For the price he had envisaged, he could have both Stearmans restored to near new condition. His heart beat so fast he could barely contain himself when he looked into Louise's eyes.

'What do you think, Lou?'

'I think we must buy.'

'And you, Dad?'

'Buy.'

'Ma?'

'Buy and let's go home and organize a celebration. Grandma's waiting for a call so she can set the kitchens on fire!'

Overcome by emotion and excitement, Joe had to sit on the grass, take out his notebook and do his sums one last time to be certain that the purchase was really feasible. Then he nodded to the salesman and took Louise in his arms.

'We're on our way at last, Lou. It's been a long time, but we'll make it.'

From that moment on, Joe organized everything. While he continued working, he devoted his evenings to planning their first display. As Louise went into a state of nerves every time she even thought of her debut as his partner, Joe had the posters printed in secret. He arranged their tour and their debut in White River Junction with meticulous care. Louise was ready, but would her nerve hold out in front of a thousand-strong crowd? Joe was certain that it would. Still, he decided not to say a word of the day and the details until the Saturday family gathering. As he looked at the posters he had had printed, his face flushed with pride. Who would have thought that the young girl who had pretended to fly his plane in England in that field near her aunt's house would become his partner, his wife and the most loved woman in the world.

They were fifteen for dinner that Saturday, with neighbours popping in and out afterwards to toast the Tanners' success. When, finally, they adjourned to the sitting-room, Louise paused, her face flushed with shock, when she saw the posters Joe had attached to the walls.

THE FLYING TANNERS
EXHIBITION OF AEROBATICS
HE FLIES THE SPIDER, SHE FLIES THE BUTTERFLY
THEY FLY TOGETHER

Louise hugged Joe to her heart, tears of emotion streaming down her cheeks.

'Are you sure I'm ready, Joe?'

'Sure I'm sure. Wouldn't take the risk if you weren't, you know me.'

The field was full of people, many of them eating hamburgers, hot dogs and candy floss. While the band played a Sousa March, a team of drum majorettes demonstrated their skills. The Tanner family were there in force, as were all the inhabitants of the town of White

River Junction. Journalists and photographers had come from as far away as Boston and some of Joe's old wartime comrades were there to cheer him on in his new career.

Louise had spent the morning being sick, lying with her feet up in the air to avoid fainting and vowing not to fly again. Joe had ignored her nerves, saying firmly, 'You're the best flier I know. After this afternoon, you'll never be scared again, Lou. So buck up and let's take our opportunity in both hands.' Louise had gone to church to say her prayers after that. Then she cried some more, ate a sandwich at Martha's insistence and dressed in her flying gear. This was the moment she had dreamed of for so long. This was *her* moment and Joe's moment and she must not let him down. She thought suddenly of her mother, the frail, delicate Camilla, and she smiled because women had changed so much it would be hard for those of the past generation to imagine a future in aviation.

First they flew in formation, wheeling like eagles above the heads of the crowd. Then they flew towards each other, as if certain to collide, causing some of the spectators to swig from their brandy flasks. There was noisy applause from the thrilled crowds. They looped the loop and did flat spins, tail spins, inverted and precision spins, until the spectators were giddy and hoarse from shouting encouragement. Vertical turns followed flat and banked turns, spiral slides and spiral spins. Then, as the orchestra played an ominous drum roll, Joe went into the famous suicide dive, the move that stressed more than any other both pilot and machine. Having dived like a shot bird, he retrieved the machine a few feet from the ground and rose in triumph, smoothing out and landing to take his bow.

The drums rolled again and everyone looked anxious.

Louise Tanner was very young and everyone knew that Joe had taught her himself, but no one really believed that a well brought up young lady could accomplish such a dangerous manoeuvre. They had no time to debate the matter, when, suddenly, Louise let the Butterfly fall, fall, fall. Screams echoed in the field. A woman fainted and had to be carried away on a stretcher. Martha closed her eyes and prayed audibly. Then, a few feet from the ground, Louise brought her plane up again, levelled out and landed gracefully, with all the skill of an expert. As she took her bow, there was riotous applause and she ran to Joe and kissed him.

'I was so scared, but I did it.'

'You were great, Lou, a natural-born flier, like I always said.'

The press took photographs of the crowd going mad and carrying the couple from the field. Joe earned a lot of money that day. His parents became overnight celebrities and the Flying Tanners started a career that would take them in the next two years to every town with a landing strip in the United States of America. Fame had beckoned and they were running fast towards it.

EIGHT

Texas, 1949

Louise looked at herself in the mirror, half closed one eye and wondered if a Veronica Lake hairstyle would suit her. Or perhaps a bare midriff and gold platforms like Carmen Miranda. She shrugged. She was more the type for baggy blue jeans, but Joe liked her to change from time to time and she liked to please him. Maybe she should dye her hair red like Rita Hayworth! Joe would be furious if she did. Louise smiled wistfully, thinking how much she loved him.

They were so happy, the only cloud on the horizon, the lack of the longed for baby. Joe was sure that it was because she had worked too hard and tired herself out, so they had decided to take a holiday with Uncle Jude in the Big Thicket area of Texas, before making their way to El Paso, where Joe was due to start work as a test pilot for an aeronautics company. They were hoping that she could be taken on too, but had decided to leave that until Joe was established. For the moment, both were agreed that Louise should try to get pregnant. It was a cause for anxiety, but also a source of endless jokes between them.

'You know, Joe, when I really start trying to get pregnant it'll be very expensive. You'll have to eat steak and eggs and iron pills for breakfast, lunch and dinner, to say nothing of tins of spinach, like Popeye.'

'Stop making light of it, Lou. You'll make me laugh so much I'll end up with severe penis wilt.'

'Have you got it now?'

'Sure have.'

'Show me. *That's* not wilting! That's in full operational condition. Shall we see if it fits? Shall we see if today's the day when we get to be a trio instead of a duet?'

Uncle Jude drove them from the station to the house in his old log wagon. He was sixty years young and had become more Texan than the Texans since his arrival in the area as a young man. For Louise it was a world apart and she gazed in wonder at the scene, as they bumped along a dirt track between sweet gum trees, the air full of buzzling parula warblers and the bay of Jude's hog dogs, as they ran alongside.

When they crossed the creek, everyone got soaked. The horses swam and Jude began to do an involuntary performance of bird and animal noises to take his guests' minds off the fact that they were in danger of drowning, because the creek was 'swimmin''. Icy water touched Louise's thighs, but she looked straight ahead, instinct telling her that the old timer was testing her courage. She wondered if there were alligators in the creek, but decided not to let her mind run riot. Then, to her relief, Uncle Jude brought the wagon out of the creek with much yelling at the horses and a faith in his own abilities. Soaking wet but triumphant, he began a brief history of the area.

'Old times, afore our grandparents, there was panthers and bears and wolves in these parts. It was a hideout for desperadoes too, but they stayed near Sour Lake, because no one else was crazy enough to go there. So they was tranquil.'

They passed one of Jude's friends returning from a hog hunt. Seeing Louise and Joe staring after the hunting party, Jude spoke out.

'Great animal the hog. He's got guts and he's smart.'

Joe continued to stare after the hunters, men who

seemed to him to be straight out of a Hollywood badmen movie.

'Any of your friends get attacked by those hogs, Uncle Jude?'

'Sure, sometimes they get themselves killed. The old boar's tusks grow in full circles, so *he* can't do much harm. He just knocks you down, bites you and leaves you bruised all over. But the males in their prime, that's another thing. You get those with your first shot or you don't get another chance!'

Louise shuddered at the thought.

'I think I'd just forget my pride and run.'

'Do you no good at all, ma'am. Hog'd outrun you for sure. He may be heavy, but he's faster than lightning. Only thing to do is climb a tree and wait him out. Helps if you shout a few curses at him. Hogs are soft hearted and they don't like curses.'

In the strange magic world of the Big Thicket, Louise learned to identify otter and beaver, the cry of a red wolf, the croak of a tree frog. She picked yellow jasmine to put on the table and once found a pitcher plant, a perfect, but deadly beauty, because it devoured everything that entered its long, thin throat. Then, on the day of their departure for El Paso, she sat wistfully watching a wood duck with her two young, paddling in the green, gloomy waters of the swamp. Louise wanted as many children as possible, but when would they come and why had they not come already? Was it possible she was sterile? The thought brought tears to her eyes, but she stifled her feelings and smiled when Joe said he was ready to leave for the station. Then Uncle Jude shouted that the horses and the hog dogs were ready to swim in the creek and he hoped they were too.

On the train, Louise snuggled up to her husband and spoke of her thoughts and reactions.

'I felt as if I stepped back fifty years in the Big Thicket. It was something I'll always remember. What impressed you most about Uncle Jude and his life?'

'The way he drove the wagon through the river. I was scared as hell in case there were alligators!'

'Me, too.'

'You know what he said about you, Lou?'

'Tell me.'

'"Got more guts than a hog that girl. You can be proud as hell of her."'

They laughed at the cock-eyed compliment. Then, as the landscape grew more arid and thoughts of wagon trains and pioneers came to mind, they just sat gazing out of the window. Names of western legend unfolded at every station: San Antonio, change here for Abilene, Fort Worth, Fort Stockton. Finally they saw the sign for El Paso and hurried to unload their bags and step down. They were welcomed by a stiff-backed, formal gentleman in clothes more suited to the staid streets of Pennsylvania than the dust-dimmed vistas of El Paso.

'Mr Tanner, I'm Elton Quaig, director of Quaig Andrews Air Corporation.'

'Nice to meet you, Mr Quaig. This is my wife Louise.'

'Hello, Mr Quaig.'

'My pleasure, ma'am. I'll drop you off at the house so my wife, Frances, can show you the ropes and teach you the necessities of local life. Then we'll go to the airfield, Joe, and you can see the plane you'll be testing.'

Louise glowered at the shiny bald back of Quaig's head.

'I'd like to see the plane, too.'

'Pardon?'

'I said I'd like to see the plane. I'm a flier, Mr Quaig, and I love planes, always have.'

Joe sighed, knowing that Quaig's traditional masculine attitudes would bring him into direct confrontation with Louise. He was surprised when his new boss spoke.

'I've read about your exhibitions of aerobatics, Mrs Tanner. What do you fly?'

'Joe and I have two Stearman P13 Kaydets. We bought them for three hundred dollars each and had them re-engined and re-motored with Pratt Whitney R-985 Wasp Junio 450 h.ps that we got from a company that was closing down.'

'We fly modern planes here.'

The implication was obvious and Louise blushed in embarrassment. Seeing her face, Joe squeezed her hand and smiled encouragingly.

'My wife's something of a mechanical genius, Mr Quaig. No man can do better than Lou in any kind of a machine and I *know*.'

The company house was a small square box, surrounded by other small square boxes that sweltered under the burning sun. There was a tiny garden like a dust bowl, full of penis-shaped cacti and half-asleep snakes. To Louise, Piedras Street looked like a place to avoid with maximum energy. All around, old men sat on their verandas, snoring peacefully in the sun. Young boys stole bicycle tyres from garden sheds, hose pipes from their hooks on the walls and cookies from the kitchen. Flies droned, babies cried and everywhere there was a heavy, leaden heat that slowed the reflexes and made even the fittest people tired.

Alone, Louise sat at the kitchen table and stared at her hands. Joe had stayed with Mr Quaig. She had come 'home' to get the house organized. She felt like crying. She put water to boil to make tea, found no tea and burst into tears. She was sobbing as if her heart would break, when she heard a child's voice.

'Mummy cried at Grandpop's funeral. Have you been to a funeral?'

132

'No, I'm just sad.'

'Come and meet Mummy. She'll know what to do.'

'Where is she?'

'Next door. She told me to bring you in for coffee. We're going to invite you and your husband to dinner if you're free and if you like tacos and frijoles refritos.'

'I don't know what they are, but I'm sure I'll like them.'

The woman next door was thirty, blonde, Scandinavian and married to another test pilot from the Quaig Corporation. Annika made coffee, served pastries and told Louise she'd take her shopping, sightseeing and out to meet folk the following day.

'Life's not bad here, Louise. The weather can be extreme, the houses aren't pretty and it's difficult to make them snug, but people are kind and the countryside's beautiful.'

'And Mr Quaig?'

'He's got the same level of tolerance for the unknown as Torquemada had for his victims. He doesn't like women, changes, socializing or being obliged to give raises in salary.'

'I'm a pilot. I'd like to work for the company.'

'There are a couple of vacancies for test pilots. There aren't many folk who want to live out here in the wilds.'

'Joe and I want to live in the sun. Tell me about the vacancies. How long have they been looking for personnel?'

'One job was vacant since March.'

'That's three months!'

'The other one came vacant last week, when the other test pilot went to California.'

'I'm going to apply.'

'Now?'

'No time like the present. Can I borrow your car to drive over there, please?'

133

'Sure, Louise, but Quaig won't take you on. Don't be too upset, will you? He simply wouldn't consider a woman for a flying job.'

Louise walked into the reception and asked to see Mr Quaig and his two joint directors. She was kept waiting for over an hour. Then the secretary informed her that Mr Quaig would see her when he had finished urgent business. Another forty minutes passed before she was led into the boardroom. Louise ignored the fact that Quaig had kept her waiting and came straight to the point.

'I'd like to apply for the post of test pilot, the post that's been vacant for three months. I'm willing to undergo any physical examination and any pilot testing you think necessary.'

Quaig answered without consulting his co-directors.

'That wouldn't be possible, Mrs Tanner.'

'Why not?'

'Because you're a woman. Maybe you're a good flier, I'm sure you are, but being a test pilot requires not only skill but nerves of steel. Women are too highly strung.'

'Test me, Mr Quaig.'

'I couldn't risk a plane testing you. I don't believe a woman could do the job and I shan't change my mind.'

Louise wondered if Quaig actually hated women or if the look he was giving her was simply his way of showing her that to him she was a nothing and a nobody. She sighed, suddenly exhausted by the effort of controlling her anger when one of the other directors spoke.

'It was a nice idea, Mrs Tanner, and maybe we could find something for you in the canteen. That way you can be near your husband and it would enable you to earn extra money. Women are marvellous at preparing meals, at least we're all agreed on that.'

'I'm a pilot, sir, not a cook. I can make burned toast and not much else.'

'We couldn't take on a woman, Mrs Tanner. We just wouldn't be confident in her ability to control her emotions.'

Louise drove back to the house, tears running down her face. From the very moment of arrival in El Paso, the moment of first meeting with Quaig, she had felt a profound and terrible disappointment. In Britain, rationing continued seemingly for ever and the nation was tired and jaded. In the States, the houses were wondrously equipped. Central heating was common, bathrooms and running hot and cold considered normal. Women were well dressed, men had more work than they could manage. She was lucky to be living in the States, but she still missed her country, because Americans were years behind the British in their thinking on the subject of women. Perhaps it was because their women had not been obliged to evolve at the same lightning speed as the British, who had driven ambulances at the front, piloted mail planes and assumed almost all the masculine jobs and roles during the long years of wartime conflict. Louise felt terribly homesick for the first time since her arrival in America.

That evening, Louise hit a new low in her anguish, as she lay in bed, looking in horror at the white walls and brutal white lights of her new 'home'. As if reading her thoughts, Joe spoke.

'These white bulbs are exactly what you'd expect from Quaig, and I think he got the furniture out of Colditz! In the morning we'll go find something much nicer to rent. Okay, Lou?'

'But this house is free!'

'Sure it is, but we hate it. We'll rent a nice place where we can be comfy together. Annika and Mrs Quaig are already planning to teach you five-star domesticity. I couldn't believe it when they showed me your programme for learning to make preserves. I'd rather have a flier than a woman who cooks all day long.'

'I'll buy all those things in the store and practise my loops while you're at work.'

'That's my girl. The women who live here stay home roasting their asses over the hot stove. They have a lot to learn.'

'Maybe I'll teach them.'

'Sure you will, Lou. You'll teach them being stubborn, getting your own way and flying instructions to be practised in bed on your husband's joystick. Maybe *we* should write a list or two. I'd like to see Mrs Quaig's face when she reads that!'

They went to bed early, groaning when the springs made such a commotion they decided that love making was out of the question, unless they adjourned to the hammock on the veranda, which they did. Then, like naughty children, they slept entwined in each other's arms until morning came, golden, hot and full of hope.

On Monday, they moved into a pretty little house behind a creeper-covered fence. On Tuesday, two friends arrived with the Tanners' planes and they did an impromptu demonstration for everyone in town before Joe went to work. Then Louise flew a personal exhibition over the Quaig Corporation airfield, preventing the test pilots from taking off for an hour.

Quaig called Joe to his office.

'I'm more than happy with your work, young man, but I want you to control your wife.'

'Oh Lou's just showing off her abilities, sir.'

'I don't doubt her flying abilities. I doubt her stability under stress. In any case, she mustn't do it again. If she does, I shall take steps to control her.'

'She's not a dog, sir, and the demonstration only lasted an hour.'

'It was an hour of lost company time.'

That same afternoon, before Joe could return home, Louise registered her protest again and Quaig carried out his threat and made a complaint to the civil licensing authorities, who withdrew her flying licence for two weeks. White hot with fury, Louise listened as her husband tried to calm her.

'You can't win with Quaig. When I've saved a bit of money we'll move on. We'll go to New Mexico or California, like all my predecessors did. They were probably bored to tears and strangled by Quaig's outdated ideas. He's a New Englander of the old school, who thinks women are for cooking, cleaning and having children, and that's about as far as his imagination takes him.'

'I love you, Joe. Come here and let's sit on the veranda and watch the sun go down.'

'In the hammock?'

'Why not?'

'Hammocks have a funny effect on you, Louise. All that rocking back and forth gets you ignited.'

'So come and get burned!'

'Now you're talking like Mae West.'

'I wish I had a figure like hers and a bank account too. I'd tell Mr Quaig to go to hell.'

'Don't think about him.'

'I'm thinking about you. Give me a kiss and then take off your jacket and let me pull those down. There's nothing but darkness and us. Kiss me again, Joe. I want to fly like an eagle and only you know how to make me do that.'

In the morning, Louise drove to the company airfield, where she and Joe kept their planes for reasons of easy maintenance and security. She had been working on calculations for their next exhibition and needed some papers kept in a side pocket near the pilot's seat. On reaching the plane, she was surprised to be questioned by a company guard.

'Mr Quaig's orders, this plane's to be impounded and put in the hangar.'

'It isn't a company plane. It's mine and I can't fly it because I've been grounded for two weeks at Mr Quaig's instigation.'

'He wants the plane under lock and key, ma'am.'

'Has he ordered you to *steal* it?'

'No, ma'am. He says it's on company land so it must be kept in a company hangar.'

'We'll see about that!'

Louise took off before anyone could stop her. Then, having checked her fuel gauge, she landed two miles from the airfield, in deserted, flat countryside. Minutes later, she saw two company vans and a police car approaching. Shaking her head despairingly, she thought that if Quaig had his way, women would remain immured in their houses for ever. There would never be women test pilots, engineers, geologists and deep-sea divers, just dimity-dressed robots who organized cake-making contests and patchwork evenings like their grandmothers before them, women who were never allowed to have the choice of doing something different. She accepted that not every woman in the world wanted to pilot a plane, but thought that it would be nice if they were free to decide their future.

Louise took off again, despite the difficult terrain, and flew to Albuquerque. Nearing the airport, she demanded permission to land and was given the all clear by the control tower. But as she taxied in, the local sheriff appeared.

'Ma'am, I'm Sheriff Towne. I have to take you into my office and charge you with flying without a licence.'

'Can I call my husband?'

'You can do it from my office, ma'am.'

Louise sat grim faced while Towne dialled the number of their house and Joe came on the line.

'Hi, Lou. You sound upset. What happened?'

'I'm in Albuquerque.'

'What are you doing there, for Christ's sake?'

She quickly told him.

'I'll go see Quaig right now,' said Joe. 'I'm due to test fly the new plane this afternoon. They're doing altitude tests today and that takes time, but I'll see him before I go up. He's already lost two of his test pilots in the last three months. I don't suppose he'll want my resignation as well. Give me your number, Lou.'

'It's Albuquerque five hundred. You'll call me back, won't you, Joe?'

'Sure will, and I'll come over for you when I've finished here. Keep your chin up, Lou, and I'll be there before you know it.'

'I love you ten million.'

'Love you, too. You're the sun and the moon and the stars to me, Lou. I'll show you how much I love you when we get home tonight.'

'It's a promise?'

'Sure is, Lou.'

At seven in the evening, uncertain what to do and puzzled that Joe had not called back, Louise rang him again at the house. There was no reply. She rang the company office, but they had closed. An hour later, Towne brought her some dinner and ate his own with her. The phone rang while they were eating their dessert. Towne listened for a long time. Then he rose, took away the empty tray and told Louise she was free to leave. She kissed him resoundingly on both cheeks.

'Was that Joe? He's fixed everything like he said he would.'

'It was a friend of his, ma'am. Shall I take you to the airport? Taxis aren't much in evidence in town at this time of year.'

It was dark when Louise flew into the company

airfield, surprised to see the office open and the runways in full operational illumination. An ambulance appeared and parked next to the two company fire engines that were always based in the compound. Louise taxied to a halt, leaped out and rushed to the office.

'What's happened? Has there been an accident? Can I do anything to help?'

Quaig was sitting with his head buried in his hands and he did not stir. Louise moved nearer.

'Are you all right, Mr Quaig?'

'I've called Frances to come at once.'

'What's the matter?'

'I've had a shock. Sit down please. Let me give you a brandy.'

Louise felt the colour drain from her face and her breath coming in fits and starts. She watched a bluebottle on the window, black against the black of night outside, its presence like a malevolence. Thoughts raced through her mind like trains through tunnels and she wanted to ask a thousand questions. She feared she already knew the answers.

'What is it, Mr Quaig?'

'I'm most dreadfully sorry to have to tell you that your husband had an accident with the B8, lost height and crashed into the Guadalupe Mountains just north of the town. He was killed outright. I swear on my life that Joe didn't suffer.'

As she heard the words, a montage of images flew through Louise's mind: the wet afternoon in Kenya, when Camilla had waved goodbye and had never been seen again. She and Joe flying together, like twin birds in total unison of heart, soul and will to succeed. She and Joe talking on the phone only a few hours previously – *You're the sun and the moon and the stars to me, Lou. I'll show you how much I love you when we get home tonight*. No tears fell, but her heart beat so fast and furiously Louise wondered if she was going to disgrace herself and faint. She went to the window and gulped in cold night air, surprised when sweat fell like rain from her brow. Her legs felt inexplicably heavy and when she tried to remember where she had left her plane she found it impossible to think. Without a word, she left the office and walked towards the ambulance, but kindly arms enfolded her and Mrs Quaig spoke.

'I've come to take you home, Louise.'

'I want to see Joe.'

'No! You just remember your husband how he was and treasure the memories. Mr Quaig'll make the formal identification and take care of all the funeral arrangements. Come dear, you're going to sleep at our place until the funeral. After that, you must contact your family and maybe return to England.'

The funeral was held in a small cemetery near the white sands that drifted like a silver sea, ever changing, ever shifting in the wilderness surrounding El Paso. Everyone was there, all of them kind and concerned. Louise wore her best yellow dress, Joe's favourite, shunning black despite Mr Quaig's exhortations because Joe hated sombre colours and even in death she longed to please him. As they sang 'Abide with Me', she thought sadly that Joe would always be with her. There would never be a day when his hand would not be in hers, his smile echoing in her mind. There would never again be a light at the end of the tunnel, except when she was flying. When she flew, Louise knew instinctively that Joe would be there at her side, encouraging, admiring, amusing, adoring.

For weeks Louise sat on the veranda, staring into space, refusing sedatives and invitations from other families. She lost a stone in weight, unable to eat without vomiting, unable to drink anything but water.

She was waiting for Aunt Flora to arrive and help her through the hell of bereavement, but the old lady remained curiously silent. Then, one Saturday morning, Joe's father appeared at the gate, hollow-eyed, haggard and ill.

'I have to talk with you, Louise. Neighbours tell me you even sleep on the veranda, that you don't eat and you vomit when you try to swallow. You're as thin as a skeleton and pale as a corpse. Won't you come back with me to White River Junction? We want you there and we'll look after you like the daughter we feel you are.'

A tear fell down Louise's cheek, closely followed by another. Bob's face was an older version of Joe's and she felt bereft and close to panic in the sudden and hideous realization that she would never see Joe again. Joe was *dead*. Until this moment, she had never really focused on the word. Now, she simply sat immobile, tears coursing down her cheeks. She barely reacted when Bob broke the news of Aunt Flora's death.

'Martha and I got a telgramme from your Uncle Ferdy in Scotland, saying the great lady died suddenly on arrival at Black Gordon. They're taking care of things and he said to come over when you want to, when you're recovered from the shock and all that. Your aunt's to be buried in the cemetery near her house in Sussex.'

'I knew something must be wrong when she didn't reply. I wanted to ring or *do* something, but I seem becalmed. I haven't the energy to get up off the chair and when I do I can't remember anything.'

'What you're feeling's normal, Louise. Grief and mourning are illnesses. We have to suffer from them and then recover from them and then have a period of convalescence.'

'I hope you're right. At this moment, I don't know

142

anything any more, except that I want to run away. But where shall I go? What shall I do? I only know about machines and flying.'

'Has the company talked about the insurance payments?'

'It's all arranged. Joe was heavily insured and there's a generous pension, but *he* won't be here any more.'

'We'll eat now, Lou, it's seven o'clock. I'll make dinner for us and you'll eat because I'm here. Life has to go on, you know. Joe always said you were the most courageous woman he'd ever met and you have to prove him right. You can't just let yourself die.'

Two days later, Bob returned home. The same afternoon, Quaig delivered the insurance cheque and told Louise to let him know where she wanted the monthly pension paid. She watched him leave, his back stiff, his face still full of shock and anguish. Then she went inside and looked at the frilly white curtains and the blue sofa she and Joe had chosen, on which they had sat in the evenings, making plans for the future, for children and flying schools and state aviation information for young people interested in the new career. They had laughed at private jokes and made love until the old marble clock had chimed midnight. Blank faced, Louise went into the bedroom, put the contents of her three drawers in a suitcase with the photographs of her wedding and then walked out of the house to her car. She did not stop driving until nightfall, when she reached Tularosa and put into a motel for dinner. Too tired to continue, she asked for a room, had a bath and fell asleep, waking at four, rising, paying her bill like a robot and preparing to leave.

Sensing her distress, the night clerk offered her coffee.

'Where are you heading, ma'am?'

'Away from El Paso, that's all I know.'

'You'll hit Santa Fe and Albuquerque soon. They're lovely. Cheer up, ma'am, today's going to be a great day.'

'There won't *ever* be a great day again.'

Louise drove north, praying for the dawn and asking herself if the desk clerk had been right about the towns ahead. All she knew was that the road led away from the little house with white lace curtains in the shadow of the Guadalupe Mountains. All she wanted was to find peace of mind and oblivion.

At sunrise, Louise saw a Spanish style town of pale pink stucco. She drove in, turning neither to right nor left until she came to a pueblo that was the town centre. There, she parked the car and sat looking about her. The columns of the Governor's Palace reflected bright white in the sunlight. Indians were holding a market under the arcades, selling vegetables, rugs and silver jewellery. The inhabitants seemed friendly. The air was clear and clean. The summer sky was cobalt blue, a perfect sky for flying. Louise locked the car, walked to the Corner Café and ordered coffee.

'I'm looking for a house to rent, something small, on a quiet street.'

'Can't help you, but I have a friend who might.'

By midday, Louise was installed with her one big suitcase in a tiny adobe house with a sculpted chimney. The living-room led to an open air portal, paved with big round stones and roofed in cedar branches held in place by rocklike upright tree trunks. The portal would become her favourite place, its cloister-like stillness a haven for her tortured mind. For days on end she sat there, alone, remembering happiness with Joe, the flying lessons, the first exhibition of aerobatics, their arrival, full of hope, in El Paso. The present was agonizing and empty, the future seemed non-existent.

Only the past made her happy, because the past was Joe.

Summer's poppies, hollyhocks and daisies gave way to the colours of autumn. The rabbit bush lost its blueness and bloomed yellow. Then, as harsh winds blew across the mesa, Louise went inside and lit the fire. Alone with her memories, she would live her first winter in Santa Fe like a hibernating animal, buried far from life in an adobe house, its shutters closed, only smoke coming from the chimney betraying the fact that someone was there. A woman who no longer existed for herself or those who passed by, Louise was waiting to emerge from the thick fog of shock and trauma into the clear skies of a new life that must, she imagined, come with the spring, when all living things reawakened from their enforced sleep. For the moment, winter held her in its icy grip and she wept for her loss and for the fact that she was hopelessly, relentlessly in love with her husband and always would be. She needed to keep Joe in her heart, where he belonged and she would do that for *always*. He had once said that nothing was for ever, but she had changed his mind. Love was for always and ever, to the ends of the earth and beyond.

NINE

Santa Fe, 1950

The lilac was in bloom. Louise rose, showered and went outside to admire the heavily perfumed fronds. Joe had loved lilac. She picked some, put it in a vase and then went to the kitchen and made coffee, stale bread toast and put everything on a tray. She carried the tray to the wicker table in the portal, its yellow walls decorated with black iron keys and ancient farm implements. The table and wicker chair were white and Louise was dressed in the same colour as the lilac fronds that trespassed above her head. Everything in the garden was in flower. Weeds covered the herb and vegetable garden and thorn bushes sprang up around the fruit trees. Louise poured some coffee and thought absent-mindedly that she really must do something about the garden. But she knew she was too lethargic to organize anything at all. She was day-dreaming about the past when she heard a screech of brakes and saw a big blue car smash through her fence and come to a halt in the middle of what had once been a vegetable patch. Louise remained immobile, flinching when a black-haired girl got out of the car, cursed and ran towards her.

'Damn! Oh ma'am, do forgive me. I'm Amy Pallister. I just passed my driving test. I was *so* excited I mistook the accelerator for the brake. I'll go get my father and he'll arrange everything.'

Louise looked into a pair of bright brown eyes set in a heart-shaped face. The girl was tall and thin and full of life. Her clothes were subtly coloured and serious, but she wore her hair in a plait around her head decorated with plastic cherries. Louise sighed, remembering when she too had been full of life and hope and plans for the future, when she would have found the idea of red plastic cherry hair slides enticing.

Amy gazed into a pair of sea-green eyes set in a pale face surrounded by a halo of blonde hair. The face was devoid of expression, as if the shock of the crash had not registered at all. She recognized Louise at once, because she had been to two of the Flying Tanners' exhibitions and had never forgotten the thrill of their suicide dives. She knew also of Joe's sudden death and had heard that his widow lived like a recluse. But nothing had prepared her eighteen-year-old mind for the shock of meeting naked anguish face-to-face. She held out her hand to Louise.

'I've shocked you, Mrs Tanner. Let me make you a fresh pot of coffee.'

On entering the house, Amy came to a sudden halt. In vases around the window ledges, there were long dead flowers. Dust half an inch thick lay on all the surfaces and the table was covered with year-old news-papers telling of Joe's career and the tragedy of his death. On one front page, Louise and Joe were pictured together, smiling into camera, after their very first exhibition of aerobatics. Amy looked from the table to Louise and then hurried to make a pot of coffee. Louise sat at the table, gazing into space until the cup was put before her. She did not answer when Amy spoke, the crash having shocked her without her realizing it. She did not even hear the words.

'Mrs Tanner, Louise, I'm going home now. I'll come back with my father. Please stay where you are and don't worry about a thing.'

Amy went out, got into her car, reversed back over the remains of the vegetable patch and disappeared from view. She drove to the hacienda, where she and her father, the world renowned photographer Nolan Pallister, lived in solitary splendour on a high hill overlooking the town.

'Are you there, Daddy? I crashed my car.'

'Before or after you got your driving licence?'

'After.'

'Are you hurt?'

'No.'

'Is anyone hurt?'

'No.'

'Then that's okay. We should celebrate with a glass of champagne!'

'I knocked down a fence and demolished a woman's vegetable garden. It was over-run with thorn bushes, but she didn't seem to have noticed. Her name's Louise Tanner.'

'Of the Flying Tanners?'

'Yes. Her husband was killed some time ago. He worked as a test pilot in El Paso.'

'What's she like?'

'She lives alone and I swear she's in some kind of shock. She's the most beautiful person I ever saw, but she just isn't *there*, if you know what I mean. She doesn't reply. She doesn't talk. I'm not sure she even *knows* I smashed her fence. Will you come back with me and talk to her? She lives in incredible disorder, with dust everywhere and old newspapers full of pictures of her husband. She needs help.'

'We'll go right down there. I'll get Alvarez to repair the fence and replant the garden.'

Nolan took his camera from habit, as always. He had seen the Flying Tanners once and knew that Joe's death had shocked the world of civil aviation. He vaguely remembered Louise, having seen her only in flying kit, skull cap and goggles. Impatient to make amends for the damage Amy had caused, he was glad when she took them swiftly into Santa Fe and parked outside a tiny adobe house.

'That's the place, Daddy.'

'You did a good job on the fence! What happened?'

'I mistook the accelerator for the brake. I was just so wild and happy that I'd passed the test. There she is, Daddy. She's sitting under the portal like she was when I first met her. Isn't she beautiful, like something out of a fairy story.'

Nolan turned and saw Louise. On a bench painted white, against a wall coloured saffron, a slim, angel-faced blonde was sitting, staring into space. Her eyes were huge and green, her hair like golden corn lit by the sun. She was wearing a slate-grey dress patterned with lilac that echoed the fronds drooping in scented profusion under the roof of the portal. Nolan photographed her from the garden and from close by, immediately aware that Louise was not registering his presence. Then he went inside the house, looked into the fridge, found nothing but tomatoes and bread. Suddenly afraid of his thoughts about this ethereal creature, he turned to Amy.

'There's nothing in the fridge except ice cubes, tomatoes and bread. Does she eat?'

'I don't think she remembers.'

'Call Dr Marcos and ask him to come up to the hacienda. Call Alvarez and give him the address. Tell him to repair the fence and put together the best vegetable patch in Santa Fe. I'm going to talk to Mrs Tanner.'

Nolan stood before Louise, taking in every detail. Her hands were long and pale, her face a too thin oval. Her body was finely boned, with full breasts, a small waist and narrow feet in Indian sandals. He held out his hand.

149

'I'm Nolan Pallister, Amy's father.'

She looked up at a tall man of forty-five, with greying temples and a mahogany suntan. His eyes were dark, their expression kind and he had a smile that was reassuring. Louise eyed his clothes and liked what she saw, the silk shirt, the navy sailor's jacket with brass buttons, the faded blue trousers. She was startled when he spoke.

'Take my hand, Mrs Tanner. When you're tired and lonely and you feel a little lost in life you need a hand to pull you out of the bad patch and into the sunlight again. This is the hand. Take hold of it.'

She heard the words and understood them. But for a moment, she hesitated. Then she put her hand in his, rising to her feet as Nolan led her to the car. His voice calmed her and she smiled wistfully when he spoke.

'You've had a shock, Mrs Tanner. I'd like to invite you to come with my daughter and me for a few days' rest at our place. All the work on the wall and the garden of your home'll be taken care of while you're absent. You don't have any decisions to make. Just lean on me for a while till you feel better.'

Louise watched the road wind higher and higher, until they stopped outside a hacienda in the most beautiful Santa Fe style. Decorated with stucco, it seemed like a citadel and as she gazed at the big thick walls, she felt secure for the first time in months. She followed without protest when Nolan opened a carved hiroko wood gate, that led to an inner courtyard with fountain and pool full of fat goldfish. The house had been constructed to take maximum advantage of the view and to give light and shelter to those who lived within the walls. It was full of wonderful canvasses by Diego Rivera, Braque and the young van Dongen, that mixed, by a mysterious alchemy, with a group of seventeenth-century Flemish paintings in the Mannerist style. Walls of leather-bound books vied with shelves of seventeenth-century Chinese bronze incense burners shaped like gourds and pumpkins. The furniture came from the four corners of the world, Nolan's creative genius mixing eighteenth-century Dutch marquetry bureaux with George I secretaires, Burgundian panels with a Mexican dresser full of German schrezheim tureens. Louise let her host lead her to a guest room done out in Nolan's idea of the English style. All in sand and white, it bore the unmistakable imprint of the Santa Fe he loved, despite an Edwardian poudreuse and a fine Burne-Jones portrait.

Suddenly, she felt overwhelmingly tired and before Nolan could speak, Louise took off her shoes, lifted back the bedcover and lay down. Seconds later, to his astonishment, she was sound asleep. She stayed asleep for most of the next four days. Then, one morning, she woke and wandered to the kitchen, where Amy was making breakfast.

'Louise! You slept for four days. Daddy was thrilled that you got so relaxed in our house.'

'Are you sure I slept for *four* days?'

'You obviously needed it, what with the shock of my demolishing your garden and not eating right, you're in a very run down condition. We've decided to give you the Pallister special recovery programme, so you can get fit and well again.'

'I don't even remember getting into bed! I'd better pack my things! In England it's considered appalling bad taste to outstay your welcome and I've surely outstayed mine.'

'Oh no! You haven't even *started* on your welcome, Louise. You've been asleep, so you didn't realize how happy Daddy and I are to have a really interesting guest in the house. Daddy's a great host and he's dying to

151

show you his photographs and enlist your help choosing shots for the retrospective at the San Diego Museum of Modern Art. He's the first photographer who's ever been chosen to exhibit there and he's getting quite nervous.'

'I know nothing about photographs.'

'You know what you like, what you think has impact. Pass an opinion. Daddy loves that.'

Louise went to the living-room and smiled down at her host, who was gazing at photographs laid out on the floor.

'Mr Pallister, I'm so very grateful to you for looking after me. I must have been more shocked than I realized by Amy's accident and I haven't been very well since . . . for quite a long time.'

'You're looking much better. After breakfast, I'd love you to help me choose the best of these. When we've chosen the black and white shots, we're going on a quick trip to my house at La Jolla to bring some colour prints back. You'll come with Amy and me? I'm as nervous as a cat about this exhibition. I need all the help I can get.'

'I'd best go home and collect some clothes.'

'No need, I bought you some. Amy and I went to the Best of Europe shop in Albuquerque. God, it was wonderful! Haven't had such fun since I was twenty-five and bought my first Rolleiflex. Hope you like the clothes anyway. Come on, I'll show you.'

He put an arm around Louise's shoulders and led her to a small bedroom off the living-room. There, on a carved Mexican bed, she saw dresses in cotton, silk and lace for morning, afternoon and evening. The range of colours had been kept in tonal shades of blue, lavender, lime and sage. The fabrics were beautiful, the styles simple but expensive. One outfit in particular thrilled Louise – a plain blue silk sailor suit with square white

152

collar and pleated skirt. She felt like a child at Christmas and knew that Nolan and his daughter had bought her the clothes to make her happy, to change her luck, to show their friendship. Turning to him, she spoke uncertainly.

'I don't know what to say. Shall I choose now or later?'

'They're all for you, Louise. Amy and I had such fun buying them. We wanted to show you that you're not alone any more. The new clothes are a symbol of our friendship and part of our prescription for getting you on the road again. Come with us to California. We'll only be away three days and it'll be a holiday for you. Give you a chance to wow the locals with your new things.'

'I can't believe all this is happening!'

'Sure, it's happening. Now we must go sit on the terrace. Amy made beef consommé to be served with breakfast like you're recovering from an illness. Nothing in the world she likes better than playing nurse!'

'Are you going to have consommé, too?'

'Of course. I'm recovering from the shock of finding the most beautiful girl in the world sitting all alone on her patio.'

Louise smiled and let him lead her to the terrace with its breathtaking view of Santa Fe. They all drank their consommé to strengthen them for the journey to California and three days of luxury at Nolan's hideaway.

Before lunch, Louise took the clothes to her room and tried everything on, staring at her reflection in the mirror and struggling to understand the strange quirk of destiny that had suddenly brought her two new friends, just when she needed to know that she was not totally alone in the world. On the wall, a lizard moved and hid behind the curtains. Louise felt that she had been like the lizard for well over a year, hiding from the light, from life, from everything. She moved the curtain, but the lizard had disappeared, as if by magic.

Louise sat for a long time on the edge of the bed in the navy sailor suit, looking at her hands. Was it possible that the suffocating weight of her sadness could be made to disappear? Was there a chance that she could be herself again someday, that she could fly her plane and run and laugh and dream and do all the things she and Joe had hoped to do together? If she could feel happy because she had some new clothes, could she feel happy for other reasons too? She took off the sailor suit, put on her own lilac patterned dress and went to the kitchen to speak to Amy.

'Your father's spent a fortune on my clothes. Will he let me repay him little by little?'

'Of course not. Daddy loves shopping and buying things. You'll just have to get used to him. He has absolutely no idea how to be economical and he doesn't need to learn.'

'But I can't let him buy me presents like that.'

'You can be a friend and Daddy's been so lonely since Mother died. Don't deny him the pleasure of giving, Louise. He's having fun. Have fun too. Relax. There's no price tag on friendship. Okay?'

'Okay Amy, if you're sure.'

La Jolla was sun-baked hills, pine trees and cobalt blue sea, indivisible from a sky of the same colour. The houses were in the Mexican style, perched over dream views or sheltered in niches, away from prying eyes. The residents were few and far between, a few artists, a group of intellectuals fleeing the tasteless concrete wastes of Los Angeles and one Texan millionaire, who wanted to be far away from other Texan millionaires.

Nolan's house was a beach shack with eight rooms. Once inside, nothing intruded on the thoughts but the sound of gulls screeching and waves lapping the shore. Louise stood on the beach, looking at the sea. There was something in the endless blue purity, the wind, the spray and the wildness that made her feel reborn. She also felt safe, because she was no longer alone and she realized with something of a shock that she was afraid when she was alone. She picked up a shell and carried it back to the house, perturbed to discover that despite her ideas on independence, she was unable to live without help.

Nolan watched from the house while Amy checked the cupboards in the kitchen.

'Louise likes it here. When you're tired and beat up the sea makes you feel better and she feels that.'

'She's been so alone and scared of everything, Daddy. You'll see, she'll start to recover now we're with her. I've put her in the blue room because it's so lovely in the mornings.'

'We'll take her to Luchino's for dinner.'

'No, I think we'll cook it here on the beach, just the three of us. She's far too disturbed for fancy places. Louise needs peace and moral support. She needs friends.'

'What shall we eat? Are we short of anything?'

'We can have prawns and mussels and oysters cooked on the fire with a little garlic. Or a paella. Or chicken with sweet and sour sauce. You like that.'

'What does Louise like?'

'I don't know, but we can ask her, here she is.'

Louise handed Nolan a large pink shell with mother of pearl interior.

'I can't afford expensive gifts like those you gave me, but this is the most beautiful shell in the whole world, so I give it to you, Nolan.'

Moved, he looked at its lustrous depths and tried to analyse the look in Louise's eyes when she gave it to him. There was an expression of almost childlike innocence and something he could not identify but that he hoped was curiosity. He went to put it beside his bed.

When they had discussed dinner, Amy and Louise went in search of the fishermen, who came ashore two or three times a day to sell their catch. A wind blew in from the sea and they stopped here and there to pocket an intriguing stone, a shell, a tiny object washed ashore from a long sunken ship.

Nolan gazed after the two women from the house. Then he sat on the edge of the bed and picked up the shell Louise had given him. Was it possible he had fallen in love with a woman he barely knew? He told himself he was being silly, but he could not stop thinking about her. He rose and went out to the water's edge. In his youth, he had loved Amy's mother, the tempestuous Mexican actress, Montalita. After her death from cancer at thirty-five, he had remained alone with his child. From time to time he had had an affair, but affairs were unsatisfying and Nolan had dreamed of finding love again. Inevitably, as the years passed, he had lost hope, until he saw Louise sitting under the portal of her adobe in a grey dress patterned with lilac.

Dinner was a great success and Louise ate with a will. Amy played her guitar and sang tunes from *South Pacific*. Nolan took them to the water's edge and showed them the phosphorescence of the oncoming waves, weaving magic spells with his words and fascinating both women. Louise told them a story of her childhood in Kenya.

'I used to play with the animals as if they were toys. At least that's what I remember. The animals were wild, but Mummy made them tame by giving them Scottish porridge for breakfast. Ostriches love porridge. Later, we went for picnics in the woods and once Mummy nearly trod on a crocodile. She was a bit short-sighted and hadn't noticed him in the mud.'

'Was she beautiful like you?'

Louise gazed at Nolan, as if the thought of being beautiful had never occurred to her.

'Oh, much lovelier than I can ever be. Mummy was the most beautiful woman of her generation and the most famous fashion mannequin in England.'

'Did she die in England or in Kenya?'

'She and Daddy were killed in a car crash after I left for England. The Invergordon family thought it was a curse come true, but I don't believe in curses. I suppose the rains came and in Kenya that makes the roads like skating rinks.'

Nolan looked thoughtful.

'You said your father was Lord Invergordon, so your mother must have been Camilla Elborne. You're not going to believe it, Louise, but I think I once did a cover of Camilla for *Picture Post* just before her marriage.'

'Oh, do find it if you can. I have so very few souvenirs of my family. Aunt Flora never talked about Kenya and the accident. Aunt Cecy said it was too upsetting to think about and I never did discover where all my mother's wonderful clothes went. I suppose they must have been stolen in transit back to England.'

The three days at the beach were sunlit and tranquil. Louise became daily more relaxed and closer to Amy. Nolan seemed more and more thoughtful. Everywhere Louise went, he went too, to protect her. Her wish was his command and he had difficulty finding time to choose his photographs for the exhibition, until Louise offered to make lists and put them in order for him. Finally, they were ready for the journey back to Santa Fe and as they boarded the train Nolan began making plans.

'When we get back, we'll check out all the photographs, frames, lists and references. That should take about three weeks.'

Amy cut in with a smile.

'Louise isn't your secretary, Daddy. She'll want to go home when we get back.'

Nolan stared at his daughter, realizing with a start that he had taken it for granted that Louise would stay on with them. The idea of her leaving troubled him intensely, but he said nothing. When they arrived at the hacienda, Louise would need to rest and see Dr Marcos for her tests. After that, perhaps, she might return to the little house in Santa Fe.

Days passed, Louise worked diligently with Nolan, organizing his pictures into some semblance of order. When she was not with him, she was trying to help Amy in the kitchen. Then Paquita, the housekeeper, returned from holiday and Louise was able to sample the family's Mexican cuisine. But finally she knew she must go home. The fence was mended, a new and resplendent vegetable garden planted. Dr Marcos had pronounced her fit, if still shocked by Joe's death. As she and Amy knew that Nolan would never agree to her leaving, they went back to Louise's house together while he was out of the hacienda for the day.

'Daddy's in love with you, Louise.'

'You can't say that. He's only known me a few weeks.'

'Makes no difference. He'll never accept that you live alone, without anyone to look after you. Daddy's a man with a lot of love to give and he's old-fashioned. He wants to protect you and shield you from unhappiness and he's right. You need someone.'

'He's been so very kind. I don't know how to thank you both. I can never repay the debt.'

'Don't thank him, just give Father the chance to make

158

you happy in his own way. You can never forget your husband and no one would want you to, but you have all your life ahead of you, Louise. Would you please give Daddy the chance to *hope*?'

Alone again, Louise sat on the wicker chair in the portal, gazing into space. She was chewing over Amy's words and trying hard to still the panic in her heart at being alone again with her memories. Dusk came, but she stayed where she was, unwilling to go inside, trying to prolong the day, because the night frightened her. She kept debating her future, as she had done so many times since Joe's death, never arriving at a firm decision. Part of her wanted to return to England, but Aunt Flora was dead and she hardly knew Uncle Ferdy. Cecy had gone back to Kenya and Louise knew she could never live there again. Africa held too many memories, most of them ones she wanted to forget. She had kept in contact with Cecy by letter, but for the moment the distance between them precluded meetings. If she stayed in America, there was no problem for money. But what would she *do*? Her plans had been to have children and a flying career in partnership with Joe. Alone, how would she fill her days, fill her life, give all she had to give to someone when there was no one there to receive it?

Nolan arrived home and kissed his daughter.

'I bought this for Louise. Isn't it wonderful? A real cheongsam. Pink's a great colour for her – at least this beigy-rose shade.'

'Daddy, Louise went back home. She invited us to lunch tomorrow so she could thank you for all your kindness, but when she knew all the work was finished she felt she had to go. She's been here a long time and she knows it's not correct to simply move in and stay.'

'Why not?'

'Louise isn't your wife, Daddy. She's a friend, but she

has her own life to lead and folk would gossip furiously if she just stayed on. They'd think she was your mistress.'

Nolan strode out of the hacienda and drove down to the valley. It was eight o'clock and getting dark. Maybe Louise would be in bed, but he didn't give a damn. Parking the car near her house, he hurried to the gate, pausing in the semi-darkness when he saw her sitting alone, under the lamp, gazing into space. She was wearing the new sailor suit she adored. Nolan moved slowly towards her, choosing his words with the greatest care.

'In India and China they choose a husband for reasons of logic and suitability. You've had a husband you loved above all else and he died. You'll always love him, because it's like that in life. But now you have to decide whether you sit on your ass on the veranda till you're old and grey or if you choose a husband who loves you and who'll do his best to wait until you learn to love him. I want to marry you, Louise. I would be miserable now without you.'

She looked into the handsome face, rose and walked towards him, relieved that he was at her side, that she would not have to go into the house alone, to spend the night with the image of a plane crashing in the Guadalupe Mountains and Joe dying when she'd thought he was coming home to her. She spoke very softly.

'I was scared to go inside the house. I'm scared all the time when I'm alone, always have been since Joe died. I like you Nolan, but I don't love you and I don't know if I ever could love you. But if you really want to marry me and take the risk, I'll accept your proposal.'

Nolan led her into the house, packed her few things, put them in the car and drove back to the hacienda. The following day, he arranged a special licence and a week later, in a very private ceremony at the hacienda, Louise Tanner became Louise Pallister.

Amy was ecstatic at the idea of her father's marriage. He had been alone for so long, aimless, unable to express himself without someone to protect and spoil. She believed that great passion only comes once in a lifetime and for Louise that passion had been Joe. But marriage to Nolan would be a new beginning and Louise obviously needed that above all else. She would be loved and cosseted for the rest of her life and in her seriously damaged state it seemed the right thing to do.

Nolan was in love, unreasonably, ecstatically in love. Louise was lost and almost alone in the world. All his protective instincts came to the surface, the instincts that were the essential base of his character and he made plans to create such a wonderland for Louise that she would never regret having accepted him. Brimming with ideas, longing to spoil her to death, Nolan thought of their honeymoon at the house on the beach and knew it was the right place to start their life together. Louise loved walking on the beach and looking into the blue infinity, that acted as a mysterious magnet for her eyes.

It was on the beach that Louise realized what she had done. Until then, the reality of marriage had not really dawned. When it hit her, her mind filled with questions. Alone, she was sure she would never recover and do the things she and Joe had planned; the flying school, the children's groups, the lectures on piloting, the foundation of a State College of Aeronautics. Married to Nolan, supported in her future life and ambitions by his love, who could tell what she could accomplish?

Louise returned to the house, where her husband was concocting a Mexican dinner. Delicious smells drifted through the window and she felt hungry and almost happy, because Nolan was there and he would take care of her. In the kitchen, she kissed his shoulder, touched when he returned the kiss on the tip of each of her fingers.

'I'm warning you, Louise, this dinner is getting bigger and bigger. We could well have to stay up till three in the morning to finish it!'

'Thank goodness, you can cook. I've never been very gifted in that direction.'

'I'll teach you.'

'What can I teach you in return?'

'I'll think of something, like talking with a British accent or whistling "God Save the King".'

Later, as they walked on the beach in the moonlight, Louise felt Nolan's body hard against her own. Her heart fluttered like a trapped bird in her chest, because she had never been touched by any man but Joe and was wondering if, at the moment of intimacy, she would weep or fight or act like a fool. Would it be impossible to give herself? She began to tremble from apprehension and Nolan, mistaking her nervousness for desire, carried her into the house and up to the bedroom. There, he loved her with tenderness, passion and all the expertise of a man of the world, relieved that she seemed so trusting. As he reached the climax of feeling, Louise cried out in a sudden moment of release, as if her control had snapped and she had finally left the past behind. Nolan took her in his arms and held her to his heart.

'I love you, Louise, and I always will. Close your eyes and sleep and think of tomorrow. From now on try always to think of tomorrow, never of yesterday.'

A solitary tear dropped down her cheek, but Nolan did not notice. He fell asleep suddenly, like a child. Louise rose and stood looking out of the window into the darkness. She saw a seagull flying low past the window, his wide wings like a glider, finely balanced on the air currents that would take him wherever he wished to go. For a moment, she watched, enthralled. Then she ran outside and tried to reach him. He was a great flier and seemed to wheel and soar and spiral, just for her. Then, like magic, he disappeared into the inky darkness of night. Louise smiled a secret smile. Joe had perhaps sent her an omen. *Was* he there? Would he understand? Tears fell as she searched the impenetrable darkness for a response to her question. But the night sky was empty. The darkness intense.

TEN

Santa Fe, 1953

Nolan sifted through a box of old files and looked with interest at his negatives of Camilla Elborne. She had been too cool and controlled for his taste, but the photographs were stunning. The articles talked of her suicide in Kenya and that of her husband, Lord Invergordon. Nolan sighed. Evidently Louise had never been told the truth. Ever protective of her feelings, Nolan thought grimly that she would never learn it from him either. He put all the cuttings on the fire and waited until they burned away. The photographs of Camilla he put aside for Louise.

As he crouched before the fire, stirring the ashes, Nolan thought deeply about the Invergordons and was troubled. Suicide ran in families, he knew. Could Louise have inherited the fatal flaw that led to tragedy? Could she become self-destructive? She was highly sensitive and had a tendency to withdraw into herself. He resolved to protect her with the utmost dedication. After the birth of their daughter, Christy, Louise had suffered from depression. Running over the situation, Nolan became daily more apprehensive that suicide might be his wife's destiny. His surveillance of Louise increased and with it his desire to do everything for her, to cosset her from the outside world to the point where she could never encounter anything that troubled her calm. He had always been impossibly possessive in love. Now, the fear of suicide gave Nolan the excuse he needed to confine his wife in a manner that made him secure and her dependent. For Nolan, love meant keeping the object of his adoration safe, preferably within the confines of home. For Louise, love was freedom, a blue sky, a plane.

Christy was a beautiful child, now two years old, a vivacious character, who danced, laughed and drew pictures to illustrate her thoughts. Only recently had Christy and her mother formed bonds. Before that, Louise's depression had submerged her and she had not been really aware of everyday life. Now, she laughed adoringly at the little girl who mimicked her every move, who drew in an original fashion and who had a talent for choosing facets of her 'sitters' personalities that even they had never noticed. They liked singing together and were given to having competitions to see who could sing loudest. Nolan christened them the Cry Twins, after Johnnie Ray, because their current favourite song was 'Too Young'. Mother and daughter also liked making toffee and looking at fashion magazines together on the sofa, preferably after making the toffee!

Christy looked at the pink cactus flower with its lime-green stamens. It was beautiful, but Daddy had said it would prick her finger and hurt terribly if she tried to pick it. Daddy always did things for her, because he was afraid that she might hurt herself and she was afraid too. But she wanted the cactus flower to give to Mummy. Christy sat on a little carved stool, gazing at the flower. Then she went to the kitchen, took the bread knife carefully in both hands and cut off the flower. Having returned the knife to the kitchen, she picked up the flower by its outer layer of petals and carried it to Louise.

'For you, Mummy.'

'Oh, that's just beautiful. Look at the colour, all

fuchsia and with green stamens. Could you draw it for me?'

Christy nodded, basking in her mother's obvious pleasure. Louise stroked the child's head, relieved to be feeling better. It was as if two years had simply slid by under a black cloud of depression. Now the cloud was lifting and she was able to appreciate the astonishing individual she had borne. She put the flower in a long, thin vase and gazed at it with pleasure. Then she took Christy on her knee and told her a story about camels and cacti, who needed little water to drink, because they were accustomed to life in the desert. When she reached the part of the story where the camel drinks and drinks and drinks at the end of the long journey, the child laughed delightedly and Louise cuddled her and smothered her with kisses.

Nolan found his daughter putting the final touches to a drawing of a cactus flower. Louise was dozing on the sofa at Christy's side. Looking at the drawing, Nolan was astonished by his daughter's already individual style. He kneeled at her side, looked into the big blue-violet eyes and spoke in admiration.

'You're two and a half and you draw so well I've decided to get you a teacher, who'll make you into a great artist. An artist paints pictures for people and they buy them for their houses and put them on the wall.'

Christy gave him a kiss, because she liked the idea. Then she returned to finishing her painting, by placing a bee high above the cactus flower. There was no bee, except in her imagination, but the picture took perspective and humour from its presence and Nolan was pleased. At that moment, Louise woke and saw the picture her child was offering her.

'Oh Christy, that's lovely, the best you've ever done. I want it framed and put on the wall of my bedroom.'

For half an hour they were all occupied framing

Christy's drawing and then hanging it in the bedroom at the side of her mother's bed.

'You know, Christy,' Louise said, standing back to admire the picture, 'when you're grown up, I shall be the proudest Mummy in the whole world, because you're going to be a great artist and we'll all be able to see your paintings in the art museum.'

'Will Amy visit the museum with us?'

'Of course, and Daddy and I and Paquita.'

Later, when Christy was asleep and dreaming of being an artist, Louise read the local paper and called to her husband.

'Look at that, Nolan. Frank Bell's coming to give an exhibition of flying. We must go and see what's new.'

'I'd rather not and I think you'd best give it a miss. It could wake memories.'

Louise looked to her husband in surprise.

'What do you mean?'

'Joe was killed in his plane. I don't want you to get depressed again, that's all. From now on, flying's out. You have a new life and new responsibilities and you must enjoy new things and learn new skills.'

'But Nolan, flying's the thing I love best in the world, always was, always will be. You can't cut it out because Joe died in his plane. I've absorbed the shock of his death thanks to you, but flying's among my very dear hopes for the future. Imagine if you had to live without a camera in your hands. From a non-human point of view that's the thing *you* love best in the world. With me, it's planes.'

'I don't *want* you to fly!'

Louise sighed wearily. Already Nolan refused to let her drive, go out alone, even go hiking with Amy on the mountain. His fear that she could be injured or depressed had made her into a prisoner instead of a wife. For Nolan, love was synonymous with protecting

167

and protecting with imprisoning. He did the same thing with Christy, who was forbidden to ride a tricycle, ski, run in the long grass, go outside the hacienda, touch cacti or any other plants, chase bees, flies and butterflies. The child was already terrified of everything. Where would it end? Louise wondered if they would both end up living in a gilded cocoon, incapable of going anywhere or doing anything, because Nolan had over-protected them to the point of making them helpless. She spoke gently, anxious not to hurt him.

'When you met me, I was in deep shock. Then, the moment we married, I got pregnant and I wasn't well in the first three months. You were wonderful and the actual birth went like a dream. It wasn't your fault that I suffered from depression afterwards. Dr Marcos told me it happens to a lot of women and it's due to chemical changes in the body. But now I'm really well, and I want to catch up on lost time. I want us to go out to dinner. I want to take dancing lessons and get fit again. I want to fly again and live again and maybe even travel to Scotland to see Uncle Ferdy.'

'You'll do lots of things when I'm sure you're well enough to be responsible.'

'I have never been irresponsible, Nolan.'

Louise resolved to speak with Amy. Only Amy knew how to manipulate her father. Only Amy understood that eagles want and need to fly and that broken wings heal.

The next morning Amy was in the kitchen with Paquita, making a giant dish of rice and chicken for Nolan's lunch guests. Louise was arranging flowers and Christy was painting a landscape with red trees, blue earth and some spectacular mustard-yellow birds. Louise spoke wistfully.

'Your birds look just like aeroplanes.'

Christy continued painting. At that moment, Nolan entered the kitchen, his face angry and hurt.

'Must you relate everything to planes and flying? Haven't they caused you enough sadness?'

Amy stared in amazement at her father, while Paquita hurried Christy to her room. Louise looked angrily at her husband, speaking sharply for the first time since they had known each other.

'When you met me, my world had always been driving, flying and aerobatics. I was deeply shocked by my husband's death, but I never lost my love of flying. The only reason I didn't continue to do it was because shock had made me so badly co-ordinated I had difficulty pouring coffee from the pot, let alone taking the controls of a plane. But now I'm well again and you'll have to let me do what I need to do. You don't want me to drive. You stop me going on the mountain. You've already refused all invitations on my behalf to dinners, fetes, balls, charity concerts and one from the authorities of Santa Fe asking me to do a charity flying exhibition. Your idea of love is for me to stay safe and a prisoner in this house, but I'm *not* a woman who can live like that and you've got to understand.'

'You've been happy till now, haven't you, Louise?'

'Of course I have, but in the beginning I was ill with shock. Now I'm better. We have to readjust our marriage and let me get used to being my old self again. Don't treat me as if I were sick or crazy, Nolan. I'm neither of those things and it hurts me very much when you say I can do things when I'm "responsible" again.'

When Louise had gone out to the courtyard to pick ivy for the table, Amy looked reproachfully at her father.

'I wish you'd never found those old newspaper cuttings! Since you read about Louise's parents and their suicide you've treated *her* as if she's unbalanced, but Louise is just fine.'

'She's fragile.'

'She *isn't*, Daddy. You'd like her to be because that appeals to your masculine instincts, but I can assure you that in her heyday Louise was a very brilliant flier and a very tough young lady.'

'Well, she isn't tough now.'

'She is. She's recovered from her husband's death. Lots of women could never have done that. Louise even has the courage to think of flying again. Don't make her feel guilty for getting better.'

On Christy's third birthday, they all went on an expedition to the far side of the mountain, with three little friends of Christy's. Everyone hunted pine cones, wild onions, buried treasure and tadpoles. They headed home about five, with their jars of tadpoles, scuffed knees and triumphant expressions, to devour barbecued steaks, paella and pancakes – served separately or all on the same plate. On the radio, Gene Kelly was singing in the rain and most of the children sang with him.

While Louise and Amy ran around refilling plates and refereeing disputes, Nolan fell exhausted on the sofa. The self-control required to let the kids wander in the wild and the desire to take Christy on his shoulders to keep her safe from harm had been almost overwhelming. But Amy had lectured him that he must stop raising the child to be terrified of everything. Had he been overprotective? Had the damage already been done? He looked over to Louise, perfectly gorgeous in her new sheath dress that showed everything she had, despite being loose, covered and correct. Nolan's eyes caressed every curve of her body and he loved her as he had never loved before. He wanted above all else to please her, but Louise's growing independence upset him. He was pleased when she came over.

'It's been a lovely day, Nolan. Don't let's have any more rows. I've been very down and depressed, but now I'm feeling fine and full of energy. Let's go to the cinema this evening. Let's do *everything* we like to do, Nolan.'

'Don't tell me you want to see Gene Kelly *again*?'

'I just love it when he sings in the rain.'

'There's an Elizabeth Taylor movie at the Plaza.'

'Maybe we should see both. You want some more cake, Nolan?'

'That cake could give me middle-age spread before dinner! Oh, by the way, I saw the Mayor this afternoon.'

'What did he want?'

'He asked if you'd reconsider doing an exhibition of flying for the Santa Fe carnival. They're trying hard to raise funds for a new children's sports stadium and you'd be a real draw.'

Louise fell silent, apprehensive that Nolan might get angry again. 'I said you'd be delighted, so you'd best start practising.'

She threw herself into his arms with a scream of delight.

'Did you really say yes? I can't believe it! I'll do the very best exhibition you ever saw.'

'It's two days in September, a Friday and Saturday.'

'Have you told Amy?'

'Sure have. She screeched louder than you did!'

Nolan watched as Louise ran to see Amy, her face radiant with happiness. It was as if someone had turned on a spotlight, that illuminated her whole being. Nolan sighed, wondering if he had done the right thing. Would Louise imagine herself back in the past with Joe if she started to fly again? He shook his head, uncertain how a return to the air would affect her. The only thing of which he was sure was that if he denied her the right to fly, she would for ever hold it against him. Worse, she could retreat into a private world of dreams in the

171

past, where she flew an imaginary plane over milk-white clouds, with a phantom as a co-pilot.

Amy was excited and Christy in a veritable fever of pride and anticipation. She and Nolan accompanied Louise to the airfield four times a week so she could practise her aerobatics. Afterwards, they formed the habit of adjourning to the ice-cream parlour for knicker-bocker glories, before returning to the hacienda.

In the past few days, the child had seen posters of her mother and understood that there would be a carnival and that Louise would be the star of the presentation. Christy already knew that she would be going on the first day to see her mother perform, but not the second, because Nolan feared too much adula-tion would go to her head. Amy would go with Nolan for the second performance and they had already planned a dinner-party in Louise's honour for after the show. Amy and Paquita had worked out the menus, sent out the invitations but kept it a secret from Louise.

When the day dawned, Louise felt butterflies in her stomach and a distinct quiver in the knees. In the past, she had flown with Joe. This would be the first time she had ever done aerobatics alone. The field was full, the roundabouts and fairground games in the adjacent meadow in full swing. A barrel organ played, a barker called and the town band rendered the title tune from *High Noon*. Louise smiled wryly, thinking she felt a bit like Gary Cooper before he went out for his final duel.

When her turn came, Louise took her plane up and went into the much practised routine, giving all her concentration to the task in hand. It was a long time since Louise had given a demonstration and she felt increasingly nervous, so for the moment she put the past – Joe, her memories – and Christy behind her, and concentrated on the precision required for the turns, spirals, spins and swoops that were a legendary part of

172

her display. She flew as well as she had ever done with Joe. The crowd roared appreciation. Once again, Louise was queen of the air. Christy saw the butterfly on the body of the plane and her mother stepping out to thunderous applause from an excited audience, who knew that she had flown alone for the first time. Someone released a hundred scarlet balloons, that floated up into an azure sky. Then the town band struck up 'The Star Spangled Banner' and Louise was carried shoulder-high until she was face to face with her husband and child. Christy ran to her, arms outstretched and Nolan rose and put his arms around both of them. They were photographed like that for the local paper, a touching front page story that headlined Christy's words: 'You were beautiful Mummy, the beautifullest in the world.'

The next morning at breakfast, Amy listened as Christy discussed the flight with the cat. Nolan sighed, hoping fervently that his child was not another budding flier. Louise stared up at the sky. There had been a favourable weather forecast and every ticket had been sold. She smiled gaily across the table at her husband.

'You know what I think? I think we should go to the beach next week and stay awhile. Christy's never seen the sea, never caught a crab and never eaten one of your special California-style clam bakes.'

'You persuaded me. We'll go Monday. You'll come won't you, Amy?'

'Wild horses wouldn't keep me away from the beach.'

Christy looked up at her father, her face uncertain.

'Crabs bite. You told me never to touch one and I don't know if I'll like the sea, because there are sharks.'

'Crabs pinch, they don't bite.'

'I'm *not* going fishing for them!'

'What are you going to do?'

'I'll paint a picture of a crab when Mummy catches

one for me. She can do anything and she never gets bitten.'

'Why don't you paint a picture of Mummy?'

'I did and you didn't like it.'

'You painted her with blue hair and green teeth.'

Christy laughed delightedly.

'I'll paint the crab black and you'll be scared.'

The next day, on a bright, sunny afternoon, Amy took her place excitedly next to her father. Nolan was tense, every second of Louise's performance torture for him, because he was terrified for her safety and even more terrified that flying would send her mind back to the days when she and Joe had been famous exponents of the aerobatic art. Applause echoed. Cheers erupted. Nolan closed his eyes as the resounding drum roll announced the suicide dive. At his side, Amy watched, fascinated, remembering the other times when the dive had taken her breath away. The crowd gasped, as it always did.

Then there were screams of horror, as the plane continued to plummet like a shot bird. Within seconds it had hit the ground and exploded with a deafening noise. Bits of metal flew towards the crowd. Flames sprang up. Firemen ran with hoses, and the people backed off from the searing heat. Children wept. The sky became black with dense smoke.

Amy rose, then sat down again, stunned by the suddenness of the tragedy. Nolan was chalk white and incapable of speech or movement. Leaving him, Amy ran to the plane, but there was nothing to be done, as firemen doused what remained of the Butterfly, a tiny heap of twisted metal, unrecognizable for what it had been. Looking in horror at the pathetic, mangled wreckage, Amy struggled to take in the reality of sudden death. Then instinct took over and she hurried back to her father, helped him from the field and drove him

174

home. Handing him over to Paquita, she explained what had happened.

'Louise's plane crashed. Call Dr Marcos and ask him to come at once to help Daddy. Then ring the guests and tell them what happened. I'll have to go back to the airfield.'

'Will you have to identify her?'

Tears sprang to Amy's eyes and she turned and ran to the car, willing herself to stay in control as she made her way to the Sheriff's office. She was moved when he waived all formalities.

'No need for formal identification, Amy. Anyway, it wouldn't be possible. We all saw Louise get into the plane, do her act and crash. I'll hurry things along, so you can get her buried with the minimum of fuss.'

'Thank you for everything, Chief Green. I don't know how to help my father and I've no idea how to tell Christy.'

'How old is she?'

'She's three and a bit and very intelligent. She worshipped her mother.'

'You want me to send Father Ordonez over?'

Amy reflected before replying.

'No, later perhaps. Christy has to be told by someone who knows her and I'll do it.'

Christy was drawing a great bird with scarlet wings. She had cut silver paper for his beak and was debating whether to stick a few poppy heads around his body to make things interesting. When Amy arrived, she ran and kissed her.

'Where's Mummy? Daddy's got tummy ache. He went to bed.'

'Have you eaten?'

'Yes, Paquita and I made stuffed sweet peppers and I ate two big ones.'

'How many did Paquita eat?'

'Half of one. I think she has tummy ache too.'

'Shall I put you to bed and tell you a story?'

'Yes. White Cat *loves* stories!'

'I'll tell you a story about a city in the sky where we all go when our life here in Santa Fe's over.'

'When we're dead like White Cat's daddy?'

'Yes. We all die, you know, and when we die the people here in Santa Fe can't see us any more, but we can see them, because we live in the sky.'

'In a house?'

'A beautiful house. We build one as soon as we arrive. First person in the family to get there has to build the house for the others when they die and arrive in the city in the sky.'

'Does it have a name?'

'It's called heaven or paradise.'

'Do you go when you're very old?'

'Oh no, people go all the time, even little children and babies. Mummy went to paradise today, Christy. Something happened and she had to leave us very suddenly, but we'll see her again when we die and go up there. She's getting us a wonderful house with a fountain and cats.'

Christy's mouth quivered and her eyes opened very wide. The silence seemed interminable and Amy bit her lip when she saw tears falling down the tiny cheeks. She took Christy in her arms, touched when the child spoke.

'Shall we go now, Amy?'

'No, we'll go a bit later, when the house is finished.'

'I never said goodbye to Mummy.'

'We'll say goodbye in a very special way, you and I. And from now on I'll be your chosen Mummy. I'm not your real Mummy, but I'll be here until you're grown up, so you can pretend I'm your Mummy.'

'I love you, Amy.'

'I love you too.'

'White Cat's crying.'

'You want to sleep in my bed?'

'Yes!'

'Come on then. I'll tell you another story about White Cat's daddy, who was the fattest cat in the whole of New Mexico and the fiercest too.'

Christmas came and went, but Nolan remained unaware of the passing months. For him, life had stopped the previous year in a field covered in bunting. Again and again he re-ran the moment, refusing to believe that it was an accident, blaming himself for the fact that Louise's suicide dive had become a real suicide, that the phantom flier who had so dominated her life had also provoked her end. Nothing seemed to assuage his anguish, even the determined efforts of the child who loved and needed him, who showed him her paintings and tried to attract his attention in a hundred different ways.

While Nolan sank into the black depths of depression, Amy did everything in her power to help Christy. On her fourth birthday, she found the child looking wistfully into the sky.

'What are you doing, Christy?'

'I was wishing Mummy could come to my party. I know she's in paradise, but I wish she'd come back, just for the day.'

'Would you like to tell Mummy about your birthday?'

'How?'

'We'll go to the cemetery, put some lovely flowers on her grave and then you can talk to her. That way you won't feel so lonely.'

Christy thought about it, then spoke with infinite sadness.

'Everything was lovely and then Mummy went away. I won't *ever* believe in lovely times again!'

'Of course you will.'

'No I won't. Every time I get that lovely feeling, I'll think something horrible's going to happen.'

Christy sighed, her child's mind anguished by the brutal disappearance of the mother she had idolized. Still, she followed obediently when Amy led her to the cemetery and put a bunch of white jasmine on the grave, next to the red roses Nolan had brought on his Sunday visit. Then, together, Amy and Christy went into the cloisters of the Spanish mission and stood looking at the graveyard, with its white stone tombs and wild flowers blowing in the breeze. Christy looked up at Amy.

'Do you really think Mummy can hear?'

'I'm sure she can. Say what you'd say if she were here with us.'

The child went to the arched entrance to the cloisters and looked out at the sky.

'Mummy, this is Christy. I want to remind you that I'm four today and I'm having lots of friends for a party this afternoon. Have you got the house ready for when we come to paradise? I miss you every single day, but now I can come and talk to you I'm going to try and cheer up. I'll tell you all about the party next week when Amy and I come to change your flowers.'

Christy took Amy's hand and together they went back to the car, a young woman shouldering great responsibility and a child struggling to find light at the end of the dark valley of despair. Both had been marked by the tragedy. Both relied on each other for support in a house deprived of its soul, with a father lost in the mists of memory.

For Nolan, nothing would ever be the same now the

beautiful blonde in the lilac patterned dress had disappeared from his world. He grieved Louise in silence. His hair turned white, his face pale and lined. He rarely left the hacienda and lost all interest in his work.

Amy and Christy watched helplessly, growing ever closer as another autumn turned to winter and winter to spring. Both hoped that things would be happy again someday, though the silence of sadness remained interminably in the house. No one felt confident that happiness was on their agenda for the near future. They tried to be hopeful, but depression reigned, like a black cloud obliterating the sun.

In the months that followed Louise's death, Nolan's already fiercely protective nature began seriously to affect his child's life. Christy was all that remained of the woman he had adored and he was resolved never to let her come to harm. Often he woke in the night and went to her room to make sure she was breathing normally. Though she adored the idea of school, Nolan decided to take on a governess and art teacher, so she could be tutored at home until she reached an age when she was less 'vulnerable'.

Amy fought her father's ideas with force, but Nolan was implacable. He accompanied Christy on walks, drove her to town himself for her ballet class and unconsciously did everything to instill in her a Pavlovian reaction, that necessitated his presence or Amy's whenever she wanted to go anywhere or do anything. Christy's desire to have her own way remained strong, her individuality already apparent, but the imprint on her young and impressionable mind of Nolan's fears was insidious. A beautiful child with talent and vivacity, she began to develop limits.

Soon, it was no longer necessary for Nolan to forbid his daughter to do things. Christy accepted automatically that if she got lost she would die, so she never left the hacienda for fear of ending up in the wilds. She disliked eating in other people's houses, in case she was food poisoned, one of Nolan's obsessions. She picked flowers in the garden but not outside and was pathologically afraid of snakes, lizards and all other reptiles. She was happiest staying in her room painting, but showed little desire to go to Santa Fe to see other people's art. The town was full of cars that might run her over, strangers to whom she had been taught not to speak and children she did not know, but whom Daddy had told her could give her mumps, measles or polio.

Amy struggled to keep the balance of normality and to an extent succeeded, but fear patterns had been deeply established, like invisible barriers in Christy's mind. Unaware of the damage his love had wreaked, Nolan lived for his child. Life continued, but for him the symphony of existence was played diminuendo. And all the while Amy watched, worried and waited for the moment when he would become more reasonable. The moment never came and finally she knew she would have to oppose him or put Christy's whole life in jeopardy.

ELEVEN

1967

Christy's strange, home-bound existence came to an end on her sixteenth birthday, when Amy, seeing the red light of real danger, tackled Nolan and finally won. The row that ensued was never again mentioned in the household, but was never forgotten either. It resulted in Amy's leaving the hacienda for good and taking up residence and partnership in a Santa Fe bookshop with a former college friend, who had been her lover for years. It brought Nolan hurtling back to his senses, too late to undo the damage his fierce love and his fears had done to Christy. And it changed Christy's life, because for the first time she learned that her grandmother and mother had committed suicide. The new-found freedom that came to her after the row was heady but showed up her limitations in stark relief against the panorama of daily life. From that day on, she lived in fear of being alone and being responsible for herself and above all of falling victim to the dark legacy of family suicide. It was generally accepted, she knew, that suicide ran in families. Christy found it very easy to add yet another phobia to her already brimming repertoire of inner conflict.

At first, in order to avoid stress and challenge, she clung even closer to Nolan, making little effort to become independent. When she did try, she went to the other extreme and did something foolish or dangerous, like driving fast and without a licence, climbing Santos Peak alone, and packing her bags to go and live with a girlfriend in an apartment in Santa Fe, an exercise that ended two days later when she returned, exhausted, hungry and penitent, to her father.

And every night, before she went to bed, Christy recalled the day of her sixteenth birthday, a summer's day full of the scent of roses, when Nolan had spoken to her of his plans for her future and Amy had attacked like the Charge of the Light Brigade. Christy shivered, remembering every word from the moment Nolan had spoken.

'Now you're sixteen, we should think about your future. I don't want you to go to art college. I'd like you to continue your studies here in the hacienda. Then, perhaps when you're older, you can take a degree at the Beaux-Arts in Paris. We could go there for a year and take an apartment so you can benefit from the different culture.'

Amy glowered at her father, knowing only too well that Christy would never go anywhere if he had his way.

'Will you take Christy to college each morning, Daddy?'

'What are you talking about?'

'You say when she's older she can do a year in Paris. How old does she have to be?'

'Twenty, twenty-five.'

'She needs to go to art college *now*. She needs full and immediate exposure to the finest professionals in the country. She has great talent, but you continue to keep her here because you're too scared to let her live a normal life.'

'Do we have to discuss this in front of Christy?'

'She's sixteen in years and ten in the head and that's how you want her to stay. What happens if you die? Have you ever thought of that? You're not immortal, you know, and you're not getting any younger.'

'Amy, can we discuss this another time?'

'Suppose I died too and Christy was left alone. How in God's name would she cope? She's rarely been out of the hacienda since she was four and never alone. She's terrified of everything, because you've instilled fear into her. It's one thing to be cautious, prudent and to take care and another to be too scared to *live*. I hold you responsible for ruining this child's life, Daddy, and if you try to spoil her future chances as an artist I'll do something about it. I won't sit by *one minute longer* and watch you controlling Christy's existence.'

'Is loving someone really so bad?'

'If loving equals the subjugation of the person, yes. If love leaves the object of the love free, then it's just fine. It's not the first time you've done this, Daddy. You tried to protect Louise to the point of making her your prisoner and *she* protested. We both know what happened afterwards.'

'I forbid you to discuss Louise!'

Amy continued her psychological charge at her father's defences, reducing Nolan to anguished silence.

'Louise died in her plane. Either it was an accident or it was not. If it was not, then there are two possible explanations, one that she had the same character flaw that provoked Camilla's suicide in Kenya. Or maybe Louise just lost her concentration, because she was fed up with being protected!'

Nolan roared his anger and his anguish, but nothing stopped Amy.

'How *dare* you say that! Christy, go to your room.'

Amy rose, towering over her father, her face white from over-controlled anger.

'You stay right there, Christy, and you listen, Daddy. I intend to apply for custody of Christy if you refuse to send her to art school and let her lead a normal life. She must have driving lessons, tennis lessons, dancing lessons and anything else that'll let her mix with people

183

of her own age and live like a normal teenager. She must be exposed to the latest techniques in the art world. She must travel and *not* with you. Open your mind, Daddy. You've had over ten years with Christy under your nose every hour of every day. I've tried to talk to you about her time and again and you've refused. Christy's your child, but you have no right at all to stunt her growth. She isn't a child any more and every day I'm scared to my roots that someone's going to tell Christy what we should have told her years ago. Someday she'll be famous, if you'll only let her learn her art, as all great talents have to learn. Do you *really* think that journalists won't look into her past? Do you really imagine that with you for a famous father Christy's origins won't be easily checked and rechecked and that awful Kenya scandal rehashed and analysed all over again? If she doesn't learn from us, she'll learn from someone who doesn't care for her. That would be destructive and you know it.'

'I won't discuss this any more.'

'If you don't agree to let Christy go to college, I intend to apply for custody of her and that's all there is to it. I've tried so often to make you see reason. This time, you take note or I'll do what I should have done years ago and take Christy out of your house until you see sense.'

'I'll oppose you, Amy.'

'If you do, I'll ask for a psychiatric assessment on you *and* Christy and expose your method of raising her. You'll lose, Daddy, if we go to court. Now you just think hard. You're in the wrong and you have to let go. Tell me your decision in the morning and we'll take it from there.'

Nolan went to his room, his mind convulsed from shock, his shoulders hunched in stress and tension. Christy sat pale-faced in front of the fire, watching Amy toasting marshmallows, as if nothing untoward had happened. Astonished by her half-sister's courage, overcome by the revelations and, above all, afraid that Amy might well be right, Christy spoke softly.

'Tell me about my grandmother's suicide. Why did no one ever say anything before?'

'They were scared of telling you because suicide makes everyone a coward.'

'Except you.'

'I'm a realist and I can't change, Christy. If we can't face reality in life, we live in a paradise of idiots and I don't ever want you to do that. Camilla was beautiful and good-natured and she married a Scottish lord, who was a drunkard. He loved her, in his way, but he was a pretty crazy person and got into trouble, so his family sent him to farm their holdings in Kenya. When he got there, he ditched Camilla and started to run with a wild crowd. She fell in love with an Englishman called John Saunders. He was a landowner, who'd never been married and Camilla took refuge in his ranch. She was cared for by Saunders and his sister, Cecy, until her husband came one night and shot the Englishman. Then Invergordon, Camilla's husband, killed himself. Camilla sent your mother back to England with Cecy and then committed suicide. She had nothing more to live for, or so she thought. Suicide was *very* much in vogue in the thirties, you know.'

'Didn't she want to live because of Louise?'

'She adored her child, but Louise had been so terrified of her father all her life that she never really got close to Camilla. I suppose in her childish mind she linked mother and father and wanted to keep her distance. She was only really happy with her Aunt Flora in Sussex and Camilla knew it. It must have been very hard for her to be rejected by her own child.'

'Poor Camilla. I'm *never* going to fall in love and have children.'

'Sure you will. Love's marvellous and children arrive and enchant us all. Camilla had the awful luck to marry a man who wasn't normal, that's all.'

'And Mummy, what happened to upset her so?'

'Louise lost *her* great love in a plane crash. Joe Tanner taught her to fly just after the war and after their marriage they dreamed of promoting aviation all over the States. When Daddy and I first met her, Louise was in deep shock because of Joe's death. She really needed us and Daddy fell deeply in love.'

'Poor Daddy. He still loves her, you know.'

'He's a truly generous and marvellous person, Christy. Don't think because of this row that I don't love him dearly. The problem is that when *he* loves someone, he's so scared they'll get hurt or have an accident or disappear from his life that he makes them his prisoner. Sure they live well and they have fun travelling with him. He buys wonderful presents and clothes and spoils everyone to death. They get so dependent on him, they're just not real people any more. That's Daddy's idea of love and he has to try to change and you have to help him and show him the way. He loves you very much, so he will try to change, I know he will. And you have to show him you're capable of being independent and that you need to be so.'

'I don't believe Mother killed herself.'

'Perhaps it was an accident.'

'You're just saying that so I won't worry!'

'No, Christy. I only know what Nolan told me and he never really wanted to discuss the event in detail. He hasn't recovered from losing Louise, that's all I know. Before, I tried to respect a certain silence on the subject. From now on, I'll continue to do so.'

'Love's horrible.'

'No, it isn't, it's the maximum. But when we fall in love, we're frightened and panicky about losing the other person. It's natural really. We just have to learn to control our fear, because no one can live their life scared all the time. We have to dare because daring's important. That's why I had the row with Nolan. *You* have to learn to dare and to do things you want to do. You can't live your life on cloud nine for ever.'

'I love being here in the hacienda.'

'And if Daddy died?'

'I'd live with you.'

'And if I died?'

'I'd be scared. Don't talk about that!'

'You see, Christy? We have to help you get so confident you can do anything you want to, whether we're here or not.'

'Shall I really learn to drive?'

'Sure you will. You'll pass your test first time, just like Louise.'

'Where will I go when I can drive?'

'In the country, to the riding school, wherever you want.'

Christy listened in disbelief, her face radiant.

'Can I learn to *ride*? Oh Amy, I always wanted to ride a horse. But what if I fall? Daddy says if you fall you can die.'

'If you fall you get bruises or break bones, but you get better. If you die, you die. That's all. You can't live your entire life worrying about whether you're going to die. Everyone dies sooner or later.'

'I'm scared of dying!'

'You're scared of everything. That's what we have to cure. You need to find the confidence to show that Christy Pallister is an extraordinary person, who can do anything she really wants to do. It won't be easy, because as we get older it's difficult to be certain. For the moment, you're not even on the first rung of the ladder. You're sixteen, with the face of a ten-year-old. From now on, you have to fill your life and your face with real experience. There's never been a great artist who painted on empty batteries.'

Christy was allowed to study and then enter the Art Department of the local university. She learned to drive, dance, play tennis, and travelled with Amy and alone to art exhibitions all over the States.

In a month she would be nineteen. Christy looked around her room, deciding that she needed a change. Teddy bears and Amish patchworks were part of her past. She was suddenly assailed by the need for something more adult. Perhaps a movie-set bedroom would inspire her to take an interest in men? She shrugged. Men were dangerous. Either they got drunk and crashed their cars or they wanted to do things on the back seat. She shrugged, deciding to ask her father if she could change her room anyway. She would put in a whole new sound system, so she could sing with Mick Jagger: 'I Can't Get No Satisfaction' . . . Christy looked in the mirror, shook her head and thought that *that* was certain!

Her mind turned to thoughts of Amy, who was in the process of buying into a bookshop in San Francisco. If the deal was finalized, Amy would move away and come home only once a month. Christy shivered. The idea of being without the support of her half-sister troubled her intensely. Nolan was kind but he was ageing fast. Suppose he got ill or died and Amy was far away?

To take her mind off such thoughts, Christy sketched a pigeon perched on her windowsill, framed by the lace curtains and lit by the setting sun. Here in the hacienda life was perfect. She could listen to the Beatles, watch TV, copy Twiggy's hairdo and try to walk like Burt Lancaster. She *loved* Burt Lancaster. Looking at her reflection in the mirror, she wondered if she could wear the filmy, ethnic, hippy clothes popular with her fellow students, who smoked pot continuously and made love under the trees that surrounded the main lawn of the college. Christy had seen them from her window and had been outraged. Then, always capable of being honest with herself, she decided that she was jealous of their 'make love not war' attitudes, because she had no boyfriend and would never dare make love even if she had. She decided she had best try to remedy that situation. Perhaps making love made you grow up fast and get independent.

Christy had few friends at college, her talent and singular nature making her more acceptable to her professors than to fellow students. She did not date and worked at her art even in the evenings, except once in a while when she went to the cinema with her classmates, sobbed at weepies, screamed at horror films and demanded a hamburger in the interval to keep her from falling asleep. Everyone knew that Christy went to bed at nine-thirty and her ability to laugh at her own limitations began to win her an admirer.

Art Brodie was the most handsome boy in the class and the vainest. He was six feet tall, drove a Mustang, disdained the hippy community and said his hero was Karl Marx. His father was President of the Dallas Investment Company and Art the only member of the family who was not a financial genius. He made up for his lack of ability in that direction by a dedication to spending money which became legendary and not at all in line with his Marxist leanings.

He took Christy to drive-ins to see *Alice's Restaurant*, *Easy Rider* or re-issues of early Bardot films, because Art was obsessed by the French actress. They had also visited the family mansion near Albuquerque and finally spent a weekend at the Brodie 'shack' on the beach at Malibu. The family shack had fifteen rooms and a spiral staircase that led from a deck jutting out into the sea up to the master bedroom. It was there that Christy finally made love. Tipsy from drinking champagne, innocent enough to go ahead despite the warning signals that Art's narcissism gave out each time he passed a mirror and paused to admire himself, she was also unaware that men who have drunk too much are not always capable of doing what they want to do.

The encounter started well enough, with kisses and Art's fevered explorations of her naked body. When he suggested that Christy kiss and taste all *his* naked parts, she burst into peals of laughter.

'Don't be silly, why would I do that? I don't believe folk do that with their mouths. I honestly don't believe it.'

'They do it before the man enters the woman. Don't you know *anything*!'

'I never did it before.'

Art pushed her back and penetrated her, disappointed that she did not scream, bleed or show resistance. Evidently Christy was not a virgin. Either that or she had done too much horse-riding in her youth. He had an orgasm almost at once, straightened his hair in the wall mirror and then looked into Christy's pale, tense face.

'You're a great friend but a lousy lover, honey. You're just not made for passion.'

'I'm scared of getting pregnant!'

'You're always scared of something.'

'I'm sorry, Art.'

'I can't stand women who apologize. Look, why don't we eat dinner at the Basking Shark. Then we'll get back

190

to Santa Fe. There are motels on the way and I love driving at night.'

Under a navy blue sky full of stars, they drove in silence. Art was dying to be home. Christy was trying to work out how anyone could get worked up about making love. She would never do it again, that was certain. She had no talent in bed. She had talent as an artist and that would be her means of existing. She must work hard, be a success and make Nolan and Amy proud of her. If she couldn't ever be sexy, she'd be a painter of acclaim. Subdued, disappointed in herself and the experience, Christy felt diminished. She had thought making love would make her feel grown up, sophisticated, independent, everything she dreamed of being. Instead, she felt like a child, who has strayed into a grown-up world and got lost. Closing her eyes, she thought that soon she would be back at the hacienda. In the light of dawn, she and Nolan would eat breakfast, like always. She wondered fearfully if Art would talk about her in college and felt a sudden desire to take flight and not return at all. But college was necessary in her quest for a stable career. When Art pulled into a motel, Christy was disappointed. Then she rallied, if it would not be tomorrow morning, she would certainly be back at the hacienda soon after. She was on her way home, that was all she needed to remember.

Before the Easter holiday Christy was given a shock by her fellow students, who elected her 'most hard-working student of the year'. Art, who had barely glanced her way since their ill-fated and solitary sexual encounter, was elected 'most handsome student' and Annie Dean, a blonde bombshell with a forty-two-inch bust 'the girl most likely to take off'. Christy asked if take off would be metaphorical or literal, given Annie's pneumatic frontage. This unaccustomed, if laconic wit earned her an invitation to lunch with Annie and her

191

group – her fiancé, Rod, and the twins Mary and Alex Western – who told her the latest college news.

'We're going to be asked to exhibit at the end of the summer term. Had you heard?'

'Where will we exhibit?'

'Here in college, of course.'

'Will everyone take part?'

'No – only us and the graduation year students. The new director has got together a group of dealers who'll come and see our work and us. He believes we can't start too young getting commercial advice and reaction.'

Christy was pensive for a long time after that. Then, remembering that she was with her fellow students, she ran and got everyone coffee and bought a box of bitter chocolate candies to eat with it. Annie smiled across the table.

'You're an awful swot, Christy, but you're not bad. You'll probably be in the Museum of Modern Art before you're thirty if panic doesn't get you by the balls.'

'That could well happen. I'm a champion panicker.'

'What happened between you and Art?'

'We split up. I've no talent for charming and seducing men. I was brought up in an isolated house and I think I'm missing a few of the essential bits and pieces.'

Annie was delighted by her honesty.

'You just think you are. You're a sleeping beauty, Christy, a late starter who'll come to life one day with an explosion like Vesuvius.'

'I hope you're right.'

'You can laugh at yourself and that's just great. It's when you stop laughing at life that the shit hits the fan.'

'I have a class. I must dash. Thanks for inviting me.'

'Come again tomorrow.'

'I will, too.'

From that moment on Christy often lunched with Annie, Rod and the Western twins. All of them worked hard to prepare canvasses for the end of term exhibition and Christy worked particularly well, because, for the first time in her life, she understood the warming glow of real friendship. Annie was adored by every man on the campus and Christy regarded her beauty and confidence with awe. Christy was a real artist of great talent and Annie knew it and returned the compliment. It was therefore understandable that it was to Annie that Christy ran when she heard the news that of two hundred paintings exhibited, the work of two artists had been selected and a major exhibition offered after graduation the following year. The two students were herself and Roderick James Holt, Annie's fiancé. Annie was not in her room and Christy ran from one part of the college to another, searching for her, Rod or the Westerns. She was returning to her room, puzzled by their absence on this so-important afternoon, when she encountered a senior lecturer, Alice Bay-Wallis.

'Have you seen Annie and the group, Mrs Bay-Wallis?'

'Why don't we have coffee in my room?'

Christy followed, surprised to be invited by a woman she barely knew. There was a tamarind tree outside the window of Mrs Bay-Wallis's private room and a still life of lemons, limes and fossils on the table that Christy wanted immediately to sketch. The teacher sat down beside Christy.

'I'm very sorry to have to tell you that Annie, Rod and the Western twins were involved in a car accident early this morning. Rod was driving and it wasn't his fault at all. Some youngsters who'd been drinking all night came towards him on an empty stretch of road and smashed into his car head-on. He and Annie were killed instantly. The twins are in intensive care. Two of the other boys were also killed.'

Christy felt drained. When she had had the happiest

moment of her life, watching Louise fly her plane, euphoria had been followed by tragedy. Now, on this wonderful day, when she had been chosen to have a major exhibition of her work, when she was happy and free and almost *real*, tragedy had reared its head again, robbing her of her friends.

Like a robot, Christy rose, thanked the tutor for the coffee and went to her room. Tears fell like rain down her cheeks and shock and anguish made her nauseous. Terrified to think, she began to work compulsively and continued throughout the night, her mind racing as she struggled to obliterate the thoughts of sudden death. She decided to do her exhibition as a tribute to Louise, Amy and Annie, three extraordinary women. She would call it 'Women of the World from Eve to Marilyn' and would paint as she had never painted before. Hollow-eyed, close to panic, but inspired by her desire to pay tribute to those she loved, Christy worked when she should have been sleeping.

Then, at sunrise, she made coffee and sat at the window, telling herself fiercely that she no longer needed friends, love, affection, company. When those you loved died, your life became insupportable, because of the pain of loss. It had been that hideous pain that had made the women in her family kill themselves. Christy hurried back to work, afraid to dwell on her thoughts. Work was the only panacea. If she could paint well, nothing else mattered. If she could create a great exhibition, nothing in the world would ever hurt her again.

Part Three

CHRISTY

The artist, like the idiot or clown, sits on the edge of the world, and a push may send him over it.   SIR OSBERT SITWELL

TWELVE

Santa Fe, 1973

Christy looked at her reflection in the mirror, pulled a face and shrugged. She had thought of wearing her new diaphanous dress, and flowers in her hair. She had decided that it was too sixties and that her late arrival in the atmosphere of the previous decade was typical of her hesitations in everything. She had chosen, therefore, a new floor-length coat by Saint Laurent, in ebony velvet frogged in plaited silk, bought for her by her father in Paris. The Louise Brooks haircut suited her well, its geometric, satiny black curves framing a face that was pale, beautiful and startling because of the vivid violet blue of her eyes. This was it, her big day, the biggest day in her whole life. Christy bit her lip, took an aspirin in case the excitement gave her a migraine, overbalanced on her platform-soled shoes and then wobbled downstairs to the hall. Realizing that she had forgotten to put on her perfume, she ran back to her room, sprayed herself with wild orchid essence and sat on the bed for a few minutes to try to calm down.

For the past fifteen months, Christy had painted with joy and inspiration her chosen theme, 'Women of the World from Eve to Marilyn'. Each canvas had been executed in the authentic materials of the period: tempera for the medieval lady chess player; oil on oak for the Countess from Palermo; gouache for scenes of Indian deities; oil on canvas and collage for a portrait of Marilyn Monroe, eyes rolling, raspberry lips pouting. Today, the critics would view her work, judge it and life would be influenced irrevocably by their reactions. Only now did Christy fully realize the enormity of what she had done, that at twenty-three, immediately after graduation from college, she was going to show her works to the finest American and international experts, in the de Vanden Gallery, known for quality, originality and a proven ability on the part of the owners to discover potentially great names.

Christy fidgeted with her stockings, put her nail through one of them, changed into another pair and then, platform shoes in hand, raced downstairs and out to the courtyard, to where Nolan was waiting to drive her from the hacienda into Santa Fe and her moment of destiny. Though he was hiding his feelings well, Nolan was even more terrified than his daughter. If Christy failed, she would have a nervous breakdown, that was certain. But the paintings were superb. He wondered desperately if the critics would be as expert in making their judgement as Christy had been at creating her miracles on canvas.

Throughout the journey, Christy remained silent, frozen by nerves, her heart pounding like a sledgehammer, her throat dry. All her life she had dreamed of being a painter and having her work exhibited, as Louise had prophesied, in a commercial gallery. Christy thought wistfully of her mother and wished that Louise could be there to share this proud occasion.

She remembered the moment at art college, when Annie had told her about the possibility of being awarded an exhibition. Annie had tried to encourage her as a woman, whilst others pushed her to realize her talent as an artist. Then, with tragic suddenness, she had disappeared. Christy had painted with dedication and love for the special people in her life. Had she done enough? Would she be accepted? Had Louise been right in her judgement all those years previously? Christy's heart began to pound again as she thought of going to the gallery and facing the public for the first time.

Twice, on the outskirts of town, Christy made her father slow down, so she could gaze at the poster of her exhibition, a startling face in red and black with the theme words in silver: 'Women of the World from Eve to Marilyn. The Works of Christy Pallister'. The posters thrilled her to the core, but made her terrified at the same time. The possibility of failure hung heavy over her head, like the sword of Damocles. Was she worthy of such attention? By the time they arrived at the gallery, Christy's whole body was shaking like a leaf in the wind.

Nolan put his arms around her.

'Calm down or they'll think you're sick.'

'I didn't expect to be paralysed by terror.'

'You'll be a great success. The de Vandens are experts and they know they have a great find. They'll have done you proud.'

'Were you nervous when you had your first exhibition of your photographs?'

'There are two kinds of stage fright, Christy. You weren't nervous while you were painting. You're nervous now, but once you pass through that door you'll wow everyone, I know you will. I wasn't nervous at all till after my exhibition began. Then I was sick in a bucket in the gallery owner's cellar. It wasn't the best start in the world, that's for sure!'

Laughing at Nolan's youthful nerves, they entered the gallery through an ancient door of carved cedar wood imported from Kashmir. Flashbulbs popped, champagne appeared in their hands and a euphoric Mitzi de Vanden hurried to welcome them. A spectacular redhead, she was dressed in a Galanos ensemble of lemon chiffon.

'Hello there, Christy, Nolan. You like the dress? Deke

199

says I look like a canary. Now let's hurry and meet everyone. We've already sold eight of the paintings and when Myron Reiss arrives he'll probably buy the rest.'

Christy's eyes widened and she looked to her father for guidance.

'Who's Myron Reiss, Daddy?'

'He's a lawyer from Dallas, isn't he, Mitzi?'

'Sure is. He buys art as investment for some of the richest businessmen in the States. He's a millionaire and his clients own half the world. Come and have a photo beside the Marilyn canvas. That was the first one we sold.'

'Who bought it?'

'A young psychiatrist called Ellie Martinez. She outbid the University of Princeton. I swear it's the first time we ever had two clients start an auction right here in the gallery!'

Christy began to relax, smiling obediently for photographers and chatting with guests. She did two radio interviews in Mitzi's office and had a preliminary discussion with the reporter from *Time Magazine*.

'Tell us about your daily routine, Christy.'

'After breakfast, I paint till three, then have a salad with my father before starting work again. At weekends I either go out sketching or I do reading research for future work. I stop at seven in the evenings and we eat dinner around eight. Then we play snooker or have friends around.'

'Who wins when you play snooker with your father?'

'I do, but only because Nolan lets me.'

'Your mother, Louise, was a famous aviatrix. Do you fly?'

'Never as a pilot. Mother was killed in her plane and I've never been able to feel at ease in the air.'

'Do you remember her?'

'Of course, I'll never forget my mother.'

'What are your skills, other than your genius as a painter?'

Christy hesitated, unable to think of anything she did well.

'I've no real skills except painting, eating and swimming.'

'What are your hobbies?'

'Sunbathing, collecting fossils, antique crucifixes and animal skulls I find in the countryside when Father and I have picnics.'

'Are you modelling your future on Georgia O'Keefe?'

'I don't believe in copying. We're all individuals with a unique viewpoint. Georgia O'Keefe lives and paints in New Mexico, but there's where the similarity ends. She was born in 1887; I was born in 1951. Women are different now. We're a new breed with a new generation of thoughts.'

'Which artists do you most admire?'

'Picasso, Schiele, Braque, Bacon.'

'All twentieth-century painters.'

'I'm a twentieth-century person. I love artists from previous centuries too, of course, but I relate to these particularly.'

'Have you a boyfriend, Christy?'

'No, I've never had time for all that.'

'Do you consider that normal?'

'I don't worry all the time if I'm normal. I paint and I think and I try not to be afraid for the future.'

'How does it feel to be hailed as the art find of the century at twenty-three?'

Dumbfounded, stunned, Christy stared at the woman who had asked the question, her mind a blank from shock and uncertainty.

'I'm not sure I understand the question.'

'That's what the critics are saying. Haven't you heard?'

A blush of pleasure, intense shock, fear, jubilation spread over Christy's face. Unable to respond, she gazed at the men and women standing before her works, analysing and admiring them. Realization was tentative, but suddenly her heart began to pound again and she had the near irresistible urge to ask her father to take her home, to give her time and privacy to savour the idea of being the 'art find of the century'. She came back to the present with a start, when the woman repeated the question.

'I haven't talked to the critics yet. I'm just bewildered by what you say. I hope you're right, but I find it very difficult to believe.'

Christy walked around the gallery, listening to comments, scrutinizing reactions and trying not to laugh at the expression of panic on Nolan's face. He was being pinned against the wall by a persistent Italian lady, who kept asking him if he was *free*. Christy turned away, tears of laughter running down her face. Nolan liked being home, doing miracles with his camera, but he was not of an age to be at ease with predatory ladies. She was eating a caviar canapé when a man in a bow tie approached.

'Your paintings are truly existential. Sartre would have adored them.'

'I never met him.'

'But you know his thoughts and you paint them.'

'No, I paint *my* thoughts and I'm not an intellectual. I don't know anything at all about existentialism. I just get the paint on to the canvas, like Van Gogh and Cézanne. They didn't know about philosophy either.'

'How very brutal.'

'I'm not brutal, I'm basic. I'm a realist and I don't ever want to become one of these artists who pontificates about her work. I don't ever want to bullshit myself into thinking I'm anything but a simple painter. That's what

I am and that's what I'll always be. And now you must excuse me.'

'Well, really!'

Christy linked arms with Mitzi and Deke de Vanden and together they went to meet the most influential critics in America. Flashbulbs popped, questions filled the air. Christy was gay, elated, high on the idea that not only was her first exhibition a success, but she was going to be famous overnight. Looking around the gallery, she smiled at the unreality of it all. Her chair for the interviews was an ancient inlaid silver throne from Rajasthan. The rugs under her feet were Turkoman kelims. And everywhere there were violets, hundreds of bunches of violets, flown in from London and placed in an upturned brass temple bell. Violets were her favourite flower, impossible to grow in the desert, because they loved shade and cool. Still, Christy kept trying to cultivate them, hiding little pots in her wardrobe in the hope that she could accomplish the impossible.

The press conference continued for over an hour.

'Has your father influenced your style of work?'

'Not directly, but obviously he's influenced my life very much and so he must have influenced my work.'

'What are your future plans?'

'I want to work well and to extend my range as an artist. I'm quite scared of the future, because for an artist there's always that basic insecurity. I'll do my best, but for the moment I have to have time to assimilate what's happened. It's all been so sudden. I'm on cloud nine and terrified of hitting the earth and reality again.'

'Your work shows great confidence, but you seem quite timid. Is it true that you've always lived a reclusive life and if so, why?'

'Father and I like to live far from the town and we like silence and peace.'

'How are you going to follow up this exhibition? It's pretty hard to top perfection.'

'It's too early to think of the next exhibition. That could be far in the future.'

'If you had to write your own epitaph, what would you write?'

'I'd say this was Christy Pallister, artist, who always worked hard and tried not to fail.'

'Are you afraid of failure?'

'Very.'

'You refer to fear pretty often. Are you a fearful person?'

'Yes, I'm afraid of just about everything, except putting paint on the canvas.'

'For you, what is failure and what's success?'

'Failure's a bottomless pit and success is Gene Kelly singing in the rain.'

It was nightfall when everyone left, having drunk the champagne and eaten all the caviar. Nolan was sitting on the throne, his eyes dazed. Deke was staring at the red dots attached to every single canvas. Sold out at the first viewing! That had never happened before in twenty years as a dealer. Mitzi took her shoes off and rubbed her feet, shaking her head as she thought of the critics' near frenzied reactions.

Christy stood in the corner, looking at the scene as if she wanted to encapsulate it in her mind for always. Stunned by the magnitude of what had happened, she walked slowly around, remembering how she had felt when she had painted each of the canvasses. And now a miracle had happened. She was not only accepted, but famous. She thought of all the paintings she longed to do in the future, all the ideas hurtling around in her head. The future was perfect. All she had to do was keep calm.

The de Vandens had done her proud, adding priceless

pieces from their personal collection to dress each section of the gallery: a fifteenth-century Cretan triptych next to a woman's portrait from the same period; a collection of ambassadorial briefcases in silver and enamel embossed leather, once used in the Sultan's court at Constantinople, to add atmosphere to a portrait of Aimée Dubuq de Rivery, the ravishing French Sultana. Christy transferred her gaze from Aimée to the venomous traits of the virago, Tz'u Hsi, fascinating Dragon Empress of China, adroitly displayed with a collection of blue and white Kang Hsi porcelain. Coming to a halt before her father, she kissed him resoundingly.

'I was very proud of you tonight, Daddy.'

'The feeling was mutual.'

'Shall we go home?'

'Yes, you drive. The shock of being the father of the art find of the century has just hit me and I'm KO'd.'

Having arranged for the dealers to come to the press conference at the hacienda the following day, they said their goodbyes. Outside, the night air was cool, clear, welcome and both paused to breathe deep to calm their feverish excitement. Christy was putting the key into the door of the car, when a white Ferrari pulled alongside and a tall, lean, grey-haired but youngish man stepped out and walked briskly past them towards the adjacent restaurant. Briefly, his eyes caught hers and he smiled. Then he was gone.

Christy stared after him, admiring his style. Then she drove out of town and up the winding road towards the hacienda. Its pink adobe walls were bright with plumbago, bougainvillaea and trumpet-shaped convolvulus. Once inside the courtyard, she stopped the engine and Nolan secured the gates. Then they entered the silent, welcome world of home, high above the town, almost in the stars. Too excited to eat dinner, they decided to settle for sandwiches and coffee on the terrace overlooking the valley and the twinkling lights of Santa Fe. Christy spoke softly, gazing into the embers of the outside log fire Paquita, their housekeeper, had lit to take the chill from the air.

'I feel as if I ran a marathon.'

'You did. To get an exhibition like that ready in fifteen months is more than a marathon. And all those questions! I hate questions. When I was young I refused to see journalists.'

'That's probably how you got your priceless reputation for being mysterious, glamorous and out of reach.'

'Probably. I did a Garbo and it worked, thank God. I could never think of all those polite things you say to their stupid enquiries.'

'Who was the man in the Ferrari?'

'I thought you'd never ask. It's rare for you to notice a man, so I expected a question right away.'

'Perhaps it was the car I noticed!'

'Perhaps nothing. The man's Dan Gray, the doctor in charge and major shareholder in the Santa Rosa Clinic on the edge of town. Handsome fellow, with his prematurely grey hair and those Paul Newman blue eyes. He's causing havoc with the female population of the area.'

'Does he like quantity or quality?'

'He's a mystery. He's charm personified but difficult to pin down. Madeleine Carson invited him to dinner, put him next to a beautiful blonde model from Dallas and he got up and left while everyone was drinking coffee. Charlie Higson invited him to their annual barbeque. Gray helped cook the steaks and was a dab hand on the piano, but when Charlie's daughter tried to dance cheek to cheek, he handed her back to her father. He knows the value of being unavailable.'

Christy leaned back, looking at the stars.

'I wish Mother could have been there tonight.'

'Me too, Christy.'

'Do you still miss her, after all these years?'

'Yes, and I always will. There was never anyone quite like Louise. I wanted to protect and love her like I never wanted to protect and love any other woman.'

'What did she want?'

'She needed me and it was good to be needed, but she needed to be free, to fly like an eagle. I always said Louise was part human and part angel.'

'You're tired, Daddy. You want to go to bed? I shan't be long. I'll stay here and think awhile. Then I'll try to sleep.'

'What time do the critics arrive? I swear I've lost my memory this evening.'

'At eleven. That gives us plenty of time to have breakfast together, like always.'

'Goodnight, Christy. I can't tell you how proud I am of your success. I hope to God I don't get big-headed.'

'Me too!'

Christy sat watching bats wheeling in silent ballet in the night sky. Too excited to sleep, she went over every moment of what had happened during the evening. She had seemed to take it all in her stride. Only now was shock filtering through her mind. Grinning mischievously, she made herself another sandwich from leftovers. Probably she could buy herself a Ferrari and some mink-lined knickers for winter. Absurd presents came to mind – a solid gold camera for Nolan and a pure silk, sexy negligée for Paquita, who weighed a hundred and eighty pounds. Red silk, because that was her favourite colour.

Then her mind turned again to the doctor, with his grey hair and grey suit and piercing blue eyes. He had long legs, thin hands and mocking eyes. A shiver ran through her body and she decided it was time for bed.

Men with mocking eyes were to be avoided. They had a talent for seeing into the mind and her mind's contents were strictly private.

Christy went to her room, with its peach silk sheets, polar bear rugs and collection of sea shells. The·cat was sound asleep on a patchwork appliquéd with scenes of Santa Fe. Christy sighed. Pushy, the cat, weighed a ton and liked to settle in the very middle of her bed, giving her cramp in her legs. She showered, inspected her shells, covered her canary and said goodnight to the orchids she was trying to train to grow up the interior walls. The clock on the landing struck one as she pushed the cat to one side and fell into bed. Exhausted, she slept.

Dawn came rose-red over the horizon. Christy looked out, smiling at the silhouette of pinon pines on the hillside nearby. A new day and a beautiful one. She sang a few bars of an ancient hymn in a booming off-key voice: 'So here has been dawning another new day. Think wilt thou let it slip useless away'. Then she dressed in her jeans and an Irish pullover, drank some orange juice and drove slowly down the hill to the stables. She was saddling Lancelot, her horse, when a flashbulb startled them both. Christy turned angrily and saw a photographer about to retake.

'Are you crazy? You startled my horse.'

'I'll do another when you mount him.'

'Where did you come from?'

'LA. Come on Christy. I have a plane to catch.'

More flashes, then he was gone, driving like a madman on the road that led to the airport. Christy shrugged and rode out on Lancelot, through the trees that would soon turn the mesa gold, past the mission and the weathered walls of a long disused fort. The earth was flecked with grey-green sagebrush and, as always, she noted the intense contrast of this fertile countryside and the approaching, encroaching desert further south, a land of sable sand and dunes, where no man could find his way. Christy shuddered at the very thought. She had always been terrified of being lost in the wilderness, of being far from civilization and help. Turning, she galloped back to the stables, elated by the fresh air and the sunshine and the moment of knowing that today she was Christy Pallister, successful artist, not Christy Pallister, art student full of insecurities. The thought made her whoop with joy and as she put the horse back in his stall, rubbed him down and gave him his bonus carrots, she spoke from the heart.

'You're famous, you know, Lancelot. You're going to have your photo in a magazine, so chin up and don't tell all our secrets to the press.'

Nolan was breakfasting from sliced mangoes, tangerine juice, toast and Paquita's melon jam. The scent of coffee was delicious and Christy hurried in, kissed him and stole one of his mango slices.

'How are you this morning, Daddy?'

'Stiff as a board, in profound shock and in agreement with Oscar Wilde. I'd do anything to get back my youth except take exercise, get up early and be respectable.'

'You're always up early!'

'I get up to be with you. I love having breakfast with my daughter.'

'I love you, you know.'

'Me too. How was Lancelot?'

'He had his photo taken. A photographer jumped out from behind the stable door and startled him with his flash.'

'Photographers are a pain in the ass, reporters too. That reminds me, we'll be fifteen at the meeting this morning.'

'I thought it was three critics and their photographers?'

'It was. Now it's five critics and their photographers and South-West TV and the de Vandens. What will you wear?'

'I'm not a fashion model, you know. I'm an artist and that's what I want to be. I'll probably wear my rubber diving-suit to be original. Reporters like artists to be original.'

Their eyes met and they laughed at the idea. Then Christy started to scan the morning papers, screaming with delight at the reviews . . . *Christy Pallister, new wonder of the art world . . . The find of the century . . . Tour de force unequalled in twentieth-century history of the art world . . . Christy Pallister, talk of the town.*

Christy read them all aloud, laughing when her father replied, 'Nietzsche said, "For women, nothing is impossible." After yesterday evening, I believe him!'

'Look at this one, Daddy: "Without doubt the most original and intensely talented art find of the past fifty years." I can't believe they're talking about me. I feel like Alice in Wonderland.'

The photo session and the interviews lasted until two, when Nolan invited everyone to lunch. The press left, finally, at five, charming, full of adulation for their discovery and anxious to congratulate Christy on her application to her work and the fact that she had dared set herself such a monumental task. The most enthusiastic critic, James Wayne of the *New York Times*, shook her hand and spoke from the heart.

'I've been a critic for twenty years and I never had such a thrill as last night, when I saw the sheer genius of your paintings.'

'You're very kind to encourage me so.'

'No, I'm not kind. It's true, they're works of genius. I just ask myself what you can do next time that will top what we saw yesterday. I can't believe that anything could. Is it true that you have a waiting list for your next paintings?'

'Yes, we have fifty names.'

'If you come to New York call me and I'll arrange for you to meet some people who'll be anxious to exhibit you there.'

Christy saw her guests to their cars and then returned to the terrace, where Nolan was looking out over the panorama that he loved, the green of pine and the strange outcrops of rock, striped in the sunlight from coral to ochre.

'That's reality, Christy.'

'I know, Daddy. I won't lose sight of it.'

'What did you think of those critics?'

'They're experts. They're famous, but it worried me that they seemed to be thrilled, above all, to have discovered someone "new". The desire for novelty always scares me.'

'Real artists are timeless.'

'They were, so were writers, but now it's the publicity that counts, that and what's novel, fresh and different. I just hope they don't need someone new each season or my status won't last long.'

'You want to eat at the Polo Club?'

'I'd love to.'

'I bought you a little gift to celebrate your success. Found it in LA when I was there last month. I was going to give it to you for your birthday, but this exhibition warrants a special souvenir.'

Christy unwrapped an eighteenth-century Chinese crystal snuffbox, painted from inside with images of lotus, carp, phoenix and flowers.

'Thank you. It's beautiful, and not at all like the rest of my collection.'

'The Chinese made them in lacquer, amber, ivory,

jade and crystal and a few rare ones painted from the inside like this one. I can't imagine how they did it.'

'It'll be the star of my collection.'

'You're the star of mine.'

'Hope so.'

At the Polo Club, they ate blue corn tortillas, steaks and chillis. The restaurant was popular, the atmosphere casual, familiar and enthusiastic. One of Christy's fellow students from college was nearby, dining with her parents. When Christy called a greeting, Janie waved, but did not come over, her face a mask of ill-concealed resentment. Christy looked at her father.

'What on earth's the matter with her?'

'A sudden attack of envy, I imagine. You have to be prepared for that. When you're a success, complete strangers want to know you and you're rejected by many old friends.'

'I can't imagine Janie being jealous.'

'All creative people compete with themselves or with other people. You've done something special and you're a winner. Janie's still got all her mountains to climb, so she's resentful. Success is a two-edged sword, Christy. You can get hurt by it.'

Christy fell silent. Then, as she looked around at her fellow diners, she caught the blue eyes of Dan Gray, who was dining with a group of trustees of the clinic. Troubled again by his direct manner, she looked away, returning to gaze when he was in conversation with one of his colleagues. Then, remembering her manners, she quickly returned her attention to Nolan, hoping he hadn't noticed her continuing interest in Gray.

They were about to finish their meal, when a woman came over and greeted them as if she were an old friend.

'Christy dear, I just loved your exhibition. I want you to do my portrait when you're ready to take a commission.'

'I don't do portraits of live people. I haven't the experience to have someone present when I'm painting. I'm sorry.'

'But I've set my mind on a portrait and after all I can pay *any* price.'

Christy frowned, furious to be harassed in a public place. Then, looking sideways, to try to avoid the woman's gaze, she caught Dan Gray's quizzical regard. This time he smiled, raised his glass and made an unmistakable indication of his feelings about the woman. Christy turned back to her.

'I'm truly sorry, but I'm not ready to do portraits, so I can't accept any commission.'

The woman walked away angrily, her face tight with annoyance at what she considered a slight. Nolan patted his daughter's hand.

'You should have been a diplomat. God only knows who you take after. Louise was impossibly direct and I would have told her I don't paint women with faces like frogs. Diplomacy gives you a heart attack. Insulting folk is very good for the blood pressure.'

Christy relaxed as her father ordered more coffee.

'What time are you leaving on Thursday, Daddy?'

'I'll be on the ten-thirty to New York and the Concorde for Bahrain the following morning.'

'Will you be away long?'

'Two weeks or so. The desert's a wonderful place and those palaces are like something out of the *Arabian Nights*. The book's due to come out for Christmas next year and I want to do something extraordinary, photograph things that just haven't been seen before.'

'I think I'll take a holiday before I decide what to do next.'

'Where do you want to go?'

'Tahiti or Samoa or Fiji. Some far away place.'

'Like Gauguin?'

'No, like Christy Pallister, daughter of Nolan, champion insulter of Santa Fe.'

'Let's go home, drink something soothing and then see if I'm still the champion snorer of Santa Fe. God, those reporters were tiring, especially that fellow who kept talking as if he'd had a revelation like Paul on the road to Damascus.'

Later, in bed, when she re-ran the day, Christy found the image of Daniel Gray intruding on her mind. She dismissed the thought with impatience. Men were complicated, a race she didn't yet understand. Still, the way he had raised his glass had been nice and when he smiled and wrinkles appeared around his eyes she had been tempted to like him a lot.

Turning out the light, Christy thought of the critic's words: *I just ask myself what you can do next time that will top what we saw yesterday. I can't believe anything could.* One of the interviewers had expressed the same sentiment at the opening of her exhibition. Christy mulled over his words . . . *It's pretty hard to top perfection . . .* Could she top what everyone considered perfection? She closed her eyes tightly and willed herself to sleep, but her brain kept repeating the phrase and she fell to realizing that if you started your career at the summit, there was only one way to go. Panic hit her as the phrases burned themselves into her mind and she felt compelled to go and talk to her father.

'Daddy, I feel suddenly very scared. That man said he couldn't believe anything could top what I did in this exhibition. And one of the other critics told me it's pretty hard to top perfection. Do you think that everything I do now'll be a kind of horrible anticlimax?'

'When you start at the top it's not easy to wow folk again. What you do is choose something different, something close to your heart, something you feel a great deal about. Your natural talent'll take you there,

Christy. You're a great success, don't start getting nervous now.'

'But if I start at the top I can only slide down!'

'No, you can stay there, but that takes a lot of courage and a lot of tenacity.'

'I'm scared.'

'Amy'll be here in the morning. She'll know how to negotiate the bends. She knows *everything*!'

At three in the morning, Christy put on the light, read for an hour and then fell asleep. She dreamed she was in a white Ferrari, but when she turned the ignition key and pushed the accelerator, the car stayed right where it was. Again and again she revved the engine, unable to make the vehicle advance by even an inch. She woke at six, soaked to the skin with sweat and utterly exhausted. When she had taken a shower and made herself a pot of coffee, she returned to bed and slept until eight, putting her nightmare down to delayed reaction to the shock of being famous.

By nine-thirty, Christy had almost forgotten all about it – almost, but not quite.

THIRTEEN

The main advantage to Christy of being famous was the relief that she had achieved it without too much pain. It meant being spoiled by people she had never met and having the best table in restaurants. The disadvantages were phone calls to the house from journalists asking for photo sessions, interviews and comments on everything from world politics to abortion. Photographers trailed her every move. Privacy became a thing of the past and tranquillity a memory. Christy soon grew apprehensive of it all, aware that every call would interrupt her work once she started painting again and conscious that she was an artist and unqualified to discuss politics, social issues or anything else outside her experience. Letters poured in from people asking for art advice, felicitating her success or demanding loans. When she did not reply, because she was not equipped to do so, the letters became offensive.

Nolan took the situation in hand when he realized that his daughter was becoming exhausted by the brutality of the sudden change in her life.

'There are two ways of handling fame, Christy, the Garbo or the Marilyn method. Either you never do photos and interviews or you do them all the time. I did none and I'm glad I didn't. I became the world's most famous globe trotting photographer without any help from such publicity. I was lucky. You've not had much choice, what with photographers hiding in the stables at the Polo Club and even trying to get into the hacienda!'

'I never thought there'd be side effects to fame.'

'There's always a price to pay for everything good in life. For my part, I find it distracting and I'm afraid it'll affect your concentration.'

'Don't say that, Daddy.'

'But you've always been so easily perturbed, dear. I've protected you as best I've been able, but everyone knows fame's a kind of disease that separates you from reality and deprives you of tranquillity.'

'Mitzi and her husband want me to go on tour with the exhibition to New York, Dallas and LA.'

'Did you agree?'

'No, I refused and they weren't very happy. They want to make me a media person, like Andy Warhol.'

'What do *you* want, Christy?'

'I want to work well, but first I need my holiday. I don't feel like painting for the first time in my life and that scares me.'

'You're just tired and shocked by the upset of your routine. Everyone who gets to be famous suddenly is hit by the same problem. You'll be fine when you get back from vacation and I'll see you're not disturbed. I'm going to take the situation in hand.'

The windows of the studio were framed in white, dazzling in the light of Santa Fe, that resembled that of Provence, inspiration for Van Gogh's genius and his madness. Everywhere there were violent contrasts and a clarity that made it seem as if every pine needle on the distant hill were visible. Christy adored her studio and the view that had been her reality, her own private world since childhood: the ruined church on the hill and the Sangre de Cristo mountains, that, in spring, had framed the scene of woodcutters in their red shirts, carting logs back to town, to be stored throughout summer in barns, farms and fincas for the coming winter.

Christy fixed a new canvas on the easel in readiness for her return to work. Looking at it out of the corner of her eye, she thought it seemed very large and ominously empty. She made a pot of coffee, put on a disc of Bob Dylan's last concert and sang with him, off key as usual. Then, having mixed her palette, she put a brushful of sepia on the canvas. She worked steadily until lunchtime, going to the window to drink in the beauty, when a sudden shower left shiny globes of water on the lilac tree leaves outside the window. Then, conscious that she had worked hard but not well, she went to the covered terrace where Nolan was waiting to eat with her.

Looking at her face, he knew that the return to work had left her downcast.

'You worked badly?'

'I did a desert scene – at least I started one.'

'Why? You hate the desert, you always did. Even as a child you were terrified of everything to do with it, getting lost, having nothing to drink, snakes, scorpions, lizards and anything else that lives there!'

'I like doing paintings of things that are difficult for me to experience. I give them more attention than things I love.'

Christy rose and went back to her studio for a few minutes, returning then to her father, her face pale and crestfallen.

'It's awful. I'll have to redo it.'

'Listen, dear, after more than a year of working for ten hours a day and the sudden shock of fame and success, I think it'll be best if you take your holiday right now. When you get back, the phone calls'll be under control. We're going to have the phone number changed.'

'I'll go to Fiji.'

'Go in the morning.'

'So soon?'

'If you don't, you risk getting worked up and tense because you're tired and that's crazy. You're empty, that's all. Have fun for a few weeks and then come home and have a fresh start.'

Scent of white flowered ginger. Tree frogs hopping around the taxi driver's feet, as he took out her bags and handed them to a huge Fijian head porter in a sulu, the fringed calf-length skirt that was standard wear for the men of the island. Delighted by the strangeness of it all, Christy thought of the moment of arrival at Nadi Airport, where the customs man had given her a massive, crocodile-toothed welcome, making her feel instantly at home. The beach alongside the hotel was scattered with shells; cowrie and sharks' eye, sonus and the spiral shaped turrida, moon shells and the nacreous nautilus. Longing to rush out and fill her suitcase with souvenirs, Christy walked briefly to the sea, smiling at its blue-green perfection. Then she followed the porter to the desk and registered, before going to a room with rattan blinds and green and white parrot motif bedlinen.

On the table, there was a bowl of fruit, a lavish arrangement of custard apples, paw-paw, pineapple and mango. Christy sketched it for future reference. A soft breeze made the blinds sway. Exhausted by the long journey, she decided to walk on the beach in the twilight and then to dine in her room. She might try the local speciality, made from powdered root of the pepper family. Yagono was said to make some folk drunk and others sneeze. Christy thought wryly that the reaction was probably whatever each individual expected.

She returned from the beach with some magnificent cowrie shells and a collector's item David's Harp, its ribbing separated by areas of what looked like a modern geometric painting. She had also collected a young stockbroker from Sydney, who remained in hot pursuit throughout the holiday.

'Look here, Christy, let's have fun. Holidays are too short to waste time. You want to come dancing tonight?'

'I'm tired after the journey. I'll go to bed early and maybe we'll meet on the beach tomorrow.'

'We could swim at dawn.'

'Aren't there sharks?'

'Sure there are, but who gives a fuck about sharks? When it's your day to get eaten by a monster, you get eaten.'

'I'm tired. We can talk again in the morning.'

'You're beautiful. You want me to come and tuck you in?'

'No thanks, I think I can go to bed without a mummy.'

Relieved when he disappeared, Christy returned to her room, ordered dinner, had a shower and put on her new, sexy, sugar-pink silk lounging pyjamas, shrugging resignedly because she knew that only she would see them. For a moment she sat down on the edge of the bed and wondered why her sex life was nonexistent. A social life with all its pitfalls did not interest her either and she was without confidence in her ability to attract a man. The fact was, she lived only to paint. Christy sighed, suspecting that she was deficient in sensuality. The experience with Art had marked her more than she had realized, but even before that she had resolved to steer clear of emotional involvements.

Christy smiled wryly, thinking that she would like, even so, to have a man of her own. The conflict made her uncertain and she decided that she would feel better when she had eaten. Looking at her watch, she wondered what Nolan was doing, ashamed by the realization that she was homesick. Damn! She was becoming more infantile as she got older instead of more adult. She decided she must review her progress in life. To recover from the physical depletion of fifteen months of excessively hard work would be easy now she was on holiday. To get her brain out of the hollow of shock that sudden fame had excavated would be difficult. She decided to start thinking about her next exhibition and what she would like to paint. That was always fun.

Hearing a knock at the door, Christy hurried to let in a giant Fijian waiter, who wheeled the dinner on a table set with yellow frangipani. Christy's spirits soared as she looked at the place setting and the food. It was a lovely start to the holiday to have a spectacular dinner on this perfect, warm, tranquil evening. Later, when she had eaten, she would telephone Nolan and tell him that she felt fine. Then she would sleep until midday. It was a family joke when Christy spoke of sleeping until midday, because she always woke between five and six. As she ate, she decided to try some surf-board lessons and if she didn't drown or get eaten by a shark, she would lie in the sun and then go to the beauty parlour to be pampered before dinner. She thought of the hotel boutique with its fabulous Chinese silks and exotic batiks. She would have Nolan some shirts made in the vivid colours that suited him well. And perhaps the batik motifs would inspire her with a baseline of new thoughts for the next exhibition?

Having eaten, Christy poured herself another cup of coffee and let her mind wander. Before the exhibition, she had been insecure, wondering if she would ever make it in the art world. Now she had made it, she was terrified of losing what she had won. Would she ever arrive at the point of feeling at ease with herself?

Changing the subject within her mind, she decided not to date the Australian. He was eager for a quick holiday romance and would be difficult when he realized she was not interested. She had come to rest, not to be hassled by a randy young man. Then her mind returned to Santa Fe and the horror they had lived through of telephones ringing at all hours of the day and night. Instead of feeling confident that everyone wanted her paintings and everyone wanted to know more about her, Christy's brain kept rerunning the critic's words . . . *I just ask myself what you can do next time that will top what we saw yesterday. I can't believe anything could.* From the moment he had said that, she had found it impossible to paint. The idea of never equalling an exhibition presented in the twenty-third year of her life was so terrifying she preferred to do nothing at all, to opt out. Wishing fervently that her admirer had kept his thoughts to himself, Christy resolved to rest and gather her strength for the return to Santa Fe. Work was her only weapon against the frightening thoughts that had suddenly paralysed her talent. If she relaxed and let her mind get used to the idea of fame, she felt sure things would return to normal.

When she was not falling off her surfboard, Christy was searching the beach for red coral, sand dollars and shells. She took trips to nearby islands, revelling in their silver beaches and the local markets, where breadfruit was sold next to paw-paw, yams, green bananas and tiny crabs threaded live on strings. She watched the changing of the guard outside the Governor's Palace, a replica of the same ceremony outside Buckingham Palace in London, except that the soldiers wore fringed skirts. Her shell collection grew until she had to buy another suitcase to accommodate it. Her list of admirers also grew, but Christy was not eager for a holiday romance. She had always avoided short-term liaisons and knew she could never change her mind. The idea of the new morality suited her fine – one man, one woman and an in-depth love affair. It was just that she had no man.

On her last night on the island, Christy dined alone in a quayside restaurant, watching a cruise liner depart, its deck lights flashing as passengers threw streamers to the crowd below and a choir of islanders, born with the ability to harmonize, sang a touching Fijian Farewell. Having paid for the meal, she rose to leave and came face-to-face with David, the Australian who had trailed her every move throughout the holiday, hoping to persuade her to change her mind.

'You're leaving tomorrow, Christy. Let me invite you to coffee and a liqueur and a taxi back to the hotel.'

'Why not?'

They talked of his work and hers, of her efforts with the surfboard and her fear of sharks and everything else that was new or strange. He touched her hand.

'When we get back to the hotel, let's go and get drunk.'

'I'm leaving at six in the morning and getting drunk's not my idea of a special occasion.'

'What is? You don't fuck. You don't socialize. You play Garbo. What *do* you do, apart from write postcards to your daddy?'

'Well, I don't make love with a man I don't know or care about.'

'You're really something – a precious type, vintage 1945.'

'No, you're wrong there, David. You belong in the sixties when everyone had everyone because they were drunk on liberation after years of soul bondage. But times have changed. We're heading for an age when everyone fights for the freedom to belong to himself or herself and to do what he or she wants and not what other people want or convention dictates. It's an important change and much nearer real liberty. This is the age of reality, it's time you woke up to it. Now this is my last night on the island and I don't intend to spoil it listening to your complaints about my lack of sexuality.'

'I'm sorry.'

'Don't be. Just leave me alone to be myself.'

As she passed through the customs barrier and ran to greet her father, Christy was happy.

'I'm so glad to be back. I loved every exotic sun-bronzed minute of my holiday, but I longed to be in Santa Fe and to see you in your panama waiting for me at the airport barrier. I've bought you some wonderful silk shirts in the sky, violet and viridian you like. You'll be quite something when you wear them.'

'Wonderful! And I've got a feast waiting for you. As you know, Paquita tends to go mad when she wants to show her love for someone. She does it with food and the kitchen's been in danger of breaking through the walls since yesterday morning. We'll have to invite a crowd to clear up the leftovers!'

'I'm hungry so that's lucky.'

They were almost at the car, when they heard the revving of an unwilling engine and saw Dan Gray at the wheel of his Ferrari, looking decidedly annoyed. Nolan called out.

'Can we give you a lift, Dr Gray?'

'I'd be grateful.'

'The clinic or the garage?'

'The clinic. I'll call the garage from there.'

'This is my daughter, Christy. She's just back from a

holiday in Fiji. That's why she's the colour of burnt toast.'

'Hello, Christy, how was the holiday?'

'Quiet but very good fun, Dr Gray.'

'Dan.'

Nolan drove to the clinic at his usual sedate forty miles an hour, dropped the doctor off and then proceeded towards the hacienda, where the feast had been laid out buffet-style in the inner courtyard. He smiled indulgently as Christy whooped with joy.

'Everything I like and then some. Oh Daddy, it's so good to be home.'

At nine-thirty, while they were drinking their after-dinner coffees, Dan called Nolan and invited him and Christy to dinner the following evening, by way of thanks for rescuing him. Nolan suggested that Dan take his daughter instead.

'Two's company, three's none and anyway I'm inclined to snore after nine in the evening.'

'I don't believe a word of it, but I'd love to invite Christy if she's free. I'll call for her at seven.'

Nolan didn't tell her about the invitation straight away, aware that if she slept on the idea she would cancel in the morning. So he told her at lunchtime, too late for her to contact Dan. She went into overdrive. She washed her hair, had a bath, spilling frangipani oil by the quart into the water to be sure to smell like a dream. Christy sang arias from *I Pagliacci* and a few hymns to give her courage. Then she tried to decide what dress to wear. Blue jeans had become a way of life and she wore little else – in summer with her paint-stained, highly fashionable tee shirts or in winter with her tartan lumberjack's coat. Blue jeans were not in line for this evening! Neither were the layered dresses, that gave her a ninety-six-inch waist measurement. Finally, she chose a black silk outfit with a handpainted jacket in

225

shades of violet that matched her eyes. She wore no jewellery, just a plain pair of black suede shoes. She was ready by six-thirty and pacing by a quarter to seven. When she heard Dan's car, she rushed out to the terrace and sat on the lounging chair, as if she were relaxed and used to being called for by the most desirable man in the area.

Nolan welcomed Dan with a drink.

'That's my tequila special.'

'I hope it's not too strong, those bends on the road up are quite something.'

'Sure are. Lots of folk have misjudged them and ended up in the valley. Here's Christy. You want a tequila special, dear?'

'No thanks. I'll have a tonic water with a slice of lemon. If I drink one of your specials I'll have jet lag, even if I didn't have it when I got back. Hello, Dan.'

'Hi, Christy, what's this you said yesterday about your shell collection getting augmented in Fiji?'

'I brought two suitcases of shells back. You want to see them?'

Following her to her room, Dan stroked Pushy, the cat, who rolled on her back and purred outrageously. He was impressed when Christy presented her fabulous shell collection.

'I've been collecting them since I was ten.'

'What are you going to do when they fill the bedroom?'

'I'll start on the bathroom, the terrace and the corridor. Then I'll have to buy another house for the spares.'

'You like having spares, Christy?'

'Oh yes, I'm very insecure. I buy spares of everything in case of a declaration of war or a sudden famine.'

'Hard to believe a woman with talent like yours and a background like this could be insecure.'

Christy hesitated, then decided to reveal the truth.

'My grandmother married Lord Invergordon, one of the richest men in Britain. Camilla was a mannequin and famous in her decade. Everyone loved and admired her, but she committed suicide because her husband was a drunk and he'd killed the only man she ever really loved. Mother was a famous flier and a household name in these parts. She was a champion skier and swimmer and very beautiful too. Louise died in a plane crash they say was an accident when she was twenty-six. Nolan knows she committed suicide. So you see, Dan, being talented or beautiful isn't enough. It isn't secure. That's probably why I buy ten of everything when I can afford it and why they may well give me the Nobel Prize for worrying one of these days.'

'Well, you have nothing to worry about this evening. Are you hungry?'

'Yes, very.'

'Steak or exotic hungry?'

'Surprise hungry.'

'Let's go.'

Dan drove her to the aerodrome, where a small private plane was ready on the runway. He was calm, solid, funny and always in command of the situation. When he brought the plane down at dusk in what seemed like a deserted area, Christy looked around her, half afraid.

'Where are we?'

'On the moon. You're an artist known for her originality so I thought I'd best be original too or you'd throw me out on my ear.'

'I can't see a restaurant.'

'Your eyes'll get accustomed to the light in a while. Look over there, fifty yards to your left.'

'I see a faint glow, nothing more.'

'That's our restaurant.'

They walked hand in hand to the massive portico of

what seemed to be a pile of boulders. Christy stared in shocked silence when Dan opened the gate, let her in and led her towards the most astonishing house she had ever seen. The architect had used giant boulders from the plain with remarkable effect, as part of the exterior and interior of the house. From afar, even from fifty yards, no house was visible, just a massive pile of rocks like all the other massive outcrops in the region.

On entering, Christy found herself in a room with a hearth of blazing logs, bright Navaho rugs and locally carved wood beams. In a long tunnel of rock lit by ingenious sky lights and the flickering splendour of a multitude of amber candles, she found the dining-room, its vast table set for two. A young Mexican maid giggled and ran away, reappearing with her parents, who carried pitchers of tequila punch, tapas, and tiny aperitif pastries, which scented the air with marjoram and thyme. Christy felt as if she had arrived in fairyland, when Dan led her to a long, wolf-fur covered sofa and put a drink in her hand.

'I saw your exhibition. It was truly extraordinary.'

For a moment, her eyes were sad, as she thought of the awful canvas painted before her departure for Fiji.

'I worked for fifteen months to get those paintings ready and I was so happy and confident doing it. There's nothing truer than that ignorance is bliss. I had no idea of the size of the task I'd set myself. I just did it.'

'What are you going to do next?'

'That's what everyone asks and me too. One of the New York critics said "I just ask myself what you can do next time that will top this. I can't believe anything could." Since he said that I'm scared to put brush to canvas and I haven't painted a single decent picture.'

'You must never try to top yourself, Christy. You just paint what comes into your head or your heart.'

'I painted one picture and it was awful. That was why I went on holiday – to get away from pestering phone calls and pestering reporters. I thought it was that that had stopped me wanting to paint. But I wonder if I was evading the real issue.'

'You think the holiday didn't work?'

'I don't know. I start work again tomorrow. We'll know then. Trouble is, when you're famous you get scared of not coming up to your own standards.'

'It's a natural reaction, you know, but you've got great talent and talent always comes up tops in the end, even if there are a few hiccups on the way.'

'And what about you? Nolan says you're the most desired man in the region!'

'He could be right: I'm desired by fund raisers, widows, patients with husbands who don't pay them enough attention and lady reporters just dying to do an exposé.'

'I'm not desired. I only ever had one boyfriend and that was a catastrophe. It was such a disaster, I acquired the reputation for being quite useless in all matters relating to the birds and the bees. So I only get harassed by journalists wanting photos, quotes and interviews.'

Dan smiled a secret smile of pleasure at her brutal honesty, so rare and so natural it moved him deeply. Then he led her to the table.

'This table's enormous. If we're to avoid shouting at each other to be heard, I vote we sit here and here.'

'Good idea. Why's the table so big? Do you entertain crowds on Sundays?'

'No, I always come alone. I live in Santa Fe, above the clinic, during the week. This place is my hideaway from earthly cares. My secret.'

'I'm honoured to have been invited.'

'You should be. I never brought anyone here before.'

Christy gulped the last of her cocktail, her heart thundering like the *1812 Overture*. She wondered why her knees had started shaking and her mind was racing like Dan's Ferrari at full throttle. She decided to talk about less personal things.

'You didn't tell me why the table's so enormous.'

'The family who work for me, Amparo and her daughter, Olivia, and the husband, who's called Matteo, came to Santa Fe from my mother's house in Puerto Vallarta. Matteo has grandiose ideas and when I asked for a table he made one suitable for the White House.'

They laughed delightedly at the Mexican's regal ideas. Then they ate roast wild turkey stuffed with pine nuts and sweet yams followed by a tart of egg yolks, chocolate and a puree of black cherries that made Christy's mouth water so much that she had to have a second helping.

'If I lived with Amparo and Matteo I should soon weigh two hundred pounds and be unable to raise my brush.'

'I often think the same thing.'

'Were you ever married, Dan?'

'I was engaged once, when I was in medical school. Lesley was killed in the Los Altos air crash on her return from vacation. I'm essentially a worker, you know. I was born poor. Then Mother inherited a vast fortune from a man who wanted to marry her but died before he persuaded her to exchange poverty for wealth. She lives in the house he left her in Puerto Vallarta and she partly financed the building of the clinic. She rings me up regularly to complain about the lack of grandchildren.'

'How old were you when she inherited the money?'

'Twenty-five, and used to being poor, working holidays and nights to put myself through school, so it was quite a shock.'

'A pleasant one!'

'Sure, but a bit like your sudden fame. It rocked the boat and disrupted the tranquillity of life. It took me years to get used to the fact that I'm the director of the clinic and I own most of the bricks and mortar.'

Their eyes met and Christy held his, glad that he understood the change that had upset her life. She watched as Dan poured coffee and moved to the fireside to drink it, indicating that she come and sit with him. Outside, a line of deep purple on the horizon made a modern painting of the evening sky. Then, abruptly, it was gone and there was no light at all, only a navy canvas, polka dotted with stars. Glancing at the painted clock on the wall, Christy saw, with something of a shock, that it was eleven o'clock. They had been together for hours that had seemed like minutes, talking of so many things, sounding each other out and liking what they heard. She smiled when Dan told her how he came to have the plane.

'Friend of mine was a flying freak. He spent more time up than he did on the ground. Then he married one of my nurses and she wouldn't set foot in the machine.'

'What happened? Did she leave him?'

'Of course not. Jake was so in love he sold me the plane and bought a Mercedes.'

'Love's scary.'

'Why?'

'The women in my family hit rock bottom when they fall in love and I've always been very wary of even thinking about it, in case I catch the dread disease.'

'That's a curious fear for a modern woman.'

'I'm a curious modern woman.'

'And a beautiful one. I'll take you back now, Christy. Sky's wonderful at night and we can stop off for a nightcap at the Pink Flamingo on the way back to the hacienda.'

'I loved being in your boulder house. It's like something out of this world. Are you sure we can take off in the dark, Dan?'

'Sure we can. Take off's no problem when you know the terrain like the back of your hand, but you can't land in the dark without lights. When I arrive at night, Amparo puts on what she calls my runway lights.'

'I'd like to see those.'

'You will. Are you free on Sunday the twenty-fourth, Christy?'

'I'm always free Sundays. It's the only day when I don't work.'

'We're having a charity auction at the clinic in the morning in aid of the new research wing. After that I'll be free for the whole day.'

'And you must come to dinner with us soon at the hacienda, give Nolan an excuse to get dressed up and show you his photographs and his collection of surrealist paintings. He'll go to bed at nine-thirty and snore loud enough to waken the whole of New Mexico, but he's great company when he's awake. If you're free next Friday do come, but I'll leave it open.'

'I'll be there.'

His eyes challenged hers for a brief moment and Christy shivered, despite her desire to appear calm and sophisticated. Then Dan put a jacket around her shoulders and led her out into the night. A flash of white in the distance betrayed the presence of a startled rabbit, a thin spiral of smoke that of a man alone in the wilderness, cooking his dinner or talking with his God. Christy felt curiously reassured when Dan took her hand and helped her into the plane. Within minutes they were airborne and flying low over the pine trees, looking at the twinkling lights of the town and the twin guidelines on the private airport runway.

In the drive through the silent countryside towards the hacienda, both were silent, conscious that when there was a true affinity, there was no need to talk.

When Dan stopped the car at the hacienda, Christy wondered if he was going to kiss her. Her heart thundered in anticipation, but he simply opened the car door and then walked with her to the gate.

'I'll look forward to dinner on Friday and our day together on the twenty-fourth. In the meantime, work well.'

'Dan.'

'Yes, Christy?'

She looked at her feet, then at the gate, wondering how to express what she wanted to say. She smiled gently.

'I haven't accepted any dates for ages, years to be honest. I always get scared at the last minute and ring up to cancel. Nolan didn't even tell me I was invited to dinner tonight until after I'd eaten lunch! I'm very glad I didn't cancel our date. I've had a really lovely evening.'

'So have I. We'll try to build this friendship to last, Christy. Solid foundations, so it can't break when the cold winds blow. Agreed?'

'Agreed, Dan.'

She watched as the car slipped out of sight over the hill that would take him back to Santa Fe. He had not tried to kiss her goodnight. He had not even touched her, except to take her hand when he helped her from the plane. Christy closed and barred the gate and ran to her room, dancing, pirouetting and humming a few bars of 'Singing in the Rain'. From her bedroom, she wandered through to the studio and looked in disgust at the painting she had started but would never finish.

Her holiday was over now and it was time to concentrate and build and consolidate. Having showered, Christy discussed her evening with Pushy, said goodnight to her orchids and slept like a log. As she slept, she dreamed . . .

The island was roughly heart shaped, its white beach fringed by casuarina trees. Two figures entwined on a rattan day bed, under the palm-fringed terrace of the hideaway. Naked, their bodies burnished by the sun, they were so engrossed in each other, they neither saw nor heard the sound of the surf or the melancholy cry of gulls overhead. His lips were at her breasts, his mouth searching, biting, savouring her hard, pointed nipples. She stretched her legs slowly, languorously, entwining them like twin snakes around his back and closing with a sudden pincer movement that pushed his hardness into the warm wetness of her core. Feeling the advent of orgasm, she began to pant as that sunburst of uncontrolled ecstasy made her cry out, because she had wanted him to fill her emptiness and he had done so without a word but with complete joy and abandon.

Christy woke alone in her bed, the cry coming from her lips as if from a distant land. Turning on the light, she saw that it was ten past four. Then, remembering the dream, she sighed because, for her, love was a stranger and ecstasy only a fantasy. Someday, maybe, she would find the strength to bury her insecurities. Someday, on a white sandy beach, she would become the woman of her dreams. But how to change? How to learn to grasp the opportunity and let someone love her as she longed to be loved, dreamed of being loved and needed to be loved? She knew only time would tell if her courage matched her desire.

Christy painted until two-thirty, then lunched with Paquita. She was thoughtful and Paquita was conscious of the strange mixture of confidence and uncertainty in the young woman she had always adored. She poured coffee for them both and accompanied Christy to the terrace.

'How was your evening with Dr Gray?'

'I had a lovely time. We flew in his plane to a house he's built in the valley from boulders, at least it seems to be built of boulders. He talked about Viennese furniture of the 1930s, Gauguin and a new cure for arthritis of the hip. He was marvellous! He's coming to dinner on Friday so Daddy can have fun, too.'

'And your painting?'

'I feel empty, Paquita. I can't explain it to you or to myself.'

'I'll ring Amy tonight. She knows what to do for this problem. Probably she will come home for a few days and tell you how to cure yourself.'

'She could always tell me how to cure myself, even when I was four years old.'

'I wish she would marry. I don't understand how a woman like Amy don't get married.'

'Not everyone wants to get married, you know, and Amy's very dedicated to her work.'

'Her bookshop! You can't *sleep* with books. You can't talk to them when you get lonely.'

'They talk to you.'

'You go to paint again this afternoon?'

'Yes, I'm experimenting with a new way of handling light. I've been thinking about it for ages, but I haven't perfected the technique.'

'I make special dinner to cheer you up.'

'You do that and we'll share it.'

When Friday came, Paquita cooked up such a storm the house smelled like Maxim's. Nolan was eager to meet Dan and the evening went like a dream, leaving Christy euphoric. Dan had arrived bearing gifts: an old bottle of port for her father and an antique copper bowl of rose petal pot-pourri for her. He had not forgotten Paquita, who received a loving cup with a porcelain frog hidden in the base. Screeching with delight, Paquita forgot herself and kissed the doctor a smacking, enthusiastic 'thank you'. Then she disappeared to the kitchen to finish the dinner and dance flamenco.

They all laughed joyfully at Dan's tales of his medical school days and a friend's affair with the matron of the teaching hospital, who, discovered in what lawyers call a compromising position with the young man, went into vaginal spasm and locked his erection inside her. Carried to the emergency ward on a stretcher together, the two had never spoken again after being 'freed'. Nolan, who had a dread of tight-arsed intellectuals, was overjoyed that, however serious his reputation, Dan had a most irreverent sense of humour.

On the twenty-fourth, Christy gave one of her small Spanish Infanta paintings to be auctioned at the clinic, watching wide-eyed as the price soared to a seemingly ludicrous level.

'Ladies and gentlemen, this painting is a genuine Christy Pallister, donated by the artist herself. Now you know she's been hailed as the art find of the century. May I have a bid please?'

'Five thousand dollars.'

'Seven thousand five.'

'Ten thousand.'

'Fifteen thousand.'

'Twenty thousand.'

Christy swallowed hard, unable to keep her mind from wandering back to the uninspired, inexplicably flat paintings she had been working on since her return from holiday. She was trying so hard, too hard perhaps, and without results. Gradually fear had filtered into her mind, making her ill at ease. What if she never found her inspiration to paint again? What if the talent never returned? Putting fear to the back of her mind, she told herself she must learn to pace herself, to play as well as work. She looked at Dan, smiling when she caught his eye. She would think of work tomorrow. She had thought of nothing but work for years. Today was for living, for learning to be Christy Pallister, woman of today.

In the smoke-blue mist of a spring evening, they sat together in front of the fire, with its fragrant, glowing logs. They had walked far into the valley, found fossils and collected strange objects long lost from times past. They had eaten their favourite foods and listened as Amparo played the guitar. Now, they were alone, tired but not so tired as to be unaware of each other.

Christy shivered when Dan's hands touched her shoulders.

'What time's Nolan expecting you?'

'He's in San Francisco. He'll be back on the third.'

'You want to stay the night, Christy? If not, I'll take you home, but there's going to be a storm and I'd prefer to stay here.'

When she didn't reply, Dan led her to a guest bedroom full of antiques, a secretaire in green lacca contrefatta, a tapestry by Jan de Bruxelles in the same olive and beige tones. The bed was enormous, its pillared corners draped in seventeenth-century Chinese silk in rose, greige and gold. Mythical birds flew from the flames of their own demise, to a lake covered in water lilies, where the reeds were gilt edged and strange faces peered out of the fronds of weeping willow trees. The bedside tables were covered in silk, embroidered in the Chinese style with cockerels of aggressive demeanour. And in the corner, pale candles in a black iron votive-holder flickered enticingly over the features of a

Madonna in oil on oak. Christy smiled happily; the Madonna was one of hers.

'I never saw a house quite like this one before. It has all the objects for a museum, but the effect is a real home.'

'Come and see your bathroom. We put in Chinese honeysuckle and old-fashioned roses to go with the furnishings. Christy, if you want to sleep, do so. If you want to come to me, I'm right next door. There's a linen wrap in the closet for after your shower. No one ever wore it before. I bought it this afternoon, in case I got lucky and you agreed to stay over.'

He saw the tremor in her hands and knew that she was out of her depth. She had stayed all the same. He smiled encouragingly.

'Take a shower and then do what you want to do.'

Christy walked from the bathroom, her hair still wet, her face reflecting a dozen conflicting emotions. She wanted Dan as she had never imagined it possible for her to want a man. Why had she changed? What was she going to do? She was useless in bed, Art had said so. Damn Art! He was nothing but a narcissistic little fart. Dan was *real*. Could he transform her into a real woman? Christy listened to the thunder and the rain teeming down at the windows. Then, without consciously making a decision, she walked from the room and knocked at Dan's door.

'I'm scared of storms.'

'I thought you might be. I've been hoping for a tempest.'

Christy felt her core contract with the onset of long-denied desire and she swayed, overwhelmed by fear and longing. Dan untied the wrap and let it fall to her waist, exposing her naked breasts and making her struggle to control the trembling of her muscles. Then, as he lifted her on to the sofa and slipped off the wrap, she stretched like a cat, gazing at the fire in contentment as he ran his hands over her breasts. Her nipples became hard as he twisted and tasted them, cupping them together so he could bite and provoke until she cried out for him to take her. Christy watched wide-eyed as Dan undressed, his suntanned body burnished gold in the firelight glow. His shoulders were wide, his arms and legs muscled but slim. His penis thrust forward, long, strong and searching. She reached out to caress it, smiling when it became moist at her touch. She was shocked to hear herself saying the words she had never believed she could say.

'I want you to love me and I want you very much.'

Dan kissed her cheeks and her nose and her lips, his tongue pushing between her teeth and exploring the warm inside of her mouth. For a moment he remained poised above her. Then, as he moved to enter her, Christy thrust forward, impaling herself on him and crying out because his strength and the urgency of his desire excited her as nothing had ever excited her before. At that moment, Dan wondered if he had ever felt such ecstasy, such deep down contentment.

Christy felt his body begin a strong, regular rhythm. She spread her legs as wide as she could and then closed them around his back, because she wanted him to fill every empty space within her. The thought was so exciting, she clutched his shoulders and began with ever increasing speed to move in unison with him, their bodies touching, their movements culminating in a moment of orgasm that felt like a bursting meteor. Wild with desire, all control abandoned, she cried out as she felt Dan give what she wanted more than anything in the world to receive. Then, embarrassed by her wantonness she bit his ear, kissed his cheek and snuggled to his chest.

'I'm so happy I'm scared.'

'I'm so tired I just hope I don't snore like your father. I never slept with an artist before. Is it true they paint you blue, green and yellow if you're not nice to them?'

Christy laughed delightedly, watching as he went to the fridge in the dressing-room and returned with a bottle of champagne. They drank and then, feeling desire return, she leaned forward and kissed his thighs and the tight buttocks that fascinated her.

'Come to me, Dan.'

'I could get to like taking orders.'

'Come to bed, please. It's not really an order. More like a royal request.'

He bent to kiss her knees and her thighs and the dark, curly pubic hair that smelled of flowers and sin. Then, as she began to writhe, he moved to kiss her cheeks and her neck and her lips, descending slowly as she waited, shuddering, when he reached the centre of all feeling. When he thrust inside her, Christy pushed him back gently, so she was astride and riding fast to the moment again when her head would fill with fireworks and her inner core would explode. As Dan grasped her, with a cry of pleasure, she fell forward, her breasts against his face. The orgasm had weakened her and she longed only to sleep in his arms. She was lying quietly at Dan's side, when she heard him whispering the words she wanted to hear.

'Sleep, think of nothing at all except the marvellous day we'll have tomorrow.'

Dan's hand touched her waist, his arms closed around her and she felt safe – safe from life, from work, from failure, from fear.

She felt something else, too, but was unwilling to admit that she wanted and needed and loved him. Love had been the catalyst that had led to disaster for Camilla and Louise. Could history repeat itself? Christy shrugged. Over-excited and tired, she thought sleepily that love had been golden. She could never turn back and had no desire to do so. Whether she liked it or not, Dan Gray was in her life and she wanted him to stay.

FOURTEEN

Santa Fe, 1974

Outside, on the wall, farolitos glowed in the cold, clear night air. The evergreens and conifers were weighed down with snow and, in the plaza, Christmas carillons were sounding. Indians had lit fires on the outskirts of the town and these shone red and gold, like a necklace of bright light.

Nolan drove from the hacienda to the clinic, stopping briefly to buy more strings of red chili ristras from a stall at the edge of the square. Then he hurried on, his face pensive. Normally, he bought Christy clothes for Christmas, but this year she was heavily pregnant, painting hard, though not well, and to say the least in a turbulent phase of her development. Nolan thought how love had changed his daughter, making her blossom. Surprisingly, the prospect of a child thrilled her, despite her sworn declaration never to love a man and never, ever to have children. But nothing assuaged the anguish she felt at being incapable of doing what she had always done with ease. Success seemed to have extinguished the bright flame of her talent and she was bereft. Without her painting, Christy felt that she did not really exist.

Nolan sighed, because he knew that work was not her only problem. When Dan proposed marriage, Christy refused and her father knew it was because she feared ending in tragedy like her grandmother and Louise. Nolan blamed himself for her fears and Amy for telling her about the family legacy of suicide. Impotent to help his daughter, he simply tried to support her and to conceal his own inner terror for her future. Christy had fallen victim to the dreaded syndrome of too much too soon, success at the very start of her career instead of a normal slow build towards the pinnacle of recognition. Fear had now completely crippled her creativity and Nolan debated if even time would help. He dreamed of her changing her mind and marrying Dan, who would protect her for the rest of her life. Then he stopped himself in mid-thought, realizing that Amy had been right and that for him love equalled protection. But what else could a man do with a fragile creature like Christy?

Nolan went at once to Dan's office and accepted a whisky and a tiny bowl of his favourite pistachio nuts.

Dan raised his glass.

'Where's Christy? I thought you might have brought her with you.'

'She's not finished decorating the house.'

'How's the new painting going?'

'Worse than the previous one. She's really lost her touch, Dan. I'm sure she'll find it again someday, because genius is genius after all, but success has just cut her off at the roots for the moment. She was too young and too inexperienced to take the strain and to a great extent I hold myself responsible. If it hadn't been for Amy, I'd have kept Christy in the house till she reached the age of forty-five, I'm just so terrified of something bad happening to her. She's always been vulnerable, or maybe I thought she was. I have a conscience about her a mile high, I can tell you, and I just don't know what to do. She knows what she's doing's bad but she just keeps on painting and hoping it'll come right someday.'

'She's tenacious. She'll make it.'

'If she doesn't crack up first.'

'How about the de Vandens? How are they reacting?'

'Christy's been avoiding them and they know it. They haven't seen the new stuff and when they do they'll have a blue fit. It just isn't Christy Pallister material.'

'That could be a real problem. They've believed in her from the beginning and any withdrawal of their support could deal a blow to her reputation.'

'They'll continue for another exhibition, maybe even two, but she'll have to come good by then or they'll never touch her again. I'm sure of it.'

Christy had decorated the chimney-breast with the traditional black and white angels from the Pueblo of Cochiti. The conifer boughs were in place and she had arranged red ristras over the door lintels. Throughout the house there was a scent of pine, a fragrance linked in her mind with home, love and family. For a few precious moments she sat alone, watching the night. It was only seven-thirty, but already she was sleepy. The child moved inside her and she thought of the past year and the wonderful times she and Dan had had together, the unforgettable moments at the Boulder House, in the countryside, in his plane en route to Albuquerque or for a weekend in paradise at Acapulco or Puerto Vallarta. Once, they had gone by car to a strangely beautiful, thinly populated settlement in Baja California, where they had rented a pastel pink house, watched pelicans diving on the shore and Pacific rollers smashing ruthlessly against the rocks. There, she had painted the only great canvasses created since her first exhibition, two big seascapes, one of fishermen catching mackerel in a vast circular net, the other of the ocean in all its restless torment, vivid in image and intensity.

Christy sat by the fire, sighing at the memory of the trip. She had wanted to stay in Baja, far from civilization, because she was happy and painting well. She smiled merrily as she recalled how she had taught Dan to swim and he had taught her about the stars. For hours on end, they had watched the sky at night and she had learned about Orion and the Plough, looking forward to the moment when he would end the lesson with kisses and caresses and love. She and Dan had really discovered each other during that trip. They had loved and laughed and been together day and night. They had grown together, become entwined, and he had told her she was the honeysuckle around the tree of his body, mind and soul, the perfume in his life. The image had stayed with her and Christy referred to it often when her confidence was on the wane. Eventually, Dan had had to return to his work at the clinic. No one could live on a pink cloud for ever and she had accepted it. Her second exhibition was getting nearer and she had come back, only to find herself once again empty of her usual vivacity and ferocity, the very ingredients that had made her famous.

The baby kicked and Christy remembered Paquita's words: *Boys are lazy, they don't move much. Girls dance from the day you first feel them.* If it was a girl, she would be called Libby Camille, after Dan's mother and her grandmother. Christy had read all the books available on giving birth. She had done her exercises in deep breathing and relaxation and was astounded to find that she was unafraid. Fearful of everything else in life, she could not comprehend why the coming event provoked nothing but positive reactions. She simply felt proud of her baby, happy with Dan and anxious to give their child the easiest possible entry into the world.

Christy turned on the television without sound and watched President Nixon talking to the nation. He had an interesting face, with chipmunk cheeks and a slightly Mafioso expression, good to paint and marvellous to caricature. When she turned up the sound, his voice and manner changed the entire image. She enjoyed the strange trickery of personality, that was the third dimension of all human beings. Then she turned to the presents Dan had bought, all wrapped in forest-green paper, and wondered what they could be. He was always original. Longing to open them, she nevertheless controlled her urge. She had painted the Boulder House for Dan, because he loved the place and so did she. The painting was in the form of a triptych, showing house and surrounding countryside from three different angles. Christy was thinking of Dan, when she saw Paquita hurrying towards her, her double chins wobbling merrily.

'Your father phoned to say he dines with Dr Gray. Then he'll come home with the doctor for the whole of Christmas. I am *so* happy. After Christmas, you go and stay at the Boulder House while your father is away and I go on holiday to my sister's place in Chilpancingo. That way you are not left alone when you get near your time.'

'Those two arrange everything between them!'

'Not *everything*. Your father want you to marry. Dr Gray want you to marry and I want you to marry too. So why don't you want to marry?'

'I will someday. Did you see this, Paquita? I'm in luck. It says here that Robert Redford's going to be a winner in the new film *The Great Gatsby* and that spring and summer fashions will be all thirties style. I shall have time to get my figure back before tight clothes are fashionable again. And Dan'll love all that filmy, romantic stuff.'

'He loves everything you wear, but don't change the subject. Since you got pregnant, your brains are like scrambled egg. Why do you hesitate to marry? He's rich and handsome and perfect and I love him and everyone loves him.'

'I love him too. He's the only man for me.'

'Then why not the marriage? Always you hesitate, like you can't decide or you can't dare. It's not a very big thing, you know. Already you live with him most of the time. Would a little piece of paper make so much difference?'

'It wouldn't change things for me, so I don't know why everyone keeps on about it.'

'I think you should marry him quick.'

'Why quick?'

'Before he changes his mind. When you get fat, fat, fat men change their minds.'

'I don't intend to get "fat, fat, fat", at least not for a long time and if a man changes his mind over externals he's not worth having.'

'No philosophy if you please!'

Paquita disappeared to the kitchen, laughing joyfully at the thought that soon the mistress of the house would be as fat as she, albeit because of her advanced pregnancy and not from habitual overeating.

Christy went to her room and changed into a caftan of green and gold silk velvet. When she had brushed her hair and checked her face, she went to the studio and looked at her paintings. They weren't bad, but they had little of the spirit of those in the first exhibition. She had chosen as her theme 'Home Sweet Home', in the hope that the critics would think the passivity intentional. The subdued palette was not her. The scenes of mothers and children, houses of past times, domestic scenes of everything from medieval cooks stuffing peacocks to Renaissance princes falconing were not her style either. But that was what had arrived in her head and she knew that an artist must paint his thoughts of the moment. The stillness of the paintings worried her most of all, because she had always painted with a restlessness and a passion that was evident. Since the last exhibition, she had been conscious of the need for

247

professionalism, the need to finish work for a given date and it had made her feel as if she was painting by obligation. But the de Vandens had faith in her and she must not let them down. Pregnant or not, jaded as she was, she must complete on time.

Christmas lunch was turkey stuffed with chestnuts, glazed in red sugar sauce and garnished with sobresadas and yellow pimentoes. The previous evening, friends had come for dinner. The farolitos had been lit and, after midnight Mass, they had enjoyed champagne on the covered terrace. Today was their private celebration, with Dan and Paquita serving at table and then sitting alongside to eat. Full of smiles, Paquita piled the doctor's plate as high as the Sangre de Cristo Mountains. Dan talked to Nolan about art and the fate of van Gogh, who lived a tragic life, only achieving fame after he was dead. Then, seeing Christy looking dejectedly at her plate, he took her hand.

'You're very quiet?'

'I'm tired after this marvellous lunch.'

'Go lie on the sofa and I'll bring you coffee and cake.'

When he had poured it and cut a slice of Christmas cake flavoured with rum, Dan took it over to Christy but found her already asleep. He turned to her father with a smile.

'She looks like a Renaissance Madonna when she sleeps.'

'She's often tired of late. She works too hard and she's unhappy with what she produces. Baby's due in a short time and then there'll be two months before the exhibition opens. I just don't know how she's going to find the strength to finish everything that has to be done.'

'She'll do it. Christy's a professional and she knows that it's important. Being tired's natural in the last two months of a pregnancy in any case. She'll soon get over that once she has the child in her arms and can go riding again. She really misses her sprees with Lancelot every morning.'

'Lancelot's a bastard. I tried to ride him the other day and he threw me down like I was a horse thief.'

'He's a one woman horse, like me. I'm a one woman man.'

Nolan looked wistfully at Dan, wishing that his daughter could appreciate the quality of the man in her life. Perhaps Christy knew it. Perhaps she was just scared of making any commitment. There was something very childlike about her that was part of her charm. He felt apprehensive without really knowing why. After all, there were lots of modern women who just didn't like the idea of marriage.

When Christy woke, she sat in front of the fire with Dan, examining the presents he had bought her and listening as he explained the significance of each.

'This is the start of a new collection for you to keep in your room at the Boulder House.'

'Tell me about them. What did they hold in past ages?'

'I don't know, unguents, honey, oil, myrrh? They're all very old, all collectors' pieces. That one's Persian, Sassanian period, motif of a three-dimensional lion that extends as a handle. Date about AD 500. This one's Japanese, Kamakura period, with the bird and flower motif of the era. The other one's Chinese, T'ang Dynasty. I like Chinese ones, because of the symbolism. That's a cassia tree and nearby the hare pounding an elixir of immortality. You remember the Kangxi bowl at the Boulder House?'

'The eighteenth-century copper one?'

'Yes, that has wonderful symbolism: peaches for long life, bats for happiness and a deer for wealth and prosperity.'

'What do the Chinese use to bring good luck to artists who aren't working well?'

'Nothing. The Chinese are very wise. They know that talent always wins in the end, even when it gets tired and goes to sleep for a while. For the moment, you have to develop an on-off switch about your work, Christy. No point in tormenting yourself all the time and going over the problem like a dog chasing its tail. You do it all the time, day in day out, and it gets you nowhere.'

'I'll try, Dan, but I feel suffocated, like the sky fell in on my head and smothered me.'

The baby was born in the worst snowstorm the area had had in fifty years. Christy and Dan were having a late lunch at the Boulder House when the pains began. There was no possibility of driving to the clinic and none of taking the plane up. Dan called Amparo, gave his instructions and the old guest bedroom, now empty, was scrubbed down, disinfected and prepared for any contingency, except Martians landing and a declaration of war. Dan was nervous, but determined not to show it. Christy was calm and relieved the moment had come.

'Dan, *do* stop pacing. This could take hours. We must relax.'

'She won't take hours. She'll probably arrive running.'

'Try not to worry. You've gone quite pale.'

'Doctors are a real pain in the ass when they're ill, Christy. They know too much and they're scared of things going wrong.'

'But you're not ill!'

'I feel very green.'

'I love you.'

'That's cured me for the moment. Say it again in half an hour.'

The birth was without complication, other than the

news that Santa Fe had been cut off by record snowfalls. The baby was born at twenty past ten that evening, weighing in at seven pounds on Amparo's kitchen scales and making enough noise to wake folk snoring soundly in Los Angeles. Christy was ecstatic, Dan exhausted, though he rallied when Amparo appeared with the family, carrying champagne and a pound pot of Beluga caviar. It was five in the morning before they went to bed, all of them euphoric that a new member of the family had made her appearance. From that very moment, Miss Libby Camille Gray would be loved and cherished and directed with deep affection.

Alone, wide awake and happier than she had ever been, Christy lay in her four-poster hung with Chinese silk and looked adoringly at her child, with her heart-shaped face and tiny hands. The baby was perfect and she and Dan were happy. For the moment, the studio full of strangely subdued paintings was forgotten.

The period after LC's birth was as near paradise as Christy had ever known. She and Dan spent every waking moment together, he collecting wood for the fire with Matteo and arranging it in the newly built store. The expeditions to collect wood were inter-spersed with periods using an electric saw or drinking hot rum and nutmeg punch to keep out the cold. Christy stayed in bed late, but went out each afternoon to sketch the snowy landscape. Around four, she adjourned to the kitchen, where Amparo was pre-paring the evening meal. She loved to sit drinking a glass of wine in the kitchen, where the beams were hung with hams and pungent herbs grown in terracotta pots on the terrace. One afternoon, she found Dan sitting on a log, looking out into the wide, open spaces beyond the house.

'Are you all right, Dan?'

'I'm great. How's LC?'

'She's content, quiet, no trouble at all.'

'We'll have to have three or four more.'

'I'd like that.'

'But not out of wedlock. I want us to marry, Christy. You're the only woman in the world for me and I want you to be my wife. Will you accept?'

She threw her arms around him and smothered him with kisses.

'I love it when you propose. I love *you*, but right now I'm so happy I'm scared to change anything. I'm in a period of intense change within myself and I've known it, we've both known it, for a long time. I need to settle down and get my life in order again. Our relationship makes me happy because it's beautiful, but it makes me conscious of lots of phantoms from the past that I have to exorcize.'

'You're talking about Camilla and your mother and suicide linked with falling in love and getting married?'

'Yes, Dan. When Camilla married, she stopped work as a mannequin and started on the slippery slide to catastrophe. After the death of her first husband, Mother married Nolan and gave up flying, because he didn't want her to take risks. After that, she just fell apart.'

'I don't want or need you to give up painting.'

'No, but I do. I never really want to paint nowadays. I just think about you all the time and want to be with you and I'm scared I'll make you the reason for never painting again, never facing up to the responsibilities of life and the challenges of fame. I'm anxious on all my levels, Dan. I want to be with you and for us to stay together for always, but I don't want to get married. I need to deny myself the possibility of hiding behind someone for the rest of my life, of abdicating the responsibility to develop as a person and as an artist.'

Dan sighed, but concealed his disappointment,

understanding the terrible tension Christy's malaise was causing her.

'I'll ask again when you're painting well. Now, we'd best go inside and see what Amparo's cooking. Once the sun goes down it's too cold for long conversations in the snow.'

They made a home movie of LC in her cot, in the bath and going out for a ride in a pram decorated with holly and pine cones. They converted one of the small store-rooms into a bedroom that interconnected with Christy's room. Disdaining conventional childish colours, they evolved a Chinese scheme for the nursery that complemented Christy's décor, putting LC in a setting of red lacquer, dragon chairs and a hand-painted frieze complete with lotus flowers and gilded carp. The cot was of Brazilian zebra wood inlaid with brass ormolu and bronze. The overhead lights of amber-tinted glass from a Venetian palazzo. Dan looked the room over with satisfaction.

'She'll grow up the only baby in Santa Fe with a T'ang tallow marble lion as a playmate.'

When Nolan returned to the hacienda, he went at once to the studio and looked at Christy's latest paintings. On the easel there was a snow scene, quite beautiful and splendidly executed, as was the scene of a baby in a cradle surrounded by striped cats with flower posies in their paws. For a moment, he felt sure she had found her touch again. Then he looked at the other paintings she had done for the exhibition and sighed. Apart from the two seascapes, there was nothing but light, dom-esticated scenes any artist of talent could have painted. Downcast, Nolan returned to the living-room and col-lided with Christy, holding LC dressed in a Chinese silk robe. On seeing her father, she kissed him tenderly and presented his grandchild.

'Daddy, meet Miss Libby Camille Gray, born in the worst snowstorm Santa Fe's had since 1920.'

Nolan took the baby in his arms and held her to his heart, tears filling his eyes as he remembered the moment when Louise had given him Christy and he had loved the tiny child as he had never loved anything before. Looking at the baby's wide blue eyes, he noted the mouth, the tuft of blondish hair, the determined chin.

'She's just like Dan but with your violet-blue eyes.'

'Dan told me all babies have blue eyes but they could change colour later.'

'Hers are *violet-blue* and very distinctive. I must get my camera. God, I shall probably never work again! I'll just bore the ass off all my friends showing photographs of my grandchild. I've always had a horror of folk who do that.'

'Dan's at a medical seminar in Boston.'

'Then I'll have you all to myself. He'll be back for the exhibition, I hope?'

'Yes, and Amy's coming over. She knows I'm scared and not optimistic of the critics' reactions, so she's booked her flight.'

The gallery had been decorated specially for the exhibition in celadon green, *bois de rose* and stone. In the entrance, giant arrangements of scented grasses and dried flowers had been placed on either side of an 1890 Mary Cassat in pastel on paper, of Hélène de Septeuil with a green parrot. The painting of the child and the parrot was a perfect way of setting the scene for the new exhibition, with its mothers and daughters from bygone ages, its depictions of domestic life from medieval times to the present day. As before, each painting was impeccably researched, each one painted in the style of the period. The difference was in the atmosphere and the artist's manner of attacking her subject. The colours were pastel or sepia, giving a dreamlike impression that came as a shock after the violence and vivacity of the first exhibition. The domestic angle jarred to many of those present, because it did not conform to their idea of Christy Pallister's character and disappointment was evident in the faces of the viewers the moment they entered. Certain friends bought in order to own a Pallister painting, the general feeling being that though this was a minor exhibition it was wise to stock up. Jokes were made that the artist's big production of the year had been Libby Camille and people smiled mechanically, as if to forgive Christy. The critics left as soon as they had finished their canapes, without asking for interviews.

Deke de Vanden looked at nine red sold stars on the paintings and remembered the previous exhibition when every single canvas had sported a red star before the end of the evening. His wife had been pushing hard with an investment banker from LA, but she had failed. Mitzi's face was tense as she turned to Amy.

'Everyone here's disappointed and so are Deke and I. Don't say so to Christy, we don't want to upset her. It's certainly a subdued and over-controlled group of paintings. Any idea what went wrong? They aren't at all like Christy's previous work.'

'We think she got scared of not coming up to her previous standard and just couldn't create. It's a common problem, not only for painters, but for actors who win an Oscar and writers who win a Pulitzer or a Goncourt. They get scared of not being great all the time – which, of course, no one can.'

Christy watched the dealers and Amy talking, then turned to Dan, trying to conceal her inner panic.

'Everyone's got faces like a funeral. I let them down,

Dan. I should have cancelled the exhibition and waited till I felt better, but I'm so scared of never wanting to paint again, I really *needed* to deliver.'

'The paintings aren't bad, Christy. They're just different. Folk expected fireworks and virtuoso Christy Pallister. Instead of passion they got control and they don't like it. Buyers want you to repeat yourself, you know. It's one of the problems of success.'

'I'll never repeat myself. I want to make progress and explore new paths. But that's surely not what I've done here. I'm so angry with myself, Dan. I'm so ashamed that I let everyone down.'

'You'll do better next time.'

'I might do worse. I'm not the most confident person in the world and when I get something wrong I tend to get so terrified of never getting it right I go worse and worse the more I try.'

'I don't think so and anyway this is Saturday and pessimism's not allowed Saturdays.'

'I hope LC's okay.'

'Sure she is. She and Paquita are probably eating steak, French fries, chili con carne and enchilladas by now.'

Christy laughed delightedly at the image of Paquita feeding the baby grown-up food. Then she went over to talk with Mitzi and her husband.

'I bombed, didn't I?'

Deke smiled wistfully, conscious of her anguish.

'Not entirely. The paintings are beautiful, but they're not what people expected of you and they're not very commercial. Folk expect passion and surprises galore. You'll get it right next time, I know you will.'

There were no interviews, no effusive clients queueing for a painting, just Nolan and Dan trying to be cheerful as they drove back to the hacienda on a cold, clear night. Christy fell silent, anguish surfacing and being smothered by iron self-control, so as not to hurt her father or trouble Dan. But inside she was torn apart by the knowledge that she had failed. This had been her chance to consolidate her incredible success. Instead, she had taken a safe route, unable to come up with anything new. In doing so, she risked being hailed as a flash in the pan instead of remaining 'the art discovery of the century'. A solitary tear ran down Christy's cheek and she prayed fervently that this state of artistic impotence would pass. But when she thought of painting, her mind rebelled and when she thought of Dan she became panic stricken. He had met her when her career was at its peak, when she was someone special. He loved winners and winning and might well lose interest and move on if she proved to be just another young person with the talent to impress but not the talent to sustain. Maeterlinck had said that what matters above all else is to last. Could she learn to stay the course? Or was it already too late?

Christy went to her room on arrival, leaving the two men to drink whisky together and to analyse, as she was analysing, what really went wrong with Christy Pallister.

FIFTEEN

Paris, 1978

The trip to Paris was something new, a working holiday suggested by Bob Hayman, star of cinema, real life and his own over-ripe fantasies. Hayman had bought three large canvasses from Christy's first exhibition and the snow scene from her second. She had not touched a canvas in the three years since the failure that had paralysed her creativity. During these barren years, she had raised her child and loved Dan. On one level she was deeply content. On another she was in profound torment, asking herself a thousand times a day if she would ever paint again. When Hayman had offered her a month's contract as 'artistic adviser' on his film, Christy had accepted eagerly. It was a chance to do something different. She wondered if the cinema was her future, an outlet for creativity blocked. Or was it just a new excuse not to paint? The actor normally played western heroes, or comic roles in which he excelled, with his twinkling eyes and the endearing quality of never being honest with anyone, least of all himself. This time he was to play a man in love with an artist. He had asked Christy 'to advise and give authenticity to the painting scenes'. She had accepted at once.

Since her arrival in Paris, she had sketched the usual scenes new to her but familiar to everyone else: queues of people buying oysters for the traditional Sunday lunch; a kiosk vendor grilling fish on a tiny charcoal brazier and then eating it at a fold-up table but with a fine linen serviette; a butcher in bloody apron, sipping

258

vin rouge at the zinc of the local bar; sparks flying from a knife-grinder's wheel and the luminescence of Paris by night, like an amber halo around a mysterious crescent-shaped moon. She had eaten alone in her hotel or the bistro across the road and had been to the cinema five times to see old American films in their original language, films she had never had time to see before. *Jaws* gave her nightmares. *Love Story* made her cry so much she was convinced her mascara would run clean down to her knees. And *All the President's Men* made her profoundly relieved that she had never had anything to do with politics. Alone in bed at night, Christy thought wryly that not many young women came to Paris to go to the American cinema! But she was happy in the knowledge that she was due to start work and was hoping to learn something. Glancing at the French fashion magazines, she was amused by the huge shoulder pads designers were going to try to impose on women, but relieved to see that the bulky seventies outline, so long in vogue, had been fined down and shortened. Things were changing. Christy hoped that she was too.

One evening she was kissing Dan goodbye fervently over the telephone, when she saw Bob Hayman standing in the hotel foyer, grinning at her. He was immensely tall, burned cinnamon by the sun, blond, lithe and confident of everything.

'Hi there, I wish I could meet someone who kissed the phone like that when she'd spoken to *me*.'

'I'm sure you're not short of affection, Mr Hayman.'

'Call me Bob. You want to go to dinner? I'm going to La Pomme on the Ile de la Cité. Come with me?'

'I'd like that.'

'The restaurant's right opposite Yves Montand's house.'

'Does that make it a better restaurant?'

'No, I just said it to impress you. Are you working on a new exhibition, Christy?'

'I should be. I'm due to show in four months' time but I haven't been inspired. I haven't even started painting.'

'Inspiration comes to women in bed.'

'Not to me!'

'You're beautiful, you know that?'

Christy smiled, amused that she was with one of the world's great sex symbols and he left her cold. Men like Hayman always said the same things, wanted the same things and thought that making love cured everything from influenza to hammer toes. With Dan it was different. Only with him did she feel secure that he said what he felt, what he knew to be true. Homesickness swept over her and she wished the month were at its end and that she was en route to Santa Fe.

The restaurant was tiny, wood panelled, with an owner who cooked delicious and original dishes and served them herself. There were four tables that seated sixteen people. Fascinated by the woman's exuberant personality and Riviera tan, Christy watched in rapt admiration. When the wine was served, she raised her glass and smiled across the table at her host.

'To your new film, Bob.'

'To you, Christy. We never met before, because I sent a guy who handles my investments to your exhibition, but I hope we can be good friends.'

A flashbulb popped as they raised their glasses, startling Christy, but leaving Hayman unperturbed.

'I resigned myself to flashbulbs when I got famous. Photographers are all born on another planet and they don't have human sensibilities. My wife divorced me when our LA house became a kind of challenge for them. Once they even broke into my bathroom and photographed me in the nude. Can't only show your prick to the woman of your choice when you're famous. Everyone wants to look!'

The morning edition of the *Herald Tribune* was full of Hayman's new romance with painter Christy Pallister.

Christy drove to the studios to start work, continuing on past the gate when she saw a crowd of photographers grouped outside. From a nearby café, she rang her French counterpart, Arlette.

'Why are all those reporters outside the studios?'

'They're waiting for you, Christy. Hayman's done his publicity stunt and latched on to you because this is a film about a man who falls in love with a famous artist. He's never anything but obvious, you know.'

'I'm going home. I'll not stay for another minute!'

'You'll be in breach of your contract if you leave Paris.'

'I never agreed to be used as publicity fodder for Bob Hayman's virility. I'm going home and I won't *ever* come back.'

Christy rolled her canvasses, paid her bill, packed her bags and took a taxi to the airport. There, she boarded the next flight to New York. Before take-off, she rang her father and asked him to meet her at the airport, explaining what Hayman had done as a publicity stunt to link the film's story-line with real life. Nolan's voice seemed strained. He'd seen the article and was angry. Worse, Dan had too. Christy felt close to panic. She had wanted a change, a moment of stimulation, hoping that her desire to paint might return with the visit to Paris. Instead, she risked losing Dan.

When the captain announced that they were coming into Kennedy, Christy cheered inwardly. Even the queue for passport control would be welcome, because she was almost home. She left the plane with a smile and walked briskly towards immigration. She was entering the transit lounge for her connecting flight to Albuquerque, when she heard a familiar voice.

'I came on the plane to meet you and I slept nearly all the way. So did Daddy and he snored!'

Christy ran to pick up her daughter and to hug Dan.

'I'm so pleased to see you, Dan.'

'Me too. You looked tired. Let's go eat. There's plenty of time before our plane leaves. Relax, Christy, you're on your way home and we won't accept any contracts again from guys like Hayman. Next time you do a film you do it for Milius or Spielberg or Coppola. They have imagination and they're real creators. You'll work well with them. Hayman's just starlet fodder.'

LC skipped alongside, delighted by her mother's return.

'Did you bring me a prezzy, Mummy?'

'Sure did. I've brought a French green velvet frog and a beret and some chocolates shaped like hearts. And I told everyone about you.'

'What did you say?'

'I said LC's favourite word is "no", and she paints lovely pictures.'

On arrival home, Christy painted Paris, using her sketches of the city as the basis. It was at the hacienda that Christy finished her Paris paintings and where the de Vandens came to see them. Dan had already told her that she was too perturbed by the Hayman incident to be in control of her craft. Nolan was in agreement. Paquita loved the paintings and so did Mitzi de Vanden. Deke said little except that they would do a small exhibition for three days. Christy agreed and had her first row with Dan because of her decision.

'Those paintings are the worst you've ever done. They're not only unfinished, they seem unbalanced! You just *don't* realize that you have to get your life and your mind straight before you can paint with all the genius you possess.'

'I have a contract with the de Vandens to do this exhibition, Dan. I don't want to break my word.'

'In future don't sign contracts. Paint when you have something to say, when you really feel something strong and deep and telling. Don't paint at all when you're empty. If you can only be a great painter every five years that's fine. You'll have rarity value and your work'll bring more than Picasso's.'

'You don't understand, Dan!'

'I understand better than you do. This is no time to play the terrier and persist in trying to exhibit when you're not mistress of your game. You could be ruined if you exhibit those postcard views of Paris. Have you any idea how they compare with the originality of what you did in your first exhibition?'

'I don't want to live my life with everything I paint being compared with my first exhibition. I have to move on, even if what I do isn't perfect.'

Christy ran to her room and locked the door, leaving Nolan and Dan together. Nolan spoke with all the wisdom of his years.

'We all have to make mistakes, Dan. That's how we learn. Christy's making a mistake, but perhaps it's for the best. When the critics see those works they'll slaughter her or just ignore her. Whichever route they choose, the heat'll be off, because she'll be finished as a serious artist. Fame'll become a memory and she'll start painting again and maybe next time she'll really make it and sustain it.'

'I can't stand by and let her commit professional suicide, Nolan.'

'She's lost and she has to find herself again. An artist who loses her capacity for self-criticism isn't an artist at all. You know that as well as I do.'

Christy sobbed until her eyes turned scarlet. Then she took a shower, lay on her bed, put blue drops into her eyes and tried to think straight. Dan's words had cut her to the core. Yet even in her distressed state, she appreciated his honesty. Only Dan had the guts to say what he really thought. But what to do? If he was right, the exhibition would ruin her. If he was wrong, nothing would be lost in keeping her word to the de Vandens. If she was ruined, all the nightmares of the past would be over and she could settle down to marriage in the full and final knowledge that she had tried but failed. If the exhibition was a success, she would be liberated from her fear and able to give all her attention to Dan and LC.

Christy did not realize that she had left out the human element, that failure to her would be unacceptable and even destructive.

The exhibition was poorly attended. Not a single painting was sold. At the end of the first hour, Deke went to talk to his wife in the office.

'Not often you're wrong, Mitzi, but this time you boobed. Christy's finished. Did you ever see such banality? In a year rich in images, she comes up with Paris pavement style!'

'She'll come back.'

'I won't handle her again. She's unstable and these days talent isn't enough. Artists have to be bankable, dependable and adaptable to current trends. She just isn't together.'

'Van Gogh's lucky to be dead!'

Christy drove home, replaying her conversation with the gallery owner while Dan and Nolan sat in silence. Deke had shown her the cover of an Italian *Vogue*, depicting a nude model wearing a medieval torture helmet and leather thongs crossed between her breasts.

'Sadomaso's in this season,' he had said. 'Why

264

couldn't you tap *that*? At least we'd have got some publicity.'

Christy had replied that she had seen protests from women's organizations at the Frox advertisements, showing a nude on her knees wearing a dog lead and being 'trained' by a man wearing the company's blue jeans. She had not wanted to follow *that* trend. Deke had become incoherent with rage. Christy winced as she remembered his verdict on her exhibition: *This stuff belongs in a bistro!* She wondered if the critics would say the same or if they would even bother to file copy.

'The art find of the century' had bitten the dust for the second and last time. It was then that Christy felt a curious sensation she could not identify, a kind of defiance, anger, even fury that entered her mind like the burning chilis in a Mexican stew. That night she mulled over the feeling until she fell asleep.

In the morning, Christy stayed in bed until Paquita came with her breakfast. The housekeeper looked perturbed when she asked for the morning papers, but at Christy's insistence returned with a pile of papers, some marked with red.

'Dr Gray went out early to buy everything and I wish he didn't!'

Christy ate her breakfast, showered and stood at the bedroom window, gazing at the aspens that coloured the mesa of Santa Fe old gold. Then, one by one, she read the reviews: *Christy Pallister equals disaster . . . Give up Christy, you're washed up . . . Exhibition of mediocrity from once great artist.* Tears began to fall, but she read on, as if needing to know the worst . . . *Exhibition farce by local artist . . . Paris banalities by Pallister.* Panic hit her suddenly and she wanted to run, but there was nowhere to go. There was no doubt about it, she had lost her priceless gift. From this moment on, she could no longer call herself an independent woman, nor even a real artist. She would live with a man who knew she had failed, a man who disliked failure as much as she did. How long would it last? Waves of fear made her nauseous and she lay back on the bed, staring at the ceiling but seeing nothing at all. The reviews ran through her mind like tickertape through a machine: *Christy Pallister equals disaster . . . Paris banalities . . . once great artist*. Had she really sunk so low? Had she really lost her judgement?

When Dan entered the room Christy was crying hysterically, as the full realization of the enormity of the catastrophe hit her. He looked down, finding her beauty even more disturbing than usual, knowing that she was an unquiet presence, a volcano ready to explode. If only she could explode on canvas as she had before! But he feared that she might explode into an unstable state from which he could never retrieve her. He took her in his arms, speaking with love and tenderness.

'There are some women who can have a child every year without problem. Others can only have them every three or four years. Doing an exhibition's a bit like having a child, except that it takes twice as long, maybe more. You've worked too hard, too fast and you're too scared to succeed. You have to re-evaluate yourself as a woman and as an artist and make up your mind to paint only when you really feel the need to do so.'

'They'll never take me seriously again.'

'Who won't?'

'The critics, the de Vandens, no one.'

'To hell with other people! Dammit, Christy, it's what *you* think that counts. The critics'll respond when you paint well and you won't paint at all till you get over the shock of your first success.'

'Will I ever, Dan?'

'That's going to depend on your force of character and your real desire to come back. It seems to me there are lots of problems here. You've lived an over-sheltered life, you've never been in need or in trouble, so you're like a newborn, with no protective cover of experience. Apart from the tragedy of your mother's death, when you were three, you haven't been placed under stress.'

'And the first time it happens, I crack up?'

'The first time a man runs a marathon he feels pretty beat, but finally he gets to the point where he can pace himself. The same'll happen to you. Sudden fame thrilled you, but it broke your back. Now you're experiencing failure and it'll be a bitter pill to swallow. Learn from it, become a bigger person. Don't ever let failure diminish you. Force yourself to learn from it and become bigger and better and greater.'

'It's easy for you, Dan. You're a success and you always have been.'

'Wrong. I was the poor boy who got excluded from invitations at college because he didn't have the right clothes for fancy occasions or even a car to get there. I had to run pretty hard to get where I am, never forget that.'

'Maybe I don't have what it takes.'

'Could be. You have it as an artist, in terms of talent, but talent isn't enough. You have to learn to ride the roller coaster of professional life. You have to mature first. You can help hurry the process along by calming down, thinking hard and remembering you're not alone in this. You have me and LC and your father and Amy and we all love you. Think, Christy. Count your advantages and stop dwelling on negative things.'

But Christy burst into floods of tears again as the reviews returned to her mind. The nice times were over. Yet again tragedy had followed triumph in her life and she was running scared. Unable to find reserves within herself, unable to control her grief, she wailed like a five-year-old. She was still sobbing at midday, and almost out of control by evening. Nolan rang Amy to ask what she advised. Dan administered a sedative, wondering if he should call the clinic's consultant psychiatrist. He decided against it. Christy simply had to grow up. Perhaps everyone had been too solicitous of her fragility in the past. Perhaps it was time to force the issue, to make her confront her fears.

For weeks Christy stayed in her room at the hacienda, refusing to go out, to meet visitors, except Dan, who had moved into the spare room. She cared for her child, but barely ate or slept and refused to take calls except from Amy, who phoned daily from San Francisco to encourage her. In the hacienda, Christy felt safe, hiding from life, reverting to childhood patterns of behaviour – until the day when Dan lost his patience.

'Christy, this situation has to stop. I'm going back to the Boulder House now. Either you come back with me and quit playing little girl lost or you see our resident psychiatrist. You just cannot hide from the world for ever. You have to get up off your ass and fight your depression or you're going to end up in a clinic for good.'

'I can't change!'

'You mean you won't.'

'I'm scared to go anywhere!'

'Then you can stay here and rot. I can't stand your fears one minute longer.'

Christy burst into tears and threw herself down on the bed, stopping with a start when Dan shouted at her for the first time ever.

'Christy, get up, right now! Get dressed and go wait for me in the car. *Now!* I'll find LC in the garden.'

When Christy stayed where she was, stupefied by his anger, Dan became furious.

'Get up *immediately*! I won't wait and I won't come back if you don't come with me.'

Profoundly shocked and terrified of losing Dan, Christy dressed and ran out to the car. She had not thought to say goodbye to her father, nor packed her things. Only love had propelled her to action after weeks of incapacity. When LC appeared, Christy took the child in her arms and kissed her, barely noticing the speed at which Dan drove towards the Boulder House. Confused thoughts raced through her mind. She must make an effort, so Dan would not stop loving her. Dear God, how he had shouted! He was mad with anger at her stupidity and her cowardice! She must *try*. She repeated the word like a mantra, to give her strength.

In the weeks that followed, Christy did just that, trying as she had never tried before to grow, to learn, to progress. Gradually, she began to win her battle with her fear of suicide and of failure. She began to go out sketching and even to drive again. And slowly, with Dan's help, the nightmare of the reviews began to fade from her mind.

It was a windy day, the sky in cumuli, like a Dali painting. In the low, pink town of Santa Fe, the tamarisk trees twitched, as gusts blew dust from the cactus lands that lay to the south.

Christy drove to the last house in town, honked her car horn and two little girls ran out. They were dressed in navy and white like LC, and it was also their first day at school. Eyeing the wilderness that stretched to the horizon after the house, Christy shuddered. There was nothing between here and the Mexican border, nothing but emptiness and trees bent into submission by the wind. She drove off in the direction of the Sarah Clayborne School for Under Fives. LC and the twins were chattering like magpies. LC was most concerned by the contents of her friends' lunch baskets.

Christy smiled as she listened to the little women,

now nearly four, in the back of the car. She turned into the fashionable Canyon Road and was almost at the school, when a car shot out of a parking lot on her left, causing her to swerve fiercely to the right to avoid being hit. Heart pounding, she manoeuvred to pass the careless driver and put herself in the path of a refrigerated lorry coming from an intersecting street on the right. There was no time to react. The driver had no chance at all of avoiding her.

Christy felt the car overturn, heard the children scream and the lorry's power brakes clamping to a halt. Through the mist of shock, she became aware of people crying out. Sirens sounded. Then the car was righted and put on its four wheels. The twins were crying.

Christy felt blood on her chin and touched the spot where her lip was cut. Stunned, she stroked a swelling on her forehead where she had hit the windscreen. Then, she realized that LC had made no sound at all. She struggled to sit up and, turning, saw that the side of the car where her daughter was sitting had taken maximum impact. LC was trapped in a mass of broken, tangled metal, an ominous red stain spreading from her shoulder to her waist. Panic screamed in Christy's mind as she leapt from the car, almost falling, because she was disorientated from her own injuries. She cried out for help and a couple comforted her. The woman spoke reassuringly.

'Calm down. The ambulance is on its way, and the fire brigade in case they can't get the child out.'

'Oh my God, *please* call Dan!'

'Is he your husband?'

'Yes. He's director of the Santa Rosa Clinic. *Please* hurry and call him for me right now.'

The woman passed Christy to her husband, who helped her to a roadside seat. Blue lights flashed on police cars, red ones on ambulances, as they converged on the scene. Her vision blurred, Christy saw two of everything, but she went to the side of the car and tried to touch LC's hand. When that was impossible, she returned to the driver's seat and sat there, her arm outstretched to reach her. Praying silently, she watched as special equipment was brought, LC freed and rushed into a waiting ambulance. Christy stumbled after her, weaving dazedly, as if she were drunk. A paramedic stopped her entering the ambulance.

'You can follow in the second ambulance, ma'am. They'll have to carry out special procedures on the child so you can't go with her.'

'I'm her mother!'

'Come with me, ma'am. You can see your daughter when she gets to the clinic.'

Christy was walking to the other ambulance, when Dan arrived, took in the scene at a glance and helped her into his car. Shock began to edge into her mind, making her feel as if her brain were lost in the fog. He spoke sharply to bring her back.

'I know you're shocked but I have to know exactly what happened for LC's sake. Tell me, Christy. You're being very brave, just be extra brave and explain *everything*.'

She tried, finishing with, 'It wasn't the truck driver's fault.'

'It wasn't yours, either. Did you see the driver of the car?'

'A young boy in a yellow Oldsmobile. A local, I think. I can't remember.'

Dan drove behind the ambulance, helping Christy to a wheelchair on arrival at the clinic.

'LC will be in emergency. I'll go right down and check on her condition. You just stay here and let Dr Scarman take care of you.'

'Come and tell me how she is, Dan.'

'Of course I will.'

Dan went at once to emergency, his face grim, his heart pounding from fear that his child might not survive. He had seen enough to know that LC's injuries were serious. At almost four years of age, the child was well, strong and vital. But would she survive? He hurried in and took the preliminary report sheet from the computer.

Libby Camille Gray. Aged three years eleven months. Compound fracture right arm, right leg, right shoulder, right hip. Hairline fracture of cranium. Possible artificial pneumothorax. Internal bleeding. Immediate splenectomy to be considered.

Dan sighed, unable to take his eyes off the child he loved. LC had a fifty-fifty chance of survival, if the internal damage was not too severe. He touched her hand, and left her to the team of experts in accident surgery. Then, alone, he walked to the clinic chapel and sat gazing at the cross painted by a local Indian artist, its halo radiating sunrays, giving the illusion of light and hope. He was on his knees praying when his secretary came to tell him that Nolan had arrived. Dan rose and went to the office to meet him.

'I came at once. How bad is it, Dan?'

'Christy's concussed. We're checking her over, but I'm sure she'll be all right. Shocked, of course.'

'And LC?'

'It's bad, Nolan. They'll be operating shortly. She has maybe a fifty-fifty chance.'

Nolan turned tallow pale and sat immobile, willing himself to be calm, to act like a grandfather should act in a sudden and calamitous emergency.

'Do whatever you have to do, Dan, no matter what it costs, no matter what we have to do or who we have to

272

bring in to save the child. I feel very helpless, but I want to offer whatever resources I have – everything I have, if it'll help. Shall I go see Christy? Do you need blood? I'm the same grouping as LC.'

'We don't need it for the moment, but we might. Go and see Christy and reassure her that it wasn't her fault.'

'Is it true?'

'Yes, she wasn't to blame.'

'Thank God for that.'

'Don't tell her how bad it is with LC. We'll wait and see how the operation goes before we talk about that.'

Nolan watched his daughter, as she stared at a spectacular sunset, an orange ball sun that seemed to be balancing on a turbulent sea of deep purple. Dan had come and gone throughout the afternoon, his anguish evident. Now, they were waiting to know if LC would live. She had survived surgery, but had gone into cardiac arrest in the intensive care unit. She was now being monitored by every expert Dan could find, aided by a battery of the very latest electronic equipment. These first hours would be crucial. If LC survived until morning, there was a chance that she would soon be out of danger. If not, they would know before midnight.

Christy moved slowly, almost trancelike in her shock. Then she saw how pale and tense her father was and kissed his cheeks.

'Go home, Daddy. I'll call you if there's any news.'

'I love you, Christy. Please don't blame yourself for all this. It wasn't your fault. The police are searching for the boy in the yellow car, which was stolen. There'll be charges against him when they find him.'

'Blaming him won't help LC.'

Nolan held her to his heart for a moment. Then he hurried from the clinic and drove towards the hacienda, his eyes streaming tears as he thought of LC and remembered her laughter and her grim determination, so reminiscent of Christy's at the same age. Would she laugh again? Would she live? Or worse, would she return to the hacienda, a pale, silent shadow of the child she had been? He went to bed immediately on arrival at the house, but could not sleep. Suddenly everything had gone wrong for Christy. The very foundations of her life were rocking precariously, like a carefully constructed pack of cards blown away in a storm.

Christy sat alone in the darkness, thinking of her child. She couldn't help feeling responsible. She had been so busy avoiding one car she had forgotten to watch traffic coming from the right at the intersection. She had forgotten to send some new sketches to the de Vandens and also to buy supplies of canvas. She had forgotten what it was like not to forget, her discipline gone with the wind, her depression hidden so that outwardly she seemed normal, but inwardly was incapable of coping. Was this why Camilla had killed herself? Had she also reached the strange and bewildering point of no return? And Louise? It was known that she had suffered from post-natal depression. Christy frowned. Depression often ran in families. Was that what had gone wrong in *her* life? Had shock at the sudden fame turned elation into depression, so she could not rise again to the heights of her talent? Treatment had not existed in Camilla's day and minimally in Louise's. Now it was known that action and an attractive goal in life were the antidotes to the crippling condition. But action was just what she seemed unable to achieve.

Christy's eyes turned steely as she thought of her child lying in intensive care, fighting for her life, her spleen removed, her insides bleeding. God damn it, she must snap out of her condition or be unworthy of LC's love and respect. Tears fell as she thought of the tiny body and the injuries sustained. She must find a way to cure herself of her malaise, her insufficiencies, her crass stupidity, her cowardice. If she was incapable of physical action, she must use mental action and occupy herself with analysing *why*, at the height of her success, she had fallen victim to failure mentality. The answer, Christy felt sure, lay in her childhood and the heritage of the past. What had Camilla and Louise had in common that destroyed their successful and seemingly enviable lives? If she had inherited it, she would cut it from her mind and body like the abscess it was in danger of becoming. She would do that for LC, no matter what the price in anguish or sheer suffering.

Christy rose and began to pace the room, exhausted, shocked, hollow-eyed, but suddenly fiercely determined to change. From somewhere nearby, the soft strains of 'Love me Tender' came to her ears and she listened, her face filled with sadness. The song brought back memories of her earliest childhood, when Amy had sung it to her to send her to sleep. Was love enough? Christy knew that it was. For love of Dan she would find her courage. For love of LC, she would become a real person, filling in the deficiencies fabricated by a loving but fear-ridden upbringing. Decision made, Christy closed her eyes, to cut out the sight of the empty bed at her side, the bed LC would occupy if ever she emerged from intensive care. She must concentrate on pinpointing the fatal flaw within herself. Then she must correct it. No excuses. No quarter given. She had been too indulgent of her weakness for too long. It was time to show that Christy Pallister was a real woman and a formidable artist. And she would do it, that was certain.

SIXTEEN

Santa Fe, 1978

LC's treatment continued. To Christy, it seemed like never ending pain without pity for the child she adored.

At first LC was semi-comatose and passive. Then, as life began to return, she became sullen and withdrawn, staring out of the window, not answering when Dan or Christy spoke to her. Gradually, as she began her precarious steps towards rehabilitation, she screamed when pain was inflicted, fought her nurses and cried as if her heart would break for hours on end. No matter how many times Dan told Christy the crying was the result of delayed shock, she suffered as she had never suffered before, conscious that her daughter was angry with her and constantly debating if the child held her responsible for the accident. Slowly, inexorably, Christy sank into an ever deepening depression, her resolve to fight it swamped by her anguish.

Dan was at his desk, listening to the nurse in charge of his daughter's case.

'LC's coming round fast, Dr Gray. She can't walk very well yet, but she's as mad as hell with everyone and that's a great sign. The passivity's gone and she wants to go home. She talks all the time about the Boulder House and painting the bats at night and finding a cat to catch mice.'

'She'll make it. We should be able to release her in a month. That'll give her time for a rest and for her bones to stabilize before she starts rushing around like a blue-arsed fly.'

'It'll be a long time before she can do that, Dr Gray, but the physiotherapy's doing wonders. More than I can say for her mother. She's heading for a breakdown if she doesn't take a firm hold of herself.'

'I'll talk to her, Melanie, don't worry.'

Dan remained alone in the office for an hour after Melanie's visit, thinking of Nolan and how over-protective he was of those he loved. Only Amy had escaped his strangling form of affection, because she had been raised by an English nanny during the period when her father had been in love with his first wife to the exclusion of everything and everyone else. Christy had come in for double measure of over-protectiveness, because of her mother's tragic death and Nolan's neurotic fear of losing his child as well as his wife. The result had been predictable. Dan knew there was a danger now that patterns established by Nolan would be repeated with LC. What should be done? What could be done?

Dan paced the room. Then he rang the clinic's psychiatric specialist, Ellie Martinez.

'Can you come up, Ellie?'

'Right now?'

'Right now.'

They talked for fifteen minutes, then went to LC's room. In reality the visit was to take a preliminary look at Christy, who was sitting red-eyed from crying at the window of her daughter's room. She looked up and smiled wanly at Dan.

'LC's sleeping, has been since she had the investigation this morning.'

'She's fine, don't worry. This is Dr Martinez, one of our resident specialists. I wanted her to have a word with LC, but it'll wait till later. I'm going to see the Hollis child in four. I'll come back later, Christy. Ellie, will you come to my office when you're through on this floor.'

Christy gazed at the beautiful woman in the white jacket and felt suddenly, for the first time in her life, furiously jealous. Ellie Martinez had thick, dark blonde hair worn in a rope-like plait around her head. Her eyes were vivid green, her teeth large and square, her skin burnished bronze. There was an aura of confidence about her that made Christy shrink inwardly and wonder if Dan was in love with this free-striding Amazon. She spoke as if to an enemy.

'What do you do in the hospital?'

'I'm consultant psychiatrist.'

'Does Dan think LC needs psychiatric help?'

'He didn't say so.'

'Does he think I do?'

'Do you think you do?'

'I have lots of problems but I'll resolve them.'

'Tell me about your problems.'

'Is Dan having an affair with you? Did he tell you to ask questions?'

'Do you believe Dan's unfaithful?'

'I didn't. Now I don't know. If he wanted me to see a psychiatrist, why didn't he tell me? He might have other secrets from me, too.'

'He didn't say you needed help.'

'But he brought you here to meet me.'

'I was passing. I thought I'd say hello to LC.'

'Well pass off! I don't want to talk to you.'

'I'm sorry you're angry, Christy. There's no reason to be. I've been at the Santa Rosa Clinic since it opened and I'm on the Board of Governors, like my parents. I'm here to help people, but only those who want to be helped. Okay? If you need anything, you know where to find me.'

Christy sat at LC's bedside when Ellie had gone, her

face mutinous. Who the hell did Dan think he was, sending along Ellie Martinez to ask questions? She rang for a nurse to come and sit with LC while she went to Dan's office. Then she marched to the second floor and demanded to see him, but he was in surgery with an emergency. Overwrought, crippled by stress, Christy flopped down in an armchair and burst into tears.

Dan's secretary, Rosemary, ran and made coffee for them both. 'Listen, you cry all you like,' she said, handing a coffee cup and a box of tissues. 'I'm a great believer in letting off steam. You've had such a difficult time and you've been so brave, the stress must be awful. Just remember that LC's getting better and you'll be able to go home soon. The worst is over.'

'I hope it is for Libby. She's going to forge ahead from now on. I'm just not sure I can do the same!'

'You'll make it to better times. You're just not the type to fail. My Grandfather Trelawney always said that some folk were failures and some destined for better things. He was English, from Cornwall and he *knew* things.'

'How did he decide who fell into the failure category?'

'He always said that failures fall at the first hurdle and never get up. Only stayers survive. You're a stayer, because after all that's happened and all you've suffered you're ready to fight a lion you're so angry. Only a real stayer could do that.'

Christy gazed at the young woman's round face with its rimless spectacles, neat features and serious expression. Then she rose and walked to the door.

'Thanks for the coffee, Rosemary, and thanks for the advice. I need all the help I can get at the moment.'

'You have it, inside of *you*, Christy. That's why I know you'll be a winner even if you have a few falls before you reach the finishing post.'

Christy smiled and walked slowly back to LC's room
. . . *You have it inside of you . . . You'll be a winner even if
you have a few falls before you reach the finishing post.* Now
she must learn to get up when she had fallen down.
The days of being scared of everything were over. The
time for confrontation had come. But how, where?

Four weeks of physiotherapy, of learning to walk
again and laugh again and return to a semblance of
normality. LC's humour reappeared and she showed
great courage in forcing her limbs back into action.
Unwilling to give in, she tried again and again to arrive
at her goal, to walk and run without crutches or sticks.
To be LC again.

Christy helped her child every hour of every day,
encouraging LC, planning picnics in the grounds of the
clinic and finally preparing her for the idea of going
home. Now the worst was over, nothing seemed to
trouble the child. Her aggression and hostility faded as
the lessons had their effect. Christy marvelled at her
resilience and wished her own matched it. During this
gruelling period, she had been forced to make many
decisions. She had slept badly and looked and felt ten
years older, her nights plagued by bad dreams, doubts
and fears of the testing to which she knew she must
submit herself. Unable to work out how to break the
cocoon of fear that had crippled her for so long, Christy
struggled with the conundrum of her deficiencies as LC
struggled with her broken limbs.

They returned to the Boulder House on a warm spring
day. LC stood gazing at the familiar paintings on the
walls, the giant pine cones she and her father had
collected and put on display, the fur rug Christy had
bought in the Indian market. Her face lit with pleasure
and she moved forward, as if in a dream. Her stay in
hospital had been bearable only when she had thought

of this room, and she had dreamed and hoped and prayed to return here.

'I'm so glad to be home.'

Dan looked at Christy, frowning at the dark lines under her eyes, the erratic movements of her hands.

'We'll have English tea shall we, LC?'

'With cake, Daddy, lots of cake.'

'Take a seat on the sofa, Christy. You look beat. I'll go ask Amparo to bring us something to eat.'

'And don't forget the chocolate cookies, Daddy.'

Dan disappeared and LC looked at her mother.

'Your dress is dirty and your face is all white. Now we're home, *you* have to get well, Mummy.'

'I will, don't worry.'

'Shall we go to keep fit classes like Amparo and Olivia?'

'They go because they're too fat.'

'You're so thin I can see your bones sticking out of your shoulders and your legs look a bit like runnerbird legs.'

'I'll start eating right now. Look, Amparo's brought tea for us and, wow, we have my favourite almond slices. We won't be able to eat dinner after all this.'

'I will, Mummy.'

When the child had eaten everything on the plates, she slept for two hours before demanding dinner. Then Christy bathed her, wincing at the terrible scars on her daughter's legs and right arm. The main thing was that LC was well and anxious to get back to normal. Remembering the impact of the crash, Christy closed her eyes as sweat broke out on her face. She was touched to feel LC's arms around her.

'What's the matter, Mummy? You've gone all wet and pale again.'

'I'll be all right when I've had a good night's sleep.

Hospital beds are so narrow I haven't slept well for weeks and weeks.'

'Get well soon and then we can go to the beach.'

'I'd like that. It's been a long time, LC.'

'We'll collect shells and you'll kill all the crabs, because you're not frightened of anything.'

With that, LC slept almost at once, and Christy went downstairs and drank a glass of iced Dom Perignon with Dan.

'She's fine.'

'I wish I could say the same thing for her mother. You need a holiday and a series of vitamin B shots, Christy.'

'I need to get my head straightened out.'

'You sent Ellie packing when I tried to get her to help you.'

'You should have asked me first if I needed help.'

Dan looked at her in disbelief.

'Christy, when I met you, you were hailed as the art find of the century. Since then you've lost all desire to paint. Now you won't drive, go out of the house or think of starting to do so again. You're twenty-seven years old and coming to a full and grinding halt. And you say you don't need help?'

'I don't need Ellie's help. I believe what needs to be done and how to do it are in my own mind. I just need to work out how to cure myself.'

'Ellie's an expert. If you don't like her, I'll find another colleague to help you.'

'Are you having an affair with Ellie Martinez?'

'She was a close friend in the early days of the clinic. But since I met you and she got engaged to the oil man, Chuck Rafferty, we're just good friends and I mean that. I love you Christy, but I'm finding it tough to watch you sliding down the slippery slope. I almost get the feeling that you want to hit rock bottom.'

'Of course I do. When you hit rock bottom you can

282

only go up. I started at the top and never stopped falling. I'm *sick* of falling. I want to start climbing and I will.'

'I hope you're right. One thing's certain, in the last three months since the accident, at a time when we should have been closer than ever before we've been reaching crisis point.'

'Can you wait a while, Dan?'

He looked into her eyes, pitying her state, angry from frustration that Christy continued to descend into fear and uncertainty and yet loving her more than anything in the world.

'I've waited four years. I'll wait for one more. Then we'll stay friends, but we won't live together any more. A man starts wondering if it's his fault when the woman he loves loses her confidence and lets herself go. It's not the only problem, as you know. I want to be married and have lots of kids, but you can't even commit yourself to love.'

'I will, Dan.'

'When?'

'When I've cured myself.'

'You have one year, Christy. After that we call it quits.'

'I'll get myself right again – and I love you, Dan.'

'Then show me. I want to marry you. Get your mind around to that and I'll believe you're cured.'

That night, Christy thought of LC's words . . . *you'll kill all the crabs because you're not frightened of anything.* There and then Christy decided to take the Jake Thackery survival course, which was the current talk of Santa Fe. Thackery had been in the marines and was said to turn out his assault course pupils fiercer than Attila the Hun. She would do the course, with its rifle, knife and unarmed combat lessons. Then, when it was over, she would prove herself worthy of her child's respect.

When LC went to her physiotherapy sessions, Christy went to Thackery's combat training. At first, she was incapable of bringing herself to make the terrifying howling war cries Thackery demanded from his pupils at the commencement of every daily session. When asked to stick a knife in a beef carcass as if it were a man, she fainted. On firing her rifle for the first time, Christy fell on the floor because of the recoil and cried because she thought she'd broken her shoulder. Then, swearing never to try it again, she stalked off back to her taxi and went home. Thackery took to calling her Yella, a name so offensive that Christy roared at him. He smiled approvingly.

'We might make something of you yet, Yella.'

'You call me that once again and I'll – '

'You stop being yella and I'll call you Christy. Now pick up your fucking rifle and start firing head shots or gut shots, but hit the target and no falling on your ass! Get your feet apart, weight even and pretend that cardboard man just raped your kid. Now go! You hear me, *go!*'

For two hours each morning Christy ran, exercised, shot and killed imaginary assailants. Then, after lunch with LC, she returned to the class for another two hours of unadulterated purgatory. When LC woke from her siesta, her mother was there, exhausted but loving. The child wiped the sweat from Christy's brow.

'Are you going to be like Charles Bronson when the course is finished, Mummy?'

'I hope so.'

'I *love* Charles Bronson, almost as much as I love Daddy.'

Dan's reaction to Christy's assault course and her new-found habit of practising her howling war cries in the countryside around the Boulder House was disbelief followed by near panic.

'Are you sure all this is constructive for an artist, Christy?'

'I'm sure.'

'What does it give you?'

'The ability to kill anything that scares me.'

'Including canvasses?'

'There's no room for sarcasm in my life at the moment, Dan.'

'Not even for jokes?'

Nolan was also visibly alarmed by the news of Christy's course.

'That fellow's as mad as a hatter, everyone agrees. He's probably paranoid, or worse, a Communist.'

'Thackery's an ex-marine. He fought his battles, and when he came home to Santa Fe and thought he was safe and secure, his wife got raped by a gang of Hell's Angels. She had a breakdown and took an overdose at twenty-seven. He decided to train folk to defend themselves and he's right.'

'But who's trying to hurt you, Christy? I've spent my life trying to protect you.'

'That's the trouble, Daddy. You over-protected me and I can't hiccup without being scared. I'm trying to learn to be self-sufficient and I will learn, no matter what I have to do and no matter how you and Dan oppose me.'

Unarmed combat was a nightmare. Christy had black, bruised legs, arms, back and bones. She cried so hard and so often Thackery regularly sent her home in disgrace. Then, one morning, exasperated by his attitude, she kicked the shin of her unarmed combat instructor, when he told her to defend herself by whatever puny means she could find. The instructor howled all over the baseball pitch where the sessions were held. Thackery came running, his eyes wide with shock.

'What the hell happened here?'

'This fucking bitch near broke my leg!'

'You're training her in self-defence. You should be pleased if she's put you out of action for the day, Sullivan. You'll make it yet, Yella. I'm starting to get hopeful.'

Christy learned to fire her rifle without falling down, but sticking a knife in anything made her vomit and unarmed combat continued to make her cry. When the day of her passing out examination arrived, she fainted in the changing-room and then appeared on the field pale grey from terror. Her performance was distinguished only by the fact that during the assault course she nearly drowned, and then shot the cardboard cutout of a police officer instead of that of the attacker specified. Still, she threw a fourteen-stone instructor so he couldn't get up to continue. She shot the target twice through the left eye, screamed from sheer excitement and did it again for good measure. Unable to stab her dummy attacker, she used the knife like a scimitar and sliced him up like salami.

Thackery sighed, handed her her diploma and shook her hand.

'Congratulations, Christy. You'll never make it to the marines, but you'll get the better of any opponent by shocking the poor jerk rigid. I cancelled the taxi, by the way. Dan left your car outside so you can drive home. If you have any problems, we'll do a couple of turns around the field to give you confidence.'

He had called her Christy instead of Yella and she was very proud. She put the badge on, the diploma in her pocket and walked to the car. But she sat for twenty minutes trying to find the courage to drive away. Every time she touched the key, she remembered the crash and the moment when she had seen blood seeping through LC's tee shirt. Tears rolled down her cheeks, despite all her efforts.

Thackery looked at her through the open window, told her to move over and before Christy could protest drove off at a hundred miles an hour around the baseball pitch, wheels screeching, shouting like a madman all the while.

'If some fuck-head follows you, you pull on your handbrake like that and, wow!, the car starts flying in the opposite direction. I love it. I'll do it again. Yahoooooooo!'

The car leapt in full circle and proceeded at a hundred in the opposite direction. Then Thackery put it in reverse and reversed around the pitch even faster.

Christy vomited in her lap.

Ignoring the stench and the lime green tint of her face, Thackery continued for another fifteen minutes, to be sure she understood what he wanted of her, finishing the performance with an emergency stop that jarred every bone in her body. Then he got out and told her to move into the driving seat and to repeat everything he had done. He sat, calm as a judge in the passenger seat, while Christy drove around the pitch at thirty-five. Then, suddenly, he was screaming, shouting, howling, animal like in his madness.

'Get your speed up, get it up, up, up, fifty, sixty, seventy, eighty – Go to it, Christy! – ninety, a hundred. Up, up, up! There you go. There you go, faster, *faster*. Now turn her. Woeeeeeeeeeeeee!'

Christy sobbed hysterically, but was too terrified to stop. The sudden reversal of direction disorientated her and she lost control of the wheel. Then Thackery was shouting again and screeching his war cries. 'Reverse again, *again*. Now you go for it, forty, fifty, sixty, seventy. Go on, Christy. I want you to break the fucking sound barrier. Ninety, a hundred, one twenty, one forty. Yahooooooooooo! Congratulations, you know you're really something. Now you'll be able to drive home without too much trouble.'

Christy drove back to the Boulder House. Slowly. The stench of vomit in the car was overwhelming and she knew she must clear it on arrival or suffer the odour forever. She barely saw the countryside and felt incapable of lucid thought, as shock took her strength away and made her want to sleep.

On arrival at the house, she saw a banner with 'CONGRATULATIONS' hung from the front door. Then LC and Dan came rushing out.

'Mummy, you won your badge. We're so proud of you, Daddy and I. We've made a celebration tea and we bought you a prezzy, even before we knew you'd passed.'

Dan smelled the vomit and helped her out of the car.

'You've made a great effort and passed your test *and* you've driven home. I'm so very proud of you, Christy. Come on in. Take a shower and then come and join us. LC and I have champagne and smoked salmon canapes as a slightly unconventional afternoon tea. Amparo'll fix the car. When you've showered hurry down and be spoiled. You deserve it.'

Christy stood in the shower, covering herself with lemon gel and trying to stop the shaking of her limbs. But she was smiling, because Dan was pleased with her and her child was proud of her. This was the first step on the ladder. She had conquered one set of fears, her terror of confrontations, attacks, driving. She was on her way back to the gold standard and nothing was going to stop her. She knew now that the only person who could stop her was herself. For the moment, she decided to enjoy the evening. She had worked hard. Now she would relax. Then, in the morning, she would make plans to complete her transformation.

LC went to bed late, joyful because her mother was

happier than she had been for ages. When she had had a story and was safely asleep, Dan and Christy sat by the log fire.

Dan poured them another glass of champagne.

'What's next on the agenda?'

'Next I have to find a way to stop being so scared of insects, spiders, scorpions and snakes.'

'That's not easy. Those are primitive fears and could be impossible to shake.'

'I want to get rid of them, or at least to diminish them. If I'm to paint again as I know I can paint and be a good mother and get married to you I have to lose all the shit in my brain and stop being a nobody. I want to be someone special.'

'You've never been a nobody, Christy. I've always thought of you as someone very special. Just ask me to help if there's anything I can do.'

'Be patient, it won't take for ever.'

'I saw a great painting yesterday.'

'Where?'

'In the home of Bob Martinez, Ellie's father. He's Chairman of our Board of Governors.'

'Was she there?'

'No, she went to Dallas for her wedding dress fittings. The Martinez family are all art collectors from way back, you know. The painting I saw was of the Empress Tz'u Hsi in all her splendour. Bob had it displayed in the entrance to the house, the only painting there next to a wonderful Chinese throne of carved lotus wood. It was one of yours, Christy. I was so proud when I saw it. And you know what he told me? Ellie bought your collage of Marilyn Monroe at the first exhibition. She has it in her all-red dining-room. She's a fan of yours. Try not to get het up about her, because she's a friend not a lover. She's truly en route for a marriage with one of the richest oil men in Texas.'

'Will she stay on at the clinic afterwards?'

'No, Ellie wants lots of kids and when she's had them she'll go into private practice. It's an easy way to do both things. The clinic's much too binding to continue after you have a large family.'

'I painted some great things for that first exhibition, didn't I, Dan?'

'You did and you've not painted anything great since. But you will.'

'You're always encouraging, but I don't paint at all now and I don't ever want to.'

'You will and better than ever.'

'How do you know?'

'Because you got your badge this afternoon. Before that I thought you were finished, but if you can learn to do a marines assault course with all it entails and pass out, you can do anything. I *never* believed you'd make it, neither did Thackery. He's in adoration of you and my idea of your future has changed radically since this morning.'

'Shall we go to bed, Dan?'

'I thought you'd never ask.'

In the still of the night, a wild cat snarled near the house. Then a car passed on the distant road. Dan untied Christy's shirt, kissed her shoulders and bared her breasts.

'I think the combat course made them even more beautiful.'

'Do they taste different?'

'I'll tell you in a minute.'

She writhed in a fever of desire. They had not made love for a long time, because she had been too tense about LC or too tired from her combat course. Now she wanted Dan and as he entered her she arched her back and pushed to meet him, sliding her body hard against his and letting him make her soar like an eagle, like in the old days when she had been Christy Pallister, art find of the century. As they reached the climax of love and then lay, tightly entwined, Christy thought how much she wanted to win her battles, how much Dan needed her to win and how much their future depended on it. For a precious moment, she was complete, a woman in love, a woman beloved, a woman about to waken from a long and enervating nightmare.

They lay in each other's arms and were content, happy, as they had been before the dark clouds gathered.

Then, Dan whispered, 'We'll make it, won't we, Christy?'

'We'll make it, Dan.'

'Maybe getting your badge has broken the bad sequence and started a new one.'

'Can that happen?'

'Sure it can. Sometimes we reach out and catch a shooting star and that changes our idea of our capabilities. You could have done that with Thackery's course. You didn't expect to get your badge. I surely didn't expect you to and in the beginning he didn't either. So you're capable of anything and clear to go forging ahead.'

When she woke, in the still of night, Christy relived the moments of the test and the precious memory of Thackery pinning the badge on her tee shirt. For the first time in all her life she had beaten her fear. More important, she had wanted to win so much she had clung on through weeks of sickening, terrifying lessons. She had beaten her fear! The thought brought tears of intense pride and happiness to her eyes and she lay there, relieved, uncertain of many things but sure that she could now beat into submission all the other obstacles in life. She had turned the corner. If she could keep her energy and her cool, she would make it.

* * *

The following day, LC invited her mother to the attic for a game of buried treasure. Chests and trunks abounded, full of Dan's mother's possessions, left to him in her will but never sorted. Some of the things had belonged to Christy's family and the joy of the game was that they always managed to find something new. There were sepia photographs, old clothes, cut-glass bottles, their perfume long evaporated, and mothballs by the score. There were paintings and old shoes, jangling twenties earrings and a fine selection of warlike bows and arrows, scimitars and machetes.

Christy took one of the perfume sprays, obviously from the thirties, and sniffed the fragrance of patchouli and vetiver, that lingered like an echo of a frenetic age when everything had changed and people who once had drunk champagne out of satin slippers learned to fight for their lives. Women, above all, had changed. They had not only learned to stand up and fight, but to get up when knocked down. They had also learned to be alone and independent. Christy took a sequinned jacket out of the trunk, shocked when it disintegrated on reaching fresh air. The important thing in life was not to disintegrate under stress, like the sequinned jacket in the bright air of morning. The important thing in life was reality – accepting and surviving it. Was the capacity to make dreams become reality inborn or part of the toughening process every modern woman had to learn? Christy realized that that was what both Camilla and Louise had lacked. Both had been able to dream, as she was able to dream. Neither had been able to make dreams become reality when life turned difficult and they were opposed by fate. Learning to accept reality was part of the act of becoming real to ourselves. Christy smiled, realizing that she had reasoned out what she lacked.

She was about to leave the attic, when she saw an

ornate machete leaning up against a beam, yet another souvenir of some journey long past. Inspecting it, she smiled at the faded inscription: *Presented to Amelia Gray by Don Alfonso Mercadal y Vilana, in recognition of her great courage, 1915.* Suddenly, Christy knew what she must do and, gathering LC in her arms, she went to her room and packed one small suitcase of cottons, her paints and a new roll of canvas bought in the hope that its presence in the house would shame her into working. LC followed, squealing with curiosity when her mother put the case, paints, canvas, water, flasks, picnic case and finally the machete into the car.

'Are we going on a trip, Mummy?'

'Yes, we're going to become modern day pioneer travellers.'

'Where are we going?'

'To Tucson and then into Mexico and the Gulf of California. I'm going to take a painting holiday. We have to pass through the desert on the way to the Gulf.'

'But you hate deserts!'

'After this trip I won't hate them any more.'

'We'd best take lots of food in case I get hungry. Since I left the clinic I can't stop eating.'

Christy took maps, a compass and her sunglasses, two big Irish tweed blankets, a ground sheet, a giant bag of Amparo's butter cookies and two two-gallon containers for water. Then she wrote a note for Dan.

I'm going after my second badge. Plan trip to Gulf Coast. Decided to start out right now, because if I wait I'll get scared again. I love you. Will ring when we reach our first night stop.
                    Christy.

They started out at two-thirty for Tucson. It was a trip Christy had often wanted to make but had never dared and she knew Dan would be furious at her sudden, unprepared departure. But if she didn't go immediately she never would and she wanted to try. She told herself that this was a test, a trip into the unknown with no one to help her. The roads were, for the most part, modern, well organized and surfaced. After the Mexican border, she would come face to face with the most destructive of her fears, the fear of the desert's emptiness, and being unaided and totally alone to make decisions and defend herself and her child. Of course, the road was good all the way to the coast and full of tourists most of the year. But it skirted the desert and was often obstructed by strange animals or broken-down trucks. To Christy the trip was approximately equal to climbing Everest.

LC smiled at her mother, thrilled to be embarking on an adventure. Christy smiled back. LC trusted her and this was the moment to prove that she was everything a mother should be. The road was well used and there was no serious danger that should preclude her taking the child with her. Her own fears were unfounded and unreasonable and it was to crush them that she would complete the long and exhausting trip. At the end of it, Christy would be a woman without frontiers, barriers, limitations. A woman of far horizons.

In her haste to leave the house, Christy forgot to listen to the weather forecast.

SEVENTEEN

She rang Dan from their first night stop at Las Cruces and then from a motel on the outskirts of Tucson. He was almost incoherent with anger that she had taken LC with her in a mad bid to find her courage.

'Where exactly are you heading, Christy?'

'Towards the coast, the Gulf Coast. The road's civilized, you told me that often enough yourself.'

'The weather can be disagreeable. I think you should come back.'

'I have to do it, Dan.'

'Do you have to take risks with the child?'

'I won't do anything foolish. Apart from you, LC's the most precious thing in my life.'

'I want you to come back.'

'Now you're talking like Nolan and being over-protective of me and LC. She has to learn too, you said so often. We don't want her to grow up like me, perpetually terrified of everything.'

'Christy, I love you. Will you please see reason.'

'I see it crystal clear. I'll call you from the coast when we arrive.'

Christy lay back, her heart pounding, because Dan was angry. In the next bed, LC was asleep, her cheeks a healthy pink, a smile on her face. Christy thought how they had enjoyed the first part of the journey, the vistas of New Mexico in summer, the valleys spotted with the bright green of the aspens. The markets were full of mounds of yellow and orange melons. They had bought some for the journey, with bowls of hot chili from a street vendor, enjoying the meal as much as if they were at the Ritz. Christy debated if Dan were right about not taking LC. Then she shook her head. When she had talked in the past of her desire to go to the coast, he had always said, 'There's nothing to it, thousands of folk go every day. The road is as modern as ours in Santa Fe. It just cuts clear through the desert.' So why was he making such a fuss?

Turning out the light, Christy closed her eyes and then put on the light again and set her alarm for five. If they started early, they might reach the coast in time for dinner. In the darkness, she wondered if they would see a scorpion or a tarantula or worse. She decided to stop for the briefest of picnics at the roadside and never to leave the car. The thought of snakes made her nervous and she had to put on the light again and drink a glass of water to calm herself. This was her test and Christy knew she must make it. There was no possibility of turning back.

In the morning, they left the motel and ate breakfast in a roadside diner. LC devoured pancakes with maple syrup, a hamburger and two glasses of orange juice. Christy was so nervous she had difficulty in swallowing a coffee. She almost forgot her daughter's presence until LC started to talk.

'Have you looked at the map, Mummy?'

'I looked at it in the night when I couldn't sleep.'

'Will we get to the beach tonight?'

'I'd like to get there for dinner, but it depends on the weather and if there's lots of traffic on the roads. Sometimes it takes hours to just pass the frontier into Mexico.'

'Will we see a Gila Monster?'

'I hope not.'

'I hope we do. Amparo told me all about Gila Monsters and she says fried rattlesnake tastes just like chicken.'

'We won't be eating rattlesnakes!'

'I was hoping we might.'

'In order to eat one we'd have to kill it first and how would *I* kill a rattlesnake?'

'You'd know how, Mummy, but if we don't see a rattlesnake we could eat an iguana. They taste just like chicken too. I *love* chicken.'

'We've got tins of fruit and rice pudding and meat loaf now. Do we really need iguanas?'

'We're having an adventure, Mummy, and on adventures you eat spiders and you sleep in the desert in your clothes. You never put your nightie on.'

'Let's go, LC.'

The child ran to the car, as eager to start the adventure as Christy was for it to be over. Passing the frontier at Nogales, both were surprised when a sleepy guard barely glanced at their papers. Christy was even more surprised that theirs was the only car crossing. It was six-thirty. Surely the long distance lorries started work early? So why was there no one on the road? Glancing at the sky, she thought it was a beautiful leaden grey, mentally filing the colour to use in the palette she dreamed of mixing someday soon. She saw only the perfect colour, the rays of pale sunlight giving an angular, biblical halo to the far landscape. Yet again, Christy had forgotten the cardinal rule for all travellers through a desert region – listen to the weather forecast before starting out.

At first things went well. They passed saguaro cacti, with their creamy white flowers and patches of mallow, each petal spotted with scarlet. By the roadside, the mysterious, poisonous, narcotic datura, showed its white trumpet shaped blooms. LC took a photograph of everything in case Christy wanted to paint it when they reached their holiday hotel. They did not see any dangerous animals or any other traffic. Christy drove on at speed, confident that they stood a good chance of reaching their destination before nightfall.

They ate a picnic of fruit, cheese, chicken and rice salad at midday. As she sat surveying her surroundings, Christy thought how deserts emphasized the omnipresence of death, not only past deaths, but the possibility of present ones. By the roadside, tiny crosses in white painted wood marked the sites of fatal accidents. Dying cactus creaked in the increasing force of the wind and a mesquite tree ceded life to a parasitic creeper that had covered its trunk and every branch. Christy shivered, packed the picnic things, put them in the back of the car and drove on towards the alkali flats and the burned out volcanic hills.

Time passed. The wind increased to a howling lament. Sand swirled like fog before her eyes and Christy debated whether to turn back. Looking at her watch, she saw that she had been driving for over four hours. She was over half way to her destination. Better to push on for the coast than retreat. She continued, a solitary white car in a sepia landscape, under a grey sky. Behind her, the road disappeared, as sand swirled so high the marker lines and boundaries were engulfed. Only the telegraph poles remained to show where the tarmac had so recently been.

It was two o'clock when Christy stopped her engine, turned on the car radio and heard nothing at all but a crackling static cacophony. Ahead, the sky had turned a menacing charcoal. To her right, a signpost to Caborca was almost interred in sand. She looked around, unable to believe that theirs was still the only car on the road. Suddenly, fear hit her hard, with the eery feeling that they were two human beings on the mountains of the moon. The road indicated by the sign looked like a sea of sand, the road behind her likewise. It was impossible to retreat and unsafe to go on. LC's voice broke into her thoughts.

'I can't see the road.'

'Neither can I, LC.'

'The road's vanished, but it'll come back like in my book *The Magic Journey*.'

To Christy, the strange darkness of afternoon had an apocalyptic atmosphere. Panic clawed at the outer limits of her mind and hurried into the full focus of her consciousness. She reminded herself that she had two two-gallon containers of water, two boxes of tins of Coca-Cola and the meat loaf, rice pudding and fruit. The coast could not be more than three hours' drive from where they were, probably less. She must stay calm. Above all, she must not let the child realize they were in danger.

By three o'clock, Christy was in an advanced state of terror. The wind had reached such a howling, raging force she wondered if the coast had been hit by a hurricane. Suddenly, she realized why no other cars or lorries had passed the frontier in the early morning. The drivers had heard the weather forecast and had decided to postpone their trip. She and LC were stranded in the middle of nowhere, alone and in danger of breaking down. If the car radiator became too full of sand and the engine clogged, they might well be there for ever.

Forgetting her terror of snakes and every other desert animal, Christy leapt out and fixed their groundsheet over the radiator with heavy-duty tape. It was then that she realized that the car was slowly becoming sub-merged by sand. Instinct told her she must seek shelter – a cave, a crag, no matter what. Otherwise, by morning, she and LC could be buried alive. Putting on a brave front, she drove forward, remembering that the

299

compass had pointed south-west at the sign for Caborca. Glancing at LC, Christy saw that she was wide-eyed with apprehension, as sand obscured the windscreen completely.

'I can't see anything, Mummy.'

'Neither can I.'

'Where are we going?'

'I must find a cave to use as a garage for a while. We'll wait till the hurricane's blown out and then continue to the beach.'

'We can swim when we get there and watch the pelicans. Daddy told me there are pelicans everywhere on the Gulf Coast.'

'They'll be waiting to say hello to us.'

'And the dolphins, too?'

'And dolphins, too.'

'Are we lost, Mummy?'

Christy hesitated, surprised by the directness of the question.

'No, but we can't go on. We have to find shelter and be very brave.'

LC looked uncertain, until a great, dark shadow loomed ahead.

'What's that, Mummy?'

'I don't know.'

'If it's a mountain we might find a cave.'

Christy drove on, terrified of taking them over a precipice, but even more afraid of remaining stuck in the sand. Edging on, she came finally to a halt under what seemed like a vast, overhanging crag. The umbrella of rock was better than nothing, curving, as it did, almost to the ground in front of her. The prevailing wind was blowing directly at the car, which was now protected by the crag.

Christy stepped out and tried to see if there was a cave nearby, but swirling sand blinded her and she saw nothing at all. Tight-faced, she hurried back to the car, put LC's seat into recline and covered the child with a blanket. Within seconds, LC was asleep. Christy closed her eyes and uttered a silent prayer. Then she unearthed the machete, carried food and water from the car boot, took out the blankets, flasks, supermarket supplies and organized the interior of the car. Having put her own seat into recline, she lay listening to the deafening blasts of wind and watching a sandstorm that brought to the surface every deep rooted, primitive fear she had ever had. Dan had been right. She should never have brought LC on a trip like this. If she needed to prove herself, she should have done it alone. Her body rigid with fear, her mind running in circles around the problem of what to do, how to proceed, Christy slept fitfully. She woke to find herself in inky darkness. The wind sounded fiercer and more turbulent, and every few seconds loose rock fell past the overhanging spur that was their only shelter. Christy looked at her watch. It was five in the afternoon and as dark as midnight.

LC was not hungry and refused even her favourite rice pudding for dinner. Christy sighed. It was the first time her daughter had not eaten since she left the clinic and she knew that the child was afraid. The idea of going to the lavatory in a hastily scooped hole in the sand relieved the situation, terrifying Christy, but making her daughter laugh. Rattlesnakes and scorpions were far from reality to the child and she remained ignorant, for the moment, of their proximity. LC was not immune to the fear that the strange weather, the terrifying wind and the fact that they could not continue their journey engendered. While Christy looked intently at the map, LC whispered a question.

'We'll be able to leave tomorrow, won't we, Mummy?'

'I hope so.'

'What if we can't?'

'We stay till it's safe to go on.'

'But what if the road never comes back?'

'Then we find a way to get to the coast without it, like real explorers in the past.'

'You're very brave. I wish Daddy was here, don't you?'

'We'll call him from the hotel when we arrive.'

The following morning, the wind had died down, but the road was invisible. By nine o'clock the heat was unbearable. Christy opened the car windows, then the doors. Then she and LC stepped out and went in search of a cave where they could shelter from the punishing rays of the sun. There were no caves. Instead, Christy rigged a makeshift tent from the blankets, attaching them to the rock face, the car and a small, jagged pinnacle in the ground. They ate sparingly, drank too much water, buried the sour milk some distance from their camp and then screamed in horror at the sight of huge ants crawling by the dozen over the empty Coke tins in the car. It took Christy an hour to kill the ants and clean out the car. Then she buried the tins of Coke far away and returned to see how LC was faring with her tidying up.

The air was heavy, the silence oppressive. As Christy neared their tent, every nerve in her body seemed to signal alarm. Instinct took over and she advanced silently, looked around the draped blanket and saw that LC was unaware of a pale yellow scorpion advancing from the rocky overhang. As she regarded the scorpion in horror, LC looked up, saw her gaze and then saw the scorpion. Her face paled, but she sat quite still. Christy took one step forward and hit the scorpion with the iron frying pan. The severed tail shot in the air and the danger was over. Her heart pounded so hard she almost fainted, but as she covered over the scorpion with sand, she knew that she had also taken the first step in severing another of the crippling fears that had ruined her life. She tried to hold back the tears, but as LC leapt into her arms, they fell like rain down her cheeks.

'It's over, the scorpion's dead.'

'Was he going to bite me, Mummy?'

'I don't know, but we didn't give him time anyway. He was probably asleep in the rock face and he fell out and felt angry.'

'You're very brave, Mummy.'

As LC clung to her, Christy longed more than anything in the world to find a way out of the desert that had engulfed them. The child loved and trusted her. She must think. She must find a way to go on. But how?

That night, while LC slept, Christy lay awake, so afraid she could not stop trembling. The heat had obliged them to leave open the windows. Fears of snakes, scorpions and tarantulas made it impossible for her to relax her guard. Only in the morning light, after six did she doze, waking with a start at eight when LC kissed her resoundingly and began the day with a shock announcement.

'There's a dog watching our car, Mummy.'

'A dog! Where is he?'

'There.'

Looking out, Christy saw a coyote, who turned on his heels and ran. In the far recesses of her mind, she remembered reading that coyote tracks always lead to the sea. Was it possible she could follow the tracks? Dare she take the risk? Dare she *not* take the risk? One two-gallon container of water was already empty. If the heat continued, they had at most two days' supply and that only with strict rationing. The roads would not be cleared for at least a week. For her and LC that would mean a slow death in a sea of sand.

Christy got out of the car, machete in hand, and went to look at the tracks. One coyote had looked with interest at the car, but there were the tracks of a whole pack. They were clear and if the wind did not rise again would stay clear at least until sunset. Christy made her decision, packed the car, shook out the blankets from their 'tent' and put them in the boot. Then she drove slowly forward on to a seemingly endless, colourless world of sand. The heat was so intense her eyes kept watering and her cheeks burned. She was terrified of having a puncture or the engine overheating. Grim-faced from stress, she thought that if she were lucky enough to return to Santa Fe, she would take a car mechanic's course.

At midday they rested for an hour, drank water but could not eat. Then they pressed on, because it was becoming urgent for them to reach the coast. The red warning light indicating water shortage was flickering on the dashboard. Christy prayed silently that they would not be obliged to follow the tracks on foot. Vistas that looked like the Sahara appeared as they reached the summit of every sand hill, provoking her to waves of panic. The skeletons of animals long dead from thirst punctuated the landscape with ominous regularity. As the cruel light exhausted her eyes, Christy began to see tracks everywhere, but she continued, relentlessly, find-ing reserves of strength within herself because her child's life was at stake. LC just watched, wide-eyed.

'Are you sure coyotes lead to the sea, Mummy?'

'Absolutely certain. I read it in *National Geographic* and they're always right.'

By four o'clock, Christy was soaked to the skin with sweat, LC likewise, but still the coyote tracks continued, as if the pack had run to the ends of the earth. When the light began to fail, Christy strained to continue, but by five in the evening she could no longer see them. Exhausted by the slowness of her pace in the sand, by the heat and lack of food, she turned to LC, smiling with a confidence she was far from feeling.

'We're nearly there. Tomorrow morning we should arrive.'

'Why aren't there any more cactus, Mummy?'

'I don't know.'

'There's nothing here except coyote tracks and those horrible black things.'

Christy stared out at black bats wheeling in the sky, their sinister silhouettes ominous against a blood-red sunset.

'Those are bats.'

'I don't like them. Do they bite?'

'Bats are very interesting animals. They fly at night. They can't see very well but they never collide with anything because they have a kind of built-in radar.'

'Like dolphins? Daddy told me about that. I'm thirsty, Mummy. Can I have some water? I drank the last of the Cokes.'

'We'll have some water and there's still tinned fruit and rice pudding.'

'I could eat a McDonald's hamburger.'

'They're not on the menu tonight.'

'I love you, Mummy. Are you sure we'll get there tomorrow?'

'Nearly sure.'

'We're lost, aren't we? Tell the truth.'

'Yes, we're lost, but we'll find our way in the morning.'

Christy slept almost at once, despite her desire to stay on guard. She woke suddenly, as dawn lit the horizon, blinking because she had no idea why she had emerged so brutally from a deep sleep. For a moment, she closed her eyes. Then she opened them, stretched and stepped out of the car, smiling at her habit of walking every-where with the machete, like a medieval warrior. A few days in the desert had changed her and she knew she would never be the same again. She was about to climb the small hillock in front of the car, when she heard LC screaming.

'Mummy! Help me, Mummy!'

Christy ran back to the car, stopping in her tracks, frozen by terror at the sight of a rattlesnake coiled on the seat she had just left. It was less than an arm's length from her child and she knew at once that that was what had wakened her, the metallic, alien rattle in this sandy chasm of emptiness. Christy moved forward and with the handle of the machete flicked the snake to the ground. Angry, it slithered towards her and she saw that it was a ring-tailed rattler, the most common and most dangerous in the region. When she backed away, the snake accelerated, so she stood her ground. The rattle echoed in the silence of dawn. The snake hesitated. Then advanced at speed. Christy narrowed her eyes, judged the distance and brought the machete down so hard the snake's head was severed. For a moment she watched the body threshing in the sand. Then it was over.

Christy took a deep breath, wiped the sweat from her face and began to walk back to the car. She was almost half way there when she heard again the same metallic rattle and, disbelieving, turned in time to see the rattler's mate advancing at lightning speed towards her. For a moment she considered running to the car and locking the door, but the snake came too fast and the car was too far away. Again, Christy stood quite still, but this time the snake did not hesitate and there was no time to take aim. Instead, she hit it again and again and again with the machete, stopping only when she saw a jumbled, mangled mass of reptilian body swimming before her blurred vision. Then, like a sleepwalker, she walked back to the car, sat down and closed her eyes.

LC remained still, shocked into silence. After a while, she took the machete from her mother's hand, stared at the chopped up rattler and tried to think what to do. Dan had taught her how to make a fire out of doors. There was coffee in the car and a frying pan and water. She got out, made a little fire, boiled water in the pan and made coffee in the jug they had used for milk. It smelled good and after checking that there were no more snakes between her and the car, LC hurried with a mug of coffee and put it into her mother's hand. Then she sat holding the machete and guarding Christy while she drank.

'You were truly great, Mummy, better than Charles Bronson. I'll never forget it. I'll tell everyone in Santa Fe when I get home.'

'I love you, LC.'

'Is the coffee good?'

'It's perfect.'

The coffee was full of grains, but Christy drank every drop. Then she drove slowly up the hill, praying there would not be another endless vista of desert. As the light hit her eyes, she stared disbelievingly, because after an expanse of sand that covered two-thirds of her view, there was the shimmering, pelucid blue of the sea. She smiled, tears of relief filling her eyes. Then, without saying a word to LC, in case it was a mirage, Christy revved the engine and drove forward, on, on, on until they could hear the seagulls and smile at the antics of the pelicans that flapped in formation above the waves, plunging like kamikaze into the surf. The beach was golden. The water clear as crystal and on an old battered sign there was the name of the area, Puerto Libertad. Tears streamed down Christy's cheeks and she whispered to her child.

'We made it, LC. We made it.'

'I love you, Mummy.'

'We made it. We *really* made it.'

'Don't cry, Mummy. If you cry, I'll cry too. Come here and let me give you a big kiss.'

They sat together, listening to the sound of the sea, staring at the sunrise, smiling at a school of dolphins far out in the bay and then, in a moment of mad, joyful folly, rushing headlong into the sea.

They smelled for the first time the unique scent of Mexico, of refried beans, ironwood smoke, manure, mesquite and old adobe. The village was occupied by fishermen and a few Seri Indian families, with two houses built by American emigrants on a beach littered with shark eggs, sand dollars, kelp and starfish. Further on, towards Kino Bay, friends of Christy from art college days had put their savings into a beach hotel and restaurant. The hotel was her planned destination and she drove towards it now, smiling. She would ring Dan from the hotel and tell him they were safe. She would tell him too that she had conquered all but her fear of painting and marriage. Those she would now wipe out of her life, like the obstacles to happiness they had become.

On the journey, Christy had realized one simple truth, that fear inhabits the mind, crippling thought and action, but that courage is there also. When they need it enough, even the most fearful of human beings have their reserves to tap. Soon, she knew, she would set up her easel and climb another mountain. She would paint again. For the first time in so long she actually wanted to paint, even longed to do so. She and LC ran into the hotel, greeted Christy's friends and were shown to their rooms. Arrangements were made for a long stay with price reduction if she felt like doing a mural for the dining-room wall. Her first call was to Dan.

'We've arrived.'

'Thank God. I thought you were dead. What happened? You were about to cross the border at Nogales when you called me last time and that was the day a hurricane hit the whole of the Gulf Coast area. Trucks have had to delay ever since and no one knows when they'll be able to clear the roads. Even now the whole area's blocked by sand. Folk can't find their way.'

'I know.'

'Did you fly down?'

'No Dan, we drove. No one told me about the hurricane warning, so I drove right into it.'

'You were in the desert? Oh my God! How'd you find your way out, Christy?'

'We sheltered and then, when the water got low, I followed the coyote tracks. Coyotes always lead you to the sea.'

There was a long silence at the other end of the line. Then Dan spoke.

'Are you both all right? No injuries?'

'We're both better than we've ever been.'

'Can I speak with LC, please?'

'Hello, Daddy. I love you.'

'Tell me about your journey, LC.'

'There was sand everywhere. You couldn't see the road in front or behind and we sheltered under a rock shaped like an umbrella. The milk went sour and a scorpion tried to bite me, but Mummy hit him with the frying pan.'

'Then what?'

'Then we followed the coyotes and they led us to the coast. Mummy killed a rattlesnake that got in the car and then, just when she was coming back to me, another rattlesnake came and tried to attack her and she cut it up in little pieces with our machete. It was wonderful, Daddy, just like Charles Bronson in *The Magnificent Seven*, except that Mummy was on her own.'

'Did you cry, LC?'

'No, Mummy went a bit pale, so I lit a fire like you taught me and made a mug of coffee for her.'

'I'm very proud of you, LC, and I'm very, very proud of Mummy. Tell her that will you, please? I'll come down soon to see you both.'

'Your voice has gone funny, Daddy.'

'Bye, LC, tell Mummy I love her best in all the world.'

LC turned to Christy.

'Daddy says he loves you best in all the world. He's coming down to see us and I think he was crying. He probably thought we were lost. We *were* lost, weren't we, Mummy?'

'Yes, we were, but when you're lost you find your way somehow. When you're tired you sleep. When you're upset you cry. Being lost is just the beginning of finding a way to get where you want to be. It's a kind of extra challenge.'

'Shall we go for a swim?'

'Why not?'

'And we'll have steak and eggs and fried potatoes and a McDonald's hamburger for lunch.'

'All at once?'

'I got a bit fed up with meat loaf and rice pudding on the journey, but now I'm very, very hungry.'

Days of sun and sand followed, of sleeping in a hammock in the afternoon and again for ten hours at night. Christy and her daughter ate and swam and dreamed sweet dreams, until the ordeal of the desert began to fade from their memory, leaving only the joyful residue of that moment when they had climbed the last hill and seen the sea.

At the beginning of their third week in the hotel, Christy began to paint. She worked fast, with fluency, urgency and avidity, scenes that had filtered like moving pictures through her mind in the long years of trying to analyse her malaise. The paintings became the exteriorization of her inner conflicts, of her battle for her place in the sun. She portrayed Camilla in delicate pastels, fragile in lace and linen, parasol in hand, gazing into the Kenyan sunset. Beauty of landscape juxtaposed with intense impact the delicacy of a flawed woman too sensitive to withstand the ugliness of a frenetic new frontier. Louise was depicted in primary colours, as the high flier, the adventuress, the woman of a new era, a golden eagle blinded by the sun.

Sometimes, when Christy found a painting was not working, she put it aside. Instead of panicking, she remembered the combat course and the days lost in the wilderness and told herself that setbacks were just setbacks and could be overcome. If the painting continued not to work, she started another, determined to let nothing stop the flow or impede the confidence that was surging within her like a long blocked cascade. Often, she recommenced her work after LC slept in the evening and continued until after midnight. Once, she fell asleep at the easel and woke covered in rose madder, where she had fallen into the palette. But she was happy and increasingly confident that she was coming back fast and painting better than ever before. Hope returned, fuelling her desire to succeed and she worked faster and faster, better and better, eager to complete the paintings for an exhibition and return to Dan in Santa Fe.

Early each morning, Christy walked alone on the beach, gathering stones, examining shells, thinking of Dan. Then, one day, he was there, sitting in the old rattan rocker when she returned from her beachcombing.

'Hi, Christy. How's it going?'

She ran to him and leapt into his arms.

'Oh, Dan.'

'I'm only here for two days, but I needed to see you both. I hear you're painting.'

Christy stiffened, afraid of his judgement, though she knew that Dan had always been her best and most scrupulous critic. She avoided the question and he pretended not to have noticed her tension.

'Let's have breakfast. Then I'd like to see your work, if you let me, Christy.'

While LC slept, Dan looked at the paintings, his face intent, his eyes solemn. Christy followed in silence, her newfound determination faltering when he said nothing at all. Then, when they were alone in her room, she saw that his eyes were full of tears.

'What's wrong, Dan?'

'Nothing's wrong. Everything's right. The paintings are the best you've ever done, including those in your first exhibition. If you can sustain that same quality, you'll be the great art find of the century again and next time you won't break under the strain of your success.'

Dan took her in his arms, kissed her and they lay together on the bed. Christy wiped his eyes, kissed his mouth and then they were making wild, violent love, as if the bad years had never happened, as if uncertainty and fear no longer blocked their way. After love, they sat on the terrace and Dan held her hand and kissed her shoulders, his eyes tender.

'Stay till you've enough paintings for an exhibition. Then the real battle'll begin.'

'You think no one'll want to know about me?'

'I'm sure of it.'

'I'll fight, Dan.'

'We all will and we'll need to. Critics think has-beens are has-beens for ever. You'll have to hit nothing but high notes to convince them, but you'll do it. You already have. You're working with great energy and force and you're fast. It won't be much longer before you're ready with enough canvasses to exhibit.'

In the early morning light of the day of Dan's departure, Christy watched her daughter throwing stones in the water with him. LC had been ecstatic to see Dan and had barely left his side. Christy sighed. Dan had loved her, judged her paintings as sheer genius, but he had not proposed marriage. Used to his frequent proposals over the years, she felt strangely deflated by the fact that he no longer wanted to marry her. She walked with him to his car, kissing him fervently and then stood watching with her child as he drove away. A faint smile hovered on her lips as she returned to her studio. She would paint as she had never painted before, then return to Dan in Santa Fe. She wrote a letter to Nolan telling him about her plans for a new exhibition. She wrote another to Amy, telling her about Dan's reactions to the new canvasses.

In the days that followed Dan's visit, Christy reflected on his words. He had been right about one thing. The real battle would begin on her return to Santa Fe, when the six-year has-been tried the impossible, to make the critics cry their adulation for the second time.

Her face intent, her mind steely in its new-found determination, Christy painted from morning to night. She must pour everything she had learned, all her pain, her fear, her anguish, her ecstasy, her new maturity into these paintings. If she failed again, she would be finished for ever. Tossing her head, she defied the thought. The hell with defeatism! It was time to come out firing all her guns. Images took form in colours that stunned the senses, emotional intensity allied with a sure and dominant hand that hit the onlookers with its passion and its force. Christy was entering the last round in her long drawn out battle with herself.

EIGHTEEN

Christy grew accustomed to the region, the silence, the solitude. There were few guests in the hotel and sometimes they drove away for a picnic and never saw a soul the whole day until their return. Without her realizing it, Christy's fear of being isolated from friends and immediate help began to recede. She learned local customs and legends, amused by the people's belief in spirits and their incredulity when someone discovered a rattlesnake that didn't rattle in a nearby town. For Christy, familiarity bred content and she felt more and more relaxed.

Often, in the pale light of morning, she went to the beach and watched the fishermen walking out, up to their knees and throwing their nets in the time honoured way. Fish that were not sold on the beach were smoked and dried, nothing ever wasted in this area of cruel poverty. Tiny black pigs ate the fish entrails, when they had been gutted, and were in their turn roasted for feast days or turned into pies to be sold by pastry sellers during Sunday religious parades. The fishermen fascinated Christy and when she watched them, learning to identify blue and green parrotfish, yellow-finned surgeon and white-spotted purple puffers, she also sketched their faces, their catches, their colours, their simple, honest ways.

Day after day Christy painted what she saw, what she felt, depicting her own struggle with life in terms of the dreaded puffer fish, for whom she had a sneaking admiration. When attacked, the puffer could take in so much water so fast his body swelled and his spikes pierced the attacker. He had also been known to eat his way out of a shark's stomach when swallowed whole. A soft, comic character in appearance, his flesh had been identified as a deadly poison thousands of years before Christ, the lethal dose of puffer being smaller than a grain of salt. When eaten, death came as a merciful release. Christy watched the deadly fish and enjoyed the thought that she was painting her way out of her prison, like the puffer ate his way out of the shark's stomach. If he could do it, so could she.

Unaware of how much she had changed and how fast, Christy fought to keep up the astonishing quality of her painting, the spontaneity she had lost and now refound. Dan had said that to neutralize critical prejudice she would surely encounter, each painting must be a masterpiece. Ignoring tiredness and her desire to return home to the man she loved, Christy continued to work twelve hours a day.

Then, one morning, Dan returned and said he wanted to take LC back with him to Santa Fe.

'She's due to start school again in a week. We don't want her to arrive late and be a misfit, left out of all the activities that form friendships at her age. She already missed so much because of the accident.'

'She doesn't want to leave the beach. I long to come home, but LC loves it here.'

'She can't live like a savage for ever, Christy. She has to go to school and get back to being a little girl with a regular life.'

'I suppose so.'

'How are you?'

'Tired, but content with my work.'

'Can I see the new paintings? I've thought of nothing

315

but that all the way here. I didn't even stop for breakfast, I was so impatient to know how you're doing.'

When he had examined every canvas Christy had completed since his last visit, Dan hugged her to his heart.

'All this absence, your crazy journey and our separation's been worth it, you know. You're back on the gold standard with a vengeance, Christy. I'll ask Amy to come to Santa Fe when you get back. Maybe when she sees these she'll have some inspired idea on how to relaunch your return.'

'Will the de Vandens not handle me like before?'

'I saw Deke the other day and he told me they're not doing twentieth-century painters any more. I don't believe him. I think they caught a cold with your last exhibition and they just won't take the risk again. Times are hard in the art world, except in auctions of the great names of the past. They're going for crazy prices.'

'I'll find someone else.'

'Come here, Christy. You know something, every night when I go to bed, I wish you were with me. Every morning when I eat breakfast I want to tell you things, share things, like always. I'm sick of being alone in the Boulder House. I'm sick of watching television night after night and working all day till I'm too tired to think. I know you had to do this, but I want you to come back soon.'

'I will. I've only one more painting to finish, then I'm through. I keep blocking it in my mind, because it's a scene of Louise flying. I've never been able to accept that she just let her plane fall and fall till it was all over.'

Dan opened his briefcase and handed Christy an envelope.

'That's one of the reasons why I came down here. When you were with LC in the hospital, I was worried about you and I tried to get Ellie Martinez to take you on. You rejected the idea and perhaps you were right.'

'How is she?'

'She got married and already she's expecting twins.'

'She didn't waste any time!'

'Ellie gave me these before she left the clinic. She was sure the main problem with you was that you'd grown up with the idea firmly implanted that your grandmother and your mother committed suicide. She said that no matter what fame and fortune you achieved, with that at the back of your mind you had no sense of permanency in life. In other words, Ellie's theory was that you were always waiting for the moment when you'd do the same thing as your mother and grandmother. These are the details of the investigation into Louise's air crash and they prove conclusively that your mother died in an accident due to a mechanical fault. She did not, repeat *not* kill herself. So there's no family legacy of suicide. Read the reports, they're clear and emphatic on the subject. I don't know why you never saw them before, Christy. I suspect your father just couldn't bear to let you read them. He still can't talk about the tragedy and I don't think he ever will.'

Christy stared disbelievingly at Dan and then at the papers.

'But Nolan believes she killed herself!'

'I think Nolan went crazy with grief and seriously thought that that was what happened. Who knows how the mind works? Maybe mechanical failure was difficult to accept because he would have held himself responsible for paying for the maintenance of the plane. I can't explain what he did, Christy. I only know he didn't do it with bad intent.'

Tears of shock, relief and anguish for her father fell down Christy's cheeks and she walked to Dan and asked him to hold her tight.

317

'I can't believe all this, Dan.'

'You will when you've read the papers. And then you'll paint those last paintings with a new outlook. You're free for the first time of that black cloud, Christy. You're *free*.'

In the scarlet sunset of a summer evening, two bodies entwined, two lovers sighed and panted and floated on clouds, their skin touched by the magic glow of evening. When they kissed, there was deep abiding understanding. Later, they walked on the beach together, fascinated by ghost crabs on long, spiky legs and fiddler crabs scuttling on one big and one small claw. The moon shone silver on the water and an old man riding by on his mule called out, '*Buenas noches*.' Dan kissed Christy as they strolled back to the hotel.

'When are you planning to come home?'

'Soon, very soon. I've only one more canvas to finish.'

'We'll have a celebration when you return. Nolan and Amy are already making plans.'

In the morning, when she saw LC sitting in the car, her face solemn, her mouth tight, Christy almost burst into tears.

Instead, she said cheerfully, 'Good luck on your first day at school.'

'I don't want to leave, Mummy.'

'LC, you'll be glad to see everyone, won't you?'

'No, I won't. I don't want to go!'

'Remember when we were lost in the desert and you made coffee and looked after me? Will you do me a favour and look after Daddy till I get back at the end of the month? I've just one painting to finish. Okay? You know, all the time we've been having fun at the beach, no one looked after *him*.'

LC hesitated before replying, 'I'll look after Daddy, but promise you'll return soon.'

'I promise.'

When they had gone, leaving nothing but emptiness, Christy broke down and cried like a child. The period of testing was almost over and she had lost all but one of her fears and maybe even that. She had only the final portrait of Louise to finish. Then she would pack and move on to the next battle, the battle against fear of failure and the prejudice of those who refuse to change their minds. Christy shuddered as she thought of the dealers and the critics. Was it too late? Would anyone ever agree to expose her? Or had her efforts been in vain? Shaking her head like a boxer, she strode into her studio. No point in thinking of all that. She must finish the painting, pack and then decide what to do and how to do it. She had come back, found her desire to work again and created some fascinating canvasses. She must not get discouraged before she even tried to find a new gallery. Somewhere in America there must be one dealer who would take the risk and a handful of critics who remembered the good times.

In the failing light, the dunes looked grey. Christy sat at the window, looking out to the sea, thinking of Louise and the final portrait she had started a dozen times, rejected and tried again. Then, as the sunset came like a great orange ball, lighting the whole landscape with its flame-like intensity, she rose and hurried to her studio. *That* was how she would depict Louise, going out in a blaze of glory and then rising like the phoenix from the ashes to live again in the memory of those who had loved and admired her. The painting would be a celebration of her talent, not a funereal memory of her death.

Christy painted with passion until three in the morning. Then she fell exhausted on her bed and slept until dawn, when the cries of the fishermen woke her. In a day or two she would pack and move out. To be home again, to be working well and dreaming again would be the best thing that ever happened to her.

They had a party when Christy arrived, just as Dan had promised. They ate wild turkey and drank champagne and no one mentioned the battle ahead. Dan already knew that Amy had drawn a blank in Los Angeles, San Francisco and even Dallas, when trying to organize the exhibition for Christy. That left local or minor galleries. He wondered what Christy would say when she knew. For the moment, she was drinking too much champagne and trying not to fall asleep on the sofa. He rose and took her hand.

'Shall we go to bed?'

In the still of night, a coyote howled and a bird swooped past the window of their room. Christy was sound asleep. Dan lay awake, wondering how he was going to break the news that no one wanted her any more, that no dealer with a gallery of quality would exhibit her. Christy needed to feel she had made it back alone, that she was dependent on no one. He decided to let her work it out with Amy, just the two of them, as in the days of childhood.

The two women sat on the terrace each morning, a list of galleries, gallery owners and exhibition halls in their hands. Each was listed under state and city headings. Amy's face was solemn.

'We've exhausted all the major galleries and prestige locations, plus those dealers who specialize in twentieth-century artists. We're on number eighty of the small galleries and there are only two left. After that it's mediocre locations and we won't touch those.'

'What do you propose, Amy?'

'Publicity maybe.'

'I hope your hair doesn't turn white overnight with the trauma of all this.'

'Yours might, but mine comes out of a bottle so no danger!'

They called a publicity agency and put the problem to them of changing Christy's luck. For a hundred thousand dollars the head of the agency offered to design a campaign that would 'neutralize the problem of Christy's failure image'. But he would give no guarantees. They thanked him kindly and showed him out of the house.

They lobbied columnists, art critics and even the President of the Museum of National Art, who had bought a Christy Pallister from her first exhibition. No one would touch her. One columnist was particularly offensive. Christy winced as she heard him on the phone.

'Christy's old news. If she kills someone, gets murdered or marries Brando maybe we'd print it. But you can forget the idea that folk are interested in her paintings, no matter how good they seem. She's yesterday news as a painter.'

Finally, knowing that Amy was longing to return home to San Francisco and the new husband she adored, Christy proposed that they both went there for the weekend.

'I need a change, so how about an invitation? We can discuss all this in detail during the weekend. I'll have to leave the idea of an exhibition until after the holiday.'

'Are you staying home for Christmas?'

'Nolan's going to Kyoto. Dan always stays in Santa Fe because they have the annual anniversary of the founding of the clinic in the last week of December and folk come from all over the States for meetings of trustees and the Governing Board.'

'How's Dan taking this?'

'He's great. You know he gave me a year to sort myself out and accept his proposal of marriage? After that we separate but stay friends. The year started last April, which doesn't leave me much time to organize my exhibition, get to be a successful and independent woman and accept the proposal. I won't marry until I'm a success in *my* idea of the word.'

'You'll just have to ask him to wait!'

'Dan's waited over five years. He won't wait any longer. He wants a big family and not a family of bastards, so he won't wait.'

Christmas carillons chimed in the plaza. Massed voices sang carols and children watched, entranced, as farolitos were lit and placed on walls and rooftops. Friends visiting the Boulder House were offered the traditional hot chocolate and biscochitos. And everywhere there was the winter smell of pinon pine fires, cut evergreens and the enticing pungency of roast red pimentoes and honey-basted turkey.

LC had replaced Amy as Christy's assistant. Feeling thirsty one evening, she drank the leftovers of everyone's champagne, plus Dan's whisky and soda. She woke the next morning, astonished to have missed dinner but in fine form for a four-course breakfast. Then, in the icy cold of a December day, she walked behind Christy, who was gathering pine cones, her expression troubled.

'I know you can't find a gallery to show your work, Mummy.'

'Don't worry, LC.'

'I'm not worried. You should have your exhibition in Daddy's clinic. Everyone loves the conference room because its walls are pink adobe.'

Christy looked at her daughter and then kneeled before her.

'Did Daddy tell you to say that?'

'No, I thought of it myself. I keep hearing you talking on the phone and everyone says no and I *hate* them! But Daddy won't say no, because he loves you. All his friends are coming for a fancy-dress party and the anniversary dinner. I heard Daddy say it on the phone. They'll love your paintings and you'll be famous again and on television like Barbara Walters.'

Christy ran back to the house, LC close behind. Out of the mouths of babes and sucklings . . . the child had seen the easiest and simplest solution. But would Dan agree?

'Can you spare a minute, Dan?' she called. 'LC, tell Daddy what you just said to me.'

Dan listened, staring in astonishment at the solemn-faced child he loved.

'We'll do it. Now! We've only got ten days to arrange an exhibition and it's not enough – nowhere near enough – but we'll do our damnedest. Agreed, Christy?'

'Agreed, Dan.'

'Agreed, Daddy.'

They worked from eight in the morning to midnight, Christmas Day included, with the help of Amparo and her family, plus two handymen, who were unmarried, alone and delighted to participate in something interesting during what seemed to them to be a very lonely time of the year. The conference room was big but not clinical, its walls of stone and adobe in the true Santa Fe style. Contour was given by a false arch erected as an 'entrance'. Furniture was borrowed from one of the clinic's directors with a penchant for the exotic. And soon the history of Camilla and Louise and the long odyssey of self-discovery through which Christy had passed were displayed in conjunction with rare pieces that accentuated their power.

A seventeenth-century four-poster bed and bible box

323

stood guard over a portrait of Camilla in her castle in the Kingdom of Fife. Twin Japanese bronze t'suru cranes and a wondrous stuffed white peacock formed partners to welcome Camilla, in Kenyan sunshine, to the lake of ten thousand flamingoes. A kelim of geometric perfection, made by the Quash'quai toned with the Kalimkari block-printed quilt draped over a painted Venetian chest of the eighteenth century, that matched the one in the portrait of Louise on honeymoon. Carved cypress tree columns echoed those on the veranda of her house in Santa Fe, where Christy had portrayed her mother, as the family remembered her, sitting on the bench against a vivid yellow wall, surrounded by overhanging lilac, the most beautiful girl anyone had ever seen and the loneliest. The astonishing final portrait of Louise, executed in flaming colours, that depicted both destruction and resurrection in Christy's mind, became the centrepiece of the exhibition, displayed between parallel pathways of miniature orange, bay and myrtle, arranged with panache by the clinic's head gardener. Paintings of Mexican beaches, tropical fish, sunrises, loneliness, deserts and rattlesnakes were juxtaposed, with Christy's sure hand, with buffalo bells from Bali, suits of Dutch seventeenth-century armour and an ivory inlaid Mudéjar cabinet. At the entrance, through which all the guests would pass, Christy's vast painting of two Mexican fighting cocks was displayed alone, next to a chair in solid amaranth and a Vallière bureau by Dubolis. On the priceless bureau, Christy had arranged a simple Mexican bowl of persimmons. It was her final gesture and made at midnight on the twenty-ninth of December.

In the corner of the room LC was asleep on a camp bed. The handymen and gardeners had gone home exhausted. Only Dan remained, finishing the final drape of a curtain, the last poster to be placed at the entrance to the clinic. It said simply 'Christy Pallister Invites . . .' As the clock struck midnight, he held up a sprig of mistletoe and kissed Christy with deep affection.

'You're white-faced and hungry. Shall we go home?'

'I'm famished, Dan.'

'We haven't eaten since midday.'

'LC ate enough for everyone!'

'She loves going to the canteen. I think visiting the clinic gives her deep satisfaction, because she's well again. She remembers when she was ill and she's euphoric, because it's all over. Come on Christy, we'll get her in the car and then we'll stop off at the Crazy Cuckoo for a take-home meal.'

'Amparo'll sulk.'

'No, she won't, she's even more exhausted than we are.'

'What do you think of the exhibition, Dan?'

'If there's any justice in the world they'll go crazy.'

'Without the critics to reassure them that what they're buying is bankable?'

'We've some pretty important collectors among our directors. I don't believe they really need critics to reassure them. But we'll soon know.'

'Will Ellie come?'

'I hope so, but she only had the twins a short time ago and Chuck told me she's very tired.'

'She'll make it to see you.'

'No, if she comes it'll be only for one reason, to see your paintings. She can see me any time.'

In the still of the night, as the coyotes howled, Christy lay awake thinking. Art was like any other commodity and folk liked to be reassured that their judgement was sound. That was why van Gogh had sold only one painting in his lifetime, but brought twenty-five million dollars at Sotheby's less than a century after his death.

She had no desire to remain a has-been. She'd fought her battles and won most of them, but this was a battle that depended on other people. The paintings had been priced astronomically high, at Dan's insistence and despite the fact that her reputation was as a washed up, faded, flash in the pan who'd hit the high notes at twenty-three and then fallen into the pits. Christy tossed and turned, terrified of failing again. Was there anyone left who believed in her, apart from the family? A roar of distant thunder echoed in the night. She snuggled up to Dan, closed her eyes and told herself that from this moment on she was in the hands of destiny.

When she had heard the clocks chime two, three, four, Christy got up to make coffee. This was no time to sleep. She could sleep when she was old! This was her moment, the moment when friends of the clinic, directors and trustees came from all over America to lunch together and plan policy. If they went in to see the paintings, as she hoped they would, she would know from their reactions whether she was in business again. Like a gunfighter preparing for his last shootout, Christy dressed in her best, brushed her hair with ferocity and went outside to face the day.

NINETEEN

The meeting of the board was scheduled for eleven in the morning. Lunch, at Dan's invitation, followed in the dining-room. It was a jolly affair with much gossiping, scandalmongering, fund raising and plan making. Then, one of the visitors enquired about the poster.

'What's all that about, Dan? "Christy Pallister Invites . . ." Are we invited and to what?'

'Christy's having an exhibition of her paintings starting tomorrow. You can have a preview if you like, Agnes.'

Ellie looked across the table to Dan.

'I'd like to go see the paintings, Dan. I'm a great fan of Christy's.'

'I'll take those who'd like to see a preview when we've finished lunch.'

Ellie followed Dan, her arm linked with that of her father on one side and her husband on the other. She had made a big effort to come to Santa Fe, fighting fatigue after the birth of her twins, because avid curiosity about the new paintings had proved irresistible. Ellie was convinced that Christy had the most amazing talent of any twentieth-century artist. She also knew that Christy had a mental block against success that had ruined everything. What had she been able to do for this last, desperate throw of the dice? Had she been able to master her fears? Entering the conference hall, Ellie came face to face with the fighting cocks, the chair in amaranth, the bowl of persimmons. Scrutinizing the cocks, she felt breathless with excitement at the energy, vehemence and virulence of the artist. It was immediately obvious that Christy had found herself again, because there, leaping out of the canvas, was all the old anger, passion and pure genius. One glance at the prices told Ellie that Dan had realized the enormous value of the works.

Showing nothing in the expression on her face, Ellie made a quick tour of the exhibition. Then she spoke to her husband.

'This will go down in the history of art as something quite sensational. We must buy, Chuck.'

'I figured you'd say that. Jesus, what happened to Christy? Last time I saw her paintings, she seemed to have done them all five fathoms under the Pacific. These jump clean out of the wall.'

'I must ring my brother.'

Ellie ran to Dan's office and phoned Mark, art critic of the powerful *Washington Post*.

'It's Ellie.'

'Wow, has there been an earthquake? This is great, but what happened? You *never* call.'

'Christy Pallister happened.'

'A has-been, sis, don't buy. Even the art museum's put her stuff in store.'

'She's not a has-been any more. You want to be in on the biggest art story since the raising of Lazarus?'

'You're joking, what's going on?'

'Christy can't find anyone to exhibit her – understandable after those last two exhibitions. In desperation she's put on a display in the conference hall of Dan's clinic. She's been away for months finding herself and my God has she found herself! If she doesn't get an accolade for these paintings, there's something wrong in the world, but anyway she has my vote for the most courageous woman of the century.'

'Where's she been all this time?'

'God knows. I think she went somewhere in the wilds of Mexico or Baja. The only thing I can tell you is that these are the greatest paintings I've ever seen by a living artist.'

'I'll come down.'

'Come fast. She'll be big news in a few days.'

'Thanks, Ellie.'

'Come soon won't you, Mark.'

'Is it really *that* urgent?'

'It is.'

'I'll be on the next plane.'

Christy watched the viewers, standing, staring, talking animatedly among themselves. No one had asked to buy. Many came and talked to her, including Ellie and her husband. Then, somewhere in the distance, a clock chimed three and folk drifted out to drink a last coffee and take a liqueur with Dan in his office suite. Christy sat alone, staring into space. There were no red sold stars on the paintings, as this was a preview. Sales would be agreed tomorrow, when the general public were admitted. Sure that the paintings were her best ever, Christy remained uncertain about the degree of influence of the critics. Did the public buy what the critics recommended or what they liked, without thought of a financial gain on their investment? For years it had been accepted that modern art would not augment greatly in value in the artists' lifetimes. But now the art situation had changed and in a world where money was worth nothing at all, art was becoming the newly fashionable investment. Tired, uncertain, but not defeated, Christy left the conference hall, pausing for a moment to look at her painting of the fighting cocks. It was then that she saw the red sold star on it. She smiled, thinking Dan had put it there to encourage her. When he appeared, she hugged him to her heart.

'Did you put the star on?'

'No, I thought you did.'

Christy stared at him, laughing despite herself.

'We have a phantom buyer?'

'More than one. The guests have gone home but they were mightily impressed. Five of them are coming back tomorrow and they're all big collectors. But someone evidently wants the fighting cocks enough to try to cinch the sale at preview!'

'Did Ellie like the paintings?'

'I didn't see her, but Chuck told me they'll be back first thing in the morning. She was tired and wanted to return to her hotel.'

'And her father?'

'Bob loved them, said he'll be back first thing, too. We'll wait and see how it goes, Christy. Either we sell out or we don't. If they don't buy here I'm prepared to take you to LA and hire the Beverly Wilshire's entire public area for your next exhibition.'

'I love you, Dan.'

'Let's go home. I'm so tired I feel like a sixty-year-old gold prospector with flat feet.'

The following morning, Ellie walked around the exhibition with her brother, amused by the look of controlled excitement on his face.

'What do you think, Mark?'

'You were right to get me here fast. I don't think we've seen this quality since Christy's first exhibition that shook the art world to its foundations. This one's going to do the same. Can you fix for me to see her? Then I'll phone in my story and take the next plane back to Washington.'

Christy smiled politely at the young man in the navy suit, introduced by Ellie as her brother from Washington. She had refused all requests for interviews and knew that whatever happened in the future she would never again let herself be dependent on a dealer, museum or critical opinion. Ignorant of Mark's occupation, she spoke easily.

'How long are you staying in Santa Fe?'

'I have to get back to Washington at three this afternoon.'

'That's really a flying visit!'

'How does it feel to be back at the top again?'

'I don't know if I am. No one's hurrying to buy. Only one of the paintings has been sold and that's the fighting cocks.'

Ellie interrupted.

'Wrong. When did you last look?'

Christy walked with Mark around the exhibition, pausing to speak with LC.

'Who bought the sunset picture of Louise?'

'I don't know, but Daddy keeps sticking stars on the paintings. Can I buy one, Mummy?'

'Which one?'

'The puffer fish we met on our great adventure.'

'That'll cost you two kisses, LC.'

'Can I stick my own star on?'

'Of course you can.'

They continued to look at the paintings, while LC remained behind sticking red stars around the frame of her personal painting. Mark spoke with deceptive casualness.

'What was the great adventure?'

Christy explained her survival course, her fears, her block after the first exhibition, her despair and finally her decision to confront her fears with the journey through the desert and the unexpected complication of the hurricane.

Mark stared at her, unable to believe that she had been capable of doing what had to be done and of coming back with such spellbinding brilliance after five

331

years. He shook hands with her on leaving, promising to do his best to rally some 'clients' in Washington.

'After the effort you've made, you deserve all the friends you can find, Christy. I'll do my best to help. Can't promise anything, but I'll be in there trying.'

The following morning, a story went out on the coast-to-coast wire: 'Christy Pallister Reborn'. It was a powerful article, detailing not only the greatness of the paintings in the exhibition and the euphoria they had provoked in the onlookers, but the story of Christy's reaction to fame, the support of Dan, Nolan and LC, who wanted a painting of her own. It ended with a challenge to the critics who had made her and also brought her down. Christy had met her fears and uncertainties and had won in a spectacular way no one would ever be likely to forget. 'Will the critics dare come out of the woodwork and pocket their clichés? Or are critics not worth their salt any more?'

Events moved speedily and with certitude once the article appeared. Every painting was sold by the second evening and critics and gallery owners were calling hourly. Christy asked Nolan to deal with the calls. The most prestigious critics were allowed a view. All gallery owners were excluded, with the exception of the de Vandens. National gallery directors were made welcome, but told that in future bids would be accepted from all comers without priority.

As she walked around the exhibition with her father, Christy looked up into Nolan's handsome face.

'What do you think, Daddy?'

'I was stupefied by your talent. I took all my cameras that first day and forgot to take a single photograph.'

'You've taken a few today.'

'Sure have. How's Dan, has he proposed again?'

'No, and I don't think he ever will.'

'Don't panic. The year he gave you isn't up yet. Shall

we eat dinner on the terrace at the hacienda, like we did after that first exhibition?'

'Why not?'

'Where's LC?'

'She's acting as my agent, informing everyone that I'm going to be exhibited in the Museum of Modern Art, because she heard Ellie saying that I should be!'

'What next, Christy?'

'Oh, I think I have one more surprise in store.'

Days of photographers and flashbulbs, of crowds and noise and strident voices cawing appreciation. Christy met clients and admirers, was charming, gay and amusing, but she signed only one contract, with the person who had supported her from the days of their lonely childhood. At the end of the exhibition, Amy Pallister Irving became her official agent. Christy also agreed to travel to Washington to discuss an exhibition at the National Gallery. The lessons of the past were well remembered, however. In the early days she had accepted every offer of an exhibition and had painted herself out. Now, she knew the value of being unavailable. No gallery owner succeeded in persuading her to sign a contract. No television station succeeded in interviewing her, except the local one, TV South-West, for whom she had a great affection, because it had always championed her talent.

One thing Christy handled with the greatest delicacy and maximum pleasure was the private celebration dinner for herself and Dan at the Boulder House. While Amparo rushed back and forth preparing the feast, Christy drove out in search of interesting items for a still-life centrepiece for the table. She collected the fossil of a scorpion, a yellow cactus flower and a small iron ring fallen from a pioneer wagon. Then she hurried to put on her new Saint Laurent black velvet dress, worn with an Indian necklace of turquoise and silver.

Dan came down at seven, elegant, as always in grey.

'That's a truly superb dress, Christy. And the table's a miracle. What does the centrepiece mean? It's symbolic of something, but you have to explain.'

As they sipped iced Krug, Christy explained the arrangement she had made specially for Dan.

'The fossil signifies my past fears and how they're as dead as the scorpion. The cactus flower's bright and full of life and it can survive all the droughts and heatwaves of life. I can, too, now, but it's taken me nearly thirty years to get to the point where I can say that. Some women dream, but their dreams have no base in reality. I wanted fame without responsibility, love without marriage, everything without committal on my part. But now I'm a real person. I can still dream and, more important, I can try to realize my dreams. The ring's probably very old. It fell off a wagon or a pedlar's cart or maybe it was a curtain ring. It signifies something very important.'

Christy kneeled before Dan and kissed his cheeks.

'You're used to proposing, but this is my first and very last time. Will you marry me, Dan? I won't take no for an answer.'

For a long time he sat quite still, his eyes on hers. Then he spoke softly, almost as if he was thinking aloud.

'When I first met you, I thought you were the most beautiful thing I ever saw, the purest and the most brilliant. Then I got to know you and I was scared that you'd never make it, that your fear and your phobias would ruin what should be a truly happy life. Your beauty and your genius just seemed like obstacles and I got very unhappy for a while. If it hadn't been for LC . . .'

Dan rose and lifted Christy to her feet.

'I want you to know that I'm very proud of you,

Christy. You've done what very few people can do in life, you've not only survived an eccentric and almost dangerously sheltered upbringing and without help from any professional, you've made it to be a very real person. I've dreamed of this moment for so long, damned if the tears aren't going to arrive and ruin my Cary Grant image. You really know how to knock a fellow off balance!'

'You haven't said yes.'

'I'll be the proudest man in the world to be married to you, Christy. You're a great artist and a very great lady and we'll make a perfect couple, though I say it myself. Now let's drink our champagne before I get tearful again!'

After dinner they watched Christy being interviewed by the local television company's anchor man. She was talking about her work.

'Yes, all the paintings are sold. The Museum of California bought three, the Municipality of Santa Fe another three and personal friends and family the rest.'

'No paintings went to dealers?'

'None were bought by dealers. I gave one to my former dealers, the de Vandens, for their kindness in the past.'

'What of the future, Christy?'

'I'll paint when I have a good idea. I shall never tour with the exhibitions. I have a mind to do a little research on last century's women of America. I love the contrasts of all that, the poor emigrées arriving from Italy and Russia and Ireland, the pioneer women in their sod houses and those wonderfully glamorous creatures in their mansions on Rhode Island.'

'You're a very independent woman, but now you're thinking of marriage.'

'I finally got my priorities right. When a woman's

truly independent, she has the courage to let herself be dependent from time to time.'

'How'd you learn that?'

'Dan taught me. Dr Ellie Martinez taught me, everyone tried to teach me, but it took a long time.'

'Did Ellie Martinez buy a painting?'

'Ellie's always bought my paintings, right from the start and I'm very proud of her judgement and that of her husband and her parents, who are famous collectors.'

Christy held out her hand to Dan.

'Remember when I was horribly jealous of Ellie?'

'I'm never likely to forget it!'

'How many paintings did she really buy?'

'Her father bought three. Her husband bought one for Mark, eight for Ellie and three for his mother. Ellie wanted them all, but most had already been sold.'

'I'm in her debt, Dan, and I'll never forget what she did for me.'

'She did it for her too, she was always your biggest fan, from the very day when she bought the Marilyn painting and showed it to everyone in Santa Fe.'

'It's been a long climb back, Dan.'

'You remember Lyndon Johnson's words: "Yesterday is not ours to recover, but tomorrow is ours to win or lose." You just won all your tomorrows, Christy.'

'Shall we go to bed, Dan?'

'I thought you'd never ask!'